Armored

EDITED BY

John Joseph Adams

ARMORED

Copyright © 2012 by John Joseph Adams

A Baen Books Original

Baen Publishing Enterprises
P.O. Box 1403
Riverdale, NY 10471
www.baen.com

ISBN: 978-1-4516-3817-2

Cover art by Kurt Miller

First paperback printing, April 2012

Distributed by Simon & Schuster
1230 Avenue of the Americas
New York, NY 10020

Pages by Joy Freeman (www.pagesbyjoy.com)
Printed in the United States of America

For
John Steakley
&
Robert A. Heinlein

CONTENTS

FOREWORD

A few years ago, Marvel Comics approached me about writing for them. They suggested I might want to work on *Iron Man*.

Now, I was no fan of superhero comics—my taste, as a kid, had been more along the lines of *Classics Illustrated* and Scrooge McDuck, with a bit of *Superboy* thrown in because he was actually a kid with a real life.

But Iron Man? He didn't even have any extraordinary powers—he just wore a really talented suit. Admittedly, he designed the suit himself, and funded it. But why not make a thousand of them and get other guys to wear them? Why did he have to wear the suit himself?

Now, I'd been studying military history ever since I became fascinated with the U.S. Civil War when I was eight years old. I was quite aware of the constant see-sawing of advantages between assault weapons and fortifications.

Enemies come and attack your village, overwhelming

you by their greater numbers and better weapons. When you gather the survivors to rebuild the city, you put it on a hill and you build a wall around it.

The next time the enemy comes, they ride around and around your walled city on their chariots while you throw rocks or shoot arrows at them. They outnumber you ten to one—but they can't get inside to harm you. Eventually, they go away and raid some village that *doesn't* have walls.

Next time they come with catapults. Or they dig a tunnel under your walls. Or they run up with hundreds of ladders.

Next time you build your walls higher and thicker, and surround them with a deep moat to foil tunnels.

Then cannons knock down the walls and a whole new kind of fortification in depth has to be invented, using miles of trenches. Bombers fly over the trenches; antiaircraft artillery and fighters and ground-to-air missiles bring down the bombers. And on and on.

Right along with the see-saw of armies and fortified cities, there's another game going on. A personal one.

Combat isn't just between armies. Even older than war is the contest between two alpha males for supremacy. It can be relatively peaceful: cocks displaying their plumage; other birds building attractive nests.

Two stags butt their heads together. Two gorillas tear up saplings and beat the ground with them to intimidate their opponent with their strength.

A man with two cutlasses displays his ferocious and skillful swordwork. Indiana Jones pulls out a pistol and shoots him.

Ah, yes—the blade! The projectile weapon! A way to overcome the other man's advantage. You're stronger than I am—but are your fists able to damage me as much as this cudgel of mine will damage you?

You have a cudgel? I'll throw a stone from this sling of mine. You have a spear? I'll shoot you with this arrow.

The goal is to damage the other fellow far more than he can damage you. To accomplish this, we develop deadlier weapons that magnify our strength, or weapons that we can use from farther away.

So the smaller, weaker man can, with craft and practiced skill, overmatch the stronger, larger one.

But the stronger man does not have to stand there helpless. Next time he carries a heavy shield on one arm and a sword even heavier than yours with the other. Now, little fellow, beat on my shield all you want—it won't hurt me, and meanwhile my sword will hack yours out of the way.

As for stones and arrows, the stronger man covers himself with thick cloth and leather; then he plates it with armor, or wears flexible metal mail. Your projectile weapons bounce harmlessly off as he comes close enough to break you in pieces. Turn and run, little man! You can't hurt him now.

Armor is personal and portable. Wearing it, an individual can get close enough to let his greater strength and skill overpower the enemy. Armor is a moving castle.

There are other ways of achieving the same end: stealth, speed, trickery, treachery. As many walled cities fell to bribery and betrayal as to sappers or climbers or catapults or cannon. The duel becomes moot if your enemy manages to poison you the day before, or slit your throat while you sleep.

Armor, by contrast, is hard to conceal. When the internal combustion engine achieved enough power to carry an armor-plated cannon-house on wheels and treads, trench warfare and machine guns lost their advantage, just as armor-plated ships were already able to rip wooden ships to shreds without sustaining any damage themselves. But it's hard to sneak a tank behind enemy lines.

It all comes down to the men inside the tin cans, whether they float or are borne by horses or automobiles or carried on the backs or arms of the men they protect. It's still personal.

Or is it? The remote-controlled drone now fires a missile while the operator is ten thousand miles away, controlling it by a combination of satellite and computer.

But such projectile weapons only work as long as your communication satellites remain in orbit and your radio signals can be transmitted and received. Jammers and satellite-killers become another kind of armor, potentially making drones as useless as stones thrown against metal plating.

Ultimately, though, these are all contests of will. What propels these tin cans forward are the men inside; shields, mail, suits of armor, tanks, and other personal enhancements are merely decorative until the will of a human being causes them to move close enough to an enemy for the contest to begin.

This book is a collection of stories about people who armor themselves in order to reduce the risk of coming near enough for someone else to cause them harm.

There is enough military history for every reader

to recognize that however fanciful the weapons and armor might seem, it is only realistic to say that there will always be someone devising armor to defeat a weapon, and a weapon to defeat the armor.

Most of us, though, will never don any kind of shield or wear any kind of armor, because most of us avoid combat for our entire lives.

Or do we? The power of a story about armor comes, not just from its roots in the real world of physical combat, but also from the fact that all humans are constantly searching for ways to armor themselves against another kind of weapon.

We build up an image, a reputation, in order to armor ourselves against lies and slanders—or against inconvenient revelation of our secrets.

When we have been damaged by personal treachery, we often armor ourselves emotionally by creating a thick emotionless shell which, though invisible, can be impenetrable.

We surround ourselves with a wall of friends to protect ourselves from the deep javelin of loneliness.

We try to control our children, building walls and fences, rules and an umbrella of constant vigilance to keep them from the consequences of their own foolish choices as well as from outside forces that endanger them.

And always, always we find that there is no such thing as armor that is impervious to all risk; or if there is, it is so heavy that we cannot move.

I think of the powerful scene near the end of *The Lion in Winter*, when Queen Eleanor's personal guard overpowers the armored knight who stands watch in front of the prison where her sons are being held.

His armor protected him until he stumbled and fell; then the same armor prevented him from escaping as the queen's man came close enough to insert a thin dagger into the helpless knight's brain through the gaps in his faceplate.

I can think of few metaphors for our ultimate defenselessness as good as that one. Whatever armor we put on to protect ourselves from risk can be turned against us.

As I began to write my series of *Ultimate Iron Man* comics for Marvel, the question I had to answer was what vulnerability in the man Stark made it imperative for him, not to invent armor, but to put it on his own body and wear it into combat himself. Why does he hate vulnerability so much that he must shield himself and then constantly test the shield against the deadliest of foes?

The armor is Iron Man's kryptonite, as well as the source of all his power.

The soldiers inside a tank cannot escape the hand grenade or Molotov cocktail dropped through the hatch. The sailors in the submarine are trapped by their thick hull when a depth charge or undersea obstacle cracks it and lets the water in.

And the person who has armored himself against emotional risk is utterly unprepared when that barrier is unexpectedly pierced. And if it is not pierced, the person wearing it finds that his armor has kept him from living his life. In the end, complete safety means complete immobility; armor is eventually overcome, or leaves us helpless.

Behind their high walls, the people of the city can only watch as the enemy ravages all the lands that supply them. There is always the possibility of terrible loss, despite or because of the thickest of defenses.

And yet we would be fools to expose ourselves to the risks of life without some kind of defense. Or else we must be prepared to sustain and bear and try, somehow, to survive the wounds that will inevitably pierce and break the thinly-covered skin, the unbraced bone, the trusting heart.

—Orson Scott Card,
October 2011

Introduction

JOHN JOSEPH ADAMS

Thanks to classics like *Starship Troopers* and *The Forever War*, and the current popularity of mega-properties such as the *Halo* video game franchise and the *Iron Man* films, power armor has become a concept everyone is familiar with. But for me, it all began with John Steakley's 1984 novel *Armor*.

Ever since reading *Armor* (and, soon after, *Starship Troopers* and tons of *Iron Man* comics), stories about soldiers going to battle in personal, powered combat armor have always appealed to me. When I first turned my hand to creative pursuits, the first thing I ever attempted to write—at around age eighteen or so—was a novel about a power-armored soldier, so in many ways I've been working toward this anthology my entire career.

Like me, many readers and gamers have long been fascinated by this concept. Yet there has never been an anthology devoted to this coolest of science fiction concepts—until now.

The stories in this anthology demonstrate the range of what can be done with the idea, exploring everything from the near-future powered exoskeleton technologies we might be seeing just a few years from now, to the powered combat armors and giant bipedal mechs of the far future.

Most of the stories included here are the kind of futuristic military SF stories you would expect to find in an anthology on this topic—"Hel's Half-Acre" by Jack Campbell, "The Johnson Maneuver" by Ian Douglas, "Contained Vacuum" by David Sherman, "You Do What You Do" by Tanya Huff, to name a few—and those stories naturally have all the requisite cool tech and ass-kicking you've all come to expect from books with the Baen logo on the spine.

Although most of the stories included do take place in the far future on strange alien worlds, some take place closer to home; "Jungle Walkers" by David Klecha and Tobias S. Buckell, for instance, takes place here on Earth in the not-too-distant future, and Michael A. Stackpole's "Field Test" is the most contemporary— taking place in Libya during the revolution of 2011.

Some of the stories take place even further in the past; in David D. Levine's "The Last Days of the Kelly Gang," we get a glimpse of what those infamous nineteenth-century outlaws might have attempted had they had a little more technology on their side. And in Carrie Vaughn's "Don Quixote," she imagines what might have happened had mecha technology been pioneered during the Spanish Civil War.

Other unusual takes on the theme include Genevieve

Valentine's tale of deep-sea scavengers on a distant alien world, "The Last Run of the *Coppelia*," and David Barr Kirtley's "Power Armor: A Love Story," about a Tony Stark-like figure who never takes off his invincible armor for fear of a lurking assassin. John Jackson Miller's tale "Human Error," meanwhile, takes a humorous look at what might happen if you're trapped out on the edge of the final frontier and the armor you ordered from HQ isn't quite what you expected. And in "Nomad" by Karin Lowachee and "Transfer of Ownership" by Christie Yant, the armor itself is in the role of protagonist, and the authors tell us *their* stories, instead of those of their occupants.

There's all that and more—a total of twenty-three different takes on what it means to be on the front lines of the future of warfare, on what it means to be part of a unique symbiosis of man and machine, on what it means to be . . . *armored*.

I made it my mission as an anthology editor to put together the kinds of books that I would like to read. And this book, perhaps more than any I've done thus far, exemplifies that. So suit up, power on, and lock and load—your mission begins on the next page.

The Johnson Maneuver

IAN DOUGLAS

The motto of the U.S. Marine Corps' Embassy Security Group was, appropriately enough, "In every clime and place." And that, Marine Gunnery Sergeant Carl Schaeffer had decided, had become something of an understatement.

The world of Pi^3 Orionis IV—dubbed Cernunnos by the human Contact/Liaison group on the surface, and something unpronounceably like "Cha'a" by the natives—was young, raw, and hot. The local gravity was a shade over six tenths of a G, the atmosphere dense and thick. The star, listed as type F5V on the main sequence, was just 27 light-years from Sol—right next door by interstellar standards—and the second-nearest planetary system found so far to have evolved intelligent life.

At least, Schaeffer thought with some amusement, *there was* supposed *to be intelligent life here.* He'd had a number of encounters with the natives during the past few weeks, and he wasn't entirely certain that the xenosophontologists had gotten that part right. He was standing now on the parapets of the Earth C/L compound, looking out over the city of Karnon—low, white domes and flat-roofed octagons. Columns of smoke were rising from several parts of the city, now, and his helmet mikes were picking up the usual chorus of deep, fluting, and disharmonic hoots and wailings that served as Cha'an language.

The crowds were working themselves up to a frenzy. It might just be another demonstration ... but the Embassy Guard Marines had been warned that the rebels might attack.

"You think they'll let us load up, Gunnery Sergeant?" Lance Corporal Carol Passerotti asked him. Like Schaeffer, she was in ceremonial dress armor—peacock-bright in bronze, blue, red, and white. He couldn't see her face behind the opaque, white visor. "It really sounds like they're building up to something big."

"I know," he told her. "Hang tough. As long as they're still talking, and the king crab still says it likes us, they shouldn't bother us."

A crowd—a big one—was gathering at the main gate, chanting as they gesticulated with clenched, multiple fists. He couldn't tell what they were saying, not without linking in to the embassy's translation AI, but they didn't sound happy. Or friendly.

"Yeah, but how can they tell if it *does* like us?" Passerotti asked.

"Beats me, Passerotti. I guess when they knock down the gate, we'll know we've worn out our welcome." He turned away. "Stay sharp, Marine."

"Aye-aye, Commander."

Schaeffer was a gunnery sergeant, a non-commissioned officer, but as head of the Marine security detachment assigned to the Pi^3 Orionis IV embassy, he held one of the very few enlisted billets in the Corps where an NCO could hold the title of *commander*. He had ten enlisted Marines under his command; his boss was the embassy's RSO, a civilian federal agent named Warner— an unpleasant piece of work.

He locked through into the embassy building and pulled off his helmet. The atmosphere outside was *almost* breathable, but there was too much sulfur dioxide from the young planet's numerous volcanic vents for human health. You could get by with a breather mask and goggles here, but Marine guards outside wore their Class A armor, which filtered out the SO_2 and reduced the high O_2 partial pressure to Earth-normal. After a moment's pause, he accessed his in-head circuitry and opened a private communications channel. "Mr. Warner?—Schaeffer," he said. "I need a word, please."

"I'm awfully busy, Commander," Warner's nasal voice shot back. *"Can it wait?"*

"No sir, but it's short. I need your authorization to go weapons-live."

"That will not be necessary, Commander."

"Excuse me, sir, but I feel it is. A large crowd is gathering outside, and it sounds like they're working themselves into attack mode."

"They've never attacked us before. We don't know what 'attack mode' for them would be."

"All I'm asking for, sir, is authorization to lock and load. Just in case."

There was a long hesitation on the other end, and then Warner's voice said, *"Come on, then."*

The office of the embassy's Regional Security Officer, the RSO, was Spartan but high-tech. Surveillance monitors covered the walls from deck to overhead, and Reginald Warner was ensconced within a desk that had more in common with the cockpit of a V/A-90 Demonwraith than a piece of office furniture.

Several screens showed different views of the mob at the front gate. The main viewall, however, was dominated by the startlingly deep-purple, cyclopean eye of Ng'g'!grelchk, the senior administrator to the ek-Cha'a Hierarchy's chief—call it the king's prime minister. Its name and title were displayed in English at the top of the screen.

"This," Warner said to the being, speaking into a microphone on his desk, "is the leader of our security guard here at the embassy. Commander Schaeffer."

Schaeffer heard in the background the computer-rendered blend of warbling, hooting, and glottal-stopped consonants that was the translation of what the RSO had just said. When they stopped, the being on the screen replied with some warblings of its own.

"I RESPECT YOU AND WHAT YOU REPRESENT." The consecutive translation scrolled up the right-hand side of the viewall, accompanied by the flat voice of the embassy AI as it spoke. "MAY LONG YOU HOLD FAST TO YOUR FEMALES. MAY LONG YOU BE KNOWN TO BE PROSPEROUS."

"Say 'thank you,'" Warner said in a harsh whisper when Schaeffer didn't immediately respond.

"Thank you," he told the image. He knew better than to add "sir." Hierarchy administrators were drones, sexless and landless, and sex-based honorifics could be misunderstood.

But not *powerless*.

The Heirarchy's ruler, Ng'g'ch'gra!ooh was also a drone. Having drones in charge was the only way the ek-Cha'a could have anything like a government without bull-male legislators slaughtering one another on the floor of the Executive Congress over minor legal disagreements.

"Commander Schaeffer," Warner added, "seems to feel that the situation outside the gate is extremely serious. He's concerned about... territorial incidents."

"THE ELDEST DRONE HAS ISSUED THE FIRMEST SUGGESTIONS," the AI both said and printed on the screen, translating the string of hoots, pops, and consonants. "THERE WILL BE NO ENCROACHMENT OF TERRITORY. YOUR FEMALES WILL BE SAFE."

Humans had been studying the ek-Cha'a language for perhaps thirty years, now. Vocabulary, grammar, and inflection all were now well understood, and translation in either direction was not a problem. Understanding the psychology *behind* the words, however, most definitely was.

"There, Commander, you see?" Warner spoke loudly now, so that his words were picked up for translation. "The Eldest Drone has assured us of our safety."

"Sir," Schaeffer said, "I still think it would be a good idea to—"

"*No!*" He shouted the word, cutting Schaeffer off. Then he continued in a calmer voice. "No, Commander. What you suggest would not be a good idea. Not *now*. The ek-Cha'a set great store in a martial *appearance*. But we do not want any... unfortunate incidents. Do we?"

Meaning, Schaeffer thought, *we can carry laser rifles, but not the batteries to charge them. He doesn't trust us.*

"I'm not talking about incidents, sir. I'm talking about what happens if that mob decides to come through the front gate."

"We have the assurance of the Eldest Drone that they will not. Am I right, Ng'g'!grelchk?" He made a pretty good approximation of the alien syllables, at least for a human limited to lips, tongue, and larynx, as opposed to paired air bladders and diaphragms.

"MY COUNTERPART SPEAKS PRECISION AND TRUTH."

"You are dismissed, Commander."

"Counterpart," meaning that the ek-Cha'a on the screen was in charge of the local army, as Warner was in charge of the security group. Schaeffer almost said something more, but the warning glare in Warner's eyes told him he would get nowhere with an argument, especially with the native looking on.

"Aye-aye, sir." He came to attention, turned on his heel, and walked·out of the office.

Damn the man! And damn all red-tape bureaucrats, all self-serving politicians, and all sanctimonious REMFs, military and civilian, who thought *conciliation* and *peace* were synonyms.

He headed back toward the security unit squad bay. He needed to *think.* . . .

For almost ten years, now, humans had been on Cernunnos. The human compound wasn't precisely an embassy, at least not as humans understood the word, but a contact/liaison facility housing the lab and research staffs for the xenosophontological mission. This world was of great interest to the planetologists; the Pi^3 Orionis system was young—only about 1.4 billion years old, not nearly enough time, according to the standard evolutionary model, for sapient life to appear. Either the standard model was wrong, or the ek-Cha'a, together with the local biosphere, were themselves relative newcomers to the world. The C/L team was here to learn as much as possible about the Cernunnans—their biology, their sociology, their culture, and their myths.

After several years of contact, the Eldest Drone had agreed to receive an Earth embassy in the principal city the humans called Karnon. It turned out that the concept of extraterritoriality—of a plot of land within the city that technically was *Earth* rather than Cha'a—was easy enough for the ek-Cha'a to understand. Much of ek-Cha'a culture was centered on the idea that bull-males claimed areas of land for themselves and their harems, and fought to defend them. The Eldest had ceded a walled-in block of buildings to the C/L mission, an area of land a little more than one hectare in size, and the Earth facility had been built there.

The *Hesperus* had arrived with Ambassador Gonzales two years ago, a blatant attempt by Geneva to force the ek-Cha'a to accept diplomatic contact with Earth. The first Marine security contingent had come with her. Schaeffer and his Marines had arrived six weeks ago on the *Bohr*, relieving the original security team, while Ambassador Tarleton had replaced Gonzales. The replacements had arrived in the middle of what amounted to all-out civil war.

The locals didn't see it that way, not as *war*. The drones ran things in ek-Cha'a society, but they had no real power save what they were granted day to day by the local dominant-bull males. Those males had initially agreed to cede the compound to the offworlders, but in recent months, more and more, the native population—both dominant and submissive males, the females, and even some of the drones— had been insisting that the aliens needed to abide by ek-Cha'a traditions.

And that meant fighting for their land.

The ambassadors—both Gonzales and Tarleton—had refused the repeated formal challenges, of course. An embassy was an instrument of *peace*, after all, of *diplomacy* . . . ideas the ek-Cha'a had difficulty understanding. Fractious and belligerent, especially over territorial matters, ek-Cha'a history appeared to be a very long saga of land grabs, territorial squabbles, alliances, betrayals, and bloodshed—not *wars*, as such, but as the niceties of day-to-day life.

And it was beginning to look as though the humans were about to be drawn into the latest round of not-quite-war confrontations.

The drone council that served as this world's government had so far resisted demands that the offworlders play along, claiming that humans were not *true* males, that they didn't understand how ek-Cha'a thought, and so were exempt from the need to claim and fight for land. While a large part of the population was still willing to go along with this, a number of the dominant males had begun organizing gangs with the goal of forcing the Earthers to fight. They'd broken into a local armory, seized military weapons, and begun a campaign of demonstrations, arson, and rioting that had paralyzed Karnon for weeks.

From their point of view, it wasn't as though it was *war*. . . .

Schaeffer didn't trust the drones. Ostensibly a third ek-Cha'a sex, they were in fact sexless, originally male or female ek-Cha'a who'd metamorphosed out of their sexual phase. In primitive ek-Cha'a society, they'd been specialized caregivers, the nurturers, child-raisers, teachers, and feeders; now they ran the planet, trying to maintain at least a semblance of peace between the hormone-drunken clans and gangs of bull-males. They couldn't give *orders* to the bulls—no one could do that except for a bigger, stronger bull—but they could make *suggestions* . . . and by long-standing tradition those suggestions generally were honored.

And the Marines understood tradition very well indeed.

"Commander Schaeffer!" The voice was Passerotti's, her call sounding from the tiny speakers implanted behind and below his ears. *"We've got trouble! Looks like the mob's coming through the gate!"*

"I'm in the squad bay. Send me a link."

His cerebral implant, nanochelated within his brain, gave him electronic control over devices nearby. He thoughtclicked the big viewall display to life, tuning in on the image feed from the camera mounted on Passerotti's helmet. Outside, the sun was setting, an intensely bright, hot, pinpoint glare casting long shadows through the streets of Karnon. He could see the high wall surrounding the embassy compound, and the six-meter-wide iron-bar gate across the entrance.

The mob filled the plaza beyond the compound wall, gesticulating, whooping, surging, a wild cacophony of angry xenophobia.

They did not, in fact, look much at all like crabs,

though they had evolved from arboreal pseudocrusta-
ceans. Each was twice as massive as a human, standing
two and a half to three meters tall, with four jointed
legs around a powerfully muscular tail kept tightly
curled up underneath, like a huge, nervous lobster. Pos-
sessing both internal and external skeletons, they were
sheathed in armor like overlapping strips of hardened
leather. Four thick-muscled arms grew evenly spaced
around what generously might be called the head—a
recessed bowl on the upper end of the highly flexible
torso protecting a single small and armor-enclosed eye,
deeply buried to protect it from the hot local sun.
The feeding pouch was located somewhere beneath
the thorax; four slits farther down the body allowed it
to breathe as well as speak. Ek-Cha'a speech sounded
like the discordant hoots and warblings from the brass
section of an orchestra just getting tuned up—*especially*
when they were worked up about something, which
lately seemed to be most of the time.

The arms were their most distinctive feature—
massive, bare of external armor, three-fingered, and
bright blue, branching out from the recessed single
eye like the petals of a flower. The ek-Cha'a closest
to the gate were gripping the bars with all-fours, rattling them furiously.

None of the natives Schaeffer could see was carrying a weapon, thank God, but those powerful arms
could do serious damage to an unprotected human.
The worst part of the situation was Warner's order
that the Marine guard not carry charged lasers. The
battery packs all were in the basement armory, sealed
and locked, and only Warner had the keypad code.

He tried another call to Warner, but got the "busy"

graphic on his in-head display. He might have been able to kick the RSO's door in and pound on his desk, and to hell with what the crab on the wallscreen thought about it, but, damn it, there wasn't *time*.

Sergeant Broder stood beside Schaeffer, looking at the mob. "What do you, think, Commander?" he asked. "Looks like the Boxer Rebellion all over again!"

"I was just thinking that."

Schaeffer had long been a student of military history—especially the history and tradition of the Corps, and that included the so-called Boxer Rebellion of some three hundred years ago. The Dowager Empress in her palace in Beijing had claimed she was trying to protect the foreign legations attacked by the fanatic, rampaging Boxers. In fact, secretly, she'd been behind much of the anti-foreign rioting culminating in the 55-day siege of the legation compound that was still a heroic footnote in the Marine Corps' history.

The ek-Cha'a Eldest Drone, Schaeffer was convinced, was playing a similar game.

The Marines called the asexual drone the king crab.

Schaeffer turned and walked to the rear of the squad bay, where the Security Group's armor lockers were kept. Schaeffer was wearing his Class As, which *should* deflect anything the locals had in the way of small arms.

Although it was always difficult to compare mutually alien technologies, the ek-Cha'a were generally thought to be a couple of centuries behind the Human Confederation—no spaceflight, as yet, no lasers, no nano, no heavy EM or plasma weapons.

Small comfort. Chemically propelled slugs could

still be lethal. And the ek-Cha'a certainly had the advantage of numbers. The city plaza outside the gates was packed with them; the embassy's AI estimate put their numbers at between ten and twelve thousand.

"What the hell are you doing, Gunny?" Broder asked.

"I'm going out there," he replied. "Maybe I can talk them down."

"'One mob, one ranger,' huh?"

"The Texas rangers aren't here. One mob, one *Marine*. But that sounds about equal to me."

"I'll come with you."

"No," Schaeffer said. He was already wearing dress armor, and the heavy, combat stuff was locked away with the laser power packs. He would have to content himself with a fresh armor power unit and a meta jump pack, both of which nestled into the curve at the small of his back, the nano-active surfaces melding with his armor and interfacing with it. As he donned his white, visorless helmet, he felt the suit systems snapping on, and the icons on his in-head display came up green.

"Damn it, Gunny, you can't go out there *alone*!"

"Maybe one man won't be as provocative as two. Besides, I want you to go up to Warner's office, okay?" He drew his 12mm pistol and checked the magazine and safeties, before putting it back in his external holster.

"And do what?"

Schaeffer turned to face Broder, the sergeant's image clear in his IHD.

"Get him to see you. Knock the door down, if you have to. Tell him we need the armory open and battery packs for the lasers and plasma weapons distributed, and tell him we need them *now*!"

"You're going out there with your fucking *service pistol*?"

"We use what we have," Schaeffer told him. He grinned, suddenly, though Broder couldn't see his face. "The Johnson Maneuver, right?"

Broder shook his head. "That mob ain't gonna back down, Gunny."

"Then I'll keep them busy until you can pass out the charge-packs. And break out the heavy armor, too. I'm sick of *diplomacy* with crabs who don't even know the meaning of the word."

"Aye-aye, Gunnery Sergeant. But I don't like this...."

"We work with what we have, Sergeant. Improvise! Adapt! Overcome!"

"Ooh-rah," Broder said, but the old battle cry was delivered flat, without emotion, and without enthusiasm.

By the time Schaeffer made it out the front door of the embassy, fifteen meters from the front gate, the mob had acquired reinforcements. Thompson and Rodriguez were on guard at the door, looking decidedly nervous. "God, Gunny!" Thompson said, pointing, "the crabs've got armored back-up!"

A saurian towered above the crowd, ponderously approaching the gate. *It could not*, Schaeffer thought, *get a whole lot worse.*

The alien armor was an ek-Cha'a military vehicle, somewhere in size and deadliness between a tank and a personal suit of military power armor. Dubbed "saurian" by Marine intelligence, it combined a tracked base with an erect, armored tower that mimicked the upper torso of a bull-male ek-Cha'a. Almost seven meters tall, the armored, segmented torso could twist and turn through more than ninety degrees vertically, and rotate a full two-seventy side-to-side. At the top, four jointed, chromium-alloy steel arms ended in massive, three-clawed pinchers; two small ball turrets to either side of the upper torso mounted 27mm rapid-fire cannons. The vehicle's sole occupant rode inside the thing's upper torso, organic arms operating controls inside mechanical arms, like waldoes, while his legs worked the torso articulation controls and the tracks. The technology was primitive by Confederation standards; the thing was fission-powered, slow, and awkward, its armor no match for Marine lasers and plasma weapons—but the Marines didn't have lasers at the moment, none that worked, and from the way the vehicle waded up through the crowd and grasped the bars of the gate with all four arms, it looked like the vehicle was about to come into the embassy compound.

"Jesus, Gunny!" Rodriguez said. "What are we gonna *do?*"

"Get inside," Schaeffer told the guards. "Go tell Warner if he doesn't distribute power packs and armor, he won't have an embassy left to guard. *Move it!*"

Though awkward and a bit slow, the servomotors behind the saurian's arms were strong. The upper torso of the armored vehicle strained, twisted from side to side, then lurched back a step, pulling the locked gate with it in a shower of powdered stone from the walls to either side. The mob crowding around the vehicle's tracks started forward....

Schaeffer stepped in front of them, drew his service pistol, and aimed it at the closest ek-Cha'a. He thoughtclicked the translate icon on his in-head. "Halt!"

he shouted, and an amplified voice boomed across the compound. *"!Ah'ih!"*

The mob came to a halt, the ones behind piling into the backs of the ones ahead in tangles of jointed legs and segmented bodies. Schaeffer's suit was now linked to the embassy's library AI; it would translate whatever he said into the principal ek-Cha'a language, clicks, glottal stops, and all.

But the saurian was clattering forward, now, tossing the gate aside and grinding ahead of the crowd with a shrill chirping of road wheels and the clash of tracks. Schaeffer pivoted, pointing his sidearm at the machine. The pistol was a 12mm Colt-Blackhawk, nearly as much of an anachronism in the modern Marine Corps as an officer's dress sword, firing solid slugs instead of light or plasma. He had eight rounds in the magazine, not enough to stop a mob of ten thousand . . . or to do serious damage to a light tank.

But maybe they didn't know that. *"!Ah'ih!"* the suit's amplified voice boomed again.

Abruptly, the saurian halted. A string of hoots, barks, clicks, and grunts thundered from the machine. The listening AI dissected them, and scrolled a running translation down the side of Schaeffer's in-head display. SUBMIT, HUMAN. I AM GA!GRE'JOOOH OF THE CLAN !DAKT'JI, AND I CLAIM YOUR LAND AND YOUR HABITATIONS FOR MYSELF AND MY COWS.

"Like hell!" Schaeffer snapped back, the pistol not wavering. "Under the terms of extraterritoriality, this compound is the sovereign territory of the Earth Confederation, and you have five seconds to get the hell out!"

The translation echoed off the surrounding walls

and buildings, as Schaeffer wondered how the AI was rendering such terms as "extraterritoriality" and "hell."

Arms spread wide, its torso bent forward and down, the saurian screamed and lurched forward. . . .

Schaeffer didn't bother firing the pistol. That had been for show only, with the hope that an aggressive stance might make the bastard back down. Instead, he flexed his knees, jumped, and cut in a quick burst from his meta pack.

Meta—He$_{64}$—was an exotic rocket fuel with an exceptionally high energy-density stored in the highly insulated tank on his back. It took tremendous amounts of energy, using high-powered lasers, to pack the helium atoms tightly together in a metastable configuration that came apart *very* easily when it was released into the jumpjet reaction chamber and heated. In Cernunnos' sixth-tenths of a G, a single burst carried Schaeffer high into the air, then dropping toward the armored giant. For a moment, he feared he'd miscalculated; objects fell here at less than 600 centimeters per second squared—just five meters and a bit in the first second. From his adrenaline-charged perspective, it felt like he was hanging in the air, nakedly exposed. The flexible torso of the machine twisted about, as though trying to locate him, then angled up, and Schaeffer found himself looking down at the transparent dome located at the joining of the four outstretched arms. Twin ball turrets on the upper torso rotated up, and the saurian loosed two streams of 27mm high-velocity needles.

Something slammed into his side as he dropped, jarring him. His dress armor was light and thin, but designed to distribute the kinetic energy of an impact across its entire surface. Schaeffer was clubbed to one side by the blow, but he managed not to tumble, managed to awkwardly grab hold of the alien tank's upper body as he struck, managed to grab and hold tight.

From half a meter away, he stared into the transparent canopy at the upturned violet eye of the saurian's pilot.

The machine's torso jerked from side to side, trying to throw him off. He jammed his left arm into the mass of interlocking metal plates that served as shutters to protect the clear dome, which appeared to be made of some kind of thick plastic.

He didn't know if a bullet would penetrate that plastic, and ricochets might hit someone in the crowd. He wanted to *stop* these people, not start a war.

Reversing the pistol in his right hand, Schaeffer brought the butt down hammer-hard against the dome. The force of the blow jarred him to his shoulder despite his armor's dissipation of the energy, and the driver on the other side of the plastic flinched, but it didn't look like he'd even scratched the bubble's surface.

He swung again, striking hard. And again. And *again*. . . .

The machine was frantic, twisting, turning, and trying to claw at him with its arms. A chirping sounded in Schaeffer's ear, an alarm triggered by his armor's radar, and he let go, dropping onto the tank chassis as one massive, mechanical fist whipped past his head and slammed into the bubble. Another arm tried to reach him, but he swarmed up the twisting torso once more, using the segmented armor plates as hand- and footholds. Tucked in close, clinging to the torso and one shoulder, he wasn't *safe*, exactly, but the clumsy thing was definitely having trouble reaching him.

The dome had been brightly starred by the impact of the machine's powerful arm. When Schaeffer climbed back into view, the metal shutters around it irised shut, protecting it. His suit's radar warned him of another incoming swing and again he ducked, clinging tightly to the massive, armored torso. The saurian's ball turret weaponry opened up, but Schaeffer was too close for the guns to bear, and with the shutters closed over the dome, the pilot appeared to be blind.

"Commander Schaeffer!" Warner's voice called over his command channel. *"What the hell do you think you're doing?"*

The saurian snapped its torso left and right. He held on.

"Having a discussion . . . with the . . . locals!" he replied, spacing his words between attempts to shrug him off. "Sir!"

"You can't stop that thing by yourself!"

"Tradition . . . sir! *Duty!*" He could hear the AI translating, but that didn't matter.

"Your duty is to obey my orders, Gunnery Sergeant!"

"My *duty* . . . is to . . . protect my people . . . and civilian personnel . . . *sir!*"

"It'll kill you!"

"Then I suggest . . . you open up . . . the armory! Sir! Let my people . . . lock and load!"

Schaeffer just hoped he could buy them enough time.

A few of the more daring members of the mob were starting to clamber up onto the deck of the chassis.

Twisting around, Schaeffer fired two shots into the air . . . then kicked at one particularly stubborn ek-Cha'a who hadn't jumped off with the gunfire. The torso behind him twisted sharply to the right, the weapons still firing blind; rounds slammed into the crowd and several of the unarmored ek-Cha'a fell, writhing.

Shit! But at least the rest began scattering. Schaeffer turned at another radar warning, ducked, dropped to the tank deck, then ducked again at another ponderous swing of an arm. He hit the pavement in front of the machine and rolled, coming up again on one knee. The alien machine loomed above him, its torso bent far forward, the arms spread apart as it reached for him.

Needle-tipped bullets slammed past him, and three shattered against his chest armor and helmet, splintering, staggering him, but he kept his position. The driver's dome was again open, and Schaeffer could see the ek-Cha'a inside, staring down at him with that single, unwinking purple eye.

Still kneeling, Schaeffer brought his 12mm up in a two-handed grip and began firing, round after round slamming into the plastic bubble and shrieking off in wild ricochets. The star brightened; the dome cracked....

The shutters irised shut again, blinding the driver. The machineguns stopped, but four arms were descending on Schaeffer from above and from either side.

An alarm shrilled in Schaeffer's helmet, and he could smell the sulfur stink of SO_2. His armor had been breached.

Again, Schaeffer triggered his jumpjets, sailing up and onto the saurian's forward deck, then clambering once more up the sharply bent torso. The saurian was firing wildly now, quick, sharp bursts that raked the pavement below or shrieked off the surrounding walls. The dome shields irised open as the driver tried to acquire his target.

Schaeffer rammed his left fist down into the moveable armor plates, freezing them, while pointing the pistol directly at the driver's eye. "You can do what you like to each other," he shouted, "but this ground is *mine!*"

For emphasis, he slammed the butt of his pistol against the cracked plastic again, and this time he felt it actually give a bit beneath the blow. He pressed the muzzle of his sidearm against the plastic. *"Get this damned thing off my perimeter!"*

For long seconds, Marine and ek-Cha'a warrior stared at one another. Two arms started to move, and Schaeffer said, *"Don't!"* The armored plates surrounding the damaged bubble tightened against his arm, straining. "I said *don't!*"

If worst came to unthinkable worst, Schaeffer had one final card to play. If he released his meta tank, slapped its nanoseal surface against the tank chassis deck, and switched off the insulation circuit, it would explode within a minute or so as the He_{64} heated up. He didn't want to do that unless he had to; he wouldn't be able to control the explosion, and the saurian, he remembered, was powered by a small plutonium reactor inside the chassis. The detonating meta would not only take out the ek-Cha'a armor and a large number of the crowd, it would also scatter an unknown amount of radioactive plutonium across the heart of the city.

Back down, you hormone-happy bastard! he thought. *Back down! . . .*

The pressure on his arm relaxed. And the saurian began backing up.

Schaeffer jumped off the front of the vehicle as it

continued to back, one track skirt scraping against a gate post with a shower of stone fragments. The crowd behind it began backing up as well, uncertain, and when they collided with unmoving members of the mob behind they began panicking. Schaeffer stepped forward, following the armored vehicle, keeping his pistol steadily pointed at the driver. He halted at the gateway.

The crowd continued to disperse. The armored saurian stood there for a moment longer, and Schaeffer was uncomfortably aware that the machine's turrets both were aimed directly at him. His armor had deflected everything those weapons had thrown at him so far, but it couldn't render him invulnerable. Another sustained volley might well deliver more kinetic energy than his dress armor could handle. His side and chest were aching—now that he could think about it—from the earlier impacts.

Perhaps worst of all, the digital counter on the side of his pistol now read "0." He'd expended all of his rounds moments ago, and the weapon was empty.

The machine raised all four arms, moving them in a complex gesture.

And then it turned on its tracks and rumbled away across the plaza.

"Your actions," Warner told him in his office later, "were . . . how shall I put it? Somewhat unorthodox."

"Yes, sir."

Schaeffer stood at attention in front of Warner's high-tech desk. He'd been summoned here immediately after the incident, fully expecting to be chewed a new one.

Damned bureaucrats....

Warner studied him for a moment, his head propped on thumb and extended forefinger. "Tell me, Commander, just what made you think you could stop that vehicle by yourself, with a *pistol* of all things?"

"Corps tradition, sir."

"Tradition. Commander Schaeffer, there is *nothing* in Marine Corp tradition—"

"Excuse me, sir, but there is." Schaeffer thought-clicked a file in his own in-head, transferring it to Warner's console. "This is a download from the embassy library. Corps history is a . . . a kind of hobby of mine, sir."

Warner pulled up the file on one of his monitors and read it. "One Marine with a pistol," he said. He shook his head. "Against a column of three tanks."

"Yes, sir. He had them outnumbered. We call it the Johnson Maneuver."

Most Marines knew the story of Marine Captain Charles B. Johnson, just as they knew the fabled exploits of other Corps heroes—Dan Daly, John Basilone, Chesty Puller, Smedley Butler, and so many, many more.

"You were gambling on the tech differential, weren't you?" Warner demanded. "That bull-male couldn't hurt you through your armor."

"Not really, sir. He did breach my armor once, though the nano systems sealed it off and purged my air. The thing is, I figured he was acting under both cultural and biological imperatives, assuming that if I was a male, I would fight for my territory and my right to mate. If I backed down—if we backed down, sir—we would have proven that we were submissive males, and would have to do what the bull-males demanded. It was simpler to just show them who was boss."

Schaeffer didn't add that the armor and the technology had nothing to do with things. It was never about the armor . . . it was about the man inside. *Always*.

"Apparently you did so," Warner continued. "The Ambassador called me a few moments ago. It seems that thirty-five female ek-Cha'a have just applied for admission to the compound. According to ek-Cha'a tradition, they're yours, now. Your, ah, 'cows,' won in single combat, fair and square."

"Well, the Ambassador is going to have to find a polite way of saying 'thanks, but no thanks,' isn't he?"

"Something of that sort." Warner shook his head, but he almost smiled. "You know, I *should* write you up for insubordination, Commander, but Ambassador Tarleton is quite happy with how things have turned out. You appear to have defused a potentially serious diplomatic situation, and resolved it in our favor."

"I'm glad to hear it, sir."

But he hadn't done it for *diplomacy*.

"By the way, you might be interested to know. When the saurian broke off the fight, it moved its arms . . . kind of like this." Warner's two-handed attempt at a four-armed gesture was not nearly as successful as his attempts at the spoken ek-Cha'a language. "According to Ng'g'!grelchk, who was watching the whole thing . . . the bull was saluting you as a worthy fellow warrior, and as victor."

"We should respect the cultural traditions of the locals, sir," Schaeffer said.

Just so long, he thought, *as the locals learn to respect* our *traditions as well*.

USMC HISTORY
CEREBRAL IMPLANT DOWNLOAD
[EXTRACT]

On February 2, 1983, Israeli forces were testing the resolve of 1,200 U.S. Marines in southern Lebanon, part of a UN peacekeeping force in the area. Seeking to discredit the Marines in order to impose their own military control over the area, Israeli infantry and armor probed Marine positions and, in one case, sent a column of three heavy Centurion tanks toward a Marine checkpoint. Captain [Charles B.] Johnson stood in the middle of the road, pistol drawn, forcing the tanks to stop. "You will not pass through this position," Johnson said. "If you go through, it will be over my dead body."

Two of the tanks broke from the third and attempted to rush past Johnson. The Marine jumped on top of the lead tank, put his .45 pistol to [Israeli Lt. Col. Rafi] Landsberg's head, and ordered the man to stop his tanks.

Landsberg complied and, after a hurried exchange of radio traffic with his headquarters, the Centurions withdrew. The Israelis tried to downplay the incident, calling it a misunderstanding on the part of the Marines.

But Captain Johnson's actions were in the highest traditions of Marine Corps commitment to honor, fidelity, and duty.

Ian Douglas is the pseudonym of William H. Keith, the author of over 100 novels, mostly military SF and technothrillers. His work includes the Galactic Marines trilogy of trilogies, *Legacy*, *Heritage*, and *Inheritance*, written as Ian Douglas. Under the name H. Jay Riker, he wrote the long-running *SEALs: The Warrior Breed* series, a lightly fictionalized look at the history of Navy special warfare. More recently, he collaborated with author Stephen Coonts on three bestselling spy thrillers in the *Deep Black* series: *Arctic Gold*, *Sea of Terror*, and *Death Wave*, while his short fiction has been extensively anthologized by the late Martin H. Greenberg.

Hel's Half-Acre

JACK CAMPBELL

The armor isn't too bad too live in once you get used to being confined in a sort of obedient iron-maiden for days, weeks, and sometimes months on end. After a while, it feels normal. That's why in the mobile infantry we joke "Just bury me in my armor so I'll be comfortable."

There's padding where padding needs to be, and an interior that flexes and adjusts to fit, because the last thing you need is a sore you can't reach for a few weeks. The air recyclers do a decent job, once your nose gets used to your smell, that is. After a few weeks in armor, you can't smell anything—including yourself—and we're all very grateful for that in the Heavy Mechanized Infantry.

We've got tubes that provide stuff that needs to go in, like food and water, and other tubes that handle what needs to go out afterwards. There's not much solid waste, since battle rations are concentrated as all hell, and the liquid gets recycled, which you learn not to think about when you're thirsty. If you run low on anything, packs can be swapped out on the outside of the armor for resupply. You can get music, video, just about anything when you're not on active ops. There's even a long-standing rumor that there's an Easter egg hidden in the programming that will activate different functions in those tubes below the waist to handle the one physical need the armor doesn't take care of and that young soldiers tend to miss pretty serious as time goes by. No one's ever found that egg, but looking for it helps pass the time.

I sat amid a tumble of big rocks that we had nicknamed "the fort," surrounded by the rest of the platoon. We call ourselves Hel's Half-Acre on account of Sergeant Hel. Lieutenants come and go, usually coming with a brand new, shiny uniform and usually going in body tubes not long afterwards, but Sergeant Hel stays. "I'm gonna outlive all of you," she predicts when we haven't done something as good as we should have. "Because you're all idiots! I'll be safe since the Canaries will use up all of their ammo killing you! That's assuming you get that far, which you won't, because if any of you low-grade excuses for soldiers ever pull that again I'll shoot you myself and save the Canaries the trouble!"

The Canaries don't look like little birds, of course. It would feel kind of stupid fighting to the death against little birds. But the way they talk sounds like canaries, and for noses they've got these hard beak things on top of their mouths. I don't know much else about them, because the only ones I've ever seen up-close were dead.

It's that kind of war.

We had dropped onto a planet named Niffleheim about a month ago, and been in our armor, every seal tight, every moment since then. The dense atmosphere was made up of various highly corrosive gases that would literally dissolve human flesh and bones.

Cady was looking toward the Canary lines east of us, just barely raising up enough to see because any time anyone shows too much above the rocks the Canaries target it with some really impressive accuracy. "Rain's coming."

"Better get your wash in off the line," Iko commented, then laughed at his own joke.

The acid droplets began pelting us and the rocks that were all that Niffleheim had in the way of landscaping, and then the winds started coming through. "Everybody anchor," Sergeant Hel ordered.

Before we could start to manually do that, the Armor Assists started punching out spikes from the arms of our armor. "Place anchor here," my AA told me, highlighting a spot nearby as I got a good grip on my spike.

My AA has a sort of mechanical voice, nothing recognizably male or female. Most soldiers set the voice for someone they know, and then grow to hate that someone as the voice nags at them. Or after a while, living literally inside this thing with a nice voice, a few soldiers get way too attached to it. When they get weird like that they get sent home for a while.

But they have to be *really* weird before they get a ticket out of a combat zone.

I planted the anchor with the boost from my armor's muscles. It went deep into the solid rock, then I just locked my armor's grip on the anchor, told the AA not to relax the grip, and relaxed myself even though the wind was trying to throw me across the landscape.

"Why the hell do we want this place?" Corporal Higgins muttered. We were all linked by the tactical net, so that even in the midst of the hell outside our armor we could talk in regular voices.

"Because the Canaries want it," Iko replied.

"So why do they want it?"

"Because it's here," Afrit suggested.

"It's worthless. You can't see more than half a kilometer under the best conditions, the storms make air transport too risky for routine use, and even orbital launches can be hairy. It's not good for anything."

The Sarge answered this time. "You thinking again, Corporal Higgins?"

"Yeah, I'm thinking."

"I warned you about that." Hel's voice was as flat and even as it was during any of her lectures. "You keep thinking and they'll make you a lieutenant. You know what happens to lieutenants."

"That last one," Gonzo said, "what was his name? He was with us like six hours."

"Stuck his head too high," Cady commented.

"Yeah. Did they ever find it, Sarge?"

"Nah. Listen, there'll be another lieutenant here soon. You apes try to keep this one alive at least a few days."

"Why the hell we gotta listen to some snot-nosed—" Cady started to grumble.

"What was that?" Sergeant Hel asked. The Sarge hadn't raised her voice, but Cady shut up fast and I was glad I'd kept my own mouth shut. "Oh, look,"

Sarge continued, "it's time for a mandatory law of war training session, and we have nothing else on the schedule."

Considering that we were all hanging onto anchors while the wind made flags out of us in our heavy armor none of us could claim any other priorities at the moment, but a chorus of moans and groans sounded anyway. "Listen up for the verbal prompts," Hel told us, then ordered our AAs to start the session.

The metallic voice of my AA started the canned lecture. "Discipline on the battlefield is critical to the success of the mission and survival of your comrades. Which of the following offenses require a mandatory death penalty if committed in a combat zone? A, disobedience of an order. B, disrespect toward a superior officer. C, absence from place of duty. D, desertion. E, all of the above."

"E," I said. *All of the above* was almost always a safe answer on military tests, even if I hadn't had this same information drilled into my brain every week.

"Correct. True or false: Planning to commit an offense is not as serious as actually carrying out the offense."

"False." I fantasized for the millionth time about dismantling my AA, teeny-tiny piece by teeny-tiny piece, while it jabbered on about "unauthorized maintenance activity" until it finally shut up when I'd taken enough of it apart.

That's the thing about AAs. They're stupid. A friend of mine who's a code geek says they used to call stuff like that artificial intelligence, but there wasn't anything intelligent about it. The artificial intelligence stuff kept running faster and faster, but it stayed just as stupid.

Hard to believe, but even someone like Cady has got a lot more brains than an AA. The AAs handle housekeeping and routine tasks for the armor, keep everything working right, assist in aiming weapons, monitor our health, life-support, and damn all else. They also monitor whether we're following orders even though they're too stupid to create orders themselves.

Which meant I had to get a passing grade on this lecture or Sergeant Hel's AA would be told by my AA, which would also inform everyone else up the chain of command that Private London had failed weekly law of war instruction. That would make Sergeant Hel very unhappy, and there's not a lot of things in this universe worse than making Sergeant Hel very unhappy.

"Failure to accompany your unit in any movement while in a battle zone is A, dereliction of duty. B, a betrayal of your comrades. C, indirectly lending aid and comfort to the enemy. D, an offense justifying summary battlefield execution. E, all of the above."

"E." When you came down to it, as long as you assumed the correct answer for any offense in a battle zone was death you'd pass the test.

Which was another reason why we hated our AAs. Summary executions didn't require firing squads, not when the AA handled everything keeping you alive. Weird soldiers might sometimes grow attached to their AAs, but the AA never got attached to the soldier in the armor. A summary execution order was just one more instruction for it to carry out, and you couldn't even run, not when the AA could freeze your armor.

The storm had finally subsided, though visibility would still be worse than usual for a few hours, and the lecture ended when my armor reported a new arrival. My systems updated automatically, linking to whoever was inside that armor, and then an ID popped up. Lieutenant Yvonne Karolla. But instead of launching into the usual "I'm your new boss and we'll work great together" speech, Lieutenant Karolla waved back behind our lines. "General MacDougal is coming through."

That made us sit up. A little. No sense in exposing anything to the Canaries on the heights facing us. MacDougal had a reputation for touring the front himself, something I gave him grudging credit for. Most high-ranking officers were happy to study the battlefield using virtual tech, but MacDougal would actually come and look it over.

"The General is coming here?" Sergeant Hel asked. "Lieutenant, the General visited this same position a couple of days after we dropped."

"Then he's visiting here again," Karolla said in a don't-ask-questions voice. Even inside our armor I could easily imagine pairs of eyes rolling at the rookie mistake. Telling a senior non-commissioned officer to shut up is almost always a bad idea.

We waited silently after that, the tension radiating from the new Lieutenant strong enough that I wondered why it didn't show up on my armor's sensors. Then MacDougal arrived, his armor worn from long use. He had a half-dozen aides and guards with him, which made things a bit cramped among our rocks.

"How's it going?" the General asked no one in particular. Generals say stuff like that. It doesn't mean anything, and it especially doesn't mean they really want you to tell them how it's going after a month in armor getting shot at and rained on by acid.

None of us answered, even though my AA prompted me. "You have been asked a question by a superior officer."

"He didn't ask me," I told it, which confused the AA enough to shut it up.

Finally, the Lieutenant spoke up, trying to sound chipper amid the noxious atmosphere swirling around us. "We're doing fine, General."

"Good. Good." MacDougal moved forward a little more, toward the Canary positions, while his aides hovered nervously. I noticed he moved a little haltingly, but word had gone around that the general had been banged up a bit on the drop so that wasn't surprising. Once the injury stiffened up inside the armor it would have made it harder to walk.

MacDougal stood there, peering through the murk toward the Canary positions he couldn't actually see from here right now, then pivoted to look south. He had done that last time he was here, too, so it made me a bit nervous. "We'll remain on the attack," the general announced.

One of the colonels linked in with the general must have said something.

"There," MacDougal said, pointing to a rise to the southeast. Axe-handle Hill, we called it. The haft of the axe was covered with Canary foxholes. "We will swing a diversion to the south of the hill, then hit the front with a heavy assault."

More conversation that we couldn't hear, then MacDougal again. "Make it happen."

He walked away, while we stared after him.

"Oh, man," Higgins muttered. "Frontal assault on the Axe-handle?"

"Are you questioning orders?" Lieutenant Karolla demanded. "Corporal...Corporal Higgins?"

"The platoon will follow orders," Sergeant Hel said. "Lieutenant, request a private conference."

"Not yet, Sergeant. I need to familiarize myself with unit personnel statistics and the local terrain first."

Lieutenant Karolla was still working on that about ten minutes later when the orders to attack came down through our AAs. I looked over the attack route, suppressing a worried whistle. "Gonna need some tactical autonomy, Sarge."

"Really, London? Why the hell do you think I've been beating tactical autonomy into all of you?"

Tactical autonomy is the loophole in terms of following orders. It lets you deviate some from an ordered route or select a different target. Stuff like that. You can't go backwards, but you can go a bit to the side. In this case, it meant we could sneak along a path shielded by some more rocks until we were fairly close to the Axe-handle instead of charging across open rock with no cover at all like the AAs were telling us to.

"Tactical autonomy?" the new lieutenant asked. "I haven't—There's—"

"Jump-off," Sergeant Hel told her as the order came in. "We have to go now, Lieutenant."

My own AA echoed the command, as did everyone else's AA. The brass didn't care whether or not the Lieutenant had time to study the plan. They didn't care whether any of us had time for that. We were just supposed to follow the plan, and the AAs would ensure we knew where to go and what to do when we got there.

We didn't even have to coordinate. Sarge had

drilled it all into us. While the new Lieutenant fussed and complained we headed out, falling into an open formation with the Sergeant off to one side, Corporal Higgins off to the other, and the Lieutenant near the rear to oversee and coordinate everything. That's all standard. Being in the back doesn't protect the junior officers much, though, because the Canary gear can spot comm nodes among armor. They can always tell who the unit commander is, and the Canaries aim everything they've got at that commander. Which is one of the big reasons why lieutenants don't last very long.

I pulled out the range on my display so I could see the diversion going in. Light Mechanized Infantry, jumping fast to hit the Axe-handle on one flank. It was crazy to use the Lights under those conditions. I waited for them to get slaughtered.

But with Niffleheim's atmosphere fouling targeting gear and the Lights moving so much faster than Heavies could, the Lights kept coming through an intense Canary barrage that didn't score many hits. The Lights were taking hits, but not too many, and we could see Canary fire all along the Axe-handle shifting to engage them.

Sergeant Hel veered to the left and we charged out of the rocks toward the Canaries, everyone dodging as they ran and keeping position on the Sarge even though the AAs kept trying to tell us where to go. The Axe-handle itself was just starting to emerge from the murk as we ran toward it, which meant we were emerging into the sight of the Canaries up there.

"Stick to the assault corridor!" Lieutenant Karolla ordered us.

We all kept our eyes on Sergeant Hel. She was

amazing. Confusing enemy targeting means being almost totally random in dodging while still moving toward your objective. Nobody could do that like Sergeant Hel, and now she kept heading pretty straight for the Axe-handle even though the assault corridor glowing on our displays was about a hundred meters to the right. "Tactical autonomy," Hel advised the Lieutenant.

"There's no justification for deviating from orders here!"

"Lieutenant, going right a hundred meters will cost time and every second counts."

"Get this platoon inside that assault corridor now! I won't tell you again, Sergeant!"

"Lieutenant, if you keep active transmitting it will make it easier for the Canaries to—"

The first couple of Canary artillery rounds aimed at us bracketed Lieutenant Karolla, then a dozen more slammed into the area between the first hits.

Her link cut off completely, which meant chances were pretty high that those rounds had already killed the new Lieutenant. We kept going.

"Less than an hour!" Gonzo gasped as the Axe-handle loomed ahead of us and we began jumping recklessly up the slope. "You got to feel sorry for Lieutenant . . . uh . . . her. She never had a chance."

Most of the Canary fire was still aimed at the Lights who were falling back now. The Canaries were starting to realize we were coming in as fast as Heavies could move, but it took time for them to shift the aim of their heavy weapons, and our armor could handle most of the lighter Canary weapons. We made the top without losing anyone else even though our armor took some damage.

Canary armor isn't as good as ours. At close range, we could put holes in it easy. On Niffleheim, holes let in the atmosphere, which dissolves Canaries just like it does humans.

We cleaned out the Canaries who tried to hold the Axe-handle, but most of them fled into the murk, leaving the top of the hill and their heavy weapons in our possession. According to our map displays there was another ridge about a kilometer onward that the Canaries could fort up on and establish a new line linked to their other positions. "Should we pursue?" Higgins asked.

"Our orders are to take and hold the Axe-handle," Sergeant Hel replied, "maintaining defensive positions until relieved. You gonna show some initiative, Corporal?"

"Hell, no, Sarge. I know what would happen to us even if we won."

"All of the above," I couldn't help adding.

"Hey, Private London's a comedian!" the Sergeant announced. "Get your funny ass back down there and find what's left of the Lieutenant."

"The Canaries are dropping artillery rounds on that area to discourage reinforcements coming up here," I protested.

"Try not to let any hit you. Get going."

A day later we were back among the same rocks we called the fort. The guys from the Thirty-Second took over defending the Axe-handle, and we trooped back to our rocks. When you're sleeping in your armor, it doesn't make too much difference which rocks you're around, but at least the rocks on top of the Axe-handle had been high ground. Now we were back with Canary positions on the ridge ahead of us looking down on us.

The latest Lieutenant joined us there. Lieutenant Cathar had the sense to make nice with Sergeant Hel, or least listen to her, and he kept his head down, so he survived for several days while we huddled among the rocks and the Canaries tossed shots our way occasionally.

"Routine servicing," my AA announced.

"What routine servicing?" Not that I cared, but I was seriously bored.

"Backing up files. Reviewing automated assist routines. Complete."

I laid on my back, staring up at the swirling mess of an atmosphere which covered Niffleheim. No stars shining down on us here.

Automated assist routines. That reminded me of something. "Hey, AA."

"Yes, Private London."

"When I found what was left of Lieutenant, uh . . . what was her name?"

"Lieutenant Karolla."

"Yeah. That Lieutenant. Her lower torso looked like it had walked maybe five meters after she got hit before it collapsed."

"Emergency full assist. When Lieutenant Karolla was incapacitated, her lower armor began walking autonomously to bring her to aid. However, system damage was too extreme and atmospheric corrosion caused additional damage, resulting in rapid total armor failure."

"Incapacitated? Everything above the Lieutenant's waist was gone."

The AA didn't answer, probably because its little code routines had decided my last statement wasn't a question. But it might have been because the answer was classified. You never knew. Those special functions for the tubes below the waist might not actually exist, but we all knew stuff was embedded in the armor that we hadn't been told about.

"The General is on the way," Lieutenant Cathar announced.

"Again?" It slipped out before I could stop it.

"Shut up, London," Hel told me. "If the General wants to come back here every week, that's his call. Everybody try to look like soldiers."

I rolled to my side and got into sort of an alert-looking crouch near a really big rock while the other members of the platoon also took up more active positions.

General MacDougal came through the same way as before, once again accompanied by his aides and guards. "How's it going?"

Lieutenant Cathar answered immediately. "Great, sir!"

"Good. Good." MacDougal moved farther forward, peering at the enemy lines. "We can't stay on the defensive. We need that position." His hand raised and pointed to the ridge.

This time I heard the Colonel who answered the General. "Sir, the initial attack from here during the first week after landing was thrown back. The Canaries have substantially strengthened their defenses on that ridge since then."

"We can't stay on the defensive," MacDougal repeated. "We need that position." He turned toward us, and I felt a strange sense of reliving the past. This was just as that first attack had happened. Mac-Dougal here, eyeing the ridge, waving us forward... That time we had just gotten a serious taste of how tough the Canary defenses were when a sudden storm blew in and we had been forced to fall back among the rocks. That storm had saved our butts, but this time I couldn't see any signs of bad weather coming.

The General's arm came up and he swung it in an arc toward the Canary lines. "Get 'em, Heavies!"

He had said that the first time, too.

Sergeant Hel said nothing, just coming to her feet as the rest of us did the same.

"General?" Lieutenant Cathar asked, his voice incredulous.

"Make it happen," General MacDougal said.

That was it. A direct order to attack right there, right now. My AA prodded me, my display flashing with an attack route aimed straight at the ridge. If we didn't follow that order, our own AAs would lock us down until the execution commands were received. But tactical autonomy wouldn't help here, not when it was just a straight shot across open ground. I looked toward the others, knowing what they were thinking and feeling even though I couldn't see their expressions. *We're dead whether we disobey the order or try to carry it out. Might as well go down fighting and take our damned AAs with us.*

We made it maybe forty meters out of the rocks before the Canaries opened up. I had never been in a barrage that intense, so heavy that the command net links fuzzed and popped. Lieutenant Cathar went first, of course. I saw Gonzo stagger, then explode.

Higgins seemed to float upward a little and then he just disappeared in a blast. Cady did a funny kind of sideways dance and fell over.

Something jerked at my legs but I didn't fall. I felt a peculiar sense of weightlessness beneath me, as if I were walking on air. My legs didn't hurt anymore from running. The view in front of me tilted as if I were falling but I couldn't feel my legs or get them under me. My AA's voice sounded oddly distant. "Major damage. Activating auto-tourniquets. Activating auto-first-aid. Activating auto-amputation to seal armor. Major damage. Wounded needing pickup."

I fell onto the rocks, wondering why the damage display on my armor wasn't showing anything beneath my thighs. Something hit me really hard and I rolled, then another hit, another roll, more damage lights flashing on my display, and somewhere in all that the drugs from the first aid and the shock hit me so I passed out with the toxic gases of Niffleheim swirling over my armor. My last thoughts were wishes that I could have seen the stars and that the stupid AA would shut the hell up.

I woke up.

The first thing that registered on my brain was that I wasn't in armor, but after a moment's rising panic I realized the air was good in here.

The low ceiling was rock. So were the walls. On either side of the med-bed I was in, and on the other side of the long, narrow room, other med-beds stretched in long rows. I couldn't make them out well, though, and I remembered they had added distortion fields to med-beds to give patients privacy.

I looked down at myself as tumbled memories surfaced. Below my waist I was locked into a rebuild unit.

I was still staring at that when a medic came by, her eyes filled with that seen-too-much look. She didn't say anything to me, just checked the rebuild.

"What happened?" I finally asked.

The medic looked at me. "You lost both legs. Your armor had to activate emergency seals at the thighs or the atmosphere would have got in and turned you to mush. We're doing a fix. This is just temporary though. We're having problems with our bone reconstruction gear so we'll do an evac of you later so a full facility can do a proper leg rebuild."

"Where is this? Are we still on Niffleheim?"

"Yeah. Underground. This was the first room they finished. Your armor was totaled. You want the AA?"

"Hell, no. Wipe it. Uh, do you know how many others from my unit—?"

"No. Sorry." The medic looked toward the front of the room as something caught her attention.

I looked down at the rebuild unit grasping my waist, recalling the last things I had seen as we attacked the ridge. Had anybody else at all survived? How had I made it?

"The General's back," the medic sighed. "Every damned day. Try to look military if he stops to talk to you."

I could turn my head enough to see the General. His aides were out of armor, but he was still fully sealed in even though this was one of the only places on Niffleheim where you could unseal.

"I wish he'd take off the armor," the medic grumbled. "He had to wear it the first couple of times he visited because the air in here was still being scrubbed and we were all still suited up, but this is a medical facility, not a combat post."

The General came down the lines of cots, occasionally pausing to talk to someone.

Then he came to me. I looked at the sealed face shield, blank and menacing in strange contrast to MacDougal's voice, which sounded bluff and comradely. "How's it going?"

I just stared back at the General until I noticed a Colonel giving me an angry look. "Okay," I said.

"Good. Good."

That made something snap inside me. "I lost my legs," I said.

"Your sacrifice is an inspiration to us all," General MacDougal said.

"My platoon got wiped out. You ordered us into a hopeless attack."

"We can't stay on the defensive. We'll do what we can for you, soldier."

I lost it. I admit it. If Sergeant Hel had been there she would have given me holy hell. But this general had ordered my platoon to be slaughtered in an attack with zip, zero, nil chance of succeeding. And now he was standing here, still in his damned armor, not even giving me the courtesy of eye to eye contact, while mouthing meaningless phrases. "You lousy son-of-a-bitch! You *murdered* my platoon! Do you understand that? Does it mean anything to you?"

The medical officers and the aides standing near General MacDougal were gaping at me, too stunned for the moment to react.

"You want to know what you can do for me, you

stinking bastard?" I shouted. "Open your damned face shield and look me in the eye! Can you do that?"

A colonel lunged for me, his hand coming to rest hard on my shoulder. "Shut up, soldier," he told me.

"Just open your face shield!" I yelled at MacDougal, ignoring the colonel.

General MacDougal's hands rose slightly toward his face, and I saw the face shield crack open and begin to rise.

Remember when I talked about how bad you get to smelling in armor after a while? What came wafting out from MacDougal's armor was incredibly bad. Bad enough that the colonel pinning me down stared at the general as the faceplate rose.

I was watching the colonel, and saw him grow really pale, so I looked toward the general.

What looked out at us from the armor had been dead for a while.

Someone screamed, other people shouted, while General MacDougal's armor just stood there. Then MacDougal's voice came from it again. "Your sacrifices will not be in vain!" the voice boomed out before another colonel managed to punch in an emergency deactivation code on the general's armor that shut down the AA.

The medic was fumbling with the rebuild unit attached to me. I felt a surge of meds hit me and blacked out again. When I woke up, everyone was gone, and so was General MacDougal's armor.

For another day nobody told me anything. The medics who walked past or checked me occasionally said they hadn't heard anything, which I knew was a lie. Rumors had to be flying all over the place.

The second day since I woke up had almost ended, the lights starting the slow dim to evening illum, when I saw her enter the medical ward.

"Sergeant? Sergeant Hel?" I couldn't believe it.

The Sarge walked up to my bed and looked down at me. "Goofing off again, London?"

"I need some new legs, Sarge."

"Pretty weak excuse for lying in bed all day. They'll grow 'em back."

"Yeah. Is there anybody else? Besides you and me?"

Sergeant Hel sat down on the chair beside my bed, her eyes on mine as she shook her head. "You and me," she repeated. "That's it."

"How did you—?"

Hel shrugged. "Cady fell on top of me. I got her up and she came apart, so I dropped the pieces and started forward again." She touched her head and I realized a faded bruise covered most of her forehead. "Something hit me hard, I went down, almost all systems in my armor dead, saw you lying there, nothing else moving, no emergency beacons visible from the others, a rain of fire coming down from the Canary positions on the ridge, so I grabbed you and hauled you back. I think I passed out before I made it to the rocks, but somebody recovered us both. They stuffed me into the concussion recovery magic box, and a half day ago they let me out and woke me up again, good as new." Hel touched her forehead again. "Almost. I hear you yelled at a general."

"A dead general."

"They were going to court-martial you," Sergeant Hel said. "Because you didn't know he was dead when you mouthed off."

"Sarge—"

"You would have deserved it, too, you stupid ape. But if they court-martialed you they'd have to shoot you, which means a lot of publicity might get out, and the brass doesn't want that. No, sir."

"How long had he been dead?" I hadn't been able to get that face out of my thoughts.

"Three weeks, a couple hours, and a few minutes according to the autopsy. He died about a week after we landed." The Sarge looked around the casualty ward. "His AA had been running everything, just going on auto. He must have ceded more and more routine tasks to it, so when he couldn't function at all anymore, the AA just stepped in and kept doing what he and it had been doing."

"Why the hell couldn't MacDougal's armor tell everyone he was dead? We can't get a sore throat without the armor alerting the medics so they can order remote treatment from the first aid modules!"

Hel sat back, still looking across the ward. "The autopsy also found out that MacDougal's heart had been failing. He'd hacked his armor so the med read-outs showed he was okay. When he actually died, well, the read-outs showed he was okay."

"He hacked his armor? Nobody caught that?"

"MacDougal wanted to be the hero of Niffleheim and he was the General, London. Generals get to play by their own rules. If they don't want their armor systems inspected and deloused, they're not inspected and deloused. You should know that by now. How long have you been in the infantry?"

"Too damned long."

"You haven't learned a hell of a lot."

It felt so normal, so routine, the Sarge telling me how dumb I was, but I was in a bed in the casualty ward and we were all that was left of the platoon. I had to blink fast to try to keep from crying.

"Let it out," Sergeant Hel said. "But I ain't gonna hug you."

So I cried for a while. They encourage that, these days. Don't bury the feelings when you bury your friends. That's the motto. Seriously. Ever since I first heard it I've wanted to kill the morons who thought up that motto.

The Sarge waited until I stopped blubbering. "You gonna be okay?"

"Yeah, Sarge. Why wouldn't anyone else tell me about MacDougal? Why are the brass so worried about keeping it quiet?"

"Think about it, London. MacDougal had been dead for three weeks. Before we were ordered to assault that ridge, how was the battle going?"

I did my best to concentrate on that, running mentally through the blur of movement and boredom and fear and waiting and fighting that made up my memories. "I think we were winning."

"Yeah. That move against the Canary position at Axe-handle Hill? Pretty sweet, huh? Perfect use of a diversion using the right kind of troops."

"Yeah," I agreed.

"That was two weeks ago. MacDougal had already been dead for a week. His Armor Assist ordered that attack, using the patterns it had learned about how MacDougal fought." Hel looked at me again. "Now, how many bosses have we worked for who never would have come up with a plan like that? And how many of those would have ordered, or *did* order, senseless attacks like the one against the ridge that we got cut to ribbons on?"

I didn't have to think hard about that. "Several. What's the point, Sarge?" Before she could answer, I understood. "That stupid AA did as good as some of the humans who've commanded us in the field? It did better than some of them? Even though it was incapable of original, independent thought?"

"Yeah." Hel stood up. "Think about it. Or don't. You might be happier that way. Now as long as you're lying in bed get some rest so you can get back on duty status as soon as possible."

I watched her go, walking steadily away between the lines of beds and the wounded on them. "Sarge?"

Hel stopped and turned, looking back at me across the distance. "Yeah?"

"I didn't die before you did."

She grinned. "Not yet."

I lay there, trying not to think, as Sergeant Hel left the building.

———————

Jack Campbell is the pen name of John G. Hemry, author of the *New York Times* bestselling Lost Fleet series (*Dauntless, Fearless, Courageous, Valiant, Relentless,* and *Victorious*). His latest book is *Dreadnaught,* the first in the Lost Fleet—Beyond the Frontier series. He is also the author of the Stark's War and "JAG in space" series. His short fiction has appeared in places as varied as the last Chicks in Chainmail anthology (*Turn the Other Chick*) and *Analog* magazine (most recently "Betty Knox and Dictionary Jones in the Mystery of the Missing Teenage Anachronisms" in the March 2011 issue). He also has stories in the anthologies *Breach the Hull*, *So it Begins*, and *By Other Means*, as well as the essay *Liberating the Future* in *Teenagers From the Future* (about the Legion of Super Heroes). After retiring from the US Navy and settling in Maryland, John began writing. John lives with his wife (the incomparable S) and three great kids. His oldest son and daughter are diagnosed autistic.

Jungle Walkers

DAVID KLECHA &
TOBIAS S. BUCKELL

"Chinese metal? What does he mean?" Dan Stilwill asked.

Corporal Faisal Jabar eyed the thick Colombian jungle around the gravel road, an old smuggler's route that ran down into Venezuala, and took a deep, humid breath. Who said that no plan survived contact with the enemy? The origin of the quote escaped him, but it was really hitting home right now. So far, their routine patrol was failing to survive contact with today.

His squad, detached fragments of a full weapons platoon, started the morning on its usual babysitting routine: escorting their State Department chump, Dan Stilwill, on his daily nature walk through the ass ends of Colombia that Camp Bell sat in.

Stilwill was a specialist in convincing drug growers

to switch to vege-plastic biomass crops, and he was, apparently, great at his job. Everyone had their niche, Jabar supposed. But neither Stilwill nor Jabar was inhabiting their own proper niche right this second.

"What does he mean?" Stilwill demanded. An officious note crept into his voice as Jabar continued to scan the jungle thoughtfully.

"Lance Corporal Rader knows his armor silhouettes backwards and forwards," Jabar said. "It means what it means. I'd recommend you stay low and stay put while I give out orders, Mr. Stilwill. You're not going to be making your next speaking appointment."

When Jabar glanced back, Dan Stilwill was crouched in the bush, his face half-obscured by foliage, his bright yellow Packers cap sticking out above it.

Jabar sighed.

A few minutes later, Jabar moved down the line, crouch-running from Marine to Marine placed in the dense jungle foliage alongside the road. "Keep your heads down," he called out. "Tell me when you see *anything*. Private Van Duine, everything good?"

"Locked and cocked, Corporal," Van Duine replied, a little louder than absolutely necessary.

"Not what I asked, Van Duine," Jabar said, sliding in to kneel beside the private. Van Duine had his shoulder pressed into the stock of a medium machine gun, the silver-gray tips of armor-piercing ammo visible on the feed tray.

"We're good, Corporal," he said. "Could use some air-conditioning, though."

"Yeah, we all could, brother," Jabar said. His men hadn't expected to be grubbing through the dirt here in the jungle. When they'd first arrived in the transport airships from Florida and started unpacking, they'd figured they'd be stomping around in full, mechanized armor with fluid coolant packs running to pull the sweaty heat away from their bodies and keep them in tip-top comfort as they operated the mechanized suits his platoon was trained to fight in.

That's what they'd trained for in Florida. But the jungle out here had been brutal to their first attempts to patrol in it. Rather than invincible metal giants, the moisture wreaked quick havoc on their delicate electronics, and green, wet wood sprung back with surprising velocity at soldiers trying to push their way through. Creepers and vines could tangle legs, and soft earth could give way with no warning.

Their first day trying the armor out in the jungle, one of his Marines had sunk to his waist in quicksand, and another had gotten his leg stuck deep in an ant colony—and Ko had an aversion to the crawly buggers ever since.

They'd figured pretty quickly that for bog-standard patrols of the nearby grower villages, helping the Colombians hunt the last, most dug-in border drug lords left, it was more effective to dismount and be an old-fashioned Marine on the ground, in the flesh.

Jabar had sympathized with the flicker of disappointment in Stilwill's eyes when Jabar had explained that to the man on their first patrol with him a couple weeks back. Now being in the flesh was going to cause problems. Somewhere out there was at least a pair of Chinese walkers, according to Rader.

That is . . . a lot of metal for us to face down, Jabar thought.

"Was it this hot where you grew up, Corporal?" Van Duine asked.

Jabar glanced down, confused. "What? No, I grew up in Toledo."

It was Van Duine's turn to look confused. "You grew up in Spain? How come you said you can't speak to the locals here?"

"Ohio," Jabar said. "Toledo, Ohio."

Van Duine had the good grace to look embarrassed. Jabar, though, had other things on his mind, and inched back away from where his Weapons Platoon Marines were positioned. A few meters along, he ran into 2nd Squad—"Sloppy Seconds"—who were on hand to back up Jabar's Marines with their heavy rifles and grenade launchers.

Sgt. Arliss, 2nd's squad leader, had deployed them in a nice, hasty zig-zag, using the terrain for cover and positioning them so they could offer supporting fire if needed. Someone remembered their dismount training from the School of Infantry. If only all the Marines remembered how to fight as well outside their armor.

Staff Sergeant Demeter had joined Stilwill in the bush, but stood upright despite the threat of Chinese powered armor out in the jungle. Jabar couldn't decide if that was from some misplaced senior-Marine bravado or if Demeter had gone soft in the head after four years pulling Embassy duty in the plush urban surroundings of Bogota.

"Everything tight up front?" he asked Jabar.

"Everything's good, Staff Sergeant. We're dispersed for two hundred meters along the jungle track— machine guns out to the flanks, anti-armor assault in the center. It's a good position for what we've got."

"Excellent work, Jabar," he replied. "We've got Third Squad backing us up on the hill to our south in case we need to fall back."

Jabar concealed a sigh of exasperation in a cough. 3rd Squad—"Third Herd"—was good enough at what they did, but dismounted operations were not their forte. He'd be lucky if his detachment of Marines survived Third Herd's "covering" fire. He hoped it wouldn't come to that.

"We're a stone's throw from the border," Demeter said, possibly picking up on something in Jabar's body language that he wasn't hiding as well as he thought he was. "It's probably just a patrol gone bad. Nav equipment off. Someone lost. Or just a test of the Colombian response. I doubt this'll end up being a full-on firefight."

Jabar nodded agreement and hoped that Demeter was right.

From his position behind the bush, Stilwill interrupted. "I still didn't get any memos about Chinese troops being in Venezuela. You'd think that'd be news."

Demeter looked over at Jabar, and the two shared a "Is this guy for real?" glance. Jabar, not for the first time, wondered if Stilwill's colleagues sent him out here hoping he'd step on a landmine.

"There probably aren't Chinese drivers in the armor, sir," Jabar explained patiently. "The Chinese sell their walkers and their exo-skins to at least ten other nations, including Peru. They have a presence in South America."

"We're on the wrong side of the country from Peru…" Stilwill said, looking off to the west as though he could see the Pacific coast nation through the hundreds of miles jungle and mountain that separated them.

"But Venezuela is right there," Jabar said, and pointed at the smuggler's track.

"They're under an arms embargo; China agreed in the UN Council to abide by this. They're hungry for buyers, but not enough to risk the black mark," Stilwill muttered.

A set of snapping branches and motion in the deeper jungle interrupted him. Jabar crouched, shoving Stilwill's head further down into the bush, and Demeter even dropped to one knee.

"Hey, don't shoot, it's Reynaldo," a heavily Colombian-accented voice said.

Jabar lowered his rifle as their guide stepped out to join them. Reynaldo had been ghosting his way through these jungles hunting FARC rebels from back when they were still considered revolutionaries by some and controlled at least a third of Colombia's territory. He'd been picking off drug lords, some of them well intertwined with FARC, long before Camp Bell had been set up by US and Colombian forces working together for the final push back of Colombia's fringe areas, where the drug lords were dug in the hardest and being funded by the Venezuelans.

"You see anything, Reynaldo?" Jabar asked.

"No. And to answer Mr. Stilwill: the Venezuelans got around the embargo by giving most of their reserves directly to a Chinese corporation that makes the heavy metal. Oil for weapons." He shook his head. "And not much of it left. Caracas is ready to riot, the lights are going out all over the country. It's desperate over there."

Desperate enough to do something stupid, like attack Colombia? Jabar wondered. That seemed beyond the pale.

But he glanced down the road, a chill running down his back despite the moist heat.

"What I do," a drunk Stilwill had told Jabar, barely a day after being helicoptered out, "is show these peasant farmers how first-world farming works."

"Where did you get that?" Jabar had asked. "Alcohol's prohibited on base."

"It's not about equipment, or technology. You'd think it was. You'd be wrong. It's really about the guarantee." Stilwill gulped the amber-colored, peaty-smelling scotch in his hand like he'd stumbled into an oasis after a week of crossing the desert. "That's modern farming. All about the subsidies. No one really wants to fess up to it, but guarantee a farmer a minimum price on his crop, so that he knows his family won't suffer, and he's willing to take a risk on what is a professional field with a shrinking user base. We talk a good talk about markets; in fact, in order to enter into trade agreements with us, you have to agree *not* to subsidize your farmers. But at the end of the day, that's how first-world farming works."

"Sir, you can't just sit out here on the edge of camp with a flask of scotch..."

"There was an African country which decided to stop using 'the market' and subsidize its farmers. Lost all US aid, but within two years, they had a stable local agro-economy and could feed themselves. So we have that dilemma facing us as we look out at these little guys sitting out there," Stilwill waved his hand at the jungle. "You're a farmer: you're offered your chance of two crops. One pays a few bucks an acre. Another pays ten times that. What do you plant?"

"Sir," Jabar insisted.

"You plant the more expensive! Problem is, until me, that's always been cocoa. Colombia needs stability, and crops. They can't subsidize their farmers or they lose agricultural assistance from the US. They can't afford all out war out here. We, on the other hand, want less drug production and are desperate for more land to grow crops for bio-plastics as oil prices hit the stratosphere. So the State Department works with foreign aid, and suddenly Monsanto is here to offer farmers a minimum crop price guarantee if they grow what the bio-plastics industry needs. Just as back home, Monsanto somehow sits in the middle of it all. Everyone's happy. Except me, because I'm in the middle. Of. Fucking. Nowhere."

"Sir, the reason you can't sit here with that is because we occasionally come under sniper fire," Jabar said.

Stilwill paled. He shoved the flask into Jabar's hands and scurried back for the safety of the sandbagged walls.

Jabar turned the flask over thoughtfully.

"That's what they look like?" Amir asked, twisting the holographic image of Jabar's rig this way and that, three months prior to his big brother's deployment to Colombia. He poked at the angular shape, freestanding but cracked open for maintenance. "What's the armor?"

"The plate armor is a poly-metal synthetic, gray with your camo painted over top. Green for jungle, sand for desert. Once you have it all strapped on, you look just like one of those videogame characters," Jabar told him.

"And you'll jump twenty feet into the air with a leap, because of the joint motors inside, right?"

"After lots and lots of training," Jabar grinned. "Do that your first day you're liable to land and break every bone in your body. The armor's tougher than you are."

"What about the big ones, Faisal? The walkers?"

Jabar flicked over to some pictures he'd taken of one of the big boys, a M-19 Mattis, out at 29 Palms. "These guys? That's more like driving a car or something. The driver sits up in the cockpit here, between the big weapons pods on the shoulders. The legs can put him up to twenty feet off the ground, and a good driver can get those legs moving like a sprinter."

Just after he had taken the picture, Jabar had watched them lope across the Mojave Desert like so many gazelle, running and bounding and chewing up distance with breathtaking speed. He'd felt like a turtle in his own armor for weeks after that.

"Can I drive one?" Amir asked, looking up at him.

Jabar rubbed the top of his brother's head. In another year, he'd be eighteen and free to enlist. "You like to tinker, maybe you can fix them, and test drive them, or something. They always need more mechanics."

"But not fight in them?"

"What I do is dangerous enough for both of us, little brother."

The chatter of a dozen heavy rifles broke the jungle's wet silence. Jabar snapped his own rifle up, and Demeter and Reynaldo both dropped into crouches.

It wasn't Weapons or Second, Jabar realized. He glanced back up the small hill where Third had set up their covering position.

"Contact front!" the platoon's comm net crackled. *"Three walkers, two thousand meters!"*

"Jesus Christ, what the hell do they think they're doing?" Demeter muttered.

"Giving away their damn position," Jabar replied. *Stupid fucking buttplates*, he thought, carefully censoring himself. Only Weapons used that term, and not in a complimentary fashion.

It was Stilwill who verbalized the changed atmosphere. "This isn't a lost border patrol; this is an attack."

Jabar and Demeter—who'd both switched from anticipating the worst (while hoping for the best) and accepted the reality that a firefight had just broken out—glanced at him. "It's a thrust of some sort, yes sir," Jabar confirmed. He looked at Demeter. "Victor's gonna light Third up with tracking software and return rocket fire."

Demeter was on the comm net already, thinking the same thing. "Disengage, disengage!" he ordered. "Fall back to Rally-Delta."

It was too late. Third was lobbing grenades out in a high arc from their hill as explosions dotted their position. It was hard to miss them.

Demeter and Jabar looked at each other. "Pull your squad back, Corporal, we can't sit here anymore," Demeter said. Third had blown their pretty little road ambush. "Keep Stilwill safe and close."

Under attack by an unspecified number of possibly Venezeulan walkers and Jabar was still on babysitting duty.

"Stay low," Jabar ordered, and rushed forward to where his squad was parked, muttering obscenities under his breath the whole way. His teams should have been on that goddamn hill, not Third Herd, but Demeter had wanted the big guns out front to act as a screen and Jabar had given in because he didn't have the nuts to stand up to a Staff Sergeant yet, even one as semi-hopeless as Demeter. He came down to the edge of the track, not far from where Rader lay in the prone, scanning left and right with his rifle.

"I don't see any—"

"Doesn't matter. Third got some, and now they're going to roll us up if we don't boogie." Rader looked appropriately annoyed at the FUBARed situation. "Fall back to Delta now. You remember the way?"

"Yes, Corporal."

"Good, you've got point. Hustle us back there and don't wait for the buttplates to get their shit together."

With a mumbled "Aye," Rader was up and moving, falling back into the jungle, dragging the rest of Assault section with him. Jabar dared to jump out into the rough road that they had been beside and ran to their southern flank first, toward where Third was still firing sporadically. Stilwill followed behind, panting and out of breath from the effort of keeping up.

"Get up, get up, go," Jabar yelled at the machine gun team there, "fall in behind Assault, *go!*" Then he ran back to the north and got that gun team moving. He plunged into the jungle at the very tail end of the line, urging his Marines onward. As they passed SSgt. Demeter's former command position, he could hear trees at the smuggler's-track starting to crack and splinter under high velocity fire. He put himself between the sounds and Stilwill, whom he kept shoving in front of him.

He still had yet to lay eyes on any enemy metal, but it was quite clear they were in the middle of a firefight.

For the first time in a month, Jabar thanked Allah for the thickness of the jungle. He even permitted himself a tiny smile, wondering if the Venezuelans had had any time to practice operating armor in the jungle. Judging by the crashing sounds and slow progress, he was willing to bet they hadn't.

"Dropkick Red, moving to Rally Delta. We have ambulatory casualties."

Jabar urged Stilwill to run faster. "Red" was Third Herd's callsign, and if they were coming down the hill with walking wounded, they would be moving slow. Hopefully the withdraw and rally path, which was little more than a foot trail that went through dense jungle, would keep the Venezuelans from rolling Third Herd up in a neat bunch. The walkers would have a bitch of a time, while Jabar and Stilwill were able to thread past the thick jungle quickly enough on the footpath.

He came up on one of the machine gunners struggling a little under the weight of the ammo he was carrying. In a training situation, he probably would have just walked alongside, berating the boot for not being in better condition—hell, he might have done it out here in the jungle if it weren't for death lurking in the trees somewhere behind them. Today, instead, he just grabbed one of the two slung panniers, draped it across his own back, and hustled on. He caught up to Rader just as his scout reached the edge of the small clearing that was Delta. They entered to find Sloppy Second, breathing hard in the thick jungle air, forming themselves into a defensive circle.

They'd made it back to Rally Delta. Stilwill was in one piece. *So the mission has that going for it, at least,* Jabar thought. The man they'd been ordered to escort and protect was still alive. Kneeling at the point where trail met clearing, Jabar counted off Marines and pointed them into position around the clearing, backing up Sloppy Second.

"Are we going to call Camp for armor?" Jabar asked, prodding Demeter.

Demeter glanced back through the jungle. "Too late for that now."

"Maybe, but you do realize we're going to be the first platoon ever to face down enemy metal in an actual firefight, and we're naked?" The walkers and power armor had only been developed in the last decade, most of it in the hands of nations rich enough to deploy it . . . and rich enough to have no vested interest in fighting each other.

There'd been metal up against flesh, though. Richer nations against less-equipped nations. Normally that didn't end so well for flesh.

"Let's see what shape Third is in," Demeter said. "We could just have spooked a patrol. We need to make sure we understand what's happening before we start calling in armor or airstrikes."

He was being cautious. And trying to cover his ass. Because ultimately it was Demeter who made the call to go out into the bush without powered armor. If this mission shit the bed then it was going to be Demeter's ass on the line. But an excess of caution would send things down the same chute, get them just as dead. There was a reason the Corps prized aggressiveness.

"Let's get some eyes in the sky," Jabar suggested. "We'll know for sure what we're looking at if we unpack the moth."

Demeter thought about it for a split second and nodded. "Okay. Unpack the drone, and tell me what you see."

Stilwill was shaking his head. "Colombia's not a narco-state anymore, Bogota's got better public transportation than my home city, and Cartagena's a vacation spot. But they're still struggling with the rural areas. If this goes south, it undoes *decades* of growth in the area, growth we were hoping would check the Venezuela problem."

The moth was a tiny collapsible radio controlled drone with memory metal wings. It took half a minute to unpack, fold the wings into place, and throw into the air. Jabar controlled it with a joystick and goggles.

He spiraled it up just over the tree canopy, and then slowly flew out well away from their position. After a few minutes of that, he jerked it up into the air and spiraled up for altitude.

The jungle jerked and stuttered and spun as he climbed, and then leveled out.

A mat of jungle top stretched for miles, emerald green, sliced by the smuggler's road they'd double-timed away from to Rally Point Delta. And all along the road stretching back into Venezuela: a long convoy of heavy, metal-clad humanoid shapes stutter-walking along, interspersed with the two legged walkers, canopies glinting in the sun.

Further back, supply trucks and older tanks ground along, following the spearhead of powered armor.

One of the suits paused, and a gauntleted, metal-clad arm rose and pointed, the finger flashing as energy stabbed out at the tiny drone.

"Sir . . ." Jabar's video feed exploded in static. He ripped the goggles off and looked up to see a cloud of debris slowly falling. "It's no patrol."

It was a goddamn invasion force.

The sound of Third Herd preceded the Marines themselves by less than a minute, and a few of them were still shooting somewhere to their rear as they moved into the clearing.

Two had clearly been wounded. One, Cpl. Barney, leaned against their squad corpsman, HM3 Danks, a blood-soaked bandage at Barney's neck. Jabar frowned when he saw that; Barney was one of the better NCOs in Third—probably the best—and they would be struggling without his influence.

"How far back are they?" Demeter asked as Third Herd's squad leader, Sgt. Maly, came into the clearing.

He glanced back. "I think we scared 'em a bit. Certainly haven't gotten past the worst of the bush back there."

"Good," Demeter said. "Good work getting your men out of there in good order."

Demeter, evidently, had a different standard of "good order," but again Jabar kept his mouth shut. His Marines would have been wounded—or killed—if he had been any slower getting them to Delta. Third Herd's "fighting withdrawal" had looked more like a half-directed clusterfuck, and they had been spraying ordnance all over the jungle. They were hopeless without their own armor's target systems. He hoped that the fact that they made it to the rally point at all boded well for the platoon as a whole.

"Dropkick White, Dropkick White, this is Dropkick

Five, over." Jabar looked over to see Demeter hold his right hand against his ear, pressing the thin boom mic closer to his face.

"Five, this is White, go ahead."

"Start getting the armor warmed up." Demeter glanced back at Jabar. "We're going to need it."

"Five, this is Dropkick Six, what's going on out there?"

"Hostile armor in the vicinity, sir. Minimum company strength, possibly the tip for a larger force."

"Jesus. Get back here, soon as you can make it. We'll get armored up and out there ASAP."

Those who were on comms—the squad leaders and dedicated radiomen—brightened up a bit at the sound of their platoon commander on the net, promising to get their armor ready to go. The trick, Jabar knew, was to make it back to them in the first place. The patrol base they had been operating out of lay a half day's walk through the jungle and across a high, steep ridge. They had come across the ridge along an east-west road that continued on down into Venezuela, crossing the north-south smuggler's track along the way, and Jabar figured that's the path the armor would naturally gravitate to, once they had spent some time getting badly bogged down in the trees and brush.

"Jabar, you got a headcount?" Demeter asked, snapping him out of his tactical review reverie.

"All present *and* accounted for, Staff Sergeant."

Demeter nodded and turned back to Maly and Arliss, kneeling in the center of the clearing with Reynaldo the guide. Jabar swore softly to himself. He scrambled over to them, keeping low, holding his rifle muzzle out of the dirt as he moved. They were planning the next move, and they were doing it without him again, without input from Weapons on how best to deploy the platoon's heavier guns. Typical, not consulting with him because he was just a corporal, or because he was just a Weapons NCO. Or both.

". . . ambush along here, which we think is their most likely axis of advance." Demeter was dragging his finger along an unrolled map flimsy, drawing a bright blue line on the softly lit surface. His finger described an arc cutting across the Venezuela road where it snaked like an S around a cluster of tiny rocky upthrusts, embryonic cousins to the Andes far to the west. Someday they'd be mountains, he figured, but for now they were barely enough cover for the Marines to set in a good position and shoot at the Venezuelans without getting chewed up themselves. Maybe.

"And if they flank us?" Arliss was asking.

"They won't," Demeter said. "The jungle is too thick for them. They'll funnel up this road, and they'll just want to get over the ridge and down the other side to take out Camp Bell. We hit 'em, fuck 'em up, and withdraw in good order back to the pass. That should keep them busy long enough to give everyone at camp time to reach us and unleash some hell. By then we'll be getting orders from higher up the chain."

"Sounds like a plan," Maly said.

"Glad you agree, Sergeant. Corporal Jabar, you and Weapons take point. I want you at the tip of the spear in case we stumble across any of them too soon."

"Aye, Staff Sergeant," Jabar replied, and gritted his teeth. That wasn't how they were supposed to be used, but he didn't have time to argue the point. The man had obviously not paid attention at the advanced infantry course, much less remembered his initial schooling. Now was not the time to teach him the finer points of ambush.

"Leave Stilwill here," Demeter ordered as Jabar moved out.

"Guys," Stilwill said, sounding scared. "Don't give me some bullshit about the size of the fight in the dog versus the size of the dog. That's enemy powered armor out there, and you guys are just—"

"Just what?" Jabar asked. "Just Marines?"

Stilwill opened his mouth to say something, but saw something in Jabar's eyes and shut his mouth.

Jabar turned away. It was time to make this happen.

Flesh against armor. Stop them from getting closer to camp, hold them down until back up arrived.

He tried not to think about the long line of armor stretched down the smuggler's road.

End of the day, none of them were really cut out for hard combat operations outside of the suits anymore. But there was no denying that they would need to be ready, and *beyond* ready even, if they were going to survive for much longer. Outside of their suits, they could engage the Venezuelans, maybe even keep them at bay for a short time, but if the Chinese had supplied them with armor in quantity, the Marines were going to need armor to match them.

Hopefully Demeter wasn't too gung-ho to realize that. Seemed like he understood, radioing back for First Squad to get the suits warmed up, but the ambush tactic smelled like a shot at glory. Jabar wasn't keen on glory. Glory got Marines killed.

But Jabar had to admit, he had no more combat experience than Demeter. They had both fired their first rounds in this jungle, chasing after drug lords suddenly fallen on hard times and trying to stake a claim on a fractured and unsettled Colombia. Demeter made himself out to be wiser and more worldly, after his four years in embassies—a shtick that had worked well in Bogota, when they had had some time to walk around on liberty. He had even busted out some Spanish well enough to impress Curazon, the machine gunner who had come from Colombia when he was a little kid, fleeing the drug violence.

Out in the field, though... There, Demeter had lost Jabar's respect. The staff NCO was all thumbs, obviously rusty when it came to the operations side of things. Though no one had said as much, Jabar knew that he was the reason half of 1st Squad was laid up back at Camp Bell, nursing a variety of minor wounds after a run-in with an exceptionally well-equipped former drug lord. A terrible assault plan had left 1st strung out and trying an end-run around the drug lord's position, and the squad had gotten chewed up.

And as bad as that had been, Jabar worried that the new situation was too far beyond Demeter's meager abilities. As an armored infantry platoon, they trained for these kinds of fights all the time, but this was far from the ideal training situation. They had to ambush the Venezuelans with arms much more suited for soft targets, and there was no chance that the Marines would be able to absorb much punishment from the heavy weapons.

"Dropkick Green, hold up, hold up, circle back. We've lost contact with you."

Jabar turned his head and growled, looking back along his line. It was a short line, just fourteen Marines, and they were keeping tight together so as not to lose each other in the jungle. But somehow, the rest of the platoon had gotten separated.

"Rader! Curl right!" he shouted, and the point scout obediently changed his path, coming around in a broad arc, back to the northeast, toward Rally-Delta. Jabar jogged in place for a moment as his squad curled around him and hustled back the way they had come.

A moment later, he heard, *"Shit!"* And then the jungle was alive with the sound of automatic weapons. Marines peeled out of the tight line they had been moving in and hit the deck hard.

Jabar watched, almost in slow-motion, as a burst of plasma from a Chinese high-energy weapon sliced through the air to hit a tree a meter or two above his head and just off to his left. He dove into the stinking, ant-infested brush as a wave of heat and charred splinters pattered his softly-armored back.

"Fuck-shit-fuck," he cried, and then his curses were lost in long, cacophonous bursts from his squad's machine guns. Licks of flame brightened the dim jungle, and then he could see the dancing, juddering figure of a lone, exo-skinned enemy as fire from the platoon converged on him.

Even as he fell, another exo seemed to appear through the maze of trees, and the Marines did not have to shift their aim far to converge on the second armored figure. Jabar moved to the kneeling position, propped himself against a tree trunk, and began jerking the trigger on his rifle. Illuminated bursts of high-velocity rounds crawled up the enemy armor, and Jabar could swear he saw his rounds impact the glassy faceshield.

Then the second figure was down, and no more appeared. Jabar hollered for cease fire, and the call was taken up along their ragged line. He got to his feet and hustled forward, passing through the line and shouting for his Marines to stay down. The two armored scouts lay where they had fallen, twisted grotesquely. One of them had obviously suffered some kind of servo failure, and broken his own back when he tried to twist and catch himself when he fell.

The other had, in fact, been shot in the face, and the cheap faceshield had shattered. He lay on his side, blood pooling under the armored head. Jabar looked quickly, and otherwise wasted no time with their first confirmed kills. Where these guys were, more would be following. Both wore blue and red flags on their right shoulders.

"Dropkick Five, this is Green, confirmed contact with Venezuelan-flagged armor. Where are you?"

"Green, this is Five. We're south east of you. New plan. You make for the pass and hold it, we're going to harass, then draw back to your pos and meet White coming up."

"Roger that, Five. Green on the move." Jabar hustled back to the line now, shouting for Weapons to get to their feet. This was more like their standard use—take and hold the high ground, support the buttplates from up there. "Let's go, let's go. Double time to the pass, *move!*"

The entire dictionary of colorful Marine curses followed the orders, but everyone obeyed. Jabar paused to get his headcount—two minor wounds from a shredded tree, but otherwise all on their feet—and fell in at the back of the line. Every third step he glanced back over his shoulder, convinced that some of the exos were running up behind them. But the jungle remained enemy-free, and blessedly noisy with the protests of birds and other jungle critters expressing their dismay at the fireworks.

They reached the road about a thousand meters short of the pass. To the west, the ground sloped up steeply, jungle trees clinging to a rocky slope that would be hell to climb with or without mechanical assistance. Jabar smiled and looked east down the road toward Venezuela. So far, nothing. The track had been paved, once upon a time, but had no doubt fallen into ruin as gasoline grew harder to come by, especially in poor rural zones like this one. The former pavement now more closely resembled gravel, which would make it ideal for laying in some remote detonated devices.

"Curazon, Ko, get up into the pass and find some nice spots for your machine guns. Double-time, go." Jabar watched them set off—and counted the lumbering machine gunners as they went, weighted down under the heavy weapons and the even heavier pile of ammunition. Then he turned back to his Assault Marines, who were already unlimbering their demo packs and opening tins of explosives.

"Save the directional mines for closer in," Jabar said. "We'll place those at two hundred meters from the machine guns. Everything else, staggered pattern up the road, get 'em down in the gravel."

One of his Marines, DesJardins, ran to the far side of the road and set up in the trees with his anti-armor rocket propped up on his shoulder. He squinted into the sights, then settled in, a disposable rocket tube twisted into the backside of the reusable launcher. The others started taping together bricks of plastic explosive and pressing in remote detonators.

They moved up the road, fifty meters at a time, each stop setting in another improvised landmine and making note of existing landmarks adjacent to the mines' positions. DesJardins moved after they did, only picking up and hurrying back when Jabar shouted for him to move.

The sounds of gunfire and explosions began to filter up through the jungle as Second and Third started their mission of harassment. The distinct crump of a Marine hand grenade was as welcome as the bass thudding of a Chinese heavy cannon was not.

They were badly outmatched here. As well-prepared as they thought they had been that morning—setting out to sweep a section of the jungle for drug lords, and watch Stilwill cajole the locals into the US-Colombian plastics program—they were not well prepared for this. The machine guns were the only ones with true armor-piercing ammo, and they only brought that because they never got issued anything else. The rest of their weapons were strictly for soft targets, and only the somewhat lucky hit on that Venezuelan's faceplate had given their small arms any utility at all in this fight.

The Assault teams were another matter, but they had used up everything but their four rockets in setting the improvised mines along the road. Once those were blown, and the rockets expended, they just had the machine gunners to help keep the enemy at bay. That, and an earnest prayer for 1st Squad to have their armor warmed up and ready to move in time.

"All right! DesJardins, bring it back!" Jabar shouted as he reached one of the rocky perches Machine Guns had chosen.

"Just a sec!" the junior Marine shouted back. The rocket leapt from his launcher and streaked down-range, a series of small pops trailing after it as the maneuvering rockets adjusted its course. Within a second of the rocket leaving the tube, DesJardins was down, then up again, hustling across the road, then up the last hundred meters to the pass.

An explosion sent a dark, sparkling cloud of dirt and debris back along the road, and then they heard the sound of something toppling into the trees. Secondary explosions followed as poorly-cushioned rockets knocked against the sides of their reload pods and detonated in the walker.

Jabar smiled as DesJardins hustled up the broken road, unscrewing and discarding the spent tube.

"It was a K-47, one of the Froggers," DesJardins said.

"Bad knee joints," Jabar said, laughing.

"Very bad," DesJardins said, then took another tube from his partner and fitted into the back of the launcher. Now they were down to three rockets, but at least they had taken down a walker and maybe obstructed the road a bit.

Jabar had to imagine it was chaos down there now, with Marines to the north harassing the armor along the road, trying to get some more lucky shots in, exploiting the weaknesses of the Chinese armor. The armor itself would be having a tough time among the trees, just like his own men had struggled in the jungle with their own powered armor.

The Venezuelans could not possibly be faring any

better. They could not have had the Chinese armor for very long without a lot of people noticing, especially since they must have mortgaged the entire country just to buy a hundred exos and a handful of walkers. Oil was close to a thousand dollars a barrel, but from what Reynaldo had been telling them, they were having more and more trouble just extracting it from their oil fields.

So now maybe they were making a play for the profitable vege-plastics farms Monsanto was setting up, or hoping to force some sort of geo-political issue.

Whatever it was, it was way above Jabar's paygrade.

The sound of Marine heavy rifles seemed to be dying away, and Jabar had not heard a hand grenade go off in some time.

"Eyes open," he said as he got to his feet again, and moved across the road. "Keep an eye out for Marines coming back up through the jungle. Let's not have any blue-on-blue, dig?"

"Roger that," a couple of Marines muttered. But mostly they crouched over their weapons, half-hidden by the rocks and trees, waiting for enemy armor to fill their sights.

"Dropkick White, this is Green. What's the status on our armor?"

"Green, this is Six. White is suiting up. We're going to bring your armor up first. Blue and Red to follow."

That was good news. Bad news was that he had not heard anything from the other squads over the net since being ordered into position.

"Green, this is Six. We also have Green-Three setting up their tubes. Do you have a fire mission for them?"

Jabar resisted the urge to cheer. The mortar section had been on a food drop off to some villagers far to the west of Camp Bell when they stepped off that morning. They usually had little enough to do when everyone else went on patrol, unless they wanted to tag along. And, as everyone in the platoon said, Mortars had the sharpest skates; they could avoid boring, heavy patrols like nothing else. But now they were back, and setting up their 81mm tubes.

Jabar hustled over to the northern machine gun position and hunkered down behind a rock. The map flimsy in his pocket was pre-marked with firing locations that Mortars had marked out of habit and practice when they had set up Camp Bell. His finger trailed over the map and stabbed a spot along the road.

"Are they zeroed still, Six?"

"Negative. The tubes got packed up last week. But they're setting them in on the same positions they started with."

"Have them lay in Fire Mission One on Phase Line Candace," Jabar said, his finger dancing over the map, lips moving silently as he did the math, "then shift right twenty, drop two. We'll call for fire when we need it and adjust them manually. Fire Mission Two is 'danger close,' final protective fire. Phase Line Dora, plus twenty." The ridge itself was Dora, and Fire Mission Two would probably pepper them with shrapnel, if they were still alive to call it in.

If Six acknowledged, the words were washed out in a long burst from the machine gun right in front of Jabar. The other one picked up as soon as the first dropped off, and soon they were chattering back and forth in a system the gunners called "talking guns."

In theory, it helped disguise the number of machine guns, though Jabar had no doubt that the Chinese armor could pick out the individual muzzle flashes of the two weapons.

He threw himself down, then picked his head up to look over the lip of their fighting position. Trees shook off to the south; enemy armor was trying to flank them. A flash of azure plasma burst up into the trees and dissipated in sparks and splinters. The guns cut off as their targets vanished, the individual team leaders shouting for the Marines to conserve their ammunition.

Jabar grunted and checked his own magazines. He had yet to reload, so he still carried a full complement of rounds, minus the dozen or so he had fired off already.

"Keep your heads down!" he shouted, covering the whole, thin line of Marines. Assault was positioned in the middle, laying flat at the road's crest between the two machine gun positions, ready to detonate their explosives or bring their rockets down on anything coming up the road. "Keep your heads down!" he repeated. "Fire on hard targets only. First 'n' Worst is coming up with our armor and more ammo."

The radio buzzed in his ear: *"Green, this is Blue. Green, this is Blue. We are cut off from your pos. We are going Alamo at Rally-Mike."*

"Sit tight, Blue," Jabar said, swallowing on a dry throat, "we'll come get you soon."

"Roger, Green." If Arliss had heard Jabar's voice crack, he gave no indication.

Merciful Allah, he thought to himself. What the fuck am I doing? He had six months to go in his first enlistment and here he was, with thirteen other Marines, trying to stave off an armored ground invasion. The thought nearly overwhelmed him and he dipped his head, not wanting anyone else to see tears at the corners of his eyes. He shook his head, and the moment ebbed away, leaving only echoes of doubt. He had thought he could do this better than Demeter, and now he was being put to the test.

Allah had a sense of humor, after all.

A walker crunched into view, fifteen hundred meters down the road. It looked like a toy at that range, a blocky thing with a tapering nose and two box-like shoulders. Squat legs lifted and fell on the crumbling road, kicking up dust as it further pulverized the old pavement.

"Team One!" he shouted, looking back at Assault. "*Target!*"

PFC Krantz popped up to one knee, a rocket already loaded in the launcher. The Marine leaned forward a little, squinting down the optics, and then yanked the trigger. The rocket popped and fluttered along the road, jinking left and right on its own to avoid potential countermeasures and to paint its target from multiple angles. Krantz was already flat again when the walker responded, its right shoulder bursting in a fusillade of unguided rockets. The Marine's shot seemed to hit square in the walker's nose, making it stagger then topple forward. A second fusillade launched as it fell, spraying up a screen of dust, debris, and glowing shrapnel.

The first impacted a second later, rippling into the road and jungle fifty meters forward of their position. The shockwaves buffeted them, and another screen of cloying dust kicked up, drifting over them and coating everything in a layer of powdered concrete.

"Keep your eyes open!" Jabar shouted.

"Corpsman up!" came a call in the next moment from the machine gun team to the south.

Doc Hurley leapt to his feet from where he had been crouching with the Assault section and hustled over to the southern machine gun nest. A moment later he was dragging Van Duine back over the crest of the road and onto the reverse slope by the strap on the back of his body armor. The Marine looked to be cursing and kicking, but one of his arms dragged uselessly along the crumbled pavement. Jabar tore his eyes away and scanned the road as the dust started to clear.

The machine guns opened up immediately, zeroing on exo-skins moving up either side of the road. Assault fired another rocket, and the team leaders and ammo bearers started plinking at guys with their rifles. The improvised explosives burst, shattering individuals and sending clusters of armored Venezuelans spinning off to either side of the road. The concussive force threatened to knock Jabar off his knees.

"Green, this is Six. Two hundred meters out."

The fourth rocket fired and whipped past a walker, spiraling off into the distance.

"Rounds complete!" DesJardins shouted.

Jabar struggled to his feet, leaning against the steep, rocky outcropping that defined the northern side of the pass. He pressed his hand to his ear, pushing the radio earpiece in tighter.

"Green-Three, Green-Three, this is Green Actual. Fire Mission One."

"Fire Mission One, roger. Splash out."

"Inbound!" he screamed, "Inbound!" But he doubted anyone could hear him. His ears had to be bleeding from the noise, but he felt himself almost adrift on a calm little island. Strangely, he could hear the mortar rounds, cutting the air overhead with that distinctive *zzzzzzzzzzzip.* A bolt of plasma burst over his head, melting rock and showering him with fragments. The mortars burst at head-height, five hundred meters up the road. Armored Venezuelans toppled as the pulse of detonation overwhelmed their armor. One stood up again just in time to catch a dud in the chest—the velocity and weight of the projectile punched a hole in the armor and almost turned it inside out.

A hand fell on Jabar's shoulder and he spun, bringing his rifle butt up and smashing it across the masked face behind him. The armored figure didn't flinch.

"At ease, Corporal."

"Jesus, sir, it's you." The mottled green armor was pure Marine Corps, decorated only with slim black bars on the shoulders, indicating that the suit contained Lieutenant Hogarth.

Hogarth and 1st Squad, meanwhile, moved forward into the pass, screening Weapons as they engaged the Venezuelans for the first time.

It was now metal versus metal ripping the jungle apart as giants smashed through trees and unleashed unholy amounts of firepower against each other. The sound of combat moved away from Jabar and his men, and was soon only visible as the tops of trees snapped and fell, distant explosions thudded, and bursts of tracers zipped up into the air as armor fell.

And then the jungle fell silent.

✧   ✧   ✧

Jabar sat next to a small table on a sealed trunk he'd dragged out near the perimeter of the camp, looking out at the jungle. He poured a finger of scotch from the flask he'd confiscated what seemed like an eternity ago.

When he held the small glass up to the sun, the light flickered with amber shadows.

"I thought you were Muslim," Stilwill said, interrupting the moment.

Jabar sighed silently. "I am."

"But you're drinking," Stilwill observed unnecessarily.

"We are all sinners in the eyes of Allah," Jabar said, and raised the glass to his lips. He breathed out mellow, expensive scotch fumes. "And that was some incredibly good scotch."

"Thirty year old Macallan," Stilwill said. "There aren't really snipers out here, are there?"

"There used to be," Jabar said. "When we first built the camp."

Stilwill laughed. "You're right to be out here celebrating," he said. "What you guys did today, that was fucking epic. You realize they're going to be talking about you, no, *teaching* what you did, today? Unarmored marines versus enemy power armor, and you *took them out!*"

"Some of them," Jabar pointed out.

"It's a first. It's huge! Awesome!" Stilwill was floating on the air, Jabar saw. "We now know for sure that flesh and blood Marines can fight effectively against powered armor. And we sent the Venezuelans packing!"

"We got caught naked. It wasn't awesome, it was a firefight. And there's always a price. A billion dollars worth of armor, or some drones, or blood. To be honest, I would have preferred not to have found out how well flesh and blood does against armor. I would have rather we paid the price in scrap metal."

That got through. Stilwill realized that people here had lost friends. That wrecked armor was scattered around the motor pool being worked on.

"I'm sorry," he said. "Enjoy the scotch."

After he left, Jabar stood up, leaned over, and opened the trunk. Inside sat the components of his powered armor.

Piece by piece he took it out and set it on the table, and in between sips of the expensive scotch Stilwill had donated, set to cleaning it and checking the diagnostic software.

—————

David Klecha is a science fiction writer living in West Michigan with his wife, three children, and no cats. After graduating from university, he skillfully parleyed his degree in History and fuzzy mastery of Russian into an enlistment in the Marine Corps and a series of entry-level IT jobs. A deployment to Iraq brought the opportunity to start a milblog, and when Dave returned home he began writing professionally, as well as climbing the IT ladder, putting his combat experience to good use. Now Dave works as a Network Administrator for a global oral care products manufacturer you've never heard of and mixes his science fiction writing with online how-to articles and sporadic blogging. His short fiction has appeared in *Subterranean Magazine*.

Tobias S. Buckell is a Caribbean born SF/F author who now lives in Ohio. He is the *New York Times* bestselling author of *Halo: The Cole Protocol*, as well as *Crystal Rain*, *Ragamuffin*, and *Sly Mongoose*. His fifty or so stories—many of which have been collected in the volume *Tides From the New Worlds*—have been published in various magazines and anthologies, including other John Joseph Adams anthologies such as *Under the Moons of Mars*, *Brave New Worlds*, *Wastelands*, and *Seeds of Change*. His next novel, *Arctic Rising*, is due out from Tor in early 2012.

The Last Run of the *Coppelia*

GENEVIEVE VALENTINE

When Jacoba saw the glint of metal she signaled without thinking, and her mech, Arva, dove past the shallows towards the deep. Jacoba just hoped Arva's hull would hold.

The comm crackled to life in her ear. *"Jacoba, we're not reading any algae down there,"* David said from aboard *Coppelia*.

Jacoba was nearly down to Hyun, who was piloting Chollima to pull the last of the algae from the crevices in the rocks, sliding both handfuls into the plasma-front storage pod each of the mechs had built-in. Hyun frowned through his faceplate as he saw her passing, and flicked on his comm.

"Nosey," she muttered.

He smirked and gave her a thumbs up. Chollima echoed it, one tentacle-finger raised.

"I'm not after algae, David" Jacoba said. "Arva

85

knocked something loose when we were picking. I'm retrieving. Two seconds."

"*Is it bio?*" David was a stickler for regs—in the four years he'd been crew they'd never gone an ounce over weight, or had an off-limits life form. They'd saved so much in fines that they'd be able to fix up Ruth's mech Polly in a year or two.

"Negative," she said. "It's tech."

David heaved a martyr's sigh. "*There's no tech in this sector but us. Arva, bring it in.*"

"Override," said Jacoba, and Arva gave an acknowledging chirp and dove like she knew time was running out, the hull beginning to hum as she moved deeper into the murky dark.

(Mechs were coded to have some loyalty to their makers, but Jacoba suspected she'd built Arva more adventurous than the rest.)

"*You're not pearl diving, Jacoba,*" snapped David. "*We're at limit. Get Arva back up.*"

"But this is tech! For all we know it fell off Polly."

Polly's pilot, Ruth, buzzed into the comm. "*Hey!*"

But Ruth didn't deny it, either. Polly was as docile a mech as you could dream of—with Ruth at the helm, she could harvest as much as Hyun in Chollima—but when a mech's AI component had the uptake of a radio, it was hard to expect a lot of good judgment from her.

A thin line of static, quiet as a heartbeat, came over Arva's sensors. Arva pinpointed the source; her legs and flipper-feet never stopped their steady, calm propulsion.

After a bemused moment, Jacoba said, "It's still on."

"*No one told you to scan it,*" said David. "*You know scavenge regs on Minerva. It's none of our business.*"

The problem with David was that his voice gave him away every time, and though he was trying his damnedest to sound angry, he was curious—and worried.

That gave her pause. It was one thing to needle David, but the two of them knew better than the rest why you don't get involved in things that aren't your problem.

A moment later, Captain Shahida's voice came over the line. *"Jacoba, you have fifteen seconds."*

Arva's depth gauge showed another forty meters before she was below regulation, and since that put her out of sensor range, Jacoba could probably fudge another ten before Arva's storage container started to leak.

The hull beneath Jacoba squealed.

Okay, she thought, *maybe five more meters.*

But the little silver flash was almost within reach—it knocked gently against the rock, slowing it down just enough for Jacoba to catch up to it. When Jacoba extended her hand, Arva's right arm moved, and when Jacoba closed her fingers and pulled back, Arva's seven slim tentacle fingers plucked it carefully from the rocks.

It looked like a jellyfish, but there wasn't time to examine.

"Arva, can you make room for some air?" she asked.

From the floor under her seat came the whoosh and whir of Arva pushing some ocean brine around in the plasma-front storage to make a dry air pocket to store the finding in. The storage space made up half the mechs' torsos, and held a grown man's weight in algae. The mechs could control how permeable the membrane was; it allowed them to push things inside that couldn't float back out again.

"Ascending," Jacoba called, grinning. For a backwater mech, Arva was still something.

Arva kicked furiously up to the platform on the water's surface. When Arva pulled herself up, Hyun was already waiting, tapping his wrist, Chollima echoing the motion with a rhythmic clanging.

"Well," Jacoba said, "where's Ruth?"

Ruth sighed over the comm. *"Dammit, Polly—I'm caught in a jelly swarm, over."*

Hyun cackled and tilted backward in his chair, and Chollima dropped off the platform and into the water.

"It's not bad," Hyun said. *"Give us ten seconds."*

"Jacoba took your last ten seconds," David snapped. *"Move it."*

Polly piped through two bars of an apologetic song.

Unloading was always a trick.

The mechs were built for water, too-long arms and dexterous hands and powerful short legs. Though the webbing in their flippers contracted under the wide toes, they were still just awkward talon-feet on which the heavy torso—with its pilot pit and storage tank—balanced precariously. They lumbered like headless gorillas across the cargo bay to the tanks.

Then it was the division of their take into enormous tanks of algae and plankton and lichen bound for Alhambra Corporation's terraforming stations. The species tended to smother one another in close quarters, so the mechs helped sort them as they poured through the membrane and into the right tanks.

It was an easy enough concept for Arva and Chollima. Polly tended to be surprised by the process every time, and three runs out of five Ruth ended up straining plankton out of an algae tank or rescuing stray squid with a noose-pole. Jacoba had done all she could for Polly—she moved just fine—but there was only so much analytic integration possible with a seven-ton SCUBA suit and a radio brain.

Jacoba couldn't wait; she slid her hand into the plasma and pulled out the silver tag. It wasn't some loose joint.

It was a data drive, trailing wires.

She looked at it, weighed her options.

Then she climbed back up into the pilot pit, plugged it into the console, and whispered, "Have a look?"

Arva knew what she meant without Jacoba having to give the command, and as Jacoba rinsed brine out of Arva's joints and checked for damage and logged their haul weights, she knew Arva was hacking the tag.

It wouldn't hurt to have a copy, just in case. Old habit. You could never have too much information in your corner; she'd learned that much long before she reached *Coppelia*.

"Done," called Hyun, as Chollima's plasma storage container slimed shut. "Six ounces under. I knew it! I told him! David can take a long walk off a short reef."

"It's his job to keep us regulation," Ruth said.

Ruth had been an athlete, before they caught her doping and the bad press had pushed her so far out that she landed on *Coppelia*. Jacoba knew that these days, Ruth had a healthy respect for regulations.

Hyun rolled his eyes. "Or what, we make an extra hundred credits on excess algae? The horror."

"That Minervan patrol ship crowded us this morning," said Jacoba. "David didn't give them an excuse to board. You're welcome."

"I think it turns his crank to nag us down the line," Hyun said, shutting the algae tank. "Petty tyrants are a dime a dozen. Guy needs a hobby."

Jacoba pressed her lips into a thin line.

"I don't see the problem," said Ruth, climbing into the crook of Polly's left arm. "I also don't see the problem with this shoulder—joints are all fine, what's causing this lock underwater I've been getting?"

"A colony of microshrimp," Hyun offered.

"A useless smartass, most likely," Ruth said, and tapped Polly's arm. "Hold still, I have to look at this."

"Let me see." Hyun swung up beside her. "It might be pressure. I had to reinforce Chollima's knees last year."

"Not buying it," said Ruth. There was the screech of metal as she peeled back the scales at the shoulder.

Jacoba reached into Arva's pilot pit for the drive. She was so exhausted it felt like Arva was shaking.

Over on Polly, Hyun whistled. "Damn, this shoulder's keyed up tighter than David after an Alhambra inspection."

"Shut up," said Jacoba.

"You should talk," Hyun said. "I thought he was going to blow a blood vessel when you dove. You can't—"

"—get you to *shut up*, which is the pity." She dropped the lid on Arva.

"What a mess," Ruth sighed, and Polly let out a sorrowful bleat.

Jacoba pocketed the data drive and made it halfway to the door before she saw David waiting.

He was looking at her like he'd been watching for a long time, and she could guess how much he'd heard.

He had his back to the wall—he always did—and his expression was furious, but she kept walking and halted facing him and didn't make way.

She looked him right in the eye until he said, a long time later, "The Captain wants to see you."

Captain Shahida owned the *Coppelia* flat-out, which had cost several years of tight profits and poor wages, but at least now they didn't have to worry about red tape coming from anywhere but Alhambra.

It also meant that when the Captain wanted something from you, nothing stopped her getting it.

"What was it?" Shahida asked as soon as they came through the door to the bridge.

David glanced at Jacoba's right-hand pocket.

In her meaner moments, from the bottom of a glass, Jacoba thought it was really no wonder he'd gotten caught.

She handed it over. "Don't know the damage."

Shahida plugged it in and watched on her monitor.

Jacoba looked over the bridge, which she hardly saw—the downside of being a half-decent mechanic on a ship like this was spending most of your time inside circuit tubes, banging things with wrenches and hoping for the best, instead of operating from anywhere with a view.

The ship was hovering, and Minerva's southern ocean spread out under them, green cut by swathes of rust-red algae. It was lovely; she had a fondness for open spaces.

Shahida pushed off from the console as if something had shorted out. "Goddammit."

Jacoba flinched.

After a moment the Captain seemed to make up her mind, and said, "Go get Hyun and Ruth," in a tone so grim it sent a chill down Jacoba's spine.

David cast one accusing look at Jacoba before he left to bring the others to the war room.

At some point before it came to Shahida, *Coppelia* had been fitted for a military op. It had probably gone badly, given the state it was in when Jacoba came aboard. But even after several years of cannibalization there was still plenty of tech, and when they had all gathered in the pockmarked wreckage and Shahida put in the drive, the image sprang to life on a bay of monitors.

"Wow," said Hyun. "There are still four monitors Jacoba hasn't torn up?"

Ruth knocked him with her shoulder.

Jacoba, standing along the back wall near David, didn't answer—hardly cared.

The video was black box footage, and she had recognized the government seal on the bridge.

"That's a Vestal ship," Jacoba said.

Vesta was a planet three months' travel farther out from this system's sun; there was no reasonable way this footage could exist, here.

"Yeah," said Shahida, and sighed.

"Low orbit," Ruth pointed out. "For a while—the hyperspace engineer's almost asleep."

Onscreen a moment later, the door to the bridge slid open and the room swelled with a dozen people, armed and angry.

Very quickly, Jacoba realized how this recording was going to end.

Vestal ships were organic; if you tortured one it would give up its secrets, and if you damaged it enough it couldn't bear witness against you.

Jacoba's stomach soured.

"Well, shit," she said.

David gave her a sidelong look she couldn't meet.

Things unfolded as she'd feared: the bridge became a standoff, the captain and the first mate rose with their hands on their heads, there was a blur of motion, the lens whited out from muzzle flash and came back into focus with all of the bridge crew down.

The intruders moved in, toeing the bodies aside and fanning out to man the bridge. One of the men approached and raised his arms—it must have been to tear out the camera, because a moment after his blurry forearm came into sight, the feed cut off.

But that moment was long enough for Hyun to suck in a breath.

Captain Shahida raised an eyebrow. "Someone you recognize?"

"The tattoo," Hyun said. "Under his sleeve."

He held out his right arm.

Hyun's forearm tattoo was an owl perched on a sword. Jacoba had seen it, but it wasn't a prison tattoo, and she hadn't thought much else about it. He had four visible; other than this one being ugliest, it was unremarkable.

"Minervan Armed Forces," Hyun said, sounding embarrassed. "Special Ops."

David went so tense Jacoba thought for a moment that he was actually going to run for it.

She didn't move to stop him—sometimes there was nothing you could do but run.

"Discharged after one tour," Hyun explained, "but I made it through boot."

When he rolled down his sleeve, Jacoba caught the tightness in his jaw, and wondered what he had done that was so awful they'd gotten rid of him. *Probably thought for himself at the wrong moment,* she thought. The Armed Forces weren't thrilled about that kind of thing.

Ruth shook her head. "So that was the Army?"

"Hyun's not," said David. "No knowing if they still are. Could be ex."

"What kind of ship is it?" Jacoba asked. "Was this a smuggling bust or did they shoot a bunch of diplomats?"

Shahida spread her hands. "There's been nothing over the transom."

Ruth said, "So we don't know who else knows?"

"There was a Minervan ship trailing us," David argued. "*Somebody* knows."

"Maybe that's unrelated," said Ruth.

"Maybe this is a frame job," said David.

"Maybe somebody had an attack of conscience," Jacoba said.

"Yeah," David said, "a lot of people have those at inappropriate times."

Jacoba looked over, but didn't apologize. The air in the room was changing, and she didn't dare back down and apologize for having found it.

"So the question is," said Shahida, "whether they know we found it."

The room went quiet as they considered what would happen if they broke atmosphere and the Minervans thought they were running with evidence.

Shit.

"That Minervan ship's still in range," said Hyun.

Ruth frowned. "So what are they waiting for?"

Jacoba knew this one.

"For us," she said. "To run and look guilty."

"Goddammit," David said, turning to her, "why couldn't you fucking have left it alone!"

"If this is footage of an attack on a Vestal ship," Hyun said, reluctantly, "and the Minervans want it, that's pretty suspicious."

"But it's none of our business!" David swept an arm to encompass them. "We're suppliers, we belong to no planet—we should stay out of it. It's suicide otherwise."

"This is important information," Jacoba said. "Someone needs to know."

"So who the hell do we show it to?" David asked, sounding a little strained.

"No one," Ruth snapped. "Why would you want to get caught in the middle of someone else's trouble?"

A little late for that, Jacoba thought.

"If this can bring someone to justice," she said, "we have an obligation."

Ruth looked over as if only the width of the room kept her from striking out. "An obligation to who? This is out of our hands! You think we can just—"

The Captain cleared her throat.

The room fell silent, waiting, as she looked at the monitors, at the floor, at the ceiling. Finally she said, "We go to port as scheduled. Jacoba, a moment."

Jacoba followed the Captain out to the bridge.

Shahida turned and folded her arms. Jacoba was reminded sharply of the moment seven years ago when she'd shown up on the docks, in dirty clothes and hair still prison-buzzed, and asked for work.

Shahida had looked at her the same way then, like she was a bad bet.

"I can't have this on my ship. You tell me whether I toss it into the water, or leave you in port with it."

Jacoba reeled. She'd been bracing for a punch; she'd still prefer a punch to an ultimatum.

"Now," the Captain said.

Her voice brooked no argument—it never did—but still Jacoba's stomach sank.

She could drop it in the water and forget it. It was what someone with an ounce of sense would do.

But Jacoba never knew how to back down if she thought she was right; it was a bad habit she recognized by now.

"Then I'll go pack," she said.

It was what she'd chosen, but it still sounded like a punishment, and even the Captain's shoulders went tight, like she'd hoped it would go some other way.

"I'll tell the others," Shahida said. "They can join you if they want—I don't conscript."

Jacoba smiled tightly and nodded.

She left through the bridge. She didn't want to see Hyun and Ruth.

She already knew what David's expression would be—what his decision would be—and that was bad enough.

Arva, crouching on hands and feet in the cargo bay, was a welcome sight.

(Other welcome sights: the sky, the transport that carried her out of prison, money, the dive bar in

Baxter, the hull of the *Coppelia* every time she came home again.)

Jacoba climbed into the pit and leaned back against the communication grid in the headrest that had started out serviceable, then gotten so uncomfortable she couldn't use it, and then had come back around to feeling like a second skin. She didn't slide on the limb controls; she liked to give Arva freedom if they weren't working.

If she stayed in port with the data drive—if she abandoned ship—Arva would be someone else's.

That stung. That was the hardest thing to imagine. She'd hand Arva over to David, maybe. David respected limits. To some stranger—it would be harder to bear.

Arva was still trembling, like she was cold.

"Did you look at the drive?" Jacoba asked.

Yes.

There was no reason to connect the drive to Arva's shaking. There was no way for Arva to be thinking about it. She was only AI; she made a thousand tiny decisions when they went gathering, but those were a series of Yes and No decision points, that was all. The clip could have no meaning beyond whether the faces were in her databanks, and if there was anything Jacoba wanted stolen.

Still, Jacoba asked, "What is your analysis?"

No.

Jacoba couldn't blame her.

"I have to take this," Jacoba said, wondering why it was hard to explain. She was getting sappy in her old age. "I found it, and it might be important, so I'll be trying to find the right person to give it to. You'll have a new pilot in the next port."

No, came back through the connection point, and then faster, overlapping on itself until for one heartbeat, Jacoba felt fear—gut fear—that wasn't hers.

She wrenched her head away from the seat and scrambled out of the pit so fast that she missed a foothold.

Jacoba looked up at Arva and decided she couldn't go up and try to say goodbye—not now. It was too sad, and she had too many questions about that wrench of fear. She had enough tough things coming up, and she knew where curiosity got you.

Instead, she said, "It's all right."

It was meant for all of them—Chollima had taken a step towards them, and even Polly had turned, the glass of her pilot pit gleaming like the front of an old scuba suit.

Jacoba had fixed the antique radio transmitter into Polly's console, back when she was a pile of scrap and there was no brain to put in her. Jacoba had always suspected that Shahida asking her to build Polly had been a test.

The first three years, it had been Hyun in Chollima and Jacoba in Polly, humming along with top hits as she dug around the water for lichen, knowing she was free.

"As you were," she said, more sharply than she meant, and walked out without looking back.

There were only a few hours until landfall, and she had to pack her things.

David was sitting, hands on his bent knees, in the V of the corridor so he could see in both directions.

It meant he saw her coming as soon as she turned down the long, empty hallway that led to her room.

Because he was who he was, he waited until she was nearly at her door before he stood up, and he moved no closer.

David could be a bastard, but some limits he never pushed.

"Don't tell me you're going ashore," she said.

"What possessed you to go after it?"

His voice was quiet—he didn't like to draw attention, unless he was angry—and it made her feel even sharper at the edges.

She left her door open, which meant it was all right for him to follow. She didn't turn to see if he had; she had her pride. Instead she yanked her bag from the cupboard and started reaching for her things.

There wasn't much: two suits of clothes, and Arva.

He slid the door shut behind him.

"I'd thought you were smarter than this," he said to the door, "after where you've been."

Sometimes she could barely understand him.

Sometimes they were so similar she might as well have spent the three years of her sentence sharing his cell.

"No one's asking you to do anything," she said, shoved a sweater in her bag. It was Hyun's, left behind after an ice-water dive when she'd had frostbite, but if he hadn't missed it by now, it was hers. She'd need it—Minerva's southern hemisphere was freezing in the winter.

"Fucking right," David said. "I'm not about to go back for withholding information."

He was pressed back against the far wall, hands fisted in his pockets.

Something she'd never doubted—he'd had a rougher time of it than she had.

If you killed a man in a bar fight and went in for manslaughter, you made your peace, or not, and you tried not to get on the wrong side of anyone who could have you stabbed in the mess, and you got used to not sleeping.

When you were out, you caught an interstellar ship that gave you something to do, and had a view of the ocean or the sky, and you never again saw the planet where you'd killed someone, and you managed.

But he'd gone in for accessory to something ugly, and at some point, the cops had convinced him to turn on the others and give up what he knew.

The cooperation had shortened his sentence by years, but Jacoba suspected it was mostly because they couldn't keep him alive in there for any longer. The one time they'd slept together properly enough to take all their clothes off, there had been a mess of white scars on his back like someone was marking days, and a knot of burned flesh on one kneecap, and sickly yellow patches near his ribs where the breaks had never healed.

"Snitch" was a nickname that followed you home and sent people with grudges through your windows at night. That name kept you locked up tight the rest of your life.

"Someone took this out for a reason," she said.

"And it's your responsibility to find out why?" He was frowning now, his gaze halfway between her and the floor. "This was a mistake, not a calling. It's a piece of metal in an ocean, that's all. That's *all*. This is none of our business."

She ran her hand along her peach-fuzz hair. Prison habit—made you harder to pin in a fight.

The thing Jacoba had never told David about prison was that she hadn't been tracked down.

After she'd killed the man, she'd stayed in the bar until the cops came, because she hadn't meant to do it, but the fight had still happened and the man was still dead.

She thought about it in her weaker moments, when she couldn't sleep and she felt like saying it out loud would help. (Never did.)

But even though there were some things David would understand—she'd erased the name of the man she killed until he was just "the man"—the idea that she could have run and hadn't, he'd never forgive.

She leaned against the bulkhead, folded her arms, and looked at him.

Then she said, "You should know the importance of information like this."

He set his jaw and didn't answer for a long time.

"You don't even know who to show it to."

"Well, then I'll have a hobby once I'm landbound, I guess."

"And what other decent ships hire ex-cons? Jacoba, come on."

He was trying to sound practical, but his voice gave him away, every time.

"What we saw is a problem," she said. "I'll make it my problem, if that gets it to the right people."

She nearly added "I'm not afraid," but she wasn't in the habit of lying and didn't want to start during their last conversation.

"You're a decent mechanic," he said. "A passable diver. You're not equipped for this. This could mean war, if you guess right about who should see it. If not—" he didn't finish. There must not be a glut of optimistic sentiments for her future.

She forced a smile. "Wrong," she said. "I'm a great mechanic."

He smiled back—reflex—but it faded.

"Someone alone with this kind of information doesn't stand a chance," he said. "Not you, not anybody."

That wasn't a worried ex-con talking, now. That was the voice of experience, and she had no answer.

He had pushed off from the wall; her cabin was so small that if he moved any closer, they'd be touching.

The hair on her arms stood up.

She watched his face. He was watching her, too, deciding.

Then Jacoba heard a far-off click, and the first chords of a symphony, off-key and thin.

Fear and recognition stabbed her.

"Polly," Jacoba said, and ran.

When she reached the cargo bay, the mechs were standing where she'd left them, and she wondered if she was imagining things.

Then she saw that two of Arva's fingers were pointing to the algae tank, which read 75 kilos over regulation.

She didn't want to alert whatever bastard was in there by having the mechs swarm him, and couldn't risk the haul by flushing the tank.

She lifted one of the noose-poles from the wall and approached. She waited for Arva or Polly to warn her if there were firearms, but all she heard was Arva shifting her weight, ready to jump to her defense.

With a single motion, she kicked open the lid of the tank and shoved the pole into the algae until she hit resistance. Then she yanked the loop tight, locked it down, and pulled.

David was in the doorway, waiting to raise the alarm; she was surprised he'd followed her into trouble.

The kid she dragged out of the muck couldn't have been more than twenty. His neck and one wrist were cinched tight in the loop, and he was coughing and flailing in a way that didn't suggest a hardened soldier.

She yanked once, hard, so his free hand flew to his neck. No tattoos.

"You have five seconds before I drown you," she said. "Impress me."

"I'm unarmed," he sputtered. "I'm here under duress. Don't kill me!"

He could choose his words, she'd give him that.

"Here to do what?"

"To retrieve something."

Jacoba froze.

"Oh shit," the kid said, "you found it."

"Were you part of it?" She tightened the noose.

"No!" He squeaked as the metal dug into the back of his neck. "I'm Vestal!"

"So why did they send you?"

He didn't answer—he'd gone white, eyes rolling back. Jacoba scrabbled to loosen the noose before he died.

Self-control was a process; sometimes you had a hold of yourself, and sometimes you had to work for it.

When she glanced up, David was gone. She hoped he'd been gone a while; this wasn't something she ever wanted him to see.

(She should compare notes with Hyun about the difference between thinking you'd kill if you had to, and standing over a body.)

"Why you?" she asked again. His face had more color under his wet mat of hair, but the glassy look lingered.

"Because I fit," he gasped, more air than words.

Jacoba fought the urge to look around—there wasn't time to think about whatever hull breach they'd made. Something was worrying her more.

"Why not just board us? Don't the Minervans have mechs?"

"They'd have to use ours," the kid said, and showed a mouthful of teeth when he grinned. "Vestal mechs outclass theirs. Their home mechs are just tanks on legs." His voice was all grim pride. "They'll be lucky to figure out how to keep their balance in ours."

Spoken like a mechanic. Jacoba loosened the noose.

"How long do we have?"

He flexed his fingers, gulped for air. "They gave me five minutes—to find it quietly and get back."

To avoid swarming two ships in two days, she guessed, but five minutes wasn't much time.

"Before what?"

Something slammed into the ship so hard it knocked Jacoba off her feet.

Chollima slammed his arms down to keep balance, and Polly braced her arms against the ceiling to stay upright.

After a second of waiting for more unwelcomes to drop into the cargo bay, Jacoba realized she was wrong.

They wouldn't attack from the cargo bay forward. Too risky.

They'd hit the bridge and work their way back.

There was no way to get a mech through *Coppelia*'s cramped corridors, and no way she could hold her own otherwise.

She released the noose and pulled it free of the kid, who was so surprised that he froze, shoulder-deep in algae.

This is how you get taken hostage, she thought.

"Move it," she snapped, and he scrambled out and didn't fight her when she dragged him over to Arva.

He glanced at the pilot pit with an appraising look.

"You wish," she said, and knocked him on the shoulder so hard that he went face-first into Arva's plasma chamber.

He jerked backwards. "You're kidding."

"I'm going to open the cargo bay," she said, already jogging to the airlock. "By all means dive, if you think you can swim to land."

She pulled the switch, and the cargo bay lights flashed red for the countdown.

When she turned, Arva was behind her, and the kid was folded in the storage tank, hands braced on the hardened plasma, looking like this was the worst day of his life.

Jacoba grinned and scrambled into the pit.

If she and Arva had to have a farewell job, it might as well be something exciting.

Polly wailed a plaintive note as the first hatch closed, a sound swallowed up by the opening of the outer hatch and the sound of the ocean below them.

Jacoba threw out her arm, and Arva caught the edge of the door and swung up onto the hull.

The Minervan ship had crowded them tight— by the time they could reach the bridge the ships were ground so tightly together that Arva couldn't break into the Minervan ship without damaging *Coppelia,* too.

She'd have to separate them and then take her chances.

"Hey," she said, "where's the equilibrium circuit?"

There was a muffled sound from inside the storage pod that sounded unhelpful.

She slammed a foot to the floor, wincing as Arva did the same and sent a shudder through the hull under them.

"Don't make her spit you out," she called.

"Halfway up," the boy said. "Through four feet of hull."

But that was probably just a floor panel away from the inside, and the hull in the cargo bay was bound to be easier to crack—the boy had gotten into the *Coppelia* that way.

"Cargo bay?"

"Behind us," he said. "Low door."

Arva turned and lumbered along the top of the hull. If she could get in and knock them sideways, the others would have some breathing room to fight back.

(She couldn't imagine any of them having given up and died already. Shahida wouldn't allow it.)

They were halfway to the cargo bay door when it slid open and three mechs stepped onto the hull.

Jacoba had never seen a Vestal mech in person. As it turned out, they were tall and lithe and seamlessly fashioned, from the expressionless helmets on their shoulders to the articulated fingers that turned into fists when they caught sight of her. They moved smoothly, better than human as they moved to flank her.

They were terrifying.

But if fear could fuel her, so could anger.

She planted Arva's talon feet wide-legged on the

hull of the *Coppelia*, stretched Arva's thin fingers as far apart as they would go, and braced herself.

The first one moved in alone—she wondered if it was a trap or if they were waiting to see if she was even worth the fuel.

Then it held out an arm, hand bent forward to make room for a gun barrel.

Jacoba snapped her right arm up, and from her periphery she watched Arva's dozen-jointed arm fly forward, the fingers' pincer tips whipping against the barrel.

The Vestal mech staggered and its arm swung backwards as she heard the familiar pop and thud of a joint locking.

That happened when you operated mech you didn't know—too nervous, not listening to the controls.

The Vestal mech tried twice to bring its arm down. Then it gave up and charged.

Jacoba dropped them to one knee. Arva struggled to balance with the new center of gravity, but she managed.

"That's my girl," Jacoba said, and Arva said, *Yes*.

One of the flanking mechs grabbed her ankle and yanked hard; Arva's standing foot gave way, and her body skidded two feet along the hull.

"You're going to kill me!" the kid shouted.

Jacoba twisted in the pit, trying to see out the top of Arva's lid. Arva's foot was twisted in its grip, the taloned toes scraping against its hand.

"Feet," Jacoba said.

Arva's flippers, thin sharp sheets of metal, sprung outward, and over the sound of the mesh shrieking along the hull of the *Coppelia*, there was a rain shower as the mech's severed fingers pinged against Arva's leg.

Arva twisted away without being told, lurching back upright and swinging from side to side to keep all three of them in sight. Jacoba could feel the strain of the battle in the hanging movements, as if Arva wasn't sure how much longer her frame would hold.

Now they were crowding her, moving fast to knock her right off the edge of the ship into the water.

By all means, she thought. *We might actually survive a water fight.*

Arva must have understood, because before Jacoba could direct her, her fingers were gripping the ankles of the two closest mechs, and Arva braced, pushed backwards, and fell.

As if in slow motion, Arva floated down the side of the *Coppelia* as the two mechs lost their footing, arms straining to catch them at the last second. The one with the locked arm fell hard, and Jacoba tried not to be pleased.

Then it was the smooth drop of them falling the four hundred feet together—Arva loosened her hold, and Jacoba just had time to shout, "Watch—" before they hit the water.

Arva was so large and so dense that they never slid into the sea like a human would; instead, they fell into water that bowled out around the impact, and had a full second of air before the sea swallowed them, crashing shut above their heads and catching them in crosscurrent.

Arva and Jacoba knew this. The others didn't.

They also knew that if your arms were close to your body, you could reach under the turmoil and sink free of it in that crucial second.

The kid was panicking beneath her—she could

feel his feet as he tried to kick free of the only thing keeping him from drowning.

"Where's the oxygen tube?" she shouted.

He froze. "Are you kidding me?"

"You want a brine atmosphere in there?"

"Between the shoulder blades," he said, and kicked the floor under her a little pointedly.

Arva was already pushing off under the disturbed water, taking advantage of the tiny current to sweep up and behind the mech with only one working arm.

But she was still half-blind from bubbles, and she was suddenly slowing as if tangled, and before Jacoba looked up she knew that the other mech had Arva gripped tight, and was reaching down to rip off the lid of the pilot pit to drown her.

From Arva, there came an aching, *No*.

Something landed in the water.

The third mech joining his friends, Jacoba thought grimly. *Overkill*.

But even as the bubbles crowded her vision, the mech's hand disappeared, and she heard the crunch of metal and a triumphant sound muddied by the water.

It was Polly.

Ruth had come for her.

Jacoba and Arva twisted back and away, and caught a quick pointed finger from Polly that meant Chollima and Hyun were above them, against the third mech.

The mech with the jammed arm had wrenched it free, and even though the gun barrel was broken, it seemed more than ready to explore other ways to kill her.

"Move," said Jacoba, and Arva sliced through the water.

The mech met them halfway, and in the rush it got hold of Arva's left arm and twisted.

Arva squealed. Below Jacoba, so did the creep.

"Override," ground Jacoba through gritted teeth, and felt Arva going slack along the controls.

Jacoba waited an excruciating moment longer, as the mech pinned Arva with one arm and fumbled with its free hand for the plasma chamber. It was labored—the mech wasn't meant for water. She had three seconds, maybe.

Jacoba calculated, tensed, and threw the punch.

Arva's right arm boomeranged around the mech's shoulders, pinched tentacles lending it speed underwater, and forming a point sharp enough that when Jacoba brought her momentum to bear, Arva's speared fingers punched right through the back of the mech.

"Arva!" Jacoba shouted, and she felt Arva's responses kicking in, spreading and looping the fingers in the ways Jacoba couldn't mimic.

But when Jacoba made a fist and pulled, Arva knew what to do.

The mech froze for a moment—Jacoba guessed the pilot was hoping desperately that it could be mended.

But tubes and wiring had come loose and were floating like jellyfish threads; the water was clouding from oil and bubbles were trailing from the oxygen hose, and Arva shoved free of a mech that suddenly had graver concerns.

For a moment the mech curled in on itself. Then there was an all-too-human burst of panic as the mech gripped its own helmet, where a throat would be.

Then the mech went slack all over, waiting on orders that were never coming.

Jacoba set her jaw against her pounding heart. Just because it was necessary didn't mean she cared for it; just because she was willing didn't mean it was easy to see.

Then she turned, and Arva spun carefully to face the skirmish behind them.

Polly was pulling her fist out of a dent in the other mech's helmet that had knocked the dome concave nearly to the shoulder. There was a faint ribbon of pink snaking out of a crack in the metal, and its grip on Polly was slackening.

But Polly had suffered damage, too—Jacoba saw that one arm was wrenched out of place, and inside her plasma storage were some punched-through panels.

But Polly and Ruth were still standing, and they had come to her aid.

Jacoba wanted to ask if the Captain and David were all right; she wanted to ask about what had happened, and who had the drive now, and if they knew who had taken over the Vestal ship and why; she wanted to be able to say something that could come close to expressing her gratitude.

Instead she flicked on the comm and said, "Any ideas how we get back up to the ship?"

Ruth laughed so hard and so long that it took the Captain two hails before Jacoba heard her.

The Vestal ship was gone by the time Ruth and Jacoba reached the surface. It was only *Coppelia* hovering in the air now, casting a welcome shadow on the water.

By the time they had been hauled back up to *Coppelia*, Hyun had already maneuvered Chollima into the cargo hold. He was the worst for wear—their mechs had no advantage in battle on land—and one of Chollima's legs was torn badly enough that someone would have to rebuild it from scratch.

Me, Jacoba thought, but who knew anymore.

Polly deposited Ruth and rested heavily on her good arm, letting the other dangle without weight.

Arva nearly spat Jacoba out, for which Jacoba didn't blame her.

Arva actually did spit the creep out.

Hyun, who was rubbing his right shoulder, froze and frowned. "Did—did you and Arva just birth a *kid*?"

"This is..." Jacoba stopped.

"Marcus," said the kid. He was curled in the pose of a patient hostage, breathing heavy and white as a sheet.

"Marcus. He's a Vestal. The Minervans who took the ship sent him to look for the data drive."

Ruth and Hyun exchanged glances.

Jacoba added, "Which I am assuming is no longer here."

"They tore up the war room for it," Hyun said.

"And the bridge?"

"They both made it," said Hyun, "but David was pretty beaten up by the time I could comm them."

Jacoba's lungs seized. She'd imagined that David would have met the strangers as they came, with the drive already in hand, looking to deal.

"Why?"

Hyun shook his head. "Don't know. Thought he was on the other side of this whole thing. Now I just know not to bet against him in a knife fight."

"Well, I'll show this one to the Captain," Jacoba

said. "Then I'll do what I can for these three. Come on, creep."

Marcus rose, looking at last a little hopeful that they weren't planning to murder him where he stood.

At the doorway, Jacoba turned. "Did the Captain tell you what she'd told me, about the drive?"

Ruth and Hyun glanced at each other.

"Yeah," Hyun said.

Ruth shrugged. "We figured that only applied until the attack. Here's hoping."

Hyun crossed his fingers and winked.

The bridge was a smoky mess, and Jacoba stepped over a body on her way inside.

The Captain's console had been gutted, and there were two or three other consoles bleeding wires. The Captain stood at the navigator's console, looking out at the water far below them.

"Authorize override with voice authentication," the Captain was saying. Jacoba heard the mournful undertone of someone whose mount had betrayed her.

As soon as she hit the doorway, she was looking for David. He wasn't there; was that better or worse?

Shahida didn't turn. "How bad are they?"

"All three with damage," she said, "but fixable."

Shahida glanced over her shoulder. "And this one?"

"Marcus," Jacoba said. "Vestal refugee from the ship."

"Then as soon as David clears out of the war room," the Captain said, looking the kid up and down, "Marcus and I have things to talk about."

"He was sent under duress," Jacoba clarified. "He was instrumental in the fight."

Marcus looked over in surprise.

"I'll keep that in mind when I'm deciding whether or not we throw him into the sea," Shahida said.

"Captain," Jacoba said. It wasn't true. If nothing else, they'd need the extra set of hands patching up *Coppelia* so they could head for port. They could pitch him over the side after he'd been useful.

"Get David out," said Shahida.

Jacoba was glad to have the order. (She and David had limits that never broke. He was wounded, and she wouldn't have gone in on her own.)

David was on the table, surrounded by a carpet of broken glass and torn-out wires, and gazing up at a hole right through the hull big enough to drop a person into.

There were several long cuts along his arms, and one shoulder had a knife wound deep enough that Jacoba fought the urge to cover his hand with hers.

His eyes were half-open, and when she came into his line of vision they narrowed further.

"Everyone make it?"

"Yes. How's your shoulder?"

"Clean wound," he said.

Jacoba debated speaking, decided she had to. "Hyun told me you defended the drive."

"I defended myself," he said, "and the Captain. The drive was just another weapon."

She rested her fingers for a moment on the edge of the table, as if that was the same as thanking him.

He took a deep, uneven breath. "Can you—I mean . . ."

That was permission, and she slid one arm under his shoulders and propped him against her as he sat up.

He didn't like to be touched when he was weakened; as soon as he could, he leaned away.

"They know we've seen it," he said, carefully, around what sounded like a broken rib. "They'll recover from this, and then they'll be back. It's useless to pretend we don't know what we know."

She'd figured as much.

Then he said, without looking at her, "You might as well ask to stay on."

Jacoba didn't have an answer for that.

After the silence had gotten uncomfortable, David said, "Just as long as it takes for us to patch up the ship and for Shahida to get the drive back. She got attached to it when they tried to take it—she'll want to have that information."

"Noted," Jacoba said.

After everyone had treated their wounds, there were a few hours of ship diagnostics and some emergency patches to the outer hull. Without mechs it was slow and slipshod going, with Hyun and Jacoba knocking sheets of metal into place and welding them by hand.

Jacoba waited until the repairs were finished and the crew had assembled before she told the Captain that Arva carried a copy of the drive.

It was the most verbal Jacoba had ever seen her.

"Arva's not your property," snapped the Captain, backed against one of the consoles like she was protecting it with her body. "I should have you under arrest for compromising her that way—this is an absolutely unauthorized act that shows a disturbing lack of trust in your colleagues and your Captain, and I am furious that, in light of events, it has turned out to be justified."

Marcus startled at the conclusion, looking up from where he sat in one corner, hands bound with wires.

Jacoba nodded. "Yes, Captain."

Shahida turned to Ruth, Hyun, and David, whose shoulder was tightly wrapped.

"We don't have long," she said. "As soon as they regroup, they'll be looking for us. We have to patch up *Coppelia*, reach a decent city that isn't deep-orbit away, and find the right people to give this to."

It was no longer a question that they would be handing the information to someone. It was no longer a question that it was war.

It was no longer a question that Jacoba would remain *Coppelia* crew.

"It might not go well," Shahida said, and now it was the voice that Jacoba remembered from that port city seven years ago, the voice that had drawn her to the *Coppelia* over every other ship. It carried, and was final. "Does anyone object?"

Jacoba glanced at David. He met her eye a moment too long, looked away.

No one raised a hand.

Shahida bit back a smile. "Places, then."

They stepped around the dust and wires to their consoles. Jacoba stood next to Marcus, who ventured a smile at her. She nudged his knee with hers.

Shahida said. "All ahead full."

Hyun reached into the chaos and flipped the fuel circuit by hand.

Jacoba kept her eyes fixed out the viewer. The

sunlight was fading, and the red algae beneath them was just beginning to glow, mapping their course across the surface of the water.

Then the engines roared to life, and the *Coppelia* began its last run.

Genevieve Valentine's first novel, *Mechanique: a Tale of the Circus Tresaulti*, was recently published by Prime Books. Her short fiction has appeared in or is forthcoming from magazines such as *Lightspeed*, *Fantasy Magazine*, *Clarkesworld*, *Strange Horizons*, and *Escape Pod*, and in many anthologies, including *Armored*, *Under the Moons of Mars*, *Running with the Pack*, *The Living Dead 2*, *The Way of the Wizard*, *Federations*, *Teeth*, and *The Mad Scientist's Guide to World Domination*, among others. Her story "Light on the Water" was a finalist for the World Fantasy Award. Her appetite for bad movies is insatiable, a tragedy she tracks on her blog at genevievevalentine.com.

2 univ. English classes were not enough for me to make sense of this writing stuff.

Death Reported of Last Surviving Veteran of Great War

DAN ABNETT

WASHINGTON (Army News Service, March 19)—America's last known Great War veteran, Cpt. Arlen Howardine, died Sunday at the age of 314.

Howardine died of natural causes at his accommodation in Longview, WV, according to a spokesman for the home, who added funeral arrangements would be announced later this week.

Howardine enlisted at the age of 17 by reportedly convincing an Army captain that he was older. He was the last living American to have served in Europe during The Great War and the last of 670 servicemen who elected for the famous hardshell program.

The President released a statement today that recognized Howardine and affirmed the

"enduring inspiration of Captain Howardine's
life and service."

I never married. I understood that limitation when
I enlisted. Some of the other boys, they always said
they were married to their shells, but it wasn't like
that for me. The shell was just what it was, though
I know I surely missed it when it was gone. When
they took me out of it in '68, I felt like I'd been
crippled. You get used to that potential. That power.
I don't mean the big stuff. I mean the thought of it,
the knowledge that the capacity is there. When you
raise your right hand, you don't have to level a town
to know what that hand is capable of.

So yes, sir, I missed it. But getting rid of the
shell, in the end it was the right thing to do. It was
just getting in the way, and there were defects and
infections. I didn't need it anymore, and the Air and
Space Museum did. So what do you do?

We were popular with the girls. Yes, sir. Ladies
would regularly send me photos, and billet dos, and
sometimes items of undergarment. It was fun, and
it reminded us we were appreciated. But, lord, if
I'd ever turned up on the doorstep of any of those
young ladies with a bunch of flowers... Like I say, we
understood the limitations. We understood what we
were forgoing when we took on the shell. We were
accepting that we'd lose most if not all of the normal
and regular expectations of a man's life.

And there lay the great irony too, of course. When
the process was first developed, it shortened a man's
span. If you volunteered for one of them early shells,
you were looking at ten more years max, what with the

surgical trauma, the cardiac stress, the organ function, the stress disorders, everything. It was a burden. It burned men out.

By the time my generation came along, the process had been refined. This was the time of the Great War. Technology had advanced. And there it is, that's the irony for you. In taking the shell, we accepted a life that would be empty of all the usual experiences and milestones offered to a man. And we also accepted that the empty life we had chosen would run longer than normal. They fortified and enhanced us to receive the burden of the shell, and that made us last forever.

Or near enough. I am three hundred fourteen years old. I have outlived thirty-seven presidents and seen twenty-four—twenty-four—generations of my family go by.

They say I'm the last, the last one still going. I believe that's so. I stayed in touch with the other boys for a while, a decade or two, then fewer and fewer of them over the passing years. Some died, of course, but mostly, we just drifted apart. Hank Peterson, in Pittsburgh, I wrote him quite often, and he would write back. I understand cancer got him in the end. Mark Remy, he was in San Diego for the longest time, and we would sometimes talk on the telephone. But then he got moved to sheltered housing, and that was all I knew until suddenly I was informed he had died. Benham, John Handley Benham—he was the last I knew of. He was in Philadelphia. We never spoke or kept up. We'd never been particular buddies. He made it to... what was it? Last year? The fall before? They came to interview me at the time, because I had become the last one, as if that was some prize, some tremendous achievement all of itself. That was not how it seemed to me. I felt like I had come in last place, dragging my heels, and that everyone else had got their reward first.

The Great War was not the only service I saw. You shell up a man and bless him with longevity, he keeps going for a long while. I saw several theaters. Fifth Iraq. Ivory Coast. The Police Action of '40. I did a lot of tours. We all did a lot of tours. Latterly, it was for show. I mean, the shells wore out long before we did. Obsolete. Old fashioned and heavy. Inefficient. By '55, you understand, your basic grunt could outperform us with his second skin and his biometrics. That's progress for you. But they would bring us out for a fly-past or a photo opportunity. We'd get a new paint job, and we'd pose with some movie star, or lift an APC full of cheering troopers above our heads and smile for the reporters. They were always draping us with flags. Sometimes they'd even load us and let us cut loose at selected targets, but it was all for show. All of it. Everything was carefully staged. They wouldn't have let veteran shells go against real, live targets. Getting one of us killed in India or South China by a separatist with a pen laser would not have furthered patriotic propaganda.

I made the cover of *Time* twice. Twice. I have a feeling that in a few weeks, I may make it once more.

I remember The Great War, but not well. When they unshelled me, they had to take modules of memory that had become impacted. I'm blank on a lot. Most of it, in fact. Ivory Coast, I remember a little. Not much. I don't have stories because they uploaded them from me for the public archive, and I wouldn't recognize them as mine anymore.

I have, of course, watched the footage. I've seen

myself and been surprised. It doesn't remind me of anything I ever did or any place I ever was because the memories are simply gone. They tell me raising the flag was me, but I only have their word for that. I suppose The Great War is the one that endures in the imagination because it was the only time we went up against our own kind. The tech wasn't the same, but the capabilities were comparable, and the design philosophy pretty much identical. I always thought they looked rather more stylish than we did. More streamlined.

I met one of theirs after the war. Theirs didn't last very long, just like our prototypes hadn't. He was interned, and he was sick. He struck me as a decent man. He was hard to look at because they'd unshelled him and there was so little of the original man left. But I saw decency. He was hard to look at because I saw myself.

He said he missed it. He missed the sense of possibility. I still had my shell, so I didn't truly appreciate what he meant. Later, after '68, I certainly did. I've spent most of my life missing the shell, feeling slow and weak and flightless, heavy, like I was leaden, but not powerful. Helpless. It's not an enjoyable sensation.

We used to know the world was looking at us. We were iconic. We were a statement of our country's technological superiority, of its moral fortitude. Don't let anyone tell you that the sacrifice was some kind of a surprise. We weren't naive, sir. We weren't stupid. Well, not all of us. We understood what we were getting into. We got to serve our country for a few good years, and we got to taste, for that short time, what it felt like to be that capable. Then, after that, we got many, many more years to reflect upon that experience.

We were built to endure, and so we have endured. I'm fairly anxious for it to be over now. I've been in this sheltered accommodation one hundred fourteen years, and before that a care home. I served my country willingly and obediently. I feel, with the benefit of hindsight, that most of the effort of that service took place after '68.

Sometimes I dream, but dreaming's not enough, not when you haven't got enough memories to build the dreams upon. I'm not bitter, but sometimes all I truly want is to properly recall what it felt like. I'm not trying to put it all behind me and forget. Being able to remember would be a great consolation.

I won't be sorry when this is over.

———

Dan Abnett is a multiple *New York Times* bestselling author and an award-winning comic book writer. He has written forty novels, including the acclaimed Gaunt's Ghosts series, and the Eisenhorn and Ravenor trilogies. His latest novel for the Black Library, *Prospero Burns*, topped the SF charts in the UK and the US. His novel *Triumff*, for Angry Robot, was published in 2009 and nominated for the British Fantasy Society Award for Best Novel, and his combat SF novel for the same publisher, *Embedded*, was published in spring 2011. He has written *The Silent Stars Go By*, the 2011 Christmas *Doctor Who* novel for the BBC. He was educated at St. Edmund Hall, Oxford, and lives and works in Maidstone, Kent. Dan's blog and website can be found at danabnett.com. Follow him on Twitter @VincentAbnett.

The Cat's Pajamas

JACK MCDEVITT

It was like approaching a cosmic lighthouse. Jake would have enjoyed watching Palomus through a viewport, but viewports didn't provide sufficient protection against the local radiation, so they'd all been covered. He had to settle for the monitors.

Palomus was a pulsar. Its twin beams swept through the night in majestic synchronicity, first one, then the other, not quite two seconds apart. They were anchored at the magnetic poles of an invisible neutron star, an incredibly dense hulk only about twenty kilometers across, all that remained of an ancient supernova.

Hutchins caught her breath. "I've never seen anything like this."

Jake smiled. He'd seen pulsars up close before, had seen this one not that long ago, but he had never gotten used to them. "The ultimate light show," he said.

"It's beautiful. I don't think I realized they move so fast. The beams—"

He checked the gauges. "Actually, Hutch, these are pretty slow compared to most. There's one out near Mikai that's just a blur. The beams rotate thirty-some times per second."

"You're kidding."

He enjoyed watching Hutchins sit entranced. She'd known what was coming, of course. But knowing about it, even seeing a virtual presentation of it during the prep, wasn't the same as actually *experiencing* it. "Benny," he said, addressing the AI, "have we picked up the station yet?"

"Negative, Jake. It's difficult to get a read in all this interference."

"Okay. Let us know." He looked across at his trainee. "You ready?"

Her dark eyes met his. "I've got it, Jake."

She had a lot of self-assurance for a twenty-two year old. But taking the *Copperhead* into that swirling mass had to be scary. And if she was telling him yes, those eyes were sending a different message. Well, if she wasn't a bit nervous, she wouldn't have been human. But it really wasn't as difficult or as dangerous as it looked. If it were, he wouldn't let her near the pilot's seat.

"We have it," Benny said. The navigation display lit up. *"Range four million kilometers."*

Hutchins glanced at the navigation screen. "Set for rendezvous."

"Will do, Hutch. Estimate arrival time approximately two days."

"Okay, Benny. Open a channel."

"*Done.*"

"*Oscillation*, this is *Copperhead*." The station had once been the *Grosvenor,* a cargo vessel. Its current name, *Ossila*, derived from Lauren Ossila, who'd managed the financing and pushed the Pulsar project to completion. But it had morphed quickly. "*Oscillation*, do you read?"

It would require a minute or two before they could expect to hear a response. While they waited, Jake wondered what sort of research the three physicists orbiting the pulsar were actually doing. He'd done some reading on the way out, but he couldn't make heads or tails of it. It had something to do with comparing misalignment of the collapsed star's magnetic poles with the pulse ratio and God knew what else.

They waited, talked about how spectacular the view was, and drank their coffee. After a few minutes, Hutchins tried again: "*Oscillation*, this is *Copperhead*. Can you hear me?"

The *Copperhead* was not named after the snake. It had been designed specifically to support missions in areas of high radiation. The ship was heavily shielded. Not with copper, of course. But that was a detail.

Priscilla Hutchins was Jake's third student pilot. It had been years since the last one. He hadn't liked it then, and didn't care for it now. He'd requested they spare him. Frank Irasco, the director, said no. Maybe, he said, with that queasy smile, they could find him another assignment in a month or two. Jake had never liked Irasco.

So here he was. It had been working out, though. Hutchins was smart for a kid. And Jake was more patient now than he'd been in the old days. Maybe he was getting a bit of perspective with age.

"Still no response," she said.

It's always a good idea to give a trainee some time alone on the bridge. Makes her feel as if she's really in charge. "Kill the acceleration for a bit," he said. "I'm going down to cargo and check the lander."

Hutchins looked good, he thought. Her black hair was cut short, and she appeared trim and athletic in her uniform. It was the eyes that stood out. And it wasn't simply that they were pretty, or that they suggested intelligence. She had that, of course, or she wouldn't have gotten this far. But there was an enhancement of some sort, a level of vitality that left him with a sense that she could be trusted. He didn't see that very often.

It was a relief. He wouldn't have wanted to flunk her. He'd been through that with one of his earlier charges, and he still wasn't certain whose fault it had been.

He released his belt and floated out of his seat. "I wonder," he said, "if we're ever going to get the antigravity they keep promising?"

She grinned. "I doubt either of us will live long enough to see that."

She was right, of course. He nodded and went back through the passenger cabin, and drifted down the tube into the cargo bay. The lander, loaded with food and general supplies, would be their delivery vehicle when they reached the station. It was, like the *Copperhead*, heavily armored.

Jake climbed into the lander, settled in behind the controls, locked the harness in place, and called the bridge. "Hutch." She didn't like being called *Priscilla.* "You can start moving again."

"*Okay, Jake.*"

The pressure of acceleration eased him back against the padding.

When he'd been here last time, there'd been three physicists, a married couple and a guy on the verge of retirement. They'd added one more since then, Jeremy Somebody. A guy he'd never heard of.

They'd been absorbed then by an effect they called "quantum wrap." (He wasn't sure about the spelling.) They'd told him how glad they were to see a new face, and then ignored him.

Their pilot was Hal Moresby, whom Jake had come to know over the years. Hal was, if you could believe him, on his last Academy assignment. When he got home from *Oscillation,* he was going to open his own interstellar transport agency. If anybody could make it work, it would be Hal. He was the original deep space cowboy. No job was too big. Nothing daunted him.

And of course there was Tawny.

The kitten. Tawny belonged to the married couple. He couldn't remember their names, but they'd gone to a lot of trouble for her, installed electronic food and water dispensers, and a litter box that used magnetic gravel and gentle suction to overcome the problems of a zero-gee environment. She was probably grown now. She'd been much friendlier than her owners.

Jake liked cats.

He sighed and turned on the screen, bringing up an old Lamplighter comedy. The stunts were too farcical to be funny, but he enjoyed them anyhow. Maybe because he'd liked them as a kid, and somehow they partially dispelled the immense solitude around him. He sat back and closed his eyes, and gradually the shouts and the noise and laughter faded out.

"Still nothing," Hutchins said.

Jake strapped in beside her. "Okay, we're still pretty far. The signal may be getting wiped out by all the radiation. I think I had the same problem last time. We might not hear anything from them until tomorrow."

"Do you know any of these people?"

"More or less," he said. "I know Hal pretty well."

"The pilot?"

"Yes." And maybe Tawny.

In time, it became clear something was wrong. *Oscillation Station* remained silent. "The only thing I can think is that their comm system has broken down," said Jake.

Hutchins didn't respond. There were other possibilities, of course.

They were about four hours away when Benny broke in: "*I have a visual.*" He put it on screen.

Jake needed a moment to locate it, a speck blinking on and off as the light beams swept over it. "Are you picking up any kind of electronics, Benny?" he asked.

"*Negative.*"

The AI kicked up the magnification. It was hard to make out details. The thing looked like an ordinary freighter drifting through the churning illumination. It reminded him of a propeller. "Freeze it," Jake said. "In the dark."

"There's a light," said Hutchins.

"Let's try again, Benny. Give me a channel."

"You're on, Jake."

"*Oscillation*, answer up, please. Hal, this is Loomis. You guys okay?"

The lights—there were several—were attached to the scanners and scopes mounted on the hull, and one to the main telescope, which dominated the area above the aft section. Like *Copperhead*, *Oscillation* wore heavy shielding. With all portals covered, no internal illumination could be visible.

"Okay, Hutch," Jake said, "let's make our approach. Go easy."

"Okay."

"They should have noticed we're here. Line us up with her cargo doors. But go slow."

She didn't return his smile. Instead she proceeded in that very serious manner that marks a kid who feels she's being trusted in a delicate situation and maybe isn't too sure she should be. *"Ossila,"* she said, reverting to official terminology, *"Copperhead* approaching. Open docking area, please."

The docking area was marked by two long doors along the lower deck, which were divided horizontally.

The doors stayed shut.

Benny broke in: *"Jake, they've taken some damage. Bridge area."*

A fresh image appeared on the display: A section of scanners, telescopes, and support towers shattered, broken, some apparently driven through the armor into the station. The armor on the underside, below the bridge and the cargo hold, had erupted. Pieces of plating and cable had been blown out.

"They got hit by something," said Jake. "A rock. Came through the overhead and out down here."

"Must have been about the size of a basketball," he said.

Hutchins stared at the images. "You think they had any chance?"

"When it happened, Hutch, the hatches would have closed everywhere. There should be some survivors. Unless they got seriously unlucky."

"So what do we do?"

"First we send a message back home. Let them know. Then we go over and see what the situation is."

By "we," Jake was in fact referring only to himself. There was only one Gonzo suit. The suit, named for its designer, Jack Gonzalez, was reminiscent of the old gear astronauts had worn in the early days before the development of the Flickinger field. But neither the early gear that astronauts had worn, nor the electronic shield that now protected people doing EVA, would have been worth anything in the soup around Palomus. The Gonzo was safe; it had heavy shielding. But it was a pain to wear. It was big. And awkward. He pulled the suit out of the cabinet and sighed.

"You'll look like a robot inside that thing," Hutchins said. "How come there's only one?"

Jake cleared his throat. "Normally, there's only one person onboard the *Copperhead*."

He climbed into it. Hutchins helped where she could. It looked like metal but it wasn't. It was a flex material of some sort. After he was safely wrapped, as Hutch put it, she helped him with the jet pack. "You look good," she said.

"Okay, let's do it."

She held the helmet out for him. It had no transparent face plate. Jake's vision would be limited to an interior display. "If you have trouble getting through the lock, Jake," she said, "come back. Don't stay out there too long. And why are you smiling?"

"You sound like my mother."

Jake locked the helmet down and switched on the imager. He looked at Hutchins, and looked around the cabin. The image produced inside the suit provided the illusion that the helmet had turned to glass.

"Testing." Hutchins's voice on the link.

"Loud and clear."

She went back to the pilot's seat and guided them in close. She was good. He had to give her that. No sudden braking or choppy maneuvers. They moved in smoothly alongside the *Ossila* until the station's airlock came into view. And she continued closing. "Careful," he said.

Her jaw tightened, but she said nothing.

She eased to a stop. They could almost have reached out and touched the other ship.

"Ready to go, Jake," she said. She sounded worried. "What's wrong?"

"I don't like disasters."

"They happen sometimes," he said. "It may not be as bad as it looks."

He walked to the airlock. Hutch opened the inner hatch. He went in, glanced back to be sure she was clear, and held up a hand. Keep cool. Then he touched the control pad. The hatch closed behind him, and the lock began to decompress. When the status lamp switched from yellow to green, he opened the outer hatch . . . and was momentarily blinded by the light. Then it was dark. And light again. And dark.

He ramped up the filter to block out the worst of it. Welcome to *Oscillation Station*. It flickered in and out of view. Hutch would be getting the same picture on her display.

He paused at the edge of the lock and shut down the boot magnets. The jetpack was there only as a precaution, in case he missed. Though if he missed at this range, he should seriously consider retirement. He launched himself, drifted across a few meters of open space, reactivated his boots, and landed directly beside the hatch.

He straightened up, stood on the hull, and his perspective shifted, as it always did in this circumstance. The side of the hull became the deck, and the hatch rotated under him. The light pulses, which had been more or less vertical, went horizontal. The *Copperhead* was now immediately overhead. It made him briefly dizzy.

"*You okay, Jake?*"

"I'm fine." But he waited until his senses cleared.

The airlock controls were protected by a cover. He lifted it, pressed the pad, and the hatch slid back.

The chamber was big. It would easily have accommodated eight or nine people. He lowered himself into it, put his feet on the bulkhead that was actually the deck, and the world rotated again.

He pressed the interior control pad, which should close the outer door, and put air into the lock. But nothing happened. The status lights didn't even come on.

The inner door had an emergency panel. He opened it, extracted a handle, and twisted it. Had there been air pressure on the other side, the hatch would not have opened.

But it did.

And he saw the carnage. There was a gaping hole in the overhead. The relentless light, bright and dark, on and off, swept in through it, illuminating a smashed deck and a tumble of scorched and broken equipment. What had been the passenger cabin was blasted beyond recognition. He climbed through the wreckage into an adjoining compartment which, when he'd been here before, had been used for planning. Now it was simply twisted black metal.

The deck was gone. The meteor had ripped through everything.

He went back through the passenger cabin and onto the bridge. Part of an incinerated corpse had been thrown against the controls. He heard Hutchins catch her breath. It was probably Hal, but there was no way to be sure.

The seats were blistered, the equipment blown apart. There were other seared body parts, and two shredded Gonzos like the one he was wearing.

"I'm sorry, Jake," said Hutchins in a voice he barely recognized.

Me too, he thought. "I know," he said. He stumbled around in the wreckage, and then followed the passageway aft. Eventually, the damage faded, and he was walking through a dining area and then cargo space.

He came finally to a closed hatch. A red light came on. DO NOT OPEN: There was air pressure on the other side.

"Can't go that way," said Hutchins.

She had a genius, he decided, for stating the obvious.

"Hutch, let me talk to Benny, please."

"I'm here, Jake."

"Is there another airlock anywhere?"

"There's one below in the cargo area. But forward."

"I don't expect that'll be much help. Anything else?"

"There's an access hatch in the aft section."

He went back out through the airlock and began walking aft along the hull. *"It's up at the base of the main telescope,"* said Benny.

He climbed atop the ship. A scanner had locked on the *Copperhead*. Several lights burned in a cluster of sensors and dishes. Farther along, a telescope was turning slowly. Beyond that lay a pair of support towers, jutting maybe twenty meters above the hull, and behind them, the main scope. The towers were connected to its base.

"The access hatch is between the two towers," said Benny.

It was smaller than the main airlock. The two towers rose over him, and the telescope, in turn, dwarfed *them.* He pressed gently on the control pad. It worked this time and the hatch slid easily out of sight. He climbed down into the chamber, closed the hatch behind him, and a yellow lamp came on. Air began flowing. "This end still has power, Hutch," he said. She knew that, of course. She'd have been watching everything, but his natural inclination was to talk to her. So he did. "You okay?"

"Sure." She paused. *"Maybe somebody survived. Someone might have been on this side of the door."*

"Let's hope." The green light came on, the inner

hatch opened and revealed an illuminated lounge area. It looked comfortable. Six empty chairs were arranged around a table. Several cabinets were set along the bulkhead. The place was untouched by the disaster up front.

He checked the gauge on his suit. Air pressure in the lounge was normal. Somewhere, an engine was running. He removed his helmet. The air felt oppressive. Thin. A vent was putting out no air flow. "Hello," he said. "Anybody here?"

Deep behind the bulkhead, he could feel the thrum of electronics.

There was a closed hatch to his left, with a red light glowing. He suspected it was the one that had barred his way on the other side. Across from him, the lounge opened into a passageway. Six closed doors, three on either side, lined the bulkhead. The corridor then emptied into a workout area. He could see a stationary bike.

He secured his helmet to the table and called again: "Anybody?" He took a deep breath. "Hutch," he said, "life support is down."

"Okay. Be careful. Keep in mind, if you get in trouble I can't come after you."

"I know." He walked through the lounge. Saw a couple of containers stashed behind one of the chairs. Turned into the passageway. He stopped at the first set of doors, touched the one on his right gently, then knocked. "Anybody there?" When no one answered, he opened it. Padded chair, bunk with sheets neatly tucked, cabinet, monitor. Curtains were still stretched over the bulkhead where once there'd been portals.

The *Copperhead* was like that, too.

One by one, he opened the other doors. One in the middle was a washroom. The others were identical compartments. He looked in cabinets and found clothes, notebooks, toothbrushes, and other incidentals.

He was opening the last door when something stirred. "Somebody's here," he said.

"I'd given up hope, Jake."

It came again. Barely audible. But not in the compartment. It was in with the stationary bike. "The workout room." He was whispering. Didn't know why. "Hello?" he said. Softly.

Still nothing.

The room had a zero-gee pool, two stretch chairs, and bands you could use to anchor yourself to the deck while you touched your toes or did sit-ups. The bulkhead was lined with cabinets. Several were open. One contained breathing gear for the pool.

Another was loaded with towels.

And in a third was a cat.

It looked out at him, stretched, and climbed down onto the deck. It was wearing magnetic booties.

Tawny.

"I don't believe it," said Hutchins.

It was calico, with a white spot on top of its head. It inspected him, walked over, whimpered, and rubbed against his ankle. "You must be glad to have company, Tawny," he said.

Its eyes were black. They locked on him, and he thought he saw fear in them. But that had to be his imagination.

"There's a litter box over in the corner," said Hutch. *"It must have been back here when it happened."*

He picked her up. Not *it. Her.* "Say hello to Tawny, Priscilla."

"You knew there was a cat on board?"

"Oh, yes. Tawny and I are old friends." He took off a glove and rubbed her head. "I wonder how long she's been caught here?"

He started back toward the passageway, but Tawny wanted to be on her own. So he put her down, but she followed him. The containers behind the chairs held her provisions. A thick plastic bag had bits of meat in a sticky gravy. The bag was fastened to the bulkhead, and it had a slit which allowed her to retrieve the food. The bag was almost empty, but there would be more of it around somewhere. As long as they hadn't kept it up front.

Her water was in a soft plastic bottle.

"So," he said, "how do we get her off the station?"

Tawny walked over to the bottle and pressed on it with her paws. A small blob of water emerged from a dispenser and floated in midair. The cat swallowed it and sat down, behaving as if this were the natural order of things.

"She's cute," said Hutchins.

"Yeah."

"Doesn't look as if anybody else made it, though."

"Apparently not. I'd guess they were all up front."

"Benny says there are two suits on the station. Maybe you could locate one of them. Put her inside and bring her back that way."

"The suits were torn up in the explosion."

"You saw them?"

"Yes." Tawny had come back to him and was pushing her head into his ankle again.

"Maybe you should go back and take a second look."

"Damn it, Hutch, I saw the suits. They're useless."

"That's not good."

Jake stared into those dark eyes.

"They're going to have to send out a salvage team. She might survive until they get here."

"It's going to take them a while. The air's already getting bad."

"Well—"

"What?"

"Nothing."

"I don't want to leave her, Hutch."

"I can't see that you have any choice."

He sat down in one of the chairs, drew a belt across his lap to hold himself in place, leaned over, and petted her. She purred. Her back rose, encouraging him.

"Jake," she said, *"the kindest thing you could do would be to put her to sleep. End it."*

"You mean open the hatch."

"It would be quick."

Tawny stared up at him.

"Jake, it's only a cat—"

"Damn it, Priscilla. Shut up." He picked up his glove and, in frustration, threw it across the room. Tawny darted behind one of the chairs.

Unfortunately there was no way he could squeeze Tawny into the Gonzo suit. So what option did he have? If they were in a normal rescue situation, he could have put Tawny in a container and hustled her across to the *Copperhead*. But here, he couldn't even open the airlock hatch for a moment without admitting a fatal dose of radiation.

He hauled Tawny onto his lap. She burrowed in between the Gonzo suit and the chair arm. And he realized why she was doing it: To prevent herself from floating away.

She pressed her head against him.

Hutchins's voice broke through: *"You okay?"*

"Yeah. I'm good."

"You're going to have to put her down."

"I'm not going to do that."

"Jake, you don't have a choice."

"Would you be quiet for a minute?" He looked around the cabin. Stared at the bunks. There had to be a way. "Hutch, how close can you get? To the airlock?"

"With the Copperhead? *Maybe eighty meters. The telescope's in the way."*

"I know. How about with the lander?"

"I can slide in a bit closer, but you've still got those towers."

"You should be able to get within forty, right?"

She thought about it. *"Yes. Why? What difference does it make?"*

"I'll get back to you in a few minutes."

He looked in the compartments. Each bunk had two sheets. He removed them. Then he searched through the cabinets and collected ten more. They were seven feet long, almost three meters crosswise from corner to corner.

He carried the sheets back into the lounge, folded them, and put them in a pile. "Hutch," he said. "We might be able to do this."

"How?"

"I'm coming back over. I'll explain when I get there."

❖   ❖   ❖

He picked up the stack of sheets, opened the inner hatch, and looked back at Tawny. He thought she appeared frightened. But it was probably only his imagination. *Amazing how we project our feelings onto pets.*

He closed the hatch, and minutes later stepped out between the towers and the telescope. He took aim at the *Copperhead* and launched. This time he was off target and had to use the jetpack to home in on his ship's airlock. Hutch was waiting when he came through into the cabin. Her eyes went wide when she saw the sheets.

"What's going on, Jake?"

He held them out for her. "Here. Take some of these down to the lander."

"Why?"

"I'll be with you in a second. I have to check something." He went into his own compartment and lifted the padding from the bed. With a zero-gee environment, a bed didn't really need much padding. He released the clips that held everything together, and lifted the pads. Beneath was a frame. He removed it and carried it out the door.

Hutch and the sheets were gone. Jake took the bed frame down to the cargo deck, got some cable out of storage, and lashed it vertically to the rounded prow of the lander.

She watched him, puzzled.

"Okay," he said when he'd finished, "we now have a flat nose."

"Is that important?"

"It's critical."

"Why?"

"Trust me."

✦   ✦   ✦

They added their own sheets to the stack, and tied them together into a line approximately sixty meters long. When they'd finished, he asked Hutch to go up to the galley and get a small piece of the turkey they'd had for dinner the previous evening. She looked surprised and then nodded. "Right," she said.

While she was gone, Jake tied one end of the line of sheets to his belt. She came back with the meat wrapped in a cloth napkin. Jake slipped the napkin inside the suit.

"We ready?" asked Hutch.

"Good luck to us," he said.

She nodded and climbed into the lander. He closed the hatch behind her, put his helmet back on, and started to depressurize the cargo deck. "Hutch," he said, "can you hear me okay?"

"I read you fine. Jake, you know this is crazy, right?"

"Relax. It'll work."

He rolled the line of sheets into a loop so he could carry them, tying the loose end to the right tread. "All set, Hutch," he said.

"I'm wondering what they're going to say to me when I go back with a cat and you're missing."

"I'll be there, kid. Don't worry."

He took his position on the tread. He thought about the cat, and the comments that Irasco would have if this *didn't* work out. Though his mother would think him a hero.

The green light went on. Depressurization complete. The launch doors opened. *"Ready?"* asked Hutch,

"Go," he said.

The cradle moved the lander into the open doorway and released the vehicle. Hutch started the engine and eased the vehicle clear of the *Copperhead*.

Jake looked over at *Oscillation*'s long crowded hull. The main telescope overwhelmed everything. They moved slowly in its direction. *"Good luck, Jake."*

The pulses swept across the scope, and across the towers. At their base, the access hatch was lost in churning shadows. "They don't make it any easier, do they?" he said.

"The lights?"

"Yes."

"I guess." Her voice had grown cold.

"Hutch?"

"Yes, Jake?"

"Listen, I know you didn't have to agree to do this. That you feel you're taking a chance."

"It's okay."

"I wanted you to know that I've logged the fact that you are proceeding under direct orders, and that you're doing it under protest."

She thought a long time before replying. *"Thanks, Jake,"* she said finally. *"I hope it won't matter."*

"So do I."

He used the jetpack to navigate down between the towers. He drifted in beside the hatch. The line of sheets was still intact, connecting him to the lander, which was floating overhead, not moving. "Perfect," he told Hutch.

"Well, yeah. I didn't want to be dragging you all over the sky, Jake."

He opened the outer hatch and entered the lock, still trailing the sheet. He pulled several feet of it in with him, then pressed the section that crossed the entrance as flat as he could and touched the control pad. The outer door slid down. He held his breath, waiting for an alarm lamp to turn on, but it didn't happen. The sheet had cleared.

He opened the inner door, and left it open. Tawny was waiting for him. She was perched on the deck, her tail swishing back and forth.

"You have a pal," said Hutch.

"If you think so, you don't know too much about cats." He removed the helmet and jetpack and climbed out of the suit. The Gonzo was a back hatch design, meaning it opened in the rear. Jake laid it face down on the deck, leaving it open. Then he picked up the cat. He petted her and, when she seemed perfectly at ease, placed her within the suit. But before he could close the locks she squirmed back out.

He waited a few minutes, pretending to be at leisure. Then he took the napkin from his pocket, showed Tawny the turkey, and put it down inside the suit, holding it in place with his fingers.

The cat came back, pushed his hand aside, and began gnawing on one of the pieces. Jake raised the two sides of the suit and, slowly, closed it over her head. She didn't resist this time. He used the control to lock the sides together. Then, while the cat still showed no sign of resistance, he secured the helmet in place. "Done," he said.

"Like a pro," said Hutch.

He picked up the suit, leaving the jetpack, and carried it into the airlock. Tawny was moving around inside. "You'll be out of here in a little while," he told her.

He heard something that sounded like a whimper.

He let go of the suit. Watched it float toward one of the bulkheads. He checked the sheet to reassure himself it was still securely fastened to the belt. Then he withdrew back into the station, closed the inner hatch, and started depressurization.

Draining the air out of the lock required two and a half minutes. But it seemed much longer. He sat down in one of the chairs and fastened the belt to keep himself from drifting away. He was accustomed to zero-gee. But at the moment he was tired of it.

He wondered what the conversations had been like in the lounge, whether they'd actually sat here and talked after a long day. Tawny had belonged to the wife, but he couldn't remember her name.

Leia. Lara. Something like that. She'd been good-looking, personable, though he'd not seen much of her. They'd all been working, except Hal, the whole time he'd been here. But Tawny had spent time with Jake and Hal.

The green lamp blinked on. Procedure complete. He opened the outer door. "Okay, Hutch, she's all yours."

"Underway," said Hutch.

He imagined the line of sheets straightening. Pulling the suit out of the airlock.

"Jake, this is going to take a while."

"No hurry."

The lander would now be drawing the cat up gradually past the towers. Past the telescope.

"The NFPA will make you Man of the Year, Jake."

"What's the NFPA?"

"National Feline Protective Association."

"I didn't know there was any such organization."

"Probably isn't. I'm going to launch it when we get home."

✧   ✧   ✧

"You need a better approach angle," Benny told Hutch. *"I'm going to back off."*

"Jake," said Hutch, *"You heard?"*

"I heard."

"Benny is going to reposition."

"How far out will he be?"

"At about three hundred meters."

Tawny was traveling at ten meters per minute. That should be slow enough to avoid damage either to her or to the suit. But it meant that moving the cat to the ship would require a half hour. Well, whatever.

The air was getting worse, but it would be okay. As long as the operation went according to plan. And after all, what could go wrong?

Now that everything was out of his hands, he wondered whether he'd lost his mind.

He wished he'd brought something to read. He decided to try *Oscillation*'s central library, but he didn't expect to have any luck with it. The fact that the AI was inoperative suggested it would be down, but that, remarkably, turned out not to be true. He looked through the files and selected *Biases* by Gregory MacAllister.

MacAllister was one of Jake's favorite writers. He didn't like anyone. He poked fun at college professors, Boy Scouts, clerics, politicians, other writers, pretty much everybody. He thought women were smarter than men, that marriage was a tactic by women to rob men of their independence, and on and on. Jake found almost nothing in MacAllister that he agreed with. But nobody could insult people the way he did. He was the funniest guy on Earth.

Just what he needed at the moment.

❖ ❖ ❖

"*We're one minute from the* Copperhead, *Jake.*"

"Okay, Hutch. You're still on target?"

"*Yes. Don't worry. This is the easy—*" She stopped. Hadn't meant to say that. But it was too late. "*—the easy way.*"

It made no sense. She'd been about to say "the easy *part.*"

"Good," he said. "Okay."

The *Copperhead*'s launch doors would be wide open. He could imagine Hutch making her final approach, turning the lander sidewise, and drifting slowly into the launch bay. At the end of the long white tail attached to the right tread, the Gonzo suit would keep coming.

"*Hutch.*" Benny's voice. "*It's a bit high. I'm going to take it up.*"

"*Okay, Benny. Whenever you're ready.*"

Tawny, caught in the confines of the Gonzo suit, was probably not happy.

"*Jake, we have her lined up. She's coming in fine. The sheets are all over the place.*"

"Don't worry about the sheets. Just don't let them get tangled in the launch doors."

"*Jake, you worry too much.*" She took a deep breath. "*Okay, here she comes.*"

"She going to be all right?"

"*Right down the middle, Jake.*"

He heard her moving around inside the lander. Then: "*Okay, we have her.*"

"Soft landing?"

"*Absolutely.*" Then she was talking to the AI: "*Okay, Benny, close the doors.*"

"*Complying.*"

"Where is she now?" Jake asked.

"*Back near the storage cabinets. I'll get her as soon as I can.*"

He looked at the cat's food and water dispensers. He should try to take them back with him.

"*Doors are closed, Jake. Benny, give me some air pressure.*"

"Hutch, can you tell if she's moving around in there?"

"*The material isn't exactly flexible, Jake. You could put a moose in there and I don't think you'd be able to tell.*"

Restoring air pressure in the launch bay normally took only a few minutes. But this time the process seemed to drag on. Eventually Hutchins reported that she had a green light. He heard her switch off the Flickinger field, which she'd kept on as a precaution while in the lander. He then heard her go through the lander's airlock. And finally: "*I've got her. And she seems to be moving around in there okay.*"

"Don't let her out in cargo," Jake said, suddenly aware of what could happen if the cat got loose on the launch deck.

"*Of course not,*" she said. More hatches opened and closed. "*Okay. I'm in the passenger cabin and am about to release your critter.*"

"Good."

He heard the clips let go. Then there was a growl. "*I don't think she's happy,*" Hutchins said.

Hutchins gave her more turkey, and then provided a blob of water. "*I'm glad you decided to save her.*"

"Wouldn't have it any other way."

"*Okay. We ready for phase two?*"

"Yes. By all means. Let's go."

She said, *"Back in a little while."* She was apparently talking to Tawny.

Hutchins returned to the cargo deck. *"We lost most of the sheets. A lot of them never made it inside. I had to cut them loose."*

"Doesn't matter. We don't need them now."

"I'm glad to hear that. Why don't we need them?"

"They'd just get in the way. Getting the suit into the airlock over here isn't like getting it past the launch doors. Keep the sheets tied to the suit and when you deliver it, they'd probably get tangled with the hatch. Then we'd have a problem. Let's just not worry about it. If the suit bounces off the airlock, all you have to do is chase it down and try again."

"Okay. But hang on. I need a minute."

"Something wrong?"

"No. I just want to check into the washroom before we do this next round."

She needed more than a minute. Or maybe it was just his nerves again. Everything seemed drawn out since he'd sealed himself in the lounge. But the rest of the procedure should be simple enough.

Hutch would tie five or six sheets together. She'd loop them around the suit, using them to hold it in place against the bed frame that was mounted on the lander's nose. But she wouldn't tie the two ends of the sheets to anything on the outside of the lander. Instead, she'd bring them into the vehicle's airlock, secure one end to the handrail, and leave the other loose, but still keep it inside the lock. Then she'd close the outer hatch.

He listened to her working.

"What's holding things up, Hutch?"

"Going fast as I can, boss."

"The air's not real good here."

"Hang on. It'll only be a few more minutes."

A few more minutes. What the hell was she doing over there?

"Okay, Jake," she said, finally. *"We're ready to go."*

"About time."

She was flicking switches inside the lander. *"Benny, depressurize the launch deck."*

"Decompression beginning, Hutch."

"It'll be good to have you back, Jake," she said. *"It gets lonely over here."*

"You ought to try a couple of hours in *this* place."

While they waited, they made small talk. Hutch asked whether things like this happened very often. (They didn't.) Jake asked why she wanted to be a pilot for the Academy. "You'd make a lot more money hauling cargo for TransWorld."

"If I were out for money," she said, *"I'd have gone into banking."*

"Any other pilots in your family, Hutch?"

"No. My father was an astronomer. My mother thinks I'm deranged."

"I hope she isn't right."

She laughed. Then Benny broke in: *"Decompression complete."*

"Open the launch doors, Benny."

She started the engines.

The problem with this part of the plan was that they didn't have enough certainty. Benny would control everything, but he had no way of knowing what the precise arrangement of the Gonzo suit was on the bed frame. But it should work.

"*Okay, Jake. We are approaching* Oscillation. *Slowly. Barely moving, in fact. I could walk faster.*"

"Okay," he said. It was the right tactic, but he was tired of waiting.

"*I'm aimed directly at your airlock.*"

"How far out are you?"

"*About two hundred meters. I can see where the airlock is. But it's hard to get a good look. The outer door is open, right?*"

"Of course."

"*Okay. I just wanted to be sure.*"

The air was becoming increasingly oppressive. The cat had survived here a couple of days, and might have gotten two or three more. But Jake was using more oxygen than Tawny did.

Benny's voice: "*Hutch, get ready to release the suit.*"

"Whenever you say, Benny."

"*Twenty seconds.*"

"Okay." He heard her get out of her seat. "*Just a little while longer, Jake.*"

He tried again to look at the MacAllister book. Something about critics going happily berserk over superficial plays. The drum-thumpers, as he called them, were led by Johnson Howard, "who had the brains of a philosophy professor."

"*Let it go, Hutch,*" said Benny.

She would be touching the control pad, opening the outer door of the airlock. That would free the loose end of the tied sheets.

She'd begin to brake. Very slowly. The suit would

continue at its present velocity while the lander and the sheets dropped behind. That would leave the suit on course for the airlock.

There was a minor problem: The suit would necessarily be dragged somewhat off course as the sheet fell away. When the sheet was clear, Hutch would come up behind the suit, catch it again on the frame, and correct its course, turning it once more toward the open airlock.

Everything went perfectly. *"It's on its way, Jake,"* she said. *"Looks good."* He shut down the book. *"It should be there in five and a half minutes."*

Hutch would be braking again, dropping behind the suit as it descended toward the space between the towers and the telescope.

He tried to relax. To divert himself by thinking about the two deliveries left before he took Hutch back to the flight school. Given a little experience, she'd probably be a decent pilot. But he suspected it was a lark for her. When she discovered that star flight was mostly sitting alone, or at the very least disconnected from real life, in a tin can for weeks at a time, she'd bail. She'd find something better to do. She'd commented once or twice how boring she thought her father's profession had been. Jake hadn't said anything. Best to let her find out for herself. But she'd probably go home eventually and sign up for law school. Or get into real estate.

"Still on course," she said. *"Three minutes."*

He had another mission coming up when this series was complete. Hauling supplies to the archeological team on Quraqua. They'd found ruins out there. Dead a long time, apparently. Thousands of years, they were saying.

He hadn't been to Quraqua before. It had been a long time since he'd looked forward to a mission. But this one should be interesting. He wanted to see what they'd found, and he expected they'd be delighted to take him down and show him. Researchers were always—

He heard the suit thud into the airlock. "Hutch," he said, "it's here."

It was the last hurdle. He went over to the control panel and pressed the pad that would close the outer hatch and begin pumping air into the lock.

But the red light came on. The hatch wasn't closing. He pushed it again.

"Hutch—?"

"I see it. Part of the suit didn't make it in, Jake. It's wedged half in, half out."

Don't panic.

He looked up at the vent.

And pushed on the pad again. "Come on, damn it."

"Give me a few minutes," Hutch said.

"To do *what*? You can't get in here with the lander."

"Bear with me. I'll have you out of there shortly."

"How?"

"Jake, I'm busy. Try to relax."

She seemed to have forgotten who was in charge. But he saw no point in hassling her. So he waited.

If nothing else, he'd go down in interstellar folklore. The guy who died to save a cat.

He tried to conserve his air. Take shallow breaths. *Hutch, what the hell are you doing out there?*

He started thinking about things he'd wanted to do

that he'd never gotten around to. There'd been women he'd simply walked away from who'd deserved better. He didn't think he'd ever expressed his appreciation to his father for all he'd done. He—

Abruptly, there was a noise in the airlock. Like someone moving around. But that wasn't possible. "Hutch?"

"Yes, Jake?" She sounded annoyed.

"You're not running around out there dressed in a Flickinger field, are you?"

"No, Jake. I like you, but I'm not going to get myself radiated—"

"Okay. I thought I heard something in the airlock."

"You did. Just sit tight and let me work."

There were times he'd been a crank. He tended to think of himself as better than other people because of his profession. Most people were ground-huggers, people who never looked above the rooftops. They were not playing the game at his level. He shouldn't have let them see how he felt. But he did. He *enjoyed* doing it.

At the moment, he wished he was one of them.

He wasn't sure how much time passed. He had no way to keep track. But he remembered once when he was a boy of about four or five he'd gone to the hospital with an inflamed liver. He'd had the impression that several days had gone by with no sign of his mom and dad. He thought he'd been abandoned. Later, he learned they'd been in the room almost from the start.

He felt that way now. That hours were passing. That he was alone.

Then something clumped into the airlock.

"All right," said Hutch. *"Try it now."*

He pressed the pad. Got a yellow light. It was working. And he could hear the hatch closing.

Thank God. "Hutch, what did you do?"

She'd ignored the plan. She'd cut several of the sheets into thin strips and knotted them together into a line the length of a football field. She'd never really released the Gonzo suit. It had been tied to the lander the whole time.

"I was afraid it would get wedged down there somewhere."

"Which is exactly what happened."

"So I just pulled it free."

"What good would that have done? You couldn't get it back into the hatch that quickly. You'd have had to chase it down."

"I set it up back on the *Copperhead*. I replaced the boot magnets with alphas that Benny could activate. They're stronger."

"That would have taken some time—Oh, that's what you were doing when you claimed you were going to the bathroom."

"Yes. When the suit got stuck, we pulled it clear, just a little bit, and turned on the magnets. It didn't work the first time; it just reconnected with the hatch. But the second try was gold. Right in the door."

"Brilliant."

They were in the *Copperhead*'s passenger cabin. "I don't mind leaving this place behind," he said.

"You going to do any more animal rescues?"

Tawny was rubbing her head against *Hutch's* ankle

now. She'd switched allegiances. "I think I've had it with that."

Jake glanced at Tawny's food and water dispensers, which he'd brought over from the *Ossila*.

"I wouldn't want to cause a problem," Hutchins said, "but she's going to need her litter box."

Jack McDevitt has been described by Stephen King as "The logical heir to Isaac Asimov and Arthur C. Clarke." He is the author of eighteen novels, ten of which have been Nebula finalists. His novel *Seeker* won the award in 2007. In 2003, *Omega* received the John W. Campbell Memorial Award for best science fiction novel. McDevitt's most recent books are *Echo* and *Firebird*, from Ace. Both are Alex Benedict mysteries, about a far-future antiquarian who specializes in solving historical puzzles. A Philadelphia native, McDevitt had a varied career before becoming a writer. He's been a naval officer, an English teacher, a customs officer, and a taxi driver. He has also conducted leadership seminars. He is married to the former Maureen McAdams, and resides in Brunswick, Georgia, where he keeps a weather eye on hurricanes.

Find Heaven and Hell in the Smallest Things

SIMON R. GREEN

They threw me into Space and then dropped me into Hell, with just a dead woman's voice to comfort me.

They should have known better. They should have known what would happen.

We sat in two rows, facing each other. Twelve people. Yes, call us people, but we certainly weren't men or women anymore. Twelve people from Old Earth, wearing the very latest hard suits. The new armour, built for strength and speed, cutting-edge science, and all the latest weapons. Along with a built-in AI to interface between the occupant and the armour ... to speak soft soothing words to us, keep us human, and keep our minds off the perfect killing machines we'd become. We sat in two rows, six hard suits staring at six hard suits—identical suits of faceless armour, except for the numbers One to Twelve stencilled on our chests. Mine said Twelve.

Looking at the suit opposite me was like looking at myself. Gleaming steel in the shape of a man, with a smooth, featureless helm where a face should be. We couldn't look out, but it also meant the world couldn't look in, and for that, we were grateful. We don't need faces. We see the world with new eyes, through the augmented senses of the hard suits.

We were all of us strapped in, very securely. To hold us steady, or to keep us under strict restraint so we couldn't hurt anyone, including ourselves. Just in case we were to go crazy. It does happen. After all, no sane person would allow themselves to be put in a hard suit.

The armour keeps us alive. The armour makes us strong and powerful. The armour is our life support and our life sentence, a prison we can never leave.

We don't use our names anymore. Just the numbers. The people we used to be are gone. We don't talk much. We never met each other before they marched us aboard this ship at gunpoint. We've never seen each other outside our armour, and we don't want to. Pretty people don't get locked inside hard suits. Not handsome, whole people, with their whole lives ahead of them. At the hospital, they let me look in a mirror once, and then they had to pump me full of tranks to stop my screaming.

The ship's Captain spoke to us through the overhead speakers. His voice sounded human enough, but he was no more human than we were. Just a memory deposit, grafted onto the ship's AI—a computer haunted by an old man's memories, the ghost in the machine.

A memory of a man, to run a starship, to take things like us to worlds where Humanity isn't welcome.

"This is the Captain of the *Duchess of Malfi*," said the human-sounding voice. "We'll be dropping into orbit around our destination shortly. The planet's official designation is Proxima IV. Everyone else calls it Abaddon. Why? Because it's just another name for Hell."

The Captain wears a ship the way we wear our armour. It occurred to me that might make him a little more sympathetic to our plight than most.

"What did you do, Captain?" I said, through my suits' speakers. "What did you do, to be imprisoned in this ship?"

"Are you crazy?" said the Captain. He sounded genuinely amused. "I asked for this. Begged for it! Thirty years service in the Fleet, running the space lanes, at play among the planets... and they took it all away from me. Just because I got old. And then they came to me, and offered me my own ship and the freedom of space. Forever. Of course it wouldn't be me, as such, just the memory of me, but still... I jumped at the chance. I only thought I knew what Captaining a ship was like. If you could only see the glories I see, through the ship's sensors. They say Space is empty, but they're wrong. They need to see it with better eyes. There are delicate forces and subtle energies out here that would put the brightest rainbow to shame. There are giants that walk among the stars, living shapes and concepts we don't even have names for. We are not alone, in the dark..."

An awful lot of people go crazy, when you take their humanity away, and lock them inside a box. Even if it's a box as big as a ship. I tried again.

"Don't you miss being human, Captain?"

"Of course not! How could I miss being that small, that limited? Anyway, the real me is still human. Somewhere back on Old Earth, probably dreaming about me out here . . . Look, whatever briefing they gave you about what you're doing . . . forget it. Abaddon isn't like anything you've ever encountered before. Here's the real deal; everything on the planet below is deadly to Humanity. The air, the gravity, the radiation, everything you might eat or drink, and anything you might happen to encounter. Very definitely including the extensive and murderous plant life. Once you're down there, you're at war with the whole world. If you get distracted, you'll die. You let anything get too close to you, you'll die. You get lazy or sloppy, you'll die. Just . . . do your job, and try to survive."

"Are there any human people at the Base on Abaddon?" said Three. The voice that issued from his speakers was neither male nor female. All our voices were like that. Anything else would have been cruel.

"Hell no," said the Captain. "No people anywhere, on Abaddon. It's not a people place. That's why they've sent you to work on the terraforming equipment, because robots and androids can't operate under the extreme local conditions. Now brace yourselves; we're entering the atmosphere."

The whole cabin shook as the *Duchess of Malfi* dropped like a stone, and gave every indication of hitting something that was doing its very best to hit back. I say cabin, but cargo hold would probably be more accurate. No frills or fancies, just a holding space for twelve suits of armour. Turbulence shook us like a dog shakes a rat, slamming us all back and forth in our reinforced straps. We didn't feel a thing, of course; feeling is one of the first things you learn to do without. The armours' servomechanisms whined loudly as they struggled to compensate for the sudden movements. My suit's AI flashed up status readouts on the inside of my helm, to reassure me we were still operating well within the armour's specifications.

Any human being would have been killed by that fierce descent, but we were never in any danger. Hard suits are designed to insulate their occupants from any danger they might encounter. I could hear the wind howling outside the ship, screeching like a living thing, hating the new arrival that pierced its atmosphere like a knife. The Captain was right. We'd come to a world that hated us.

"The landing pads are almost two miles from Base Three," said the Captain. "Once I've dropped you off, find the beacon and head straight for the Base. Don't let anything stop you."

"What happened to Base One and Base Two?" said Seven.

"They really didn't tell you anything, did they?" said the Captain. "How very wise of them. The whole planet is covered by one massive jungle, and everything in it hates you. Base One was entirely mechanical: drones and robots run by the Base AI. Plants overwhelmed the whole thing inside a week. You can't even see the Base anymore, it's buried so deep in vegetation. Base Two had a human crew; they lasted almost two months before they stopped answering their comm. The rescue party found the Base completely deserted. Force shield down, main doors wide open; no trace of a living person anywhere. Not a clue anywhere as to what happened to them. Maybe you'll find out. Maybe you'll last longer."

A holoscreen snapped on, floating in mid air between our two rows, showing remote sensor imaging of what was waiting for us down on Abaddon. At first, all I could see was the light: bright and vicious and overpowering. My suit's filters had to work hard to compensate in order for me to see anything at all. The landing pads were still some distance below us, shining like three crystal coins dropped into an overgrown garden. In reality, each pad was almost half a mile wide, specially designed to absorb the destructive energies that accumulate from starship landings. The jungle came right up to the edges of the three pads, surrounding them with tall rustling stalks of threatening plant life.

"Why do they allow plants to grow so close to the landing pads?" said Nine.

"Base Three sends out drones to burn it all back, once every hour," said the Captain. "But the jungle grows back faster than the drones can suppress it. If it weren't for the radiation the pads generate, the jungle would have buried them too. Base Three has its own force shield; nothing gets past that. Remember; once we land, watch yourselves. You've got no friends down there."

You'll be fine, Paul, said a warm, comforting female voice in my head. The hard suit's AI. *Just follow your training, and everything will be well. I'm right here with you.* I didn't say anything, but I shuddered in spite of myself.

The whole ship cried out as we slammed down onto the landing pad. The holoscreen disappeared, replaced by a flashing red light and an emergency siren. The Captain's voice rose over it. "Out! Out! Everybody out! I'm not staying here one moment longer than I have to!"

Our straps flew open, releasing us at last, and we all stood. Guns and other weapons appeared and disappeared quickly, as we ran our system checks. Servomotors whined and whirred loudly as we checked our responses, like knights in armour about to set off on a crusade. And then a hatch opened in the far wall, a ramp extended down to the landing pad, and we went slamming heavily down the steel walkway to meet whatever was waiting for us.

The light hit us hard, almost blinding us despite our suits' filters, but none of us hesitated. We just kept pressing forward, wanting to be well clear of the ship before it took off again. The ramp disappeared the moment the last one of us stepped off, and the hatch slammed shut. We were down, on Abaddon.

We moved quickly to stand back to back, in squads, the way we'd been trained. The light was just about bearable now, but the air seemed ... sour, spoiled. Two suns blazed fiercely in the sky, too fierce to look at directly. The sky was the crimson of fresh blood, the roiling clouds like dark masses of clotted gore, outlined by great flurries of discharging energies from storm patterns higher up. A heavy wind blasted this way and that, howling and shrieking. Abaddon: just another name for Hell.

The jungle was all around us: unfamiliar plants a good ten, twelve, fourteen feet high in places. The colours were harsh and gaudy, primal and overpowering, clashing blatantly with each other in patterns that made no sense, in a manner openly upsetting and even disturbing to human aesthetics. There were things like trees, with dark purple trunks and massive spiked branches, weighed down with masses of serrated, puke-yellow leaves. All of them bended and bowed at impossible angles, as though they wanted to slam their tall heads down on us. And all around the trees were every variation or type of plant you ever saw in your worst nightmares, thrashing and flailing with endless hate and vitality, whipping long barbed flails through the air, pushing and pressing forward as though they couldn't wait to get at us.

They'd seemed restless enough on the holoscreen, but once we appeared on the landing pad they all went crazy, absolutely insane with rage and bloodlust. Every living thing strained towards us, churning and boiling like attack dogs let off the leash. I actually saw some of them rip their own roots up out of the dark wet earth and lurch forward on roots curled like claws. There were huge flowers with mouths full of grinding teeth, wild with the desire to drag us down. Seed pods hurtled through the air to explode among us like grenades, but the razor-edged seeds clattered harmlessly against our armour.

It was as though the whole jungle was coming at us at once, struggling against each other in a vicious urge to get to us, with no sense of self-preservation at all. We stood together in our squads, taking it all in.

"There aren't any animals," said Three. "It's all . . . plants. But plants aren't supposed to act like this!"

"The Captain was right," said Seven. "This whole world hates us. How refreshingly honest."

"We are definitely not welcome here," said Four. "You think this world knows we're here to terraform it?"

"Don't anthropomorphise," said One. "Just deal with what's in front of you."

"We have to get to Base Three," I said. "Power up all weapon systems. Remember your training. And try not to shoot me in the back."

Well done, Paul, said my AI. *Take charge. You'll get through this okay. Paul? I wish you'd talk to me, Paul.*

We strode forward, off the landing pad and into the jungle, and opened up with everything we had. I had an energy weapon built into my left hand. I fired it, and a huge mass of seething vegetation just disappeared. Good weapon, very effective, but it took two minutes to recharge between shots. My right hand held a projectile weapon, firing explosive flechettes. I moved my hand back and forth, cutting through all the plants in front of me like an invisible scythe. But my armour only held so much ammunition. So I used both weapons to open up a trail, and then stepped forward onto it and kept going.

Nine was right there beside me. He had a flame-thrower working, burning the thrashing plants right back to the ground. Two moved in on my other side. He had a grenade launcher. Lots of noise and black smoke, and bits of dead plant flew through the air. We worked well together, opening up a wide path before us. My armour was locked onto Base Three's beacon, and all I had to do was head straight for it.

We all felt the shockwave as the *Duchess of Malfi* took off, throwing itself back up into the sky again, but none of us could spare the time to watch it go. We had to keep all our concentration on the plants trying so hard to kill us. They pressed in from every side, clawing and scraping and hammering at our armour, searching for weak spots, for a way in. The various fires we started never seemed to last long, and for every plant we killed there were always more pressing forward to take their place. The jungle had already closed in behind us, cutting us off from the landing pads.

We moved slowly, steadily forward, all twelve of us together, an oasis of calm rational thought in a sea of violence, heading for Base Three. I'd tried contacting them on the open channel, but there was no reply. I remembered the Captain's voice, telling how Base Two had been found wide open and deserted... But I couldn't think about that. Not when there were still so many plants to kill.

With my ammunition reserves already running low, I had no choice but to shut down my guns and fall back on the amazing strength built into my armour. I grabbed striking plants with my steel hands, tore them apart as though they were made of paper, and threw them aside. Some twisted around my hands as I held them, still trying to get at me. A long bristling creeper wrapped itself around my arm, constricting furiously, but I tore it loose with one easy gesture, crushing it in my hand. Thick and bloody pulp spurted through my fingers. It couldn't touch me. Nothing could touch me. And it felt good, so good, to be able to strike out at a world that so openly hated us.

Two was pulled down by a mass of lashing creepers. They just engulfed him in a moment, crushing him with implacable force. His armour cracked in a dozen places under the incredible pressure. The creepers broke the armoured joints, and pulled Two apart. He died quickly, the plants soaking up his spurting blood before it even reached the ground. Seven ran out of ammunition, or his gun jammed. Either way, he just stood there looking at it, and the top of a tree came slamming down like a massive bludgeon and slammed him into the ground. All his joints ruptured at once, and blood flew out of his armour at a hundred points. He didn't even have time to scream. We never saw what happened to Ten. We just looked around and he wasn't there anymore. We heard him screaming over the open channel for a while, and then there was only silence.

The rest of us ploughed on through the jungle, killing everything that came at us. It was only two miles to Base Three, but it seemed to last forever.

We finally burst out of the jungle and there it was, right before us. Reassuringly solid, rising tall and majestic into the blood-red sky, untouched by the world it had come to change forever. There was a shimmering in the air around it, from the force shield. It made the Base look subtly unreal, as though we'd fought all this way just to find a mirage. But the energies the field generated were more than enough to hold the plants back, and we stumbled across a wide-open perimeter and entered the Base courtyard. The force shield had been programmed to let us through, and we strode through the shimmering presence like walking through a sparkling waterfall, out of danger and into safety.

A few plants got through the force shield by clinging stubbornly to our amour. We quickly ripped them away, tearing them apart and then trampled them underfoot until the pieces stopped moving. Some of the larger growths clung to our armour as though they were glued there; so we all washed each other with our flamethrowers, just to be sure. We didn't feel anything inside the hard suits. When we were finished, we turned to face the main doors and found that gun barrels had appeared on either side of the doors, covering us. Possibly to assist us against invading plants, possibly to remind us that Base Three was ready to destroy any or all of us should the need arise.

Because the armour made us too powerful to be trusted. And because everyone knew that if you weren't crazy before they put you in the suit...

The main doors slid smoothly open, and those of us who'd made it through the jungle stamped heavily forward into Base Three, tracked by guns all the way. Once we were all inside, the doors closed very firmly behind us. Human lighting, and a human setting, seemed strangely pale and wan after the extreme conditions of the planet's surface. The Base Commander's voice came to us through overhead speakers. Like the ship's Captain, he was just a memory deposit imprinted on the Base's AI. I doubted he was as happy about it as the Captain had been.

"Welcome to Base Three," said a very male, very authoritative voice. Military to the core. Presumably intended to be the kind of voice we'd accept orders from. "Welcome to Abaddon. None of you can leave until the job here is completed. I have been assured that once the terraforming equipment has been assembled, and tested, you will all be picked up and sent...somewhere more pleasant. You can believe that or not, as you please. I see nine of you. How many left the ship?"

"There were twelve of us," I said. "Three of us died just getting here."

"Get used to it," said the Base Commander. "Nine out of twelve is a lot better than the last crew they sent."

"How many crews have there been, before us?" said One.

"That's classified," said the Commander. "But learn the lesson well. Now you know what to expect from Abaddon. Everything here hates you. Every living thing on this planet wants to kill you. The air is poison, the gravity is deadly, the radiation levels would fry your chromosomes. We are at war with the world."

"Will we be allowed access to information compiled by the previous crews?" I asked.

"Of course," said the Commander. "Study the files all you want. Profit from their mistakes. But all you really need to know is that every other crew who came here is either dead, or missing and presumed dead. So stay alert. And kill everything you see, before it kills you. Now: go to your quarters. Get what rest you can. You start work first thing in the morning."

We all had more questions, but he didn't want to talk to us anymore. Eventually we gave up and followed the illuminated arrows set into the floor, guiding us to our private, separate, quarters. We didn't want to be around each other. We had nothing in common, except what had been done to us, against our will. No one ever volunteers to be put into a hard suit.

There was a common room, but we had no use for it. We had nothing to say to each other, didn't even want to look at each other. That was too much like looking at ourselves.

My room was a steel box, with a basic bed to lie on. No comforts or luxuries, because those were human things. My AI opened up the front of my armour, and I fell out of it. Or what was left of me fell out. A mess of tubes and cables still attached me to the inside of the suit, delivering nutrition and fluids and taking away wastes for recycling. I lay on my side on the bare bed, my back and all its attachments still stretching away into the suit standing upright in the middle of the room. Like a guard watching over me.

I breathed heavily, slowly, disturbed by how different the Base air seemed after the familiar recycled air of my hard suit. *Seemed* was the best I could manage; I had no sense of smell or taste anymore. I didn't have much of anything, anymore. No legs, and only one arm. Half my torso replaced by medtech holding me together and keeping me alive. No genitals. Half my face gone, replaced with smooth plastic. The rest of me was mostly whorled and raised scar tissue. I lay on my side on the bed, my eye squeezed shut, so I wouldn't have to see myself. I can't sleep inside the suit; if I could, I'd never leave it, and never have to look at what they'd done to me in the name of Science and Mercy.

Are you all right, Paul? The warm female voice of the suit's AI drifted through my mind. I was never free of her, even when I wasn't in the suit.

"I'm fine," I said. "Leave me alone. Please."

You know I hate to see you like this, Paul. It breaks my heart. Or it would, if I still had one. I wish I still had arms so I could hold you. But I'm still here, still with you. Even if all I can do is comfort and reassure you. Be the one sane voice left in your head. You might be a thing in a hard suit, and I might be just a memory imprinted in silicon, but we're still man and wife. I'm still Alice, and you're still my Paul.

"You're the voice they put in my head to keep me from going psycho," I said. "Let me sleep..."

Why are you so hard to talk to, Paul? We always used to be able to talk about everything.

"That was then; this is now. Please, let me sleep. I'm so tired..."

Yes. Of course. I'm sure things will seem much better in the morning. Just remember: whatever's out there, you don't have to face it alone. I'll be right there with you. Are you crying, Paul?

"Goodnight, Alice."

Goodnight, Paul.

They dragged me from the wreckage of the aircar, more dead than alive. They saved my life, and then expected me to be grateful. They told me my wife was dead. Alice was dead. I was so badly injured they had to cut more than half of me away, and then they decided the only way to save me was to seal me into a hard suit. Only the really badly damaged go into hard suits, because the bond is forever. And the process is extraordinarily expensive. But the Empire has a desperate need for people in hard suits, to do all the really dangerous work on truly hostile alien worlds, so they're always ready to cover the bill. And people who might have been allowed to die mercifully in their sleep wake up to find they've been sealed in a steel can, forever. Indentured for life, to cover the Empire's expenses.

Is it any wonder so many of us go crazy?

These days, every hard suit has its own built-in AI, to interface with the occupant. To talk with them and console them, encourage them in their work and keep them sane. To help with this, the AIs are programmed with the memories of someone close to the occupant, someone who cared about them. A wife or a husband, a father or a daughter. Anyone who could provide a memory deposit. Everyone is encouraged to make regular deposits at the Memory Bank, in case there's an accident, and the brain needs to be reinforced with old memories. The Empire doesn't tell you that they have the right to those deposits, once you're dead. They don't want you to know. It would only upset you.

They imprinted my dead wife's memories onto my suit AI from a memory deposit made some years earlier. She always meant to update it, but somehow she never got around to it. She had no memory of dying in the car crash. She had no memory of the last three years. *You've changed,* she kept saying to me. *You haven't,* I said. And I cried myself to sleep every night, even as she tried to comfort me.

First thing in the morning turned out to mean five A.M. Base time, of course. With its two suns, Abaddon had a planetary cycle that would drive anyone crazy. The alarm drove me out of my bed and back into the armour, and then I followed the arrows in the floor to the transport ship kept inside the Base, where the plants couldn't get at it. The ship blasted up through the top of the Base, through the force shield, and out across Abaddon to the unfinished terraforming equipment we'd come to work on.

We sat in two rows, looking at each other, strapped firmly in place. No windows, no holoscreen, no sense of where we were or where we were going. It was, at least, a fairly smooth ride compared to the trip down. The transport ship dropped us off in a clearing full of crates and half-assembled machinery, and shot off again the moment we'd all disembarked. The Commander didn't want to risk his ship; he'd have a hard time replacing it.

For a while, we just stood there together, looking around us. Piles and piles of wooden crates and something really high-tech in the middle of the clearing, looking distinctly unfinished. It didn't look like something that would eventually transform the entire planet, something that would tame the jungle and make Abaddon a place where people could live—where plants would behave like plants.

At least we had a pretty large clearing to work in. The ground had been specially treated so nothing could grow on it. It was grey and dusty, and solid enough that even our heavy footsteps sounded dull. The jungle had grown right up to the edge of the perimeter, and, once again, the moment we appeared everything went absolutely insane with rage. Every living thing strained forward, frantic to get at us.

I did ask why the terraforming equipment couldn't be surrounded by a force shield, like the Base, but apparently the field's energies would disrupt the delicate terraforming equipment. So it was up to us to defend it the hard way. Only three of us were scientists, specially trained to assemble the equipment; the rest of us were just grunts, trained to walk the perimeter and slap down the plants as they pressed forward.

They couldn't survive long on the grey ground, but it didn't stop them making mad suicide rushes to get at us and the equipment.

So the six of us divided up the perimeter and walked back and forth, each of us protecting our sector. The plants surged endlessly forward, as though just the sight of us drove them out of their minds. We walked back and forth, shooting them and frying them, blowing them up and cutting them down, and still they kept coming. To preserve our ammunition, we quickly learned to meet them with the built-in strength and speed of our armour.

The plants lashed us with barbed flails, ground at us with bony teeth inside flower-heads, tried to force their way in through our joints, or just crush us under coil after coil of constricting creepers. We tore them up and ripped them apart, and our armour ran thick with viscous sap and sticky juices.

The violent colours and clashing shades didn't get any easier to deal with. The light was still painfully bright, and the wind slammed back and forth so viciously our armour had to fight to keep us upright. We set fire to the jungle, but it never lasted. We blasted the plants with heavy gunfire and ravening energies, and they just kept coming. We tore the plants up out of the ground, with their roots still twitching, and still they fought the hands that held them, as though our presence on this planet alone was an offence beyond bearing.

There was a kind of sentience in the plants, in the jungle. I could sense it. They knew what they were doing. They hated us. The plants must have known they would die, that their continuing assault was suicide for every individual plant... but the jungle didn't care. We were the hated enemy. We had to be fought. The plants came at us again and again, their barbs and teeth and thorns clattering viciously against our armour with almost hysterical rage. And all the time they were keeping us occupied, other plants were trying to break through on some unguarded front, to get at the scientists and their equipment. As though the plants knew they were the real threat. The six of us worked the perimeter, killing everything we came into contact with. One, Three, Eight, Nine, Eleven, and me. We didn't talk to each other. We had nothing to say. Occasionally we'd overhear the three scientists on the open channel, discussing some technical matter. It might as well have been machines talking.

There wasn't much left of my senses. Torn flesh and brain damage had seen to that. The armour replaced them with specially-calibrated sensors, channelled through the suit AI. So I could see and hear for miles, and the pressure sensors built into my steel hands were sensitive, as well as strong. It wasn't touch, but it would do. I was isolated from the world, but I could still experience it. I missed taste and smell, but it's wasn't like I had any use for them anymore. It was all tubes, now.

My vision was sharp enough that I could see every detail, every colour and shade and shape, of every plant I killed. I could hear every scream and howl they made as they pressed forward, all the sounds of rage and pain and horror. I wondered, briefly, how that was possible. Plants didn't have vocal chords. Wind blowing through seed pods, or reeds, perhaps... It didn't matter. I was here to kill the plants, not understand them.

And killing them did feel so very good. I was strong inside my suit, strong and powerful in my armour. Stalks and flails and creepers tore like paper in my steel hands, and I could rip apart the largest plant with no effort at all. I broke everything I hit and everything I stepped on died; I smiled so very broadly behind my smooth featureless helm. Another reason why people don't trust us: Because any one of us could do a hell of a lot of damage to people, if we ever lost control.

Three cried out suddenly, and I looked around just in time to see his hard suit disappear under a mass of writhing blue and purple creepers. They wrapped right around him in a moment, burying him under layer upon layer, until he'd disappeared in a cocoon of pulsating vegetation. And then they just jerked him off his feet and hauled him into the thrashing jungle.

I ran forward and ploughed into the jungle after him, forcing my way through the active plants by sheer strength. Nine was right there at my side. The others yelled for us to come back, that defending the terraforming equipment was far more important than rescuing one missing grunt. That we were all expendable. I knew that. So did Nine. That's why we went after Three. Because you have to hang on to some of your humanity or you really would go crazy.

Strangely, the plants had left a trail for us to follow. A ragged path between tall plants, from where they'd dragged Three away. The surrounding vegetation hadn't blocked or overgrown it, though they'd had plenty of time. So Nine and I pressed steadily on, the earth shaking under the heavy pounding of our steel feet. And the plants on either side of the trail ... held back. It took us a while to realise they weren't attacking us anymore. And the further from the clearing we went, the quieter everything became; until we were just walking through a still and silent forest, with no need to kill anything. Nine and I looked at each other; and kept going.

It could be a trap, Paul. But it doesn't feel like a trap. This is something else. Something new.

"Watch my back," I said to the AI, on our private channel. "Full sensor scans. Don't let anything creep up on me."

Of course, Paul. I have Three's beacon. Straight ahead. He's not moving. He isn't answering my calls. Neither is his AI.

We finally found Three standing alone and very still, right in the middle of a small clearing. Or rather what was left of Three. The hard suit was standing entirely motionless, and it only took me a moment to discover why. The armour was empty. It had opened itself, and there was no trace of the occupant anywhere. Just the broken ends of tubes and cables, hanging limply from the suit, from where Three had broken free of them. Nine and I looked around very carefully, but there was no sign of any body. No blood, no signs of violence. Nothing.

His AI is dead, Paul. Wiped clean. Suicided.

"Could Three still be alive here, somewhere?" said Nine.

"Without his tubes and cables?" I said. "Not for long. Why would he open his suit? The air alone would kill him."

"Could the plants have forced it open, from outside? There's no sign of violence on the front of the armour."

"The plants couldn't have reached him," I said. "He would have had to persuade his AI to open it for him."

"But why?" said Nine. "Why has his AI suicided? Where's the body? None of this makes any sense!"

We searched the surrounding jungle, looked and listened with our sensors set to their fullest range, and found nothing at all. The jungle was still and quiet, and the plants made no attempt to interfere with our search. They just stood there, swaying this way and that under the urging of the gusting wind. Almost like normal plants. As though they weren't mad at us anymore. Or, perhaps, because they were satisfied with Three's death. Maybe even sated, if they'd eaten the body...

And then I stopped dead where I was. I'd caught a glimpse of movement, right at the edge of my sensors. Human movement, not plant. Or at least, something very like human. I pointed it out to Nine, but he couldn't see anything. And now neither could I. I had my AI replay the sensor images, and share them with Nine. Just a glimpse, of something that looked human but didn't move like anything human...

"Not Three," I said. "Whatever that was, it was a complete human figure. Not like us."

"Could it have been a survivor from Base Two?" said Nine.

"I don't see how," I said.

"We have to check this out."

"Yes. We need to be sure what that was."

We strode quickly through the jungle, and the plants let us pass. Soon enough we came to another clearing, and in it, another hard suit—standing still and silent and very empty. Its steel armour had been chaffed and smoothed by wind and weather, and the stencilled number on its open chest was Thirty-Two. Nine and I stood very still, studying it from a safe distance.

"It's an older model," I said. "This could have come from Base Two, I suppose."

"But you saw something moving," said Nine. "This thing hasn't moved in ages."

We eased forward, one careful step at a time, and peered into the hard suit's interior. The hanging tubes and cables had withered. The interior of the suit was full of flowers, alive and flourishing—blossoming with wild psychedelic colours.

"This...is getting seriously strange," said Nine. "Did the suit's occupant...turn into flowers?"

"I doubt it," I said. "He opened up his suit and left it, just like Three. Somehow they left their suits behind and went...somewhere else. Except there's nowhere for anything human to go on Abaddon." I turned slowly around in a complete circle, studying the jungle. "Tell me, Nine: what's wrong with this picture?"

"The plants are quiet," said Nine. "Nothing's attacked us since we left the others to follow Three."

"Maybe they're not hungry anymore," I said. "After Three."

"I never got the feeling they wanted to eat us," said Nine. "Just kill us. They wanted us dead. Wanted us gone." He looked at me sharply. "We *are* gone. We left the clearing. We have to get back! This could all be a distraction, to lure us away while they launched an attack on the equipment!"

We raced back down the trail. The plants had kept it open. Nine had his guns at the ready, and I had my flamethrower; but we didn't need them. The plants just watched us pass, misshapen multi-coloured heads bowing and bobbing in the wind. And when we finally burst back into the clearing, all was just as we had left it. The three scientists were still working on the terraforming equipment, while the others patiently patrolled the perimeter. They all looked round as we crashed back into the clearing, and demanded to know where we'd been, and what had happened to Three. But Nine and I were too busy looking back at the jungle. The plants had gone mad again, straining forward with everything they had, desperate to get at us and kill us. In the end I just said *The plants got Three.* And Nine said nothing at all.

We went back to guarding the perimeter. And the long hard day wore on.

Somehow the rest of us made it through to the end of the shift alive. Bone-deep weary and exhausted from fighting back the plants all day, but alive. The perimeter was heaped with torn-apart, bullet-riddled, and flame-blackened pieces of vegetation, some of them still twitching. We were all out of ammunition and power cells, reduced now to fighting the jungle with brute force. The armour did all the heavy lifting, but we still had to work the armour. The real tiredness came from the unrelenting concentration, because you couldn't relax, couldn't let your guard down, even for a moment. Or you might end up like Three.

We were all searching the blood-red skies for the transport ship long before it was due to appear, and when it finally did touch down we immediately turned our backs on the job, and headed for our ride home. I looked back, just as I was about to climb aboard, and the plants had fallen still again. They were only violent when we were around to make them mad...

I thought about that, all the way back.

We sat in silence in our two rows, securely strapped in, facing each other. None of us had anything to say. I reported Three's death to the Base Commander. He didn't seem too surprised. Or upset. After we landed, and we were walking back to our quarters, it occurred to me to ask Four, one of the scientists, how long he thought it would take to finish assembling the terraforming equipment. *Unless we get a lot more help,* he said, *three years, maybe four.* I tried to think of years like the day we'd just had, and couldn't. Years of constant fighting against an enemy that would never give up? Maybe the Captain was right. Maybe this was Hell, after all.

In my private quarters, lying on my bed on my side—so I could keep an eye on my tubes and cables and make sure they didn't get tangled—I remembered the crash again.

We were flying over the Rainbow Falls, my Alice and me, in our old aircar. We were arguing. We were always arguing, back then. We had been so much in love. But it hadn't lasted. That was why I crashed the car. I drove it quite deliberately into the side of the mountain, at full speed. Alice was screaming; I was crying. I wanted to kill us both, because she said she was going to leave me, and I couldn't bear the thought of living without her. So I crashed the car, she died, and I lived. They saved me, the bastards. And then they put me in a hard suit, and they put her voice in my head, forever. I couldn't bear to live without her, and now I couldn't bear to live with her. Because the memory deposit came from the time when she still loved me. She didn't remember the crash. She didn't remember the arguments, or not loving me. She thought we were still happy together, because we were when she made the deposit. She still thought we were in love, and I didn't have the heart to tell her.

They gave her to me as a kindness, but every kind word she said was a torment.

On the transport ship out, the next day, I told the Commander about the old empty hard suit I'd found.

"I'm not supposed to talk about that," said the Commander's voice. "But you'd just dig it out of the old records anyway, if I didn't. The crew of Base Two were mostly hard suits. Like you. Their superiors were human, but they stayed inside the Base. Only the hard suits went out into Abaddon to work. And some of them... learned to love this world. This hateful, ugly world. They decided they didn't want to fight anymore. So they just walked out into the jungle, and opened up their suits."

"But... what happened to the bodies?" I said. "Did the plants eat them?"

"There's never been any evidence that the plants here are carnivorous," said the Commander. "The hard suits' occupants just... disappeared. Now and again, some of the work crews would report seeing ghosts, moving through the jungle."

"Ghosts?" said Nine. I knew he was thinking of the moving human figure I'd seen.

"Illusions. Mirages," said the Commander. "It's just stress. This planet wears you down. If you see anything like that, don't go after them. You won't find anything. No one ever does. It's just something else the planet does, to distract you, so it can kill you while you're not looking."

"What happened to the human crew in Base Two?" I said. "Did they learn to love this world too?"

The Commander had nothing else to say. We flew the rest of the way in silence.

Out in the jungle again, we walked the perimeter. Maddened raging plants pushed forward from all sides, and I ripped them out of the ground, crushed them to pulp in my terrible grip and threw them aside, or trampled the more persistent ones under my steel feet. I blasted them with fire and bullets and energy bolts, giving it everything I had, just to hold the line. The plants never fell back, never slowed down, never for one moment stopped trying to kill us. I thought again of living through years of this, of endless killing, destroying living things that were only fighting to defend their home. Years...of living with my murdered wife's kind and loving voice in my head.

In the end, it only took a moment to decide. I hadn't gone native. I hadn't learned to love this ugly, vicious, vindictive world. It still looked like Hell to me. I was just so very tired of it all.

I stopped fighting, and walked out from the perimeter and into the jungle. The plants immediately stopped fighting me, and actually seemed to fall back, opening up a path before me. I walked on through the jungle, the plants bobbing and nodding their heads to me, as though they'd been waiting for this. Even the wind seemed to have dropped. It was like walking through a garden on a calm summer's day. Part of me was thinking; This is how they do it. This is how they get to you. But I didn't care. I just kept walking. I could hear the others calling out to me, on the open channel, but I had nothing to say to them.

Paul? Why are you doing this?

"Because it's the right thing to do. Because I'm tired of killing."

I don't understand, Paul. You know I could override your control. Walk you back to the perimeter.

"Are you going to?"

No. I was put here to help and comfort you. I know I'm not really Alice, but I'm sure she would want you to do the right thing.

I walked until I couldn't see the perimeter anymore, and then I just stopped and looked around me. Hideously-coloured, horribly-shaped plants, for as far as the sensor could see. Under a sky of blood, with air that would poison me and gravity that would crush me. Abaddon. Just another name for Hell. Where I belonged.

"Alice," I said. "You know what I want. You know what I need you to do for me."

I can't, said the warm, familiar voice that was all that was left of my dead wife. *I can't let you just die. Please, don't ask me to do this, Paul.*

"I can't go on like this," I said. "I want out. Just... open up the suit. I want this to be over. Open the suit, and let me out into this brave new world that has such ugly wonders in it. I don't want to live like this."

I can't do that, Paul. I can't. I love you.

"If you love me, let me go."

Like I should have let you go, I thought. I was still sane enough to see the bitter irony in that.

Paul? What is that? Who is that? Who are those people?

I looked around. Not far away, this time, not far away at all; the ghosts came walking through the jungle. Just vague human shapes at first, moving easily and unharmed among the plants, as though they were at home there. Not walking in a human way. They stopped, and one of them raised an overlong arm, and beckoned to me. I plunged forward, and the plants really did fall back, encouraging me on. The ghostly figures retreated before me, one of them still beckoning, and I followed them deeper into the jungle, away from the terraforming equipment, away from Base Three, and all that was left of my old human life.

What are you doing, Paul? Where do you think you're going?

"I'm chasing a dream," I said. "Of a life when I still had hope, and options, and choices that meant something."

I could stop you.

"But you won't. Because you still love me."

She didn't stop me.

I followed the vague figures that were somehow always ahead of me, no matter how much I increased my pace. I stopped once, to look back. The trail had closed behind me. There was only the jungle. The plants watched, still and silent, to see what I would do. I turned my back on my old life, and hurried on.

And finally the ghosts stopped. One of them came

back to meet me. It stepped out of the concealing jungle to stand right before me, and I took my time, looking it over. Not human. Humanoid, but not human. Taller than me, smoothly slender, different in every detail. Its basic shape was stretched out and distorted, the arms and legs had too many joints, and the face... had nothing I could recognise as features, let alone sense organs. Only yesterday I would have described it as hideous, alien, inhuman. But I was trying to see the world with better eyes. And anyway, compared to the broken half-thing inside my hard suit, I was in no position to throw stones. I nodded to the shape before me, and to my surprise it nodded back, in a very human way.

"You're not a ghost," I said.

"No," it said. Complex mouth parts at the base of its head moved, producing something very like a human voice. "Not ghosts. But we are dead men. Technically speaking. We are the surviving crew of Base Two. Made over, made new, made to walk freely in this best of all possible worlds. We came here in armoured suits, just like you, but we have found a better way. If you want answers, if you want a way out of that suit and your old life, come with me. Come with us, to the Cave of Creation. And be born anew."

I didn't even have to think about it. "Does this Cave of yours have a can opener?"

I went with them, walking through a calm and peaceful garden, with humanoid things that only remembered being human. They bobbed and bounced around me, as though their bones were made of rubber, as though the heavy gravity was no concern of theirs. And I trudged along inside my steel can, and dreamed of freedom. The jungle suddenly fell back on all sides to reveal a larger than usual clearing with a great earth mound at its centre. You only had to look at it to know it was no natural thing. The dark earth had been raised up by conscious intent, given shape and form and meaning. There was a large dark hole in its side. My guides led me forward across the clearing, right up to the earth mound, and then the one who'd spoken to me strode easily up a set of steps cut into the earth mound, heading for the opening. The others stood and looked at me. I didn't hesitate, but I had to go slowly, carefully, so the earth steps wouldn't collapse under my weight.

By the time I reached the dark opening, my guide had already gone through. I stepped into the darkness after him, and a great light sprang up, blinding me for a moment. When I could see again, I was standing on an earth ledge, looking down into a great cavern that seemed to fall away forever, packed full of strange alien technology. I had no idea at all what I was looking at. Shapes so strange, so utterly other, that my merely human mind couldn't make sense of any of it, even with my armour's sophisticated sensors. My thoughts whirled at forces and functions without obvious meaning, or perhaps too much meaning. Parts and sections that seemed to twist and turn through more than three physical dimensions at once. Wonders and marvels, intimidating and terrifying. Heaven and Hell, all at once.

My guide stood beside me, waiting patiently for me to come to terms with what it had brought me to see. "We were not the first to find this world," it said finally. "Another species came here, long ago, determined to change this world and remake it in their image. And this is the machine they built to do that. Except, they learned to love this world. And they decided, why change the planet when you can change the people? So that's what they did. They reprogrammed the machine to remake them, and when it was done, they went out into the world and lived in it. The machine still works. It can change you, and make you a part of this world, like us. It's a good world, when it's not fighting for its own survival. Join me. Become like us. Hell can be Heaven, if you look at it with the right eyes."

"Do you think it's telling the truth?" I said to Alice, on my private comm channel. "I want to believe... but I could be wrong."

I don't know. I can't tell. Is this really what you want, Paul?

"You know it is, Alice."

Then do it. Because... I'm not real. I'm not really Alice. Just a memory, a ghost, imprinted on silicon. I'm the past, and this is the future. I know about the crash, Paul. I know you crashed us deliberately. I'm a computer. I have access to records. Why did you try to kill us both, Paul?

"Because... you changed, and I didn't. You didn't love me anymore. You were going to leave me."

And now you've changed... and you want to leave me.

"Yes. You have to be better than me, Alice. You have to let me go."

Of course I will, Paul. She laughed softly, briefly. *Memories shouldn't linger. Time for both of us... to move on.*

She opened up the front of the hard suit and I fell out, onto the hard packed earth of the ledge: a small, crippled, dying thing. I cried out, once, as I felt the AI shut itself down, forever, and then all my umbilical tubes and cables jerked out of my back, no longer connecting me to the armour.

The great alien machine blazed bright as the sun, and when I could see again, I was something else.

Outside the earth mound, everything was different. I moved easily, freely, marvelling at the world I found myself in. The plants were beautiful, the jungle was magnificent, the sky was astounding and the sunshine was just right. But more than that, the whole world was *alive*; the jungle and everything in it was singing a song, a great and joyous song that never ended, and I was part of that song now.

I could remember being human, but that seemed such a small and limited thing now. I was whole and free, at last. I knelt down and studied a small flower at my feet. I put out a hand to touch it, and the flower reached up and caressed my hand.

Simon R. Green has written over forty books, all of them different. He has written eight Deathstalker books, twelve Nightside books, and thinks trilogies are for wimps. His current series are the Secret Histories, featuring Shaman Bond, the very secret agent, and The Ghost Finders, featuring traditional hauntings in modern settings. He acts in open air productions of Shakespeare, rides motorbikes, and loves old time silent films. His short stories have appeared in the anthologies *Mean Streets*, *Unusual Suspects*, *Powers of Detection*, *Wolfsbane and Mistletoe*, *The Way of the Wizard*, *The Living Dead 2*, *Those Who Fight Monsters*, *Dark Delicacies III*, and *Home Improvements: Undead Edition*.

Power Armor: A Love Story

DAVID BARR KIRTLEY

It was quite a party. The women wore gowns. The men wore tuxedos. Anthony Blair wore power armor.

Armor that was sleek and black and polished, and made not a whisper as Blair paced the lawn behind his mansion, passing a word here or there with one of his guests. In those days the most advanced exoskeletons were crude affairs, and Blair's armor seemed decades, if not centuries, ahead of its time.

But he was an inventor, after all, one who in the past several years had introduced any number of groundbreaking new technologies. And that was about all anyone knew of Anthony Blair, reclusive genius. He was seldom seen, and never without his armor, and he politely rebuffed all inquiries into his past.

So it had attracted considerable interest when he'd purchased a house on the outskirts of Washington, a move that seemed to signal him taking a greater interest in public affairs. For his housewarming, he'd sent out scores of invitations—to politicians, pundits, business leaders, celebrities, and scientists. Such a gathering of notables, along with the chance to get a rare glimpse of Blair himself, would have been enough to make this the hottest ticket in town, but there was more. Blair had let it be known that tonight he'd be making an "important announcement." Speculation was frenzied.

Finally Blair hopped up onto the patio and called for everyone's attention, his voice amplified by speakers built into the torso of his suit. From what could be seen of him through his transparent visor, he seemed a handsome man of about forty, with a penetrating gaze and a sardonic grin. He proceeded to lay out his plans for a new nonprofit group, the Anthony Blair Foundation, dedicated to promoting civil liberties worldwide, and he invited his guests to get involved.

He wrapped things up with a toast, thanking everyone for coming. He pointed an armored finger down into his wine glass, and a large plastic straw emerged, and began suctioning up the wine, which Blair then drank, moments later, from a tube inside his helmet.

As his guests sipped their drinks, they conferred in puzzled tones about whether that had been the "important announcement," in which case the evening was proving a terrible letdown. When no announcement of any greater import seemed likely to be forthcoming, they began to drift away.

Blair moved from conversation to conversation, wishing everyone a good night. A distinguished-looking gentleman said to him, "Mr. Blair, I'd like to introduce you to a colleague of mine, Dr. Mira Valentic."

She wore a red dress and had inky black hair. Blair

reached out with his giant metal fingers and lightly shook her hand. "Pleased to meet you, Doctor."

He asked about her work, and she described her research into gene sequencing. He listened intently and asked many questions, which led her to describe her graduate studies, then a childhood obsession with amphibians. As they talked, the other guests excused themselves one by one, and the lawn slowly emptied, until Blair and Mira stood alone.

"And now I've told you everything about myself," she said. "But I still don't know anything about you."

"Not much to tell," he said.

She chuckled.

After a moment, he said, "I've had a very nice time talking with you, Dr. Valentic."

"Please, call me Mira."

"Mira," he said. "I don't know what it is, but I just feel like we're on the same wavelength somehow."

"Yes," she said. "Me too."

He lowered his voice. "So I'm going to tell you something I've never told anyone."

He had her full attention now.

"I'm from the future," he said.

She regarded him uncertainly, as if this might be a joke. "People wondered," she said. "I didn't believe it. It seems impossible."

"It's not impossible," he said. "Just very difficult."

She thought for a moment. "So what's it like? The future?"

"Maybe I'll tell you," he said, "next time I see you."

"Next time?"

"There will be a next time, won't there? I should certainly hope your bosses would arrange for us to meet again, now that you've managed to wrangle one big secret out of me."

"My bosses? At the museum?"

"No, in the government, I mean."

"I don't—"

He waved a hand. "It's fine, really. I don't mind being spied on. My armor and I are big unknowns, and I don't blame folks for wanting to keep an eye on us. That's their job. Your job."

She was silent.

Finally she said, "When did you know?"

"When I first saw you."

"What?"

"From across the yard. I'm awfully clever, Mira."

"Bullshit," she said. "No one's that clever."

"I am," he said. "I didn't rise to my position by accident, you know."

"What position?"

"Maybe I'll tell you," he said. "Next time I see you."

The next time was two weeks later, downtown, at the first public fundraiser for the Anthony Blair Foundation. She approached him as the event was winding down.

"Mira," he said. "So nice to see you again."

"Well, you were right," she said. "Keep feeding me information and you'll be seeing a lot more of me."

He smiled. "In that case, what would you like to know?"

"Your armor," she said. "Where'd you get it?"

"I stole it."

"Oh," she said. "We thought it must be one of your inventions."

"It is," he said. "I invented it, and then I stole it."

"Sounds like there's a story there."

"There is," he said. "But let's not go into it just now."

He glanced about the room, then turned back to her. "Hey," he said, "do you want to get out of here?"

Later, as they walked along the river, beneath a sky full of stars, he said, "I'd like to take you out to dinner some time."

"I'd like that."

He was silent for a while.

Finally he said, "If we're going to keep seeing each other, there's something I have to tell you."

She waited.

"My armor," he said. "I never take it off."

"What?"

"It's sort of . . . something I swore."

"Never?"

"Right."

"But . . . how do you eat?"

"Through the straw. It filters poisons."

"And I mean, how do you bathe? Go to the bathroom?"

"The armor handles everything. It's very advanced."

"Wow," she said.

"I know that sounds strange," he said. "But you'll understand. Once you hear the whole story."

After a moment, she said, "So what's the whole story?"

He sighed. "You know I'm starting this new foundation. Don't you wonder why?"

"Because you care about civil liberties?"

"But why?"

She said nothing.

"It's because in the future, where I come from, there are no civil liberties. None."

"Oh," she said.

"I had never been disloyal," he said softly. "You can't be, where I come from. Our thoughts are monitored. I'd been identified early as a promising scientist, and had risen through the ranks to head of my research division. We'd developed a high-energy device that possessed some unusual properties—like, it could project a man-sized object into the past, creating a branching timeline. Theoretically, at least. Completely useless, as far as our leaders were concerned, but interesting. Then one day the thought popped into my head: I could escape."

He stopped and stared out over the water. "Once I'd had the thought, I knew it was only a matter of time before I'd be picked up for 'neural re-education.' So I had to act fast. The problem was, even if I succeeded in traveling into the past, my voyage would create a temporal wake large enough for them to send someone after me."

He met her eyes. "I don't mean to scare you, Mira, but where I come from there are...secret police. Unlike anything you can imagine. Cyborgs. Shapeshifters. I'd have no chance against one of them. Unless..." He showed the hint of a smile. "In the same lab was something else we'd been working on. This armor." He raised his gauntleted hands. "Wearing this, I'd be impervious to anything. So I could escape, but at a cost—I must never take off the armor, not for an instant. Because if I did, the agent sent to punish me would surely strike."

She glanced around at the trees, the shadows. She shivered.

"And that's the story," he said. "So, do you still want to grab dinner sometime? I'll understand if you say no."

"I . . . I'll have to think about it," she said. "This is a lot to take in."

"I know," he said. After a moment, he added, "I should probably be getting back."

"All right."

As they retraced their route, she thought: He never takes off the armor. Never. Not for an instant, he said.

That was going to make it very hard, she thought, to kill him.

He took her to one of the finest restaurants in Washington, and it made quite a sight to see him sitting there in his armor, with a napkin in his lap, suctioning up his entree through the straw in his finger. In spite of that it was a pleasant meal. That is, until the middle of dessert, when he suddenly said, "I have to ask you something."

"Yes?" she said.

"About your bosses."

"At the museum?" she said sweetly.

"No." He smiled back. "In the government, I mean."

"All right. Yes. What?"

"Do they know what you are?" he said, suddenly serious.

"What do you mean?"

"Do they know," he said calmly, "that you were sent from the future to kill me?"

"What?" She laughed.

He waited.

"You think I'm—?"

"Yes," he said.

She put down her fork. Finally she said, "Yes, they know."

They watched each other.

"They want your armor very badly," she said. "They've made repeated overtures, and have concluded that you'll never cooperate."

"They're right," he said.

She shrugged. "So . . . they want the armor, I want you. We have an understanding."

"I see."

"When did you know?" she said.

"When I first saw you," he said. "From across the yard."

She laughed. "Bullshit. Why didn't you say anything?"

"I was having a nice time. I didn't want to spoil the mood."

"I think you're lying," she said. "I think you figured it out just now."

He shrugged.

"So I guess that's that," she said, tossing her napkin out on the table and reaching for her purse.

"Wait," he said. "I want to say something."

She paused.

"We find ourselves," he said, "in a branching time-line. We can't return to our own time, and no one else can follow us here. So they'll never know whether you succeeded or not."

"You're suggesting," she said coldly, "that I abandon my mission."

"I'm suggesting you do what's right," he said. "What's best for both of us."

She stood. "I am not a traitor. You are. And the

punishment for that is death, as you well know. I was assigned this mission, and the faith of my superiors was not misplaced. Your armor is a clever gadget, I'll grant you, but no defenses can hold forever, and no matter how long it takes, no matter how safe you think you are, before this is over I will watch you drown in blood."

People at nearby tables were staring.

"Thanks for dinner," she said, and strode away.

He called her the next day.

"I had a really nice time last night," he said.

She stared at the phone. "Are you out of your mind?"

"No," he said. "Do you want to come over some time?"

She hesitated. "Is this some sort of trick?" she said. "Some trap?"

"No," he said. "I mean, what are you? A class eight?"

"Class nine," she said.

"We're in the twenty-first century," he said. "You could probably fight off a tank platoon. I don't even have a gun. I just want to talk."

"About what?" she said. "Treason?"

"No. No treason. I promise."

"What then?"

"Old books, shows, people. We're the only ones who remember the future."

"You're not afraid?"

"No. The armor will protect me."

"How can you be sure?"

"I designed it," he said.

"And what if I find a weakness?"

"You won't."

After a moment, she sighed. "All right. Fine."

"Swing by around eight," he said. "I'll cook dinner."

She drove over to his mansion, and he cooked her dinner, and they had a very nice time talking about old books and shows and people that were now known only to the two of them.

Finally she stretched and yawned. "Well, it's late."

"You're welcome to stay," he said. "I have a spare bedroom. Eight, actually."

"I don't think so," she said.

"Why not? It makes perfect sense."

"Does it?"

"I mean, what's your plan?" he said. "To disappear, change into someone else, and try to catch me off guard? It won't work. I never take off the armor, not for you or anyone. Your only hope is to find a weakness in the armor, and you won't get a better chance to study it than by staying right here with me." He added, "Besides, I like the way you look now."

She chuckled. "So what's in it for you?"

"The pleasure of your company. Plus I'll know where you are, and I won't have to go around wondering if everyone I meet is a secret assassin."

"That's it? Sounds like the risks outweigh the benefits."

"Let me worry about that," he said. "Anyway, I think you're underestimating the pleasure of your company."

"Ha."

"Also, if you get to know me better, you might decide you don't really want to kill me."

"I doubt that," she said. "Actually, I'm getting the opposite vibe."

He laughed.

"...and you said no treason. You promised."

"You're right. Sorry."

Finally she said, "All right, I'll think about it. Let's see the room."

He gave her a tour of the mansion, and when she saw the guest room she said, "Hey, this is really nice." She sat on the mattress and bounced a few times, testing it. "All right, I'll stay. For a bit."

"Great," he said.

She sprawled on the comforter, grinning. "You want to slip into something more comfortable?"

He laughed. "Goodnight, Mira. I'll see you in the morning."

She stayed with him for weeks, and they talked and talked, until they knew practically everything about each other. They went out to dinner, and to movies and plays, and they went on long, long walks. (Much longer than any normal person could walk, thanks to his armor and her cybernetics.) Many nights they simply lounged about doing nothing at all.

One night they played chess.

The first game ended with his king pinned in one corner. She put him in check with her queen, and he moved to an adjacent square. She moved her queen to put him in check again, and he moved back to the first square. This was repeated several times. The game was declared a draw.

The second game ended the same way. And the third.

"I suppose you think this is terribly funny?" she said.

He shrugged.

She swept the pieces onto the floor, and stood.

As she strode away, he called, "I'm sorry. Mira..."

She ignored him.

But when she was out in the hallway, she smiled. Her anger and frustration were feigned. Actually, things were going quite well.

She'd discovered a weakness in his armor.

They took vacations together—to London, New York, Tokyo. In Paris, at the top of the Eiffel Tower, as they stood looking out over the rivers and rooftops, she said, "Well, you were right, dammit. As always. I've grown awfully fond of you, Blair, and now the future seems like such a long time ago. So I guess you're safe."

"I'm glad to hear it," he said. "Though you'll forgive me if I don't strip off the armor just this second."

She laughed. "Of course."

Six months later though, it was starting to become an issue.

One night at dinner she said to him, "We need to talk."

"Yes?"

"Are you ever going to take off that armor?" she said.

He set down his utensils and studied her. He said, "When I fled into the past, I swore I would never take off this armor. Not for an instant."

"Because of me," she said. "Because I'd be sent after you. But that's all changed now."

"I knew there would come a time," he said, "when I'd start feeling safe, start letting my guard down. That's why I made the resolution then, when my sense of the danger was at its most acute."

After a moment, she said, "You still don't trust me."

He said nothing.

"Look at me," she said. "Can't you just look at me with your super-genius gaze and see that I'm telling the truth?"

"No," he said.

"Then I guess you're not as smart as you think you are," she said. "As you pretend to be."

"Do you remember what you said, Mira? When we first met? 'No matter how long it takes, no matter how safe you think you are—'"

"I know what I said. Look, I'm sorry, all right? I was a different person then. It was a stupid thing to say. I wish I could take it back, but I can't."

There was a long silence.

Finally she said, "What are we doing here? If you're never going to trust me, what's even the point of this?"

"Enjoying each other's company? That was the point, I thought."

"And in five years?" she said. "Ten? Will we still just be sitting across a table from each other, with you in a suit of armor?"

"I don't take off the armor," he said. "You knew that from the start."

"So there's nothing I can do? To prove myself?"

"There's one thing," he said, very serious. "You can hold my life in your hands and choose to spare me."

"But how can that ever happen?" she said. "If you won't take off the armor?"

"I don't know," he said.

When he woke the next morning, she was gone. He paced the empty rooms, seeking her. "Mira?" he called, his voice echoing.

He tried her phone, but got no response. He left message after message.

Finally she answered. "Please stop calling me," she said.

"Where are you?"

"Away," she said. "Away from that house, away from you. There are other men, you know? Who aren't afraid."

"Please come back," he said.

"Will you take off the armor?" she said. "Ever?"

"You know I can't."

She hung up.

Six weeks passed without a word. Then one night his doorbell rang, and he opened the door to find her standing there.

"I'm sorry," she said.

He made her tea, and she sat in the kitchen and said, "Look, I understand why you wear the armor. It's all tied up with who you are and why we're here together, and I accept that. I hope someday I can prove myself to you, but even if you never take it off I don't care. We understand each other in a way that no one else ever will."

"Let's fly to Paris," he said. "Tonight. We had good times there."

"Yes," she said. "All right."

They hopped a private jet, and by the next morning they were in Paris. They revisited all their old haunts. On their third night there, they ate dinner at the hotel, then took a midnight walk down a cobbled street beside the Seine.

Suddenly Mira said, "We're being followed."

A hundred yards behind them lurked three men dressed in black. One carried a briefcase.

"Are they from the future?" she said.

"No," Blair said. "Impossible."

"Then what threat could they be to us?"

"I don't know," he said. "Let's not find out. Come on."

He began to hurry. Suddenly he halted. "Uh-oh."

"What?" she said.

"I can't move."

She glanced about as more men appeared from the shadows.

"They're special forces," she said. "Black ops."

"How do you know?"

She smiled. "Because they're with me."

Eight men surrounded Blair. Several carried boxes.

"I told you you weren't the only man in my life," she said.

One of the men stepped forward. He had a heavy jaw and short gray hair and cold, hard eyes.

"Captain." Mira nodded.

The man set his briefcase on the ground and bent to open it.

"How are you doing this?" Blair said.

She knelt over the briefcase. "We introduced a virus through the suit's communications array."

"That's impossible," Blair said. "Equipment to interface with the suit won't even exist for—"

"What, you mean like this?" she said, rising, gadget in hand.

Blair studied it, his face pale.

"All right, I'm impressed," he said. "Cramming that much R&D into so short a time. But it won't matter. In a few minutes—"

"You don't have a few minutes," she said.

The men opened boxes, yanked out equipment. Blair's eyes darted about.

"Laser cutters?" he said. "Diamond-tipped saws? You can't honestly believe those will even scratch this armor?"

"No," Mira said, nodding at the men. "But they did." She added, "What can I say? They're not geniuses."

The captain frowned. Then Mira backhanded him across the face, and his head flew a hundred feet through the air and splashed into the river.

The men screamed and drew weapons. Two ran. Of course it did them no good. A minute later Mira was piling their bodies on the ground at Blair's feet.

"I admit I'm a bit nervous now," he said.

She grinned. "Told you I'd make you drown in blood."

She fiddled with her gadget, and the armor knelt stiffly, and its right hand reached out and plunged its straw deep into the chest of the nearest corpse. Blair grimaced and turned his head aside as blood bubbled from the tube inside his helmet.

"Wow," he said. "Paris is definitely not as much fun as I remember."

"Keep laughing," she said. "While you can."

The straw drained corpse after corpse. Soon the blood rose above Blair's lips and threatened to engulf his nose.

"Any last words?" she said.

"Mmmm-mmmm-mmmm-mmmm," he said.

She came and stood inches from his visor. "Sorry, I didn't catch that?"

He watched her, his eyes wide.

"Do we agree," she said, "that there's absolutely nothing stopping me from killing you?"

"Mmmm-hmmm," he said.

"Good." She smiled. "Then take off that stupid armor and kiss me."

She flipped a switch, and suddenly Blair could move again. He tore off his helmet and hurled it to the ground, then swept her up in his arms, pressing his lips to hers.

Later, as they lay naked on a hotel bed, he murmured, "I knew about your device."

She stirred and said drowsily, "Hmm?"

"I could have stopped the blood," he said. "I was never in any danger."

"I know," she said. "The armor is flawless." After a moment, she added, "It only ever had one weakness."

"Me," he said, rolling onto his side, studying her. "We understand each other perfectly, don't we?"

"Yes," she said. "I think so."

"You still haven't decided whether or not to kill me. Have you?"

"No," she said.

"But either way you wanted me out of the armor."

"Yes," she said. "And you took it off, even knowing the danger."

"I love you, Mira," he said. "I couldn't stand being separated from you another moment."

"Sounds like the risks outweigh the rewards," she said.

"I think you're underestimating the rewards," he said, and she chuckled.

He added, "If your mission is that important to you, then go ahead and kill me. You might as well, if you don't love me."

"I think that's the sweetest thing anyone's ever said to me," she said.

And for a long time after that they lay curled together, drifting in and out of sleep. And if they dreamed, it was of the future—not the distant future from which they'd come, a cold and sterile place of surveillance and mind control, but the immediate future, of the breakfast croissants they'd soon enjoy and the stroll they'd take through the fresh morning air, hand in hand. And the armor stood in a nearby corner like some exotic decoration, like some improbable furniture, watching over them with its transparent visor, a silent presence, waiting there, sleek, black polished, empty.

David Barr Kirtley is the co-host of *The Geek's Guide to the Galaxy* podcast. His short fiction appears in magazines such as *Realms of Fantasy*, *Weird Tales*, *Intergalactic Medicine Show*, and *Lightspeed*, or podcasts such as *Escape Pod* and *Pseudopod*, and in anthologies such as *The Living Dead*, *The Way of the Wizard*, *New Voices in Science Fiction*, and *Fantasy: The Best of the Year*. His most recent stories are "The Ontological Factor" in *Cicada* and "Three Deaths" in *Under the Moons of Mars: New Adventures on Barsoom*. He lives in New York.

The Last Days of
the Kelly Gang

DAVID D. LEVINE

Old Ike awoke to the sound of heavy fists on his little shack's door. Sighing, he dragged his creaking body from under the covers, letting in June's winter cold as his foot sought the slipper under the bed. "I'm coming, I'm coming," he called as the pounding came again.

No one ever visited Old Ike's shack, especially not in the middle of the night with a winter storm threatening. Annoyed, he kindled a tallow candle and shuffled his way across boards worn smooth by twenty years of his footsteps.

"Yes, yes, what is—"

Ike's voice seized in his throat at the apparition revealed in the open door. A tall man in a long duster coat, his face dominated by a huge raggy beard and capped by a battered leather hat, stood limned by a flash of lightning. A moment later came the clap of thunder, followed by a deep uncultured voice: "I'm

looking for a man called Crazy Old Ike." The man's
accent combined broad Australian vowels with the lilt
and crisp consonants of the Irish.

"I'm called Ike," he acknowledged, deliberately
broadening his vowels to conceal his own comfortable
Hampshire origins. Poor Irish-Australian farmers and
free-selectors had little love for the English. "And I'll
own to the Old. What business have you with me?"

"I'm told you . . . make things."

"I've been known to do so."

"Can we come in?"

Ike glared at the man, who'd roused him from a
sound sleep, but there was a storm coming. Perhaps,
at the age of seventy-four, he was finally mellowing.
"Oh, very well. Wipe your feet." He lit a lantern from
the candle as they entered.

The stranger wasn't alone. There were four of them
all told, lean filthy young men with beards the size of
shovel blades, all spurs and leather and the stink of
horse-sweat. The pistol handles that protruded from
each duster pocket were decidedly worrisome, but Ike
tried to reassure himself that out here in the bush
such implements were not necessarily a sign of bad
intent. "I'm Ned Kelly," said the first man, removing
his hat. "This here's my brother Dan, and them's Joe
Byrne and Steve Hart." A small grin crept onto his
weathered face. "You may have heard of us."

Ike's old heart hammered, but he tried to keep his
voice level. "Indeed I have."

The Kelly Gang were the most notorious bushrangers, horse thieves, and bank robbers in the entire
colony of Victoria and there was an eight thousand
pound reward on their heads. But they were also

beloved of the small farmers and free-selectors; it was said that when they robbed banks they burned all the mortgages they found, and afterwards distributed the cash to their relatives and sympathizers. With the help of the populace of the area—what was known as "Kelly country"—they'd been at large for months.

"I . . . I keep myself to myself up here," Ike continued. "I try to stay clear of all affairs of government. You've nothing to fear from me."

"That's good." Ned's eyes flicked around the room, taking in the forge, the lathe and bending brake, the taps and dies, the drive belts that ran every which way. Apart from the bed and a small cook-stove, the place was more workshop than home. "And you do appear to be a clever dick." He pursed his lips and nodded slowly. "I think you might be just the man for the job."

"And what job might that be?"

"I want you to build us four suits of armour." He handed Ike a scrap of paper with some crude sketches on it.

The paper showed a cylindrical helmet, front and rear plastrons on the torso, curved flaps over the shoulders, and an apron-like panel protecting the groin area. It would be uncomfortable, encumbering, and—most offensive of all to his engineering sensibilities—ineffective. Ike snorted and tossed the paper back. "It won't work."

"It will!" Joe insisted. "It's just a matter of hammering them ploughshares we stole into shape, cutting a few slots in 'em, and fitting 'em with straps. Surely a bright spark like you can do that."

"I didn't say it couldn't be *built*," Ike countered. "I

said it wouldn't *work*. The legs and arms are completely unprotected—one well-placed bullet could kill you right off. And if you added armour to those areas without changing the design you'd lose too much mobility."

Joe started to protest, but Ned cut him off with a gesture. "You said 'without changing the design.' You got a better?"

Ignorant this ruffian might be, but he wasn't unobservant. "Not immediately, no. But given time I suppose I could think one up."

Ned leaned forward, the eyes above the ratty beard fiercely intense. "Then you'd best think fast, cobber, as we've a train to catch. On June twenty-seventh." Less than three weeks away.

"I'm terribly sorry if I gave the impression I would do the work for you, sir. I was merely offering a critique of your design." Ike straightened, bringing himself to his full five-foot-four. "It's been over twenty years since I did any work on contract for any other man."

"Well then, you have a bit of a choice to make." With a movement swift and sure as a piston stroke, Ned brought the revolver from his pocket and levelled it at Ike's head. Despite the bushranger's filth and stink, the gun was well-oiled and the hammer gave a precise click as it was drawn back. "You can build us the armour, or you can learn how to do without that big brain of yours."

Trembling, Ike stood his ground. "So that's how it's to be."

He regretted having pointed out the flaws in the gang's design. This wasn't the first time his intellect had gotten him into trouble by outrunning his common sense. But still . . . armour was only defensive, after all, and the Kellys did have some support from the population; they couldn't be all bad. He'd build them what they wanted and they'd go on their way.

Besides, it would be an intriguing engineering challenge.

He licked his lips. "Let's see that paper again."

Ike lay his weary head down on his drafting table, just for a moment. The gang had settled in for the duration outside his shack, snug in their bedrolls around a pungent mallee-wood fire. But they slept in shifts, one or more of them keeping watch on him at all times, constantly demanding progress.

He'd responded with a series of increasingly detailed sketches, then paper models—knee and ankle joints, helmets, the insanely difficult shoulder joint. The gang members had scoffed at his "playing with paper dolls," but Ned, who comprehended Ike's design drawings despite being unable to read or write, had cuffed Joe across the ear. "Let the brainbox work," he'd said. "He knows how many beans make five. Unlike you lot!"

At the moment Ike was working on a model of the leg assembly, stiff vellum curved and held into place with pins. He flexed the leg and sighed. The design was sound—fully covering the limb without unduly restricting movement—but if built from the heavy mould-boards and other cast-iron scraps the gang's supporters were still delivering by wagon, it would be far too cumbersome to walk in. Yet no lighter material was available that could stop a single bullet, let alone the full police onslaught the gang said they expected to face.

As he pondered the problem, a high distant sound

penetrated his consciousness and his eyes automatically flicked to the clock. It was the 2:15 train, pulling into Glenrowan half an hour late as usual.

He'd been pleased when the North East line had been extended to Wangaratta back in 1873, making it far easier for him to obtain the instruments, materials, and few comforts he required from overseas, but its whistle also served as a daily reminder of the life he'd left behind in England. He'd had his successes there, to be sure—a few tunnels and trestles he'd designed had been entirely satisfactory to himself and his creditors—but his constant, overweening ambition had not been satisfied, had always stretched for faster, bigger, better, *more*. In the end it had brought him nothing but failure, disgrace, and heartbreak.

But there had been a joy in engineering—the eternal duel between weight and power, the combat with recalcitrant materials, the exaltation of victory over an obstinate technical conundrum. And when the pieces did fit together, when the ship that *he*, by God, had designed actually floated, or the engine moved, the speed and power of it had made him laugh like a schoolboy.

Power.

Steam power. That was the ticket.

It was the only way.

Dual pistons would be required on each leg. Lift assist of some sort on the arms. The weight of the boiler would be a serious problem, and the heat.

But it could work. It could *work*, damn it!

Grinning, he swept the drafting table clean and brought out a fresh sheet of vellum.

✧　　✧　　✧

"Try it now."

Ned moved his left leg forward. Through the rat's nest of rods, tubes, and cables that formed the prototype leg control assembly, Ike observed Ned's knee and ankle as they contacted the actuation levers. Steam hissed and the framework lurched forward to match Ned's motion. "Still kind of touchy."

"Hmm." Ike selected an extra-long screwdriver from his tool chest and tweaked one of the verniers. "Again."

This time the framework matched the motions of Ned's leg perfectly. Ike stood back, arms folded, watching it move and visualizing the armour plating that would cover it. The back of the knee would be tricky.

"This is quite a piece of kit," Ned admitted. "You gonna get a patent on it?"

"Patents?" Ike scoffed. "I've never taken out a one. They are supposed to encourage innovation in the useful arts, but in reality they smother innovation in the cradle!"

Ned raised his hands against Ike's vehemence. "Sorry I mentioned it."

Later, after being unbuckled from the prototype, Ned wiped his brow with a bandana. "So how does a toff like you wind up in the Wombat Ranges anyway?"

It was a very good question. Ike looked past him, staring through the wall, ten thousand miles of desert and ocean, and twenty years. "Failure."

Ned snorted. "I can't credit that. Look at all this kit." He gestured at the expensive imported tools and machinery that filled the shack. "I doubt you've ever spent a day hungry, never mind in gaol."

Ike returned his focus to Ned, realizing that the gulf between them was nearly as large as the distance he'd just been contemplating. "That's true. But I failed at my chosen profession—failed repeatedly and disastrously, all due to my own ambition and pride. The tunnel under the Thames...the atmospheric railway... the broad-gauge locomotive...they were all the best possible designs, in theory, but every one of them met calamity in execution. And then, worst and last, that damnable steamship of mine." The tidy, cluttered shack faded from Ike's sight, replaced by memories of great chains and hydraulic rams. "She should have been my triumph. The greatest ship ever built! But it took us over a year just to launch her. And then, on her very first foray into the Channel..." He shook his head. "Explosion. Disaster. Death." He looked Ned in the eyes. "She broke my heart, sir, and ruined my health. It was my own dear wife who suggested I pretend death and flee the country, to escape the professional and financial catastrophe that would surely follow."

Ned regarded Ike contemplatively. "You said all them locomotives and steamships and what-all was the best possible designs. Did you build 'em yourself?"

"No, of course not. There were technicians, labourers...hundreds of workmen."

Ned nodded, a decisive little jerk of his chin. "So then. You and I, we're not so far off each other. We've both been victimized by the errors of lesser men."

"I wouldn't say that I've—"

"You were let down by your workmen," Ned insisted, "while I—ever since I was fourteen years of age, and due to no fault whatsoever of my own—have been chased and hounded by a parcel of big, ugly, fat-necked, wombat-headed, big-bellied, magpie-legged, narrow-hipped, splay-footed sons of Irish bailiffs or

English landlords which is better known as officers of Justice or Victorian Police, who some calls honest gentlemen!"

At this vehement outburst Ike could do no more than gape.

"The difference between us," Ned went on, "is that you chose to run from your tormentors, whereas I choose to fight." He leaned in close, his breath hot and sour and foul. "And with the armour you're building me, I'm going to win."

The work went slowly, endless rounds of design and test and fittings peppered with interruptions and arguments.

The biggest argument came on the twenty-second of June, after Ike finally had to admit that there would not be sufficient time or materials to produce more than one set of armour. For hour after screaming hour he feared that at any moment his head would be blown off his shoulders, but in the end even Steve, the youngest and most hot-headed of the gang, was forced to concede that building four full sets of the complex armour was not humanly possible.

But even with his workload reduced by three-fourths, Ike's task was still hideously daunting. Day after struggling day, night after sleepless night, he dragged and pounded and forged and bent an endless pile of stolen iron mould-boards, until his eyes were red and his white muttonchop whiskers had gone entirely black with soot. The gang helped out with the lifting and hauling, but all of the design and fine work was Ike's.

Three complete boilers were built, found wanting, and discarded. Every time Ike thought he'd steered a safe course between the Scylla and Charybdis of power and weight, he realized that the boiler would either weigh so much that the armour would never budge, or would burst asunder under pressure as that damnable steamship had done. In the end he found a solution, involving reinforcing bands of chromium steel, that seemed satisfactory...though distressingly close to the material's tolerances.

Finally, just before dawn on June twenty-sixth, the thing was done.

It had long before grown too large to be accommodated inside Ike's shack, and he had moved his workspace to the yard behind it. Ike had been working by the light of a windproof lantern, but as he tightened the last bolt and stepped back to inspect his work he found that it was no longer necessary and snuffed it out.

The rising sun traced the edges of the armour's riveted plates, outlining its black manlike shape with a tracery of glowing orange. It stood over eight feet high. Each leg was big around as a tree trunk—a proper English tree, not the stunted wrist-thick mallees of the Wombat Ranges—and the torso bulked as large as a butt wine cask. Within that giant shell lay the pistons and rods that drove the legs and arms, great quantities of wool padding to insulate the operator from the heat and motion of the mechanisms, and of course the operator himself. *Operator* was the term Ike preferred, not *wearer* as Ned insisted—though Ike had carefully positioned the control levers so that the natural motions of the operator's legs would cause the suit to walk, the suit's occupant would also be required to constantly direct, adjust, and monitor its workings.

The helmet was the only thing about it that resembled Ned's original sketch, a bucket shape with a horizontal eye slit.

Twin smokestacks rose above the shoulders.

It weighed over three thousand pounds.

It was a thing of beauty.

Breast swelling with pride, Ike lay his abraded and blackened hand on the armour's side—it was as high as he could reach—cleared his throat, and spoke. "I dub thee . . . *Goliath*."

A sharp sound from behind Ike made him whirl in surprise. Ned stood there—had apparently been there for some time—and was applauding, slow measured claps. "Well done, mate," he said, and stepped forward to slap Ike on the back. "Well done. But it could be even better."

From his duster pocket he drew one of his revolvers, and fitted it into the armour's right hand. Sunlight gleamed greasily on the pistol's barrel.

"Now we're all set for tomorrow's festivities."

Ike felt sick at heart.

"Feed valve for the left leg's here," Ike reminded, pointing. "Right leg here. Arms, here and here. Relief valve's here; don't adjust it unless I tell you to." The sweat-stink of Ned's body fought in Ike's nostrils with the tang of hot iron and the greasy kerosene smell of the naphtha-powered boiler as he leaned in to tighten the strap across Ned's chest. Even with the chest plate open the heat was nearly intolerable. "Do you understand?"

"Feed. Legs. Arms. Relief." Ned touched each valve in turn. "Right. All sorted. Close me up."

Ike closed and dogged the chest plate shut and

stepped back. He could see only darkness through the slit in the helmet. "Can you see?"

In reply Ned raised the armour's arm—the mechanisms hissing and groaning as steam shrieked from the shoulder and elbow joints—aimed the pistol over Ike's head, and fired. A moment later came a tearing *crack* and a shiver of leaves as a limb fell from a nearby mallee-tree. A flock of pink galahs burst into the air, chirping their distress.

"Well enough," Ned said, his voice echoing and metallic. "Now let's get to work."

It was the morning of Sunday, the twenty-seventh of June. On the previous day they'd hauled the disassembled armour, in two wagons, down the hill to the outskirts of the little town of Glenrowan and made camp there. All was in readiness for whatever the gang had been planning for so many months.

Smoking and spewing steam from every joint, *Goliath* jolted down the hill toward town, shaking the ground with every step. The other three gang members followed, dragging Ike along "in case anything should happen to go wrong."

He didn't know if he was intended as engineer or hostage. Perhaps both.

Glenrowan was little more than a loose assemblage of buildings and tents surrounding a railway station, with a population of perhaps seventy. Dan, Joe, and Steve fanned out through the town, rousting the populace from their homes and businesses, while Ned, inside *Goliath*, stomped toward the tiny train station, which also served as post and telegraph office. "Don't you dare get out of my sight," Ned growled, and Ike followed him.

One blow of *Goliath*'s iron fist shattered the telegraph office door into flinders. "You inside!" Ned roared, pointing his revolver into the office. "Telegraph man! Come out, and bring your pad and pencil!"

The postmaster, a slim sandy-haired gentleman, soon emerged, holding the requested items high in his trembling hands.

"Take this down and send it to all the newspapers," Ned said, his voice booming metallically. "Let it be known to all and sundry that I, Ned Kelly, together with my compatriots, have bailed up and taken hostage the entire populace of Glenrowan. The Felons' Apprehension Act of 1878 having expired on June the twenty-sixth, we are no longer outlaws, and therefore the common people may aid and abet us without fear of government reprisal." Ike blinked up at Ned, the fierce sun haloing his cylindrical helmet. So *that* was why he had been so insistent that the armour be completed by this day! "We invite all people seeking innocence, justice and liberty to join us here. Today, June the Twenty-Seventh of the Year of Our Lord Eighteen-Eighty, marks the birth of the Republic of North-Eastern Victoria!"

After Ned's proclamation had been copied down, repeated back, and transmitted to his satisfaction, he clomped around to the side of the station, straightened the armour to its full height, reached up one mighty arm, and wrenched the telegraph wires down from the wall.

But that act of destruction wasn't enough. Ned clanked out onto the railroad track, walking several hundred yards toward Melbourne. Then *Goliath* bent down, grasped one of the rails in its vice-like hands, and— groaning and with steam shrieking—straightened up.

The rail cried out as it was torn from its bed, bending into a useless twist of metal. Its sibling rail protested its demise equally loudly and with equally little effect.

Ike had spent most of his engineering career building railroads. The inevitable consequence of this vandalism was as clear in his mind as if he'd already witnessed it with his own eyes. The next train to arrive would come barrelling around the curve at full speed, slam into the damaged section, and tumble off the tracks in a shower of sparks and flying metal. Everyone on the train would surely be killed.

Ned walked back to town and brought *Goliath* to a halt near the shattered telegraph office. Then the chest plate clanged open. "Now we wait," Ned said as he emerged, running with sweat. "They'll send a train full of constables to hunt us down like dogs. But they'll find a bit of a surprise when they arrive." He gestured to the torn-up track, his face set in a hideous leering grin. "It'll be spectacular."

Ike gulped. This was monstrous. What had seemed at first little more than an interesting engineering problem had turned into insurrection, treason, and slaughter, and now he was right in the middle of it.

He had to find some way to warn the officers that they were speeding into an ambush. But how?

The gang herded the population into the Glenrowan Inn, a wood-framed pub and hostelry that was the settlement's largest structure. Many of the townspeople were Kelly supporters, and the occupation had more the mood of a celebration than a siege, with dancing, card playing, and drinking.

Ned left the armour standing where it was, hidden

behind the station from the view of any inbound train, with a low flame under the boiler to keep it ready for action. One member of the gang stood watch over it at all times, which incidentally prevented Ike from approaching the station in search of some means to signal the train.

Ike was pacing behind the bar when Steve came in from guard duty. "Hey, brainbox," he said. "It's stopped making that noise, and it's gone all cold. Is something wrong?"

"I'll have a look," Ike said. "I'll need my tool chest."

Staggering with the weight of the heavy chest, Ike allowed Steve to chivvy him along to the armour, which stood beside the station like a triumphal statue to a battle that had not yet occurred. No hint of smoke rose from the stacks; plainly the naphtha flame had simply run out of fuel.

"Get to it, brainbox," Steve said, gesturing sharply with his pistol. He fidgeted nervously, bouncing on his toes.

Then Ike spotted the telegraph cable's broken end, lying in the dirt a few paces away, and a plan began to formulate itself in his mind.

"Looks like a framulated wazigummit," he said aloud. "Might be a bit."

Ike puttered industriously and pointlessly for long minutes, keeping an eye on Steve and an ear out for the oncoming train. Steve grew increasingly agitated, shifting from foot to foot, and Ike feared the bushranger's patience was wearing thin. But then a miracle occurred. "Gotta visit the dunny," Steve said, backing away around the corner of the station. "Don't you dare break nothing."

As soon as he heard the sound of pattering liquid, Ike set his plan into motion. Grabbing a small electrical battery from his tool chest, he scuttled to the point where the broken telegraph cable's catenary curve lay tangent to the ground. Twisting one of the exposed wires onto one battery terminal, he touched the other wire to the other terminal in a rapid series of Morse code pulses: TRACKS TORN UP IN GLENROWAN STOP NED KELLY HAS ARMOUR STOP USE ALL CAUTION STOP.

Just as he finished the message, Ike realized the sound of Steve's urine had already stopped. Slipping the battery into his coat pocket, he hurried back to *Goliath*'s side, arriving just as Steve returned. "Found the problem," he gasped.

Steve looked up from buttoning his trousers. "What's wrong? You're all flushed."

"Just the excitement of a difficult engineering problem." He struggled to calm himself as he filled the armour's fuel reservoir and lit the pilot light.

Soon the boiler was rumbling to itself as it had before, and Steve herded him back inside. As he lugged the heavy tool chest along, Ike wondered whether he should have tried to sabotage the armour somehow as well as warning the police about the torn-up track.

But as soon as they arrived at the inn, Ned got up and left to check on the armour, giving Ike a penetrating look as he passed. He had worked so closely with Ike on *Goliath*'s development that he would know immediately if anything were wrong. And if Ned even suspected Ike of shady dealings, or if the armour suddenly malfunctioned . . . one word to his gang would put a bullet through Ike's head.

No, sabotage was out.

All Ike could do now was hope that someone in authority had received his message and would believe it.

Hours passed. The sun set. The card-playing and dancing grew desultory and then ground to a halt. Many people bedded down in corners, laid low by drink or by simple exhaustion. Only a few remained seated at the table, including Ike and the four members of the gang, sitting quietly and drinking cold billy tea.

At two o'clock in the morning, Ned finally gave in. "All right, everyone," he called out. "You can all go home. No excitement tonight. But I want all of you to remember one thing—"

But no one would ever know what Ned wanted. He was interrupted by the distant cry of a train whistle.

The gang immediately roused themselves, smiling and slapping each other's shoulders, joking about how they would pick off any constables who survived the crash "like stomping ants as they scurry from a crushed ant-hill." Ned then ran to the armour and strapped himself in. Even as he closed the chest-plate, Ike heard the boiler coming up to full pressure.

The inn's lights were extinguished, Ike and the other hostages shushed and told to keep still or be shot. The three gang members ducked down behind windowsills, anticipating a fine view of the upcoming train wreck.

They waited.

The tension mounted as the wait went on, seemingly interminable. Ike felt that he had never in his life waited so long between the sound of the whistle and the arrival of a train.

And then came the chuffing of the engine, and Ike realized that his telegraph had been received. The train was not rushing toward disaster! Instead, it was slowing!

Slowly, slowly, the train pulled up to the damaged section of track and stopped. The three gang members, muttering amongst themselves, slipped out of the inn and arranged themselves in the deep shadows of the veranda; Ike and some of the townspeople took their vacated positions at the window sills so as to see the proceedings.

By the light of a gibbous moon Ike saw men boiling from the train, carrying pistols and rifles and taking up positions behind barrels and buildings. "Ned Kelly!" came a voice through a speaking trumpet. "This is Superintendent Hare. We have you outnumbered and outgunned. Surrender peaceably and you will be given a fair—dear God in Heaven!"

The reason for Hare's outburst was clear. Ned had just stomped into view, with moonlight gleaming on the armour and sparks drifting from its chimneys. Pistols were fitted into their slots in both hands. "I will shoot no man if he gives up his arms and promises to leave the police force!" he called, the armour magnifying his voice into a resonating iron boom. "But let any policeman or other man who does not throw up his arms directly know the consequences, which is a speedy dispatch to Kingdom Come!"

In the veranda's darkness Ike heard the other gang members shifting into position and cocking their weapons, but he knew that if he called them out to the constables he would immediately be shot. Heart pounding, he could do nothing more than wait.

Ned and the police stood facing each other for long minutes.

No one moved or spoke.

And then a shot broke the night's silence, followed immediately by the bell-like tone of the ricochet off Ned's armour.

In one smooth move Ned swivelled at the waist, levelled his pistol, and fired. One of the constables fell with a shriek of pain.

The night erupted into a bedlam of flashes, gunshots, and screams. Most of the shooting came from the police, and all of that was directed at Ned, who strode rapidly toward the train as though the storm of bullets were no more than a summer shower. He fired only sparingly, but each shot brought another policeman down. Meanwhile the gang was firing with abandon from their concealment on the veranda, but the police ignored them—between the noise of their own guns and the obvious target of Ned's armoured figure, they did not seem to recognize that they were being killed from two directions.

It was a slaughter.

Ike bit his lip until the iron taste of blood filled his mouth. *Goliath*, his wonderful creation, was performing spectacularly—but what a terrible task it performed!

The armoured suit strode through the chaos like a juggernaut, extracting a deadly toll from the police. A few brave officers rushed it, hoping perhaps to find some weakness, only to be smacked brutally aside by an iron fist or smashed into the earth by a piston-like leg. The remaining police fell back behind the train engine, but with mechanical persistence Ned pursued them. So did the other gang members, who slipped from the veranda and fell in behind Ned to snipe at the police from behind the impregnable wall of *Goliath's* bulk.

It seemed that within minutes the rout of the police would be complete.

And then, rising above the rattle and bang of gunfire and ricochets, Ike heard a terrific sound he'd heard only once before in his life: the high keening whistle of a steam boiler under too much pressure.

The last time he'd heard that sound had been on his great steamship's shakedown cruise. Moments later the boiler had burst, with sufficient force to throw the No. 1 funnel into the air. Five stokers had died in the explosion.

Ike knew *Goliath's* boiler design was near the limits of the materials. It had been the only way to achieve the necessary power-to-weight ratio. But now, it seemed, those limits were about to be exceeded.

All of Ike's engineering instincts demanded he tell Ned to throw the relief valve wide open. A simple twist of one knob would release the excess pressure and prevent an explosion—preserving the equipment, the lives of those nearby, and Ike's sense of himself as an engineer.

He shook himself, surged to his feet, and ran towards the battle.

"Close the relief valve, Ned!" he cried at the limit of his lungs. "*Close* the relief valve!"

In the midst of the gunfire, the clanging and hissing of the armour, and the shriek of the overloaded boiler, Ike heard a tiny squeak. The pitch of the anguished boiler's whistle rose as the pressure built. Ike's mind roiled with equations of tensile strength, steam pressure, and temperature...

And then, with a Brobdingnagian thunder, the armour exploded. Fragments of metal flew in every direction.

Blown backwards by the blast, Ike sprawled across the veranda steps. A series of crashes, loud enough to penetrate the ringing in his ears, followed as chunks of the armour landed all around him.

Then came a blow to the head, and darkness.

"He's coming around!"

The words sounded as though they were pushing their way through a half-mile of cotton batting. Ike's eyes blinked open, then immediately clenched shut against the pain of daylight. He clutched his aching head and felt bandages. "Ohh . . ." was all he could manage.

"Here, sir, have some tea!"

The tin cup scalded his lip. The tea was vile, bitter eucalyptus. He sipped gratefully.

"Constable Phillips, sir!" the man introduced himself. His face showed that he was shouting at the top of his lungs, but the words were barely audible. "I'll need to take a statement, sir!"

The resulting shouted conversation would have been laughable if the matter hadn't been so serious. So many had died—more than thirty police officers, eight of the hostages, and of course Ned himself, as well as all three members of his gang. Ike tried to give an honest report, as best as he could manage with the ringing in his ears, and not to try to excuse his own part in the debacle.

At least, in the end, he'd forced common sense to triumph over engineering instinct. For all the damage he'd caused, at least he'd managed that.

"You must have been terrified, sir!" the constable shouted. "With those bushrangers holding their guns to your head, making you build that armour, sir!"

Ike's hearing was beginning to return, but that wasn't the only reason he winced at the constable's words. "Well, to be frank, I—"

But before Ike could explain, another policeman approached—an older and apparently superior officer—and the two men held a conversation Ike couldn't hear. The second man addressed Ike. "Senior Constable Kelly, sir. We're trying to identify the person who sent the telegram that warned us about the ambush."

"That would be me."

The senior constable's face lit up with gratitude. "Then you are the hero of the day, sir!" He pumped Ike's hand with painful enthusiasm, then ran off. Ike saw him conversing animatedly with a crowd of civilians, pointing in his direction. They immediately came running, shoving each other. "Well done, sir!" cried one, and "What's your name, sir?" another.

There was no point in denying the truth. "Brunel," he admitted. "Isambard Kingdom Brunel."

The man who'd asked his name seemed nonplussed. "Isambard Kingdom Brunel? Like the famous engineer?" He studied Ike's face. "Dear Lord—you *are* Brunel!"

"Who?" asked another man.

"The designer of Paddington Station, man! The Clifton Suspension Bridge! The Great Eastern, the greatest steamship in all history!"

Ike waved a dismissive hand. "Greatest *failure* of a steamship—"

"Not much of a passenger liner, perhaps, but she laid the great transatlantic telegraph cable!" The man blinked. "I'm John McWhirter, from *The Argus*, Mr. Brunel. Where have you *been* all these years, sir? The public think you dead!"

The press. Of course the press would be here; they'd come on the train with the constables, to report the apprehension of the notorious outlaw Ned Kelly. But they had gotten far more of a story than they'd dreamed of—the dramatic siege, the unprecedented steam-powered armour, the spectacular explosion, and now the discovery of a celebrated engineer thought dead for twenty years.

As they bombarded him with questions, the reporters insisted that *Goliath* was his crowning achievement. "You'll make millions, sir," said the man from the *Herald*. "Every military on Earth will want a thousand of 'em!"

The idea was tempting—very tempting. To return to England, to see his sons and his wife's grave, to reap the financial rewards that had eluded him in his previous life...a very attractive notion indeed.

But then Ike considered the consequences of such a return. To be the father of an army of those death-dealing machines? Just one had caused more carnage and destruction in a single hour than Ike had witnessed in the rest of his entire long life.

And yet, now that the principle had been demonstrated, the genie was out of the bottle. He couldn't just go back into hiding.

Though patents were anathema to his engineering sensibilities, common sense told him there was only one thing to do.

"No, gentlemen," he said, shaking his head, "I will return to England, but only to patent *Goliath* and all the innovations that made it possible, licensing them for peaceful purposes only. I will do all I can, in whatever years remain to me, to prevent any such machine from ever being used to harm human beings again."

The reporters clamoured questions. "But surely," one of them shouted, "not even the great Brunel can prevent progress in the machines of war?"

Ike held up a hand for silence. "The way will not be easy, I admit. But today I have learned that the *Great Eastern* recovered from the disaster she suffered on her shakedown cruise and went on to serve mankind in another capacity." He drew himself up to his full five-foot-four. "If a steamship can reform herself and change the world, then so perhaps can her builder."

———————

David D. Levine is a lifelong SF reader whose midlife crisis was to take a sabbatical from his high-tech job to attend Clarion West in 2000. It seems to have worked. He made his first professional sale in 2001, won the Writers of the Future Contest in 2002, was nominated for the John W. Campbell award in 2003, was nominated for the Hugo Award and the Campbell again in 2004, and won a Hugo in 2006 (Best Short Story, for "Tk'Tk'Tk"). A collection of his short stories, *Space Magic*, from Wheatland Press, won the Endeavour Award in 2009. In January 2010, he spent two weeks at a simulated Mars base in the Utah desert, which you can read about at bentopress.com/mars. He lives in Portland, Oregon with his wife, Kate Yule, with whom he edits the fanzine *Bento* (BentoPress.com). He also has a story forthcoming in John Joseph Adams's anthology *The Mad Scientist's Guide to World Domination*.

Field Test

MICHAEL A. STACKPOLE

The UAV cockpit was almost finished with its warmup sequence, and Major Sarah "Mock" Ashton fought her rising annoyance. Just as she would do the walk-around on any plane she was going to be piloting herself, she preferred to start up her Unmanned Aerial Vehicle station and personally make sure everything loaded. *My bird, my responsibility. I don't want screw-ups.*

A slender young man turned toward her as she entered the room and at least had the good grace to flinch from her glare. "I signed you in."

"I see that." She brushed past him. "Where's Trask?"

"Mr. Trask is, um, tasked with another assignment. I'm Frost. He gave me this, to run, you know."

Oh, he must hate you a whole bunch to let me *take your mission cherry.* She slid into the command chair. "Does this mean my suspension is over?"

"Major Ashton, Mr. Trask said that you were the

last person we wanted on this mission." Frost glanced nervously at his tablet computer. "Works out, you really *are* the last person who could."

She wanted to snap off some quip that would sting him, but Frost had that eager-to-please puppy-dog anxiety that she normally loathed. The fact that she'd actually been called in meant the situation was serious, so she decided to give him a break. "How black is this op?"

"I, ah, well... really, really black?" He glanced at the door, his head tucking down like he was expecting a cuff. "When you're ready I'll give you the brief."

She slid herself forward and locked the command chair into position. Fingers flew over the keyboard, adjusting the UAV Flight Control System displays to her liking. She pulled on a headset and adjusted the microphone as the system worked through the hand-shaking that would let her drive a drone. "Spill it."

"Support for a recovery op. At zero-three-three-zero hours local..."

He reached out to punch a button on her console, but she slapped his hand away. She punched the button, which parked a small picture-in-picture image down into the main display's lower right corner. She touch-flicked it to a smaller auxiliary monitor. It blew up into a satellite image of a city on the coast of somewhere. The computer laid two colors over the image. Green dominated the eastern half, with a salient thrusting into the west. The western half had been colored red, and the two halves locked together like pieces of a puzzle.

A little gold star twinkled just inside the red zone, near the tip of the salient.

"That's Zlitan, in Libya, you know, where—"

Sarah cursed under her breath. "I have cable, Frost."

"Right. So green represents rebel forces controlled by Hassan Kayar, local tribal leader. He fought for Libya against Sudan, then fought for the Sudanese central government as a mercenary in the civil war—"

"No more History Channel." Sarah poked the star and a tiny window popped up. "Twitpics, really? The Agency can't do better than that?"

Frost looked crestfallen. "I was, um, trying for innovation, you know, showing initiative. That's only twelve hours old."

"Okay, good job." *You're a virgin, I'll be gentle.* "What's so important about Hotel Malta?"

"The Agency was developing some information—"

She laughed. "Agents got trapped?"

"Gaddafi's forces proved more robust in their assault than we expected." Frost chewed his lower lip. "Um, the guys there, at Langley—"

Sarah nodded. "You're not leaving buddies in trouble. Got it." She banished the hotel as her main screen flashed with the image that was mostly sky and just the hint of a destroyer's fantail. She punched up the system diagnostics and frowned. "You've got me driving a Predator. What am I supposed to do with that?"

"Trask said he wants less collateral damage than last time, Major." Frost smiled weakly. "Really, all you have to do is act as eyes for our man."

"Man? As in one man?" She shook her head. "What did we do, trade the Brits SEAL Team Six for James Bond?"

"Please, Major: launch. You're five minutes to station." Frost pulled on a headset, started pacing and glancing from his tablet to her screens and back. "I'll keep tabs on the political situation and—"

"Yeah, eyes for our guy. Got it." Sarah settled her right hand on the flight controller, punched the engines up, then eased her joystick back as the Predator drone shot into the sky. It responded to controls very well, despite the fact that they had to travel from Nevada up to a satellite, across to another and back down. The Predator, with its payload of only two Hellfire missiles, flew easy. She preferred its bigger brother, the MQ-9 Reaper, since it carried fourteen missiles and had much more powerful engines. Her problem, as Trask saw it, was that she liked using the missiles a bit too much.

She came in a kilometer above the city. A small white star appeared on the tactical map, right at the port. She tapped it and one of the small communications displays lit up at the edge of her main screen, right above a glowing red mute button. She punched it, opening a channel. "Kane, this is Mock, orbiting above you."

Static crackled though her earphone, then resolved itself into a bass voice. *"Mock, this is Kane. You'll put me on target, right?"*

"I'm eyes only, but I do have a one-two punch if needed."

"I'll bear that in mind, thanks."

The guy didn't sound like a soulless Agency drone, which should have made Sarah feel better. It didn't. Her having been recalled, coupled with Frost's virginal jitters and Trask's being AWOL, convinced her something wasn't right.

Sarah brought the drone back around and kicked

the targeting camera on. She flicked it to a secondary monitor, then zoomed in on the docks. She was about to flick the white star up onto that monitor, when something disturbed the harbor waters.

I knew it. Trouble.

A thing emerged from the sea between two boats, water sheeting off it. From her angle she couldn't guess its height, but it was moving on legs that bent back at the knees, like a bird. It had an ovoid body and two arms—the left ended in a pincer.

"Kane, you're screwed. Head south fast. I'm not sure what I just saw come out of the sea, but I'm pretty sure you don't want it on your ass."

"You're right, I don't."

"You have eyes on it?"

"Not really, but it's okay." Light laughter rolled through the radio. *"You see, that is my ass."*

"You know Halloween isn't for another five months."

Francis Xavier Kell, nestled safely in the cockpit of the XMWP-1, couldn't help smiling at the shock in Mock's voice. "I wanted to be a pirate, but this isn't Somalia."

"You look like Humpty Dumpty."

A new voice cut in: *"I don't think your chatter . . . well, it should be mission specific."* The apprehension in that voice couldn't disguise its youth.

"Who's that?"

"Spook handler. Calls himself Frost."

"Where's Trask? Job came through his team."

"How well do you know him?"

"Well enough. Know how his nose is broken?"

"You did that?" Mock laughed. *"Why?"*

"I felt much better *after* doing it."

"Really, please, guys, he could listen to the tapes—"

"Roger that, Frost, I'll play nice." Kell turned his head and the projected holographic hyper-spatial display provided a visual-light image of Zlitan's harbor. At the bottom a red ribbon scrolled past, providing him running diagnostics on the energy output from the hydrogen fuel cell engine strapped to his back. Weapons displays ran down each side in green, but did little more than track ammo. Still, all weapons were green, so he was loaded for bear.

"Mock, you got a tac-map?"

"Sending."

The puzzle-piece image of the city dropped into the lower left corner of his display. The gold star designating his target pulsed, and seconds later, on his main display, a golden arrow appeared in the air, stabbing down toward his goal.

He cleared his throat. "Kane, overlay IR, pump vis-light, and give me 20% on mag-res."

"Talking to yourself, Kane?"

"Negative, Mock. I'm Kell. Kane is the ride."

"Killer of men?"

Kell chuckled. "I suggested Fluffy. Agency nixed it."

"So, what is your ride?"

Frost moaned. *"No, please, need to know, and you don't need to know, Major."*

Kell ignored Frost. "Mobile Weapons Platform One, experimental. Technically this is a field test. I'm the G. I. Joe of the future. Anything this side of a thirteen millimeter cannon isn't supposed to bother me, whereas, I'm supposed to annoy the hell out of everybody."

"Doesn't sound like you have a problem with that." Mock laughed and Kell decided he liked the sound of her voice. *"On your tac-map, green's the safe zone, red's the bad guys. Head south."*

"Roger that." Kell started forward, walking as close to normal as he could manage. Sensors sewn into his spandex suit let his onboard computer track the position of his legs. They extended into the machine's legs but only to the knees. The computer translated positioning information to the onboard gyro-stabilizers and the motors which fed electrical charges into the electro-convulsive polymeric fibers that served as muscles. As he picked up speed, the cockpit shifted position, leaning him forward so he could feel as if he was running. Locomotion within the XMWP-1 had taken the most getting used to, but once he had the ten-foot tall machine moving, there wasn't much that was going to stop it.

He moved up from the harbor and through the warehouse district. He tried to run close to the line dividing the map. The green zone might be home to "friendlies," but they were friendly only in the sense that they weren't supporting Gaddafi. *They see me cruising through their area, they're going to open up.*

The main display, as per his previous command, had collected more light, turning the cityscape into that hazy greenish-blue where everything looked like it was trapped in the tube of a dying black-and-white television. He'd added infrared data, and the heat signatures showed up in reds and golds. The city had cooled enough that he could discern the faint glow of appliances and, thankfully, saw no one huddled in homes on the firing line.

The magnetic resonance information etched faint skeletons on buildings, showed old pipes and reduced vehicles to vector-graphic outlines. There wasn't as much metal as he'd have liked, since it had its uses for cover.

Ahead, to the right, four loyalists raised AK-47s. Fire lanced from muzzles. A few bullets hit, pinging off, then the shooters ducked behind a car. "Mock, I have small arms fire, forty meters, south by southwest."

"Roger, looking for their friends."

"I'll take them." Kell brought Kane's right arm up. The XM-25 was one of two weapons built into the cylindrical forearm. Using a joystick, he dropped a golden crosshair on the vehicle, raised it over the top. "Kane, XM-25, range plus one meter."

A gold dot pulsed at the crosshair's heart.

Kell hit the trigger.

The XM-25 fired a smart bullet equipped with a computer chip. It emerged from the barrel, chased by fire. The chip tracked the bullet and was able to calculate its location in real time, based on the bullet's rotational speed. As per the programming command, the bullet traveled a meter beyond the range designated by Kane's laser range finder. The High-Explosive Air-Burst projectile then exploded, spraying the area behind the car with a lethal storm of metal fragments.

"Kell, break left, now. Incoming on your two."

Taking Mock at her word, Kell sprinted the XMWP-1 to the other side of the street. As he did so, his computers pulled an image from Mock's camera and popped it in an unused corner of his display. Lines traced it, then a box opened beneath it, identifying the vehicle as a Russian-built BTR-60 armored personnel carrier.

The eight-wheeled, slope-sided vehicle had a turret with a 14.5 millimeter KVPT heavy machine gun mounted front and center.

Before he could bring weapons online to deal with it, light streaked down from the sky. The Hellfire missile hit it dead on. Golden fire blossomed along the side street. Windows shattered, buildings sagged, and the armored personnel carrier flipped into the sky, burning merrily. It crashed down through the roof of small store, its tires boiling.

"Nice work, Mock."

"My pleasure."

Frost appeared at her left. "This isn't good. You're not supposed to shoot unless *I* give the authorization."

"I'm just protecting our man."

"He's not supposed to be there, Major, and you're blowing the place up."

She gave him a hard stare and Frost almost melted. Hey, Kell, looks like this is one of those missions that never happened. How did you get stuck being expendable?"

"Broken nose, remember?"

"Frost thinks someone will notice one more explosion in a war zone." She frowned. "I only have one more punch, so you might have to play hide and seek."

"That was kind of my plan, but I'm not complaining about the help."

Frost's eyes narrowed. He tapped a finger against the tablet's screen, then grunted. "There's an update to the tactical map."

Sarah glanced down. The red line near where she'd blown up the APC pulled back. "Well, well."

Frost shot her a sidelong glance. "It wasn't your shot that did that. We have phone chatter. Loyalists are pulling back. Kell, move it."

"Roger that. What's up top?"

"One klick out to the big square in the salient, hang a right to your target. Looks clear, I'll do a sweep."

Kell cut toward the east, keeping on the political divide. He shot a glance down the street where Mock had blasted the Russian APC to bits. Though Kane had no viewport, the hyper-spatial imaging display gave him a full 360 degree view. The designers had initially tried to shrink that into a 180 degree field using a box to show him what was in his forward firing arc, but turning the head was just too natural a motion to train pilots out of.

The display automatically faded the infrared imaging of the fire, but he saw nothing beyond it. Kane bounced forward smoothly, despite moving on bird's-legs. He'd disliked how they looked until he remembered that velociraptors had the same kind of legs. He asked the designers to weld big claws on the front of the feet but they refused, saying there would be no practical use for such a thing. He argued it would scare the enemy, which they thought would be a good idea, so they painted Kane up like a ninja: all black.

No imagination, these people. Hello Kitty would have been a lot more scary.

Kell pushed south, moving fairly quickly along the main road. He passed easily enough beneath electrical and phone wires. His sensors picked up a few Wi-Fi networks. He really couldn't imagine many folks checking email while Rebel and loyalist forces

vere shooting in the middle of the town, but during
iis Army career, he'd seen stranger things happening.

A single bullet pinged off Kane's armored shell.
Iis sensors read the disturbance in the air created
)y the passing bullet, and immediately traced it back
o an upper story window one hundred fifty meters
away. IR sensors painted a faint ghost of a crouched
nan. Kell brought Kane's left arm up and around. Its
rosshair materialized in blue. He dropped it on the
ed-gold outline, got a pulse, and pulled the trigger.

The .50 caliber bullet blew through the wall. The
niper disappeared. Kell smiled, though not at the death
r even making the shot—the sensors and computers
nade it more difficult to miss than hit. His pleasure
ame from using one shot where others would have
red hundreds. The XMWP-1 had an AR-15 built into
he right arm, right beside the XM-25. Another pilot
night have just sprayed the window with a couple
ozen bullets to accomplish the same objective. Those
vere the same sort of men who would feel invulner-
ble in the warmech. It would make them into Lords
f Death, stalking through the streets, killing people
imply because they knew they couldn't get hurt.

Kell hated that idea. War was brutal. *No need to
iake it any worse than necessary.*

"Mock, we still good?"

*"Movement south. The kid called it. Loyalists pull-
ng back."*

"Good, coming up on the square." His first glimpse
natched the photographs in his briefing, though those
vere daytime shots. The square itself had a four lane
oundabout circling it, with a tall obelisk in the cen-
er. It memorialized something to do with Gaddafi's

revolution. Four major streets met there, and fou
minor streets headed out at in-between angles. Th
sensor display revealed several dead cars, and anothe
BTR-60 APC that had been shot to pieces.

As he moved forward, looking for whatever ha
riddled the APC, his tactical map shifted. What ha
been green suddenly went red.

And across the square, hidden in shadows, the thin
that had killed the BTR-60 opened up with all fou
of its 23 millimeter cannons.

"What the hell just happened, Frost?"

"Oh my god, oh my god, oh my god." Blood draine
from Frost's face as he pounded on the tablet's screer
"Gaddafi just bought out Kayar. There's no safe zone
We can't evac our people."

Kell's voice crackled through the headset. *"Hang i
there, Frost. We're not done. We can get them out.
just need some help."*

Sarah brought the Predator back around. "Hol
shit. Is that a Shilka?"

*"Yeah. Should be shooting at you, but wants groun
targets."*

"Let me take care of that." Sarah smiled as sh
swiveled the gun camera onto the Soviet era ZSU-23-
mobile anti-aircraft vehicle. It looked like a baby-tan
with a radar ball on top. She launched her remainin
Hellfire and reduced it to a fiery circle of debris.

*"Damn, Mock, with you up there, the Agency coul
have gotten their guys out in a taxi."*

"Roger that. You better move. Kayar's people ar
coming up to take control of the city."

❖   ❖   ❖

Kell sprinted to the BTR and studied the tactical map again. The whole town was red now and gave him one advantage: Now he didn't have to be too particular about sorting friend from foe. Even so, Mock had been right. He'd do better playing hide and seek than gunslinging, and *seeking* was first order of the day.

The gold star marking his target blinked about three hundred meters to the west. Kane rose from the BTR's shadow and headed that way. The warmech had gotten ten yards from the BTR when Kell caught a flash of gold in the corner of his left eye. He turned to look. The golden images of two men glowed fifty yards away behind a sandbag emplacement on a second story balcony. Magnetic resonance sensors drew a .30 caliber machine gun on a post beside them. The way they crouched, Kell assumed they were trying to get a belt of ammo ready to go. He contemplated turning to shoot them, but instead just increased his speed.

That gave him a half-second to puzzle over the fact that his departure seemed to make them more anxious than less. He couldn't imagine why that would be.

And then the world exploded around him.

Fire sprayed out in a brilliant arc from the square's western edge. It hit Kane hard. The armored figure tumbled forward. Shrapnel ripped past, shredding cars, including the old VW Bug that Kane's bulk crushed when the warmech finally went down.

"Kell! Kell!" Sarah glanced at Frost. "What was that?"

"I don't know."

"Kell, get moving." She zoomed her gun camera out. "Kell, I have a BTR coming in through the square, at your nine. You have about thirty seconds Kell, can you hear me?"

A well-manicured finger reached out and stabbed the mute button on her display as the room's door clicked shut. "It's best he can't, Major."

"Finally crawled out from beneath your rock, Trask?"

"This mission is done, Major Ashton." Trask shot the French cuffs on his shirt. Diamond chips glittered coldly from his cufflinks. "Paint him."

"What?"

"Paint Kell with your targeting laser. I have assets in the area that will clean up this mess."

Frost glanced at his tablet. "Assets? What assets? I don't have—"

"Shut up, Frost, and save yourself jail time."

Sarah shook her head as the BTR continued to roll toward Kane. "That *mess* is a man, Trask. He's in there to rescue your gold-star buddies."

"And he has failed." Save for his broken nose, the blond man had the elegant looks that could have made him the Agency's answer to James Bond. "The XMWP-1 is a prototype weapons system which will reshape warfare. If our enemies get any piece of it they'll eliminate our advantages for the next fifty years. Kell knew the risks."

"He knew breaking your nose was a capital offense?"

Trask pointed to the screen. "Paint him."

Sarah rotated the weapons camera and dropped the laser on the downed ovoid form. Then she popped her hand up off that controller and punched her communications circuit on. "Hey, Kell, Trask wants you dead."

Trask lunged to mute the radio again. Sarah smiled

His attempt to shut her up gave her all the time she needed.

Kell wasn't sure if he'd blacked out or not. He tasted blood from where he'd bit his tongue. His ears rang. He shook his head to clear it, and fought the claustrophobia of being trapped inside Kane's dark shell. He tried to move his arms and legs, which he could do, and that meant he was okay.

The XMWP-1, on the other hand, remained inert. *This ain't good.* Kell punched the ignition button and a secondary screen flickered to life. He swiped a hand across his mouth and it came away bloody. He dried his hand on his chest, then settled his communications headset in place again.

His main computer came up, and he punched a button starting a replay of the last ten seconds of activity. He didn't see much but a bright light, then static, but the computer made sense of it. It picked out a small curved rectangle that had been hidden near the BTR-60.

A Claymore. Now it makes sense.

The mine, which was packed with C-4 and filled steel balls, was intended for use against an advancing mass of troops. When it detonated, it vomited its deadly payload in a sixty degree arc. Kane had been square in the middle of the metal storm. Steel shot had peppered his armor and had tossed him into a parked car.

"Mock?"

The radio remained silent, but computer diagnostics said it should be working. The computer also picked up a fire back in the square. It was having a hard time identifying weapons, but picked out the hulk of a burning BTR-60 and what looked like pieces from a Predator drone's engine.

Kell took a guess at what had happened. He'd been down, so Mock had driven her drone into the APC, buying him some time. Now he had no support in a city where everyone was against him. As nearly as he could tell, however, his objective was intact. *If I can move, it's time to move.*

The secondary computer screen resolved itself into diagnostic graphs. The engine was coming up on forty percent capacity. Kell shunted power to the muscles, then to his sensors. Yet before the latter could come up, he felt the limbs respond. Blind though he was, he heaved the machine back onto its feet and raised both arms, happy with the ease and range of motion.

His visuals came on. He had vislight and magres, but IR kept flicking in and out. It was enough, however, so he turned west and trotted toward the Hotel Malta. Two hundred and fifty meters further along, he cut to the right and into the hotel's courtyard, arriving just in time.

Four soldiers were forcing a trio of civilians into the back of troop transport. An armored Mercedes was parked in front of the truck, with flags at the nose, ready to lead the procession away. A man in uniform and his driver stood on the hotel's steps, their look of satisfaction dissolving into one of horror as Kane loomed into view.

The Agency folk made his work much easier. As the guards turned assault rifles on the warmech, the Americans dove to the ground and rolled beneath the transport. Ignoring the bullets bouncing off the armor, Kell brought the right arm up, snapped the

AR-15 online, and tracked fire from left to right. The four soldiers went down immediately, and bullets tagged the two National Police officials before they'd reached cover.

Kell flicked on his external speakers. "Kayar's defected. Can't evac through his zone."

The agents emerged from beneath the truck. "Then we're screwed unless you have a plan."

Kell smiled and wished they could see his face. "Get the dead guy's cell phone and keys. Call the Agency in Rome. They'll put you through to the sub that's waiting for me. Drive fast to the harbor and you're good."

"I don't think the Benz can outrun a bullet."

"We'll give them something else to shoot at. This is how we sell it. You come tearing out, I'll be chasing you, guns blazing." Kell laughed easily for their comfort. "They'll let you through."

The youngest of the agents, a woman, stared at him. "But not *you*."

"I'll hang for a bit, take in the sights."

"Kayar has a half-dozen mainline Soviet era T-72s battle tanks, twice as many BTR-60s, and enough RPGs and assorted Soviet hand-me-downs to kill you."

"Then I'll play hide and seek until they get tired."

"It'll be a short game." She snapped a picture with the cell phone, then turned it toward Kell. He zoomed in.

Kane had been painted black for the mission, but its whole left side had been scoured silver by the Claymore. Armor on his leg and arm had a lot of pitting. *Damn.* Another mine or a clip from an assault rifle and bullets would be banging around inside.

Kell shook his head. "The job is to get *you* out of here. Move."

"You're nuts."

"Let me just Tweet that while you're loading up."

The three agents piled into the Mercedes and pulled out into the street. Kane followed. The driver hit the gas, swerved wide onto the harbor road, and barely missed the BTR-60 at the square. The warmech raced after them, the right arm coming up. Kell tightened his finger on the trigger.

The AR-15 lipped flame. Bullets flew above the Mercedes' roof and tore into the troops on the street. Kayar's men had used an APC to set up half a roadblock, and soldiers had been moving debris to cut off the street's east side. Kane's bullets scattered them.

The Mercedes fishtailed around the APC and vanished.

Kell cut to the east himself, trotting through Predator scraps. *I hope that doesn't come out of her paycheck.* He laughed. *I hope Kane's new paint job doesn't come out of mine.*

He pushed on north, hugging storefronts and watching west. As long as he kept moving and shooting, Kayar's men would have to react—and the agents could get clear.

The radio's continued silence told him everything else he needed to know about his situation. There was no way the Agency could let Kane be captured. Too much tech, too new and too secret. Once the agents were clear, the Agency would direct a NATO cruise missile strike to obliterate the warmech.

If I knew where that rat-bastard Kayar lived, I could park there—two birds, one Tomahawk.

It surprised him that he didn't feel angrier about being abandoned, but he'd known that was a distinct possibility the second he'd started working on black ops. It occurred to him that he only had two regrets: that he'd not been able to break Trask's nose *again*, and that he'd not been able to thank Mock for saving his life.

The BTR-60 from the roadblock pulled forward, its turret swiveling around to cover him. He brought Kane's left arm up. "Kane, load API." As the turret gun on the APC opened up, Kell dropped the blue crosshairs on the boxy vehicle's front end. A gold dot flashed and he pulled the trigger.

The fifty-caliber rifle fired a single round of M221 Armor Piercing Incendiary ammunition. The 671 grain bullet punched through the BTR-60's side armor easily and reached the center of the vehicle. To get there it passed through the driver. Once there, the incendiary charge detonated, filling the APC with fire. The vehicle continued rolling forward and clipped the burned-out BTR before smashing into the obelisk's base.

Kell keyed external microphones. "Give me that car, and you don't have to die!" He shouted it again and again as he drove toward the corner and rounded it. Survivors of the initial roadblock attack ran, arms waving, screaming in terror.

He cut north down the harbor road, then ducked east onto a side street. He leaned the machine left for a second so his sensors could take a reading, then ducked back behind cover. Another BTR was traveling south fast, and infantry trotted behind it.

Not giving them a chance to think, Kell stepped into the street and covered the BTR's turret with the blue crosshairs. He got the gold pulse and triggered another round. As fire flashed within the BTR, he continued crossing the street and launched two smart bullets from the XM-25. They burst amid the advancing infantry squads, and the light show caught the attention of another vehicle further down the line.

The computer identified it. *Oh, shit!*

The T-72's main gun belched flame. The corner of the building behind Kell exploded. The blast knocked him forward, tumbling the warmech into the sliding steel door protecting an electronics shop. Metal screamed then pulled from the rails. Kane's heavy feet tromped their way through display cases. The warmech scraped its head against the ceiling. Kell considered shooting out the security cameras in the shop's corners, but that would have been a waste of bullets.

The collapsing facade spilled bricks, shattered dishes, and dented pans into a heap behind Kane. A smoldering couch teetered on the edge of the second story apartment. Little fires burned below, and a hole had been blown into the next building west.

Kell brought magres up enough to catch the metal from assault rifles and a knee replacement on infantry as they advanced. The T-72 lumbered along after them. He could deal with the infantry, but for the tank, he had nothing. The T-72's armor was fifty times thicker than that of the BTR-60, and it sported machine guns and an anti-aircraft cannon that could rip him apart.

He took one step toward the street and fired a round from the XM-25. It burst in the crowd that had started swarming over the debris. Then he turned and smashed Kane backward through the store's stock room. Two more steps and he crashed through the store's rear wall.

That worked well.

He slammed his way through the next shop—one chock full of carpets, draperies, and linens. He got to the middle of it before he realized it had no stock room. The far wall was its back wall. A step later, the floor's center-joist snapped beneath Kane's weight. The floor crumbled. Kane fell through splintered boards down into a deep basement filled with piled carpets. The store's display stock fell, draping him. That cut off all visual sensor data, but the shock of the landing jogged the infrared sensors back full time.

That small miracle did not help. The basement had been dug to a depth of twenty feet and filled with shelves, most of which he'd crashed through. Kane, with a bit of a running start, might have been able to leap over a six foot obstacle, but it had never been built for climbing out of a square-cut hole. He was as trapped as a tiger in a pit.

He caught ghostly images of men peeking down at him. A few thrust their assault rifles into the hole and burned clips. The bullets clicked like hail on a tin roof. Then a couple other soldiers appeared, holding up what had to be cell phones, snapping pictures. Kell imagined that Kane looked like the star of some forgotten cartoon titled *When Casper the Friendly Ghost Went to War.*

He was tempted to shoot back, but there was no sense to it. Magres and IR showed that two other T-72s had joined the original, one to the east, and the other to the west. They all pulled back sufficiently far that their main cannons could depress enough to blast him out of the ground. It might take a few shots, but they'd get him.

He popped open an access panel and reached for the circuit board controlling the hyper-spatial imaging apparatus. If he smashed that, then redlined the engine and used the excess energy to melt the polymeric muscles, that would pretty much take care of recoverable tech. The fact that doing so would also fill the shell with toxic gasses really didn't please him, but if Kell wasn't getting out, he could at least go out on his own terms.

One of the soldiers stepped to the edge of the pit with a video camera salvaged from the electronics store.

Kell brought one of Kane's arms up and waved bon voyage.

The soldier waved back, then gave him the finger. Then vanished.

A Hellfire missile streaked down and hit the nearest T-72 just aft of the turret. The warhead exploded on impact, creating a fireball so hot that it fried Kane's IR sensors completely and disintegrated the soldier. The explosion evaporated the tank's armor and melted through the chassis. The turret, looking to magres like a blocky lollipop, flipped high into the air, turning over and over.

Two more blasts shook the area, raining more draperies and debris into the cellar. The buildings to the west collapsed beneath the tandem assault that destroyed the two tanks over there. Another explosion, followed by a pair shortly thereafter sent thermal plumes into the air.

"Kell, tell me I didn't get you, too!"

He laughed and closed the access panel. "I'm fine, Mock. Need a carpet? There's a fire sale here."

"Screw the souvenirs. No room on the sub."

"Package made it to the dock?"

"Said they weren't leaving without you." Mock laughed. *"Go. This Reaper has eight more Hellfires. I've got your back, now get yourself home."*

"Obliged, Mock. I imagine you're going to be in a world of hurt for this. Sorry about that."

"Don't be, I think we have it covered."

He smiled at the joy in her voice. "Then I owe you one."

"Come to Vegas. I'll be happy to collect." Mock chuckled. *"First round is yours. Mock out."*

Sarah watched as the sheet-shrouded warmech climbed up the debris pile and out of the basement. She fed him her gun camera visuals and Kell ran Kane straight up the harbor road. At the docks a small boat pulled away as the warmech plunged into the waters. By the time she took one more pass over Zlitan's docks, a bobbing boat adrift in the harbor was the only sign anyone had been there.

She punched the controls over to automatic recovery, then swiveled in her chair. Frost stood there, looking down at Trask's crumpled form. "You finished?"

Frost nodded and tapped his tablet's screen. "Okay, done."

Sarah dropped to a knee beside Trask and slapped him. "Wake up."

The man groaned, a hand snaking down to protect crushed manflesh. "I am going to bury you, Major."

"Yeah, about that." Sarah grabbed the man's tie and used the knot to force his chin up. "Frost works in your section, gets all your assets together, is eager to run an op. You have him set up this op, knowing it's a loser, but you generously give him his shot. If he pulls it off, it's a miracle, and you get the credit. If it fails, he's burned, I'm burned, Kell's burned. You came here to stop us, but it was too late because Frost went rogue and we went with him. That the picture?"

Trask eased himself up against the wall. "Worked like a charm."

"Not really." Sarah jerked a thumb at Frost. "Frost got me a Reaper, so Kell's coming back. And the agents in Zlitan had their cover stories built around being humanitarian aid workers. They're just normal, bleeding heart, innocent kids. In the last fifteen seconds, those kids have posted updates to Facebook that tell about their rescue from Zlitan by a super-soldier, complete with wonderfully grainy and indistinct photos of the XMWP-1. Couple more folks in Zlitan have been Tweeting about the fight. #ironmaninlibya is trending. Your field test is going viral. So, this op, it's a *big* success, but your ability to keep a secret project a *secret*, not looking good."

Trask lay there, gasping. "No, you couldn't. You didn't."

"Oh, but we did. Well, Frost mostly. And it *will* get worse, depending on what your report reads." Sarah straightened up and turned away from him. "You're done, Trask."

He scrambled to his feet. "Now you see here." He grabbed her left shoulder and spun her around.

She reacted.

Kell was right. After breaking Trask's nose, she felt much better.

Michael A. Stackpole is a *New York Times* bestselling author, best known for *Rogue Squadron* and *I, Jedi*. The author of over forty novels, he's won awards for his work in the fields of game design, computer game design, podcasting, screenwriting, graphic novel writing, novel writing and editing. He has an asteroid named after him. His most recent novel is *Of Limited Loyalty*, the second in the Crown Colonies series. He lives outside Phoenix, Arizona and in his spare time plays indoor soccer and enjoys swing dancing.

Trauma Pod

ALASTAIR REYNOLDS

When I come around I'm in a space about the size of a shower cubicle, tipped on its side. I'm flat on my back, resting on a soft padded surface. Curving around me, close enough to touch, are walls of antiseptic white. They wrap around to form a smooth ceiling, broken by hatches and recesses. Cables and tubes emerge through gaps. There's the soft whirr of pumps, the hiss and chug of air circulation. And looking at me right now, peering down from the ceiling just above my own face, is a pair of stereoscopic camera eyes.

I twitch, trying to raise my head enough to get a good look at myself. I've been stripped of my armor. I was wearing combat exo-cladding, but the outer shell's gone now. All that's left is the lightweight mesh suit, and that's ripped and shredded pretty badly. I try and get a better look at my extremities but a pair of hands gently pushes me back down. They poke through a pair of hatches above my sternum, as if there's someone just outside, reaching in.

They're perfectly normal human hands, wearing green surgical gloves.

A woman's voice says: "Stay still, and don't panic, Sergeant Kane. You're going to be fine."

"What..." I start to say.

"That's good. You can hear us, and understand my words. That's very positive. You can speak, too. That's also encouraging. But for the moment, I'd like you to let me do the talking."

They must have pumped something into me, because for the time being I don't feel like arguing with anyone or anything.

"Okay."

A panel has slid open to reveal a screen, and on the screen is a woman's face. Green uniform, black hair tied back under a surgical cap. She's looking right at me—close enough that it's almost uncomfortable. Her lips move.

"You've been wounded, Sergeant."

I manage a smile. "No shit."

I remember fragments, not the whole story. A deep recon insertion gone wrong. Me and the two others... I'll remember their names in a moment. Loiter drones above us, enemy Mechs too close for comfort. Armored support too dispersed to help us. Extraction window compromised. Not the way it was meant to go down.

The white flash of the pulse bomb, the skull-jarring concussion of the shockwave.

Someone screaming "Medic!"

Someone who sounded a lot like me.

"You were lucky. One of our field medical robots was able to reach you in time. The bot deployed its trauma pod and hauled you inside. That's where you are now: in the pod. It's armored, independently powered, and fully capable of keeping you alive until we have an extraction window. The field medical unit has secured the area and established an exclusion volume around your site."

My mouth is very dry, and now that I have some sense of location I begin to pick up on the fact that my head doesn't feel quite right.

"When," I say. "How long. Until extraction."

"Waiting for an update on that right now. Best guess is six to twelve hours, but that may be wide or short of the mark, depending on how things evolve in theatre."

For a second I think: operating theatre, and wonder why the hell that should be my problem. Get me the fuck out of here, then worry about when you can slot me in for surgery.

Then I realize she's talking about a different kind of theatre.

"Have I got that long?"

"That's what we need to talk about. Your injuries have been stabilized, but you're not out of the woods just yet." She pauses. "I'm Doctor Annabel Lyze. I'm linking in from the forward surgical unit in Tango Oscar. My colleagues and I will be with you the whole time you're in the pod, and we'll be handling your case once you've been extracted. I know you feel pretty isolated right now, Sergeant Kane, and that's only natural. But I want you to know that you're not alone."

"Call me Mike," I say.

"Mike it is." She nods. "And you can call me Annabel,

if that helps. I'm right here, Mike. Never more than
a screen away. Look, I can even touch you. These are
my hands you're feeling."

But they're not, and she knows it.

Under the surgical gloves lie bones and sinews of
plastic and metal. They're teleoperated robot hands
which can emerge from any part of the trauma pod that
the situation dictates. Somewhere back in Tango Oscar,
Annabel's wearing haptic feedback gloves—similar to my
own mesh-suit—that provide an exact tactile interface
with their robot counterparts. She can feel every bruise,
every swelling, as if she's right here in the pod with me.
I couldn't ask for better care.

But she's not with me, no matter what she wants
me to think.

"You said my injuries have been stabilized. Are you
ready to tell me the score?"

"Nothing that isn't fixable. You took a bad hit to
your right leg and I'm afraid I had to amputate.
But we can grow that back easily enough. That's not
our main concern here. What I'm worried about is
a bleed on your brain that we need to treat sooner
rather than later."

So the pod's surgical systems have already been busy.
While I was sleeping my damaged leg was removed,
the stump sewn up, my ruined limb ejected through
the pod's disposal vent. I know how it works with
trauma pods, and she's right; they'll grow me a new leg.

But brain surgery?

"You want to cut into my skull, while I'm still in
this thing?"

"Minimally invasive intervention, Mike. There's
a risk, certainly. But there's an even greater risk in

leaving things until later. You may not make it unless we intervene now."

"I was under, and you brought me back to consciousness. What the hell was the point of that?"

"I wanted to talk things through. Give me the word, and I'll go in. But if you'd sooner take your chances and wait for extraction, I'll respect that decision."

The tone of her voice, the look in her eyes, make it abundantly clear what she thinks of my chances if I decide not to opt for surgery. About as good as if I was still out there in the battlefield, gushing blood into the dirt. But I can't just give in, without knowing the odds of rescue.

"Show me what's outside the pod."

"That won't help, Mike."

"Show me anyway. I'm still a soldier. I need to know what's out there."

Annabel purses her lips. "If you insist."

I'm still wearing my military contacts, although I only realize as much when the view of the trauma pod's scrubs out, replaced by a visual feed from the pod's own external camera.

It's not good. I can tell that much from a glance.

I do a slow pan, taking in the blasted, toxic landscape as far as the camera can see. I'm lying flat, or flattish, on a cratered plateau, hemmed in by the craggy ruins of what were once office blocks or retail developments. A vehicle, maybe a school bus, lies on its back fifty meters from me. Some kind of transmission tower or pylon has come down, sagging over the ground contours like the skeleton of some saurian monster. Overhead, the clouds are mustard colored, sagging with airborne toxicity. The horizon ripples with chemical murk.

Pulse bombs flash in the distance. Plasma bolts gash the clouds. Mechs, humanoid and giant-sized, stalk and stride the hellscape that was once a city. I do another full visual sweep and I don't see a single human combatant.

Which isn't too surprising. Since the war went almost entirely robotic, we living soldiers have been increasingly thin on the ground. I wonder if the others got out. Maybe some of them are in pods like me, awaiting extraction. Or maybe they're all dead.

What the fuck was I doing here anyway?

Ah, yes. Deep recon squad. I remember the others' names now. Me, Rorvik, Lomax. Robotics specialists, tasked to observe the behavior of our Mechs, and our enemy's units, under real-time combat conditions. The reason? No one was saying. But the rumors weren't hard to pick up. Some of our units were going rogue. It was said to be happening to the enemy machines as well. No one had a clue why.

Actually, we had some theories. We cram our Mechs with sufficient autonomy to make them independent of human control. We give them wits and smarts, and then wonder why they start doing stuff we didn't ask them to.

Not my problem now, though.

I figure I'm safe for the moment. The field medical robot has done its work, not only of dragging my wounded remains into the pod, but of securing the pod itself. I'm surrounded by a low wall of rubble and battlefield junk, shoved hastily into place to act as a screen. Not to bury me, or complicate my extraction, but to shield me from enemy eyes, cameras, and weapon systems.

I can see the field medical unit. The four-meter

ll robot is circling the pod, keeping the area clear.
ly contacts drop an ident tag on the robot. Unit
X-457 is a headless humanoid chassis with an oval
ap in its torso, a hole I can see right through. Its
rms are muscle-bound with guns, countermeasure-
aunchers, and specialized military-surgical devices.
ts titanium-pistoned legs look spindly, but they're as
trong and shock-resistant as aircraft undercarriage.
'he unit is scary to look at, but it's on my side, and
aat makes all the difference.

I don't remember what happened, what became
f Rorvik and Lomax. They're not my problem now.

I was screaming "Medic!" out of pure reflex. I
idn't need to. As soon as my exo-cladding detected
hat I'd been injured—which was probably sooner
aan my own nervous system—it would have squawked
ne nearest field medical unit. My armor would have
ndertaken some life-preserving measures, but that
vas only a stopgap until the robot arrived. KX-457
vould have detached the pod from its belly recess,
aid it on the ground, and—after a preliminary medi-
al assessment—slid me inside.

Under ordinary circumstances, while the trauma
od was fixing me up, the robot would have plugged
ne pod back into its belly and high-tailed it out of
he combat area. Not an option today, though: too
auch risk of the robot being intercepted and taken
ut. I'm a high-value asset, or so they tell me. Better
o keep the pod in-theatre, under robot protection,
ntil a full extraction squad can come in under close
erial cover.

Meanwhile, the field medical unit maintains maxi-
aum vigilance. Every now and then KX-457 raises one

of its arms and zaps the sky with a plasma cannon
Sometimes, a drone falls out of the clouds. Most o
the Mechs on the ground are friendly, but occasionall
I'll spy an enemy scout unit on the limit of visibility
testing our defenses. They're out there.

I've seen enough. It's clear that I'm not bein
bullshitted. It really would be suicide to go for extrac
tion now.

Which means that if Doctor Annabel Lyze is righ
about the brain bleed, I do need to go under the knife

I pull my point of view back into the pod. Th
battlefield scrubs out. White surroundings again, th
hum and chug of diligent life-support. Disembodie
hands reaching through the walls.

I give Annabel my consent. Go in and fix the bleed
Then get me the fuck out of here.

I come around. The first thing that hits me is tha
I'm safe, back in Tango Oscar. I know this because I'n
definitely not in the trauma pod anymore. Althoug
it has to be said that I'm still in a kind of pod, an
it has the same kind of white interior as the first.

But it can't be the one I woke up in originall
because there just wouldn't be room. I know thi
because there's another body squeezed into this one
another wounded soldier, and that simply wouldn't b
possible in the first pod. Obviously, while I was ou
cold, being operated on, KX-457 was able to complet
the extraction. They've got me in this bigger pod whil
I await my slot in the operating room, or whateve
they've got in mind. Pretty soon it'll be smiles an
high-fives. Welcome home, soldier. You did a goo
job out there.

I wonder what happened to the other guy, the one jammed in next to me?

Then something dawns. Through the pod's insulation, and beyond the background noise of the medical systems, I can still hear the occasional pulse-bomb or plasma cannon discharge.

Either the front moved a lot closer to Tango Oscar while I was out, or I'm not home just yet.

"Can you hear me, Mike?"

"Yes."

Annabel swallows. "It's mostly good news. We arrested the bleed, and I'm very happy about that."

"I don't like that 'mostly.' Why is there another soldier in here with me? Why did you swap me to a bigger pod?"

"It's the same pod, Mike. We haven't moved you. You're still exactly where you were before I put you under."

I try and budge to one side, suddenly uncomfortable. Although I don't achieve much, I have the impression that my silent companion has budged by exactly the same amount, as if glued to my side.

"I'm telling you, there's someone else in here."

"Okay." She pulls back for a moment, whispers something to a colleague before returning. "That's... not unexpected. There's been some damage to your right frontoparietal regions, Mike. Part of it was caused by the original bleed, and part of it was occasioned by our intervention. I stress that we had no practical option; if we hadn't gone in, we wouldn't be having this conversation now. But what you are experiencing now is a hallucination: a kind of out-of-body experience caused by the shutdown of the inhibitory circuits that normally keep your mirror neurons functioning normally. You really are alone, Mike. You just have to take my word for it."

"Like I took your word that the surgery was going to be straightforward?"

"We have to consider this a success, Mike. You're with us and you're stable."

I try and move again, but my skull feels as if it's clamped in a vice. It's not painful, but it's a long way from anything I'd call pleasant. "Is there a fix for this, or am I stuck with it forever?"

"There's a fix for most things. As it happens, we can try some workarounds while you're still in the pod. During surgery I inserted some neural probes at strategic sites around the injured part of your brain. Apart from giving me a much better insight into what's going on in there, compared to the crude resolution of the pod's own scanner, I can also intervene in some critical pathways."

I'm still creeped out by my displaced body image. The body next to mine breathes with me. But it feels dead, like an appendage of me that should have withered and dropped off already.

Still, I need to keep focus. "Meaning what?"

"The neural circuitry involved in your out-of-body sensation is pretty well mapped, Mike. At the moment signals aren't getting where they should due to the damage caused by the bleed. But we can route around those obstructions, using the probes I inserted. Think of them as jumper leads, wiring different parts of your head together. If you're willing, I can attempt to reassert your normal body image."

"Again: why wait until I'm awake, if there's something you can do?"

"Again, I need consent. I also need your subjec-
ve evaluation of the effects. I said the circuits were
ell-mapped, and that's true. But there's enough
liosyncratic variation from individual to individual
) mean we can't be a hundred percent sure of the
utcome of any given intervention."

"In other words, you'll poke a stick into my head,
ir it around and see what happens."

"It's a tiny bit more scientific than that. But it's
ntirely reversible, and if we can lessen your distress
a any way, I think that the small risk involved is
cceptable."

"I'm not distressed."

"Your body says otherwise. Stress hormones peak-
ig. Galvanic skin response off the chart. Fear centre
ghting up like a football stadium. But that's under-
andable, Mike. You've been badly injured, in a war
one. You're being kept alive in a technological coffin,
hile the war continues around you. Under those
ircumstances, who wouldn't be a little rattled?"

For all that she's right—I am rattled—and for all
rat I have no desire to spend another second with
ry phantom self crammed into the pod, my combat
rstincts momentarily trump all other concerns.

"Give me the external feed again."

"Mike, there's no need to concern yourself with
ratters beyond your control."

"Just do it, Annabel."

She mumbles a curse and then I'm outside again,
eing the world through the pop-up camera fixed to
re outside of the pod like a periscope. I spin through
rree hundred and sixty, assessing my surroundings.
m still where the field medical unit left me, still

hemmed in by a makeshift cordon of rubble and junk
But I must have been out for hours. It's dark now
the camera viewing the world in grey-green infrared
It's only when the horizon flashes with an explosion
or something strobes the cloud deck above, that I get
any real sense of the tactical environment.

How long was I under the knife? More than
few hours, evidently. And yet it didn't feel like any
time at all.

"I want you to be straight with me, Annabel. The
brain surgery. How long did it take?"

"It doesn't matter, Mike."

"It does to me."

"All right, then. Eight hours. There were complica
tions. But you came through. Isn't that the main thing?

"Eight hours and you're still on duty? You said the
best guess for my extraction was six to twelve hours.

"And there's still every possibility of it happening
within that window. Look, I couldn't abandon you
Mike. But we'll be getting you out very soon now."

"Don't jerk me around. You and I both know they
won't try until daybreak, at the earliest." She can
argue with that, and she doesn't try. The combat
zone is hazardous at the best of times, but at night
as the ground cools, it's almost impossible to move
without being detected, scoped, targeted. I visualize
my trauma pod, lit up like a neon gravestone. And
know I can't just sit here doing nothing.

"Let me address that body image problem," Anna
bel says.

Something snaps inside me. It's time to start being
a soldier again. "Give me full-theatre oversight. I want
to know what's really out there."

"Mike, I'm not really sure this is in your best—"

"Just do it."

She really has no option but to give me what I want. I may be injured, but I'm still a high-value asset and my active authority means that I still get to call the shots.

The oversight is a real-time map of the battle zone, out to a radius of fifteen kilometers. It's compiled from intelligence gathered by Mechs, drones, cameras, even the still-functioning armor of dead or immobilized combatants. Most of that intelligence originates from our own side, but some of it comes from intercepting enemy transmissions, and doubtless they're doing something similar with ours. The data is woven together and projected onto my contacts. With subvocal commands I can scan and zoom at will.

I take in what the map has to tell me, knowing I should have done this sooner, rather than take Annabel's word that everything was going to be moonbeams and kittens. Because it's not.

And I'm in a world of trouble.

A phalanx of enemy machines is coming my way. They're ten kilometers out, but making steady progress. They may not know I'm here yet, but there's no guarantee of that. The deployment of a field medical unit is a gold-plated giveaway that someone's taken a hit, and there's nothing the enemy would rather do than capture or eliminate a high-value human asset. I study the numbers and the distribution of the advancing formation, measuring the enemy's strength against my sole ally: the lone medical unit. KX-457's weapons and countermeasures aren't to be trifled with. But against a dozen or more enemy Mechs and drones?

There's no contest. Nor is there much hope of my little resting place remaining undetected, when the enemy units arrive en masse.

That's when the fight or flight response kicks in. It's a hard nitrous surge, as if fear itself is being pumped into my blood. I'm not going to just stay here and hope that luck's on my side. We need to be moving, and moving now.

Yes, there's risk in that as well—especially at night. That's why my extraction is still on hold. But set against my chances of surviving the arrival of those enemy units, running suddenly looks a lot more attractive.

I pull my point of view back into the trauma pod.

"Tell the field medical unit to scoop me up. We're shipping out."

"I can't issue that order, Mike."

"Can't or won't?"

"We're running simulations now, and they're telling us that you have a statistically improved chance of survival if you remain right where you are."

"By what margin?"

"Enough of a one that I'd really urge you to consider this course of action very thoroughly."

If the odds were that persuasive, she'd tell me up front. My head's still clamped tight. But if I could shake it I would. "Bring the medical unit in."

"Mike, please."

"Just do it. There's no point putting a human being in the combat zone if you won't trust their judgment."

She relents. I don't need to see KX-457 approaching; I hear the boulders being dislodged around me and then feel the trauma pod lurch and tilt as the robot hauls it from the ground. I'm rotated through ninety

degrees, until my head is higher than my feet—or
rather, I remind myself, foot. Then I feel the reassuring clunk as the trauma pod is docked with the oval
recess in the medical unit's torso. Systems interface:
power, control, sensory. I'm no longer a wounded
man in a humming coffin. I'm a baby in the belly of
a killer robot, and that has to be an improvement.

"What are your orders?" the robot asks me.

Recalling the disposition of enemy forces, I start
to tell KX-457 to get me as far west as it can. Then
I think of something better than being taken along
for the ride. I don't need to be able to move my own
body to control the robot. What remains of my own
mesh-suit layer should be more than capable of detecting intentions, the merest twitch of a neuromuscular
impulse, and giving me appropriate feedback.

"Let me drive you."

"Mike," Annabel interrupts. "You don't need this
extra task load. Let the robot extract you, if that's
what you insist on doing. But there's no need for you
to drive it. In your present condition, your reflexes
are going to be no match for the robot's own battle
routines."

But if I'm going to die out here, I'd sooner be doing
something than just being carried along for the ride.

"I know what I'm doing, Annabel. KX-457, assign
me full command authority. Maintain the link until
I say otherwise."

My point of view shifts again. The field medical
unit has no head, but there's a suite of cameras and
sensors built into its shoulder yoke, and that's where
I seem to be looking down from.

I look down at myself. I feel exactly as tall as

the KX-457—there's no sense that I'm contained in a much smaller body, down in the belly pod. And those titanium legs and arms move to my will, just as if they were part of me. I feel whole again, and strong. That phantom image is still there, but it's much less troubling than when I was jammed into the trauma pod.

I'm still *in* the pod, of course. Need to remind myself of that, because it would be easy to lose track of things.

We move, the KX-457 and I. I should say the KX-457, Annabel, and I, because when those hands reach through to adjust my leg dressing, or the catheter in my arm, or the post-operative clamp on my head, it's hard not to feel that she's along for the ride, my wellbeing never less than uppermost in her thoughts. And while it's clear that she doesn't entirely approve of my decision to ship out, I'm still glad to have someone to talk to.

"How long have you been in Tango Oscar, Annabel?" I ask, as I work my past way the shallow, smoke-blackened remains of what was once a glorious air-conditioned shopping mall.

She considers my question carefully. "It's been eighteen months now, Mike. They cycled me in from Echo Victor, and before that it was Charlie Zulu."

"Charlie Zulu." I say it with a kind of reverence. "I hear it was pretty intense there."

She nods. Her face is projected into a small window in my view, fighting for attention with an ever-changing dance of tactical analysis overlays, flagging every potential threat or hiding place. "We had our work cut out." She gives a small dry laugh, but it's clear that the memory's still raw. "That was before the new pods came on-line. The old units didn't have anything like as much autonomy as the ones we're used to now. It was hands-on telesurgery, day and night. We were dying on our feet from exhaustion and stress, and we weren't even out there, in theatre. We saved as many as we could, but when I think about those we couldn't help..." She falls silent.

"I'm sure you did everything you could."

"I hope we did. But there are limits. Even now, we can't always work miracles."

"Whatever happens to me, you've done all that anyone could expect, Annabel. Thanks for sticking with me, all those hours. You must be worn out."

"Whatever it takes, Mike. I'm not going away."

"I hope we get to meet up," I risk telling her, even though it feels like I'm jinxing my chances of ever getting out alive. "Just so I can thank you in person."

Annabel's smile is radiant. "I'm sure we will."

In that moment I don't doubt that I'll make it.

That's when oversight picks up a squadron of enemy scout drones, coming in low just under the cloud deck. My own sensors haven't seen them at all.

I scan my field of view for concealment options, and decide to duck into the corrugated shoebox that used to contain an indoor amusement park. I pick my way through rubble and the blackened, snaking wreckage of a roller coaster, until I'm sure the drones won't pick out my infrared or EM signature. There are fallen machines under my titanium feet, and bodies. I crunch through the shattered carcasses of plastic horses and ride-on centipedes.

"We'll need to lie low for a couple of hours, until those drones are out of the area." I squat, shutting down essential systems. Just a bleed of power to the trauma pod, and another to the KX-457's central processor core.

"How will you know it's safe?"

The building's shell is blocking ambient comms, interfering with oversight. "I won't. But if they're on the usual sweep pattern, we'll be fine once they've passed over."

"Then there's no reason for me not to take a look at that body image issue, is there?"

"It's not bothering me as much as it did."

"Let me fix it anyway. If you don't nip these things in the bud, they can become a big problem during recovery."

I offer a mental shrug. "If you think it's for the best."

"I do," Annabel says. "I do."

I give it two hours, then three to be on the safe side. I creep my way out of the amusement park, until I'm almost back under the open air. I'm expecting full oversight to be restored as soon as I regain normal comms, but that's not what happens. Coverage is still patchy. I pick up intelligence from nearby eyes and ears, but nothing further out than a few kilometers. The fault may be in my own systems, but it's much more likely that there's been an attack against a critical node in our distributed grid. Those drones may not have been looking for me at all, but for a vulnerability in our comms network.

It's still dark, and the drones could still be out there. But I have to trust that they've left the area, and that the phalanx of heavy Mechs has continued on its original vector. It might take days to repair oversight, assuming the fault isn't in me. I can't wait that long. I'd rather die moving, than waste away hiding from an enemy I can't see.

"We'll give it until dawn," I tell Annabel. "It should be okay to cross open ground then, even with limited oversight."

"How do you feel now?"

"Different."

That's an understatement. But it's true. My phantom twin has vanished. I don't feel another body tagging along next to mine. And I guess I should be glad of that, because it means Annabel's neural cross-wiring has had some effect. But I don't feel the slightest flicker of elation.

Something else is different.

It's not a question of being distressed by my phantom twin anymore. He's gone, and with good riddance. But now it's my own body that's changed. I can sense it, hanging beneath my point of view like some withered, useless vestigial appendage, but it doesn't feel like any part of me. I don't inhabit it, and I have no wish to. All I want to do is flinch away from it. I was indifferent before, but now it repulses me.

I retain enough intellectual detachment to understand that this response is neurological. On some level, something has gone catastrophically wrong with my body image. It's as if my sense of self, what really matters to me, has extracted itself from my injured human body and taken up residence in the armored perfection of the field medical unit.

Clearly this is fucked-up.

But even knowing this, I don't want to go back to the way things used to be. Definitely not: I'm stronger now, and bigger. I stride this ruined world like a colossus. And as much as that revolting thing disgusts me, it's a small price to pay. I have a certain dependency on it, after all. That's a no-brainer.

But there's one other detail I need to address.

Comms is shot to shit. Oversight is a patchwork of blind spots. So how in hell is Doctor Annabel Lyze able to reach over from Tango Oscar and teleoperate her magic green hands?

More than that: how is Doctor Annabel Lyze able to talk me at all? How am I able to see her always smiling, never-tiring face?

"Don't do that, Mike."

"Don't do what?"

"Don't do what you're about to do. Don't check the comms registry. It won't do you any good at all."

I hadn't thought of checking the comms registry. But you know, now that she's put the idea in my head, that's an excellent fucking idea.

I call up the history. I scroll through the log, going back minutes, tens of minutes, hours.

15.56.31.07—zero validated packets
15.56.14.11—zero validated packets
15.55.09.33—zero validated packets
...
11.12.22.54—zero validated packets

And I learn that KX-457 has been out of contact with Tango Oscar—or any command sector, for that matter—for more than nineteen hours. In all that

ime, it's been acting entirely autonomously, relying
on its own in-built intelligence.

So has the trauma pod. From the moment it was
deployed—before I was hauled in and treated—the pod
was also operating independently of human control.
There was no kindly surgeon on the other side of that
screen. There was just... software. Software clever and
agile enough to mimic a reassuring presence.

Doctor Annabel Lyze.

Doctor Annabel lies.

The question is: was that software running in the
pod, or in my own head?

It's day when they find me. Not the enemy, but
my own side. Although by that point I suppose the
distinction is moot.

I find voice amplification mode. My words boom
out, distorted and godlike. "Don't come any closer."

There are two of them, both wearing full battle
armor, backed up by a couple of infantry Mechs.
The Mechs have shoulder and arm-mounted plasma
cannon batteries locked onto me.

"Mike, listen to me. You've been injured. You went
in the trauma pod and... something got screwed up."

Some part of me recognizes the voice—Rorvik?
Lomax? But it's a small part and easily ignored.

"Get back."

The figure who spoke dares to stand a little taller,
even as their companion maintains a nervous, bent-
at-the-knees crouch. I admire the speaker's boldness,
even as I don't pretend to fully understand it. Then
the figure reaches up and does something even riskier,
which is to undo their face mask, allowing it to flop

aside on its hinge. Framed by the airtight seal of a helmet I see a woman's face, and again there's a flicker of recognition, which I instantly crush.

"Mike, you need to trust us. There's only one way you're going to get help, and that's to relinquish control of the field medical unit. You have brain damage, very severe brain damage, and we need to get it fixed before it gets worse."

"I am not Mike," I tell her. "I am field medical unit KX-457."

"No, Mike. KX-457 is the machine treating you. You're experiencing some kind of body image crisis, but that's all it is. A neurological fault, caused by the damage to your frontal cortex. You're inside the robot, but you are not the robot itself. This is very, very important. Can you understand what I'm saying, Mike?"

"I understand what you are saying," I tell her. "But you're wrong. Mike died. I couldn't save him."

She takes a breath. "Mike, listen to me carefully. We need you back. You are a high-value asset, and we can't afford to lose you, not with the way things have been going. Where you are now, in the machine . . . you're not safe. We need you to give up control of the field medical unit and allow us to decouple the trauma pod. Then we can take you back to Tango Oscar and get you fixed up."

"There's nothing that needs fixing."

"Mike . . ." she starts to say something, then seems to abandon her train of intent. Maybe she thinks I'm too far gone for that kind of persuasion. Instead she turns to her comrade, fixes her mask back on, and nods in response to some exchange I can't intercept.

The plasma batteries open fire. I'm strong, and well

armored, but I'm no match for two infantry units. They don't mean to take me out, though. The shots skim past me, wasting most of their energy against the sagging, geologically-layered shell of a collapsed parking structure. Only a fraction of the discharges cause me any harm. I register peripheral armor ablation, loss of forearm-weapons functionality, some sensor blackouts. It's enough to remove my capacity for retaliation, but they haven't touched my processor core.

Of course they haven't. It's not that they care about me. But foolishly or otherwise, they're still thinking of the soldier I was meant to save. They want to disable me, but not to do anything that might endanger the still-breathing corpse I carry inside. And now that I've been de-clawed, now that I've been half-blinded, they imagine they can take me apart like some complex puzzle or bomb, without harming my human cargo.

Needless to say, I'm not having any of that. .

"Stop," I say.

They stop. The plasma batteries glow a vile pink. My two human watchers crouch in wary anticipation. The woman says: "Give us Mike, and we'll leave you be. That's a promise."

What they mean is, give us Mike, and we'll happily blast you to slag.

"You can have Mike back," I say. "All of him."

There's that wordless exchange again. "Good…" The woman says, as if she can't quite believe her luck. "That's good."

"Here's the first installment."

I've been a busy little beaver, while we've been having our little chat. Even holding up my side of

the conversation, even being attacked, hasn't stoppe‹
me from working.

And what work! Exquisite surgery, even if do sa‹
so myself. There's really very little that a trauma po‹
can't do, with all the gleaming sharp instruments a‹
its disposal. The beauty is that I don't even have t‹
know anything about medicine. I just tell the pod wha‹
must be accomplished, and the autonomous system‹
take care of the rest. I no more need to know abou‹
surgery than a human needs to know about digestion‹

So, for instance, if I were to say: remove as muc‹
of Mike as is compatible with the continued integrit‹
of his central nervous system, then the trauma po‹
will enact my order. And when the work has bee‹
done, the surplus material will be ejected throug‹
the waste disposal vent in the pod's lower end fairing‹
Not incinerated, not mashed, but spat out whole, s‹
that there can be no question of its biological origin‹

That's important, because my witnesses have t‹
understand that I mean what I say. They must gras‹
that this is no hollow threat. Mike means nothing t‹
me, but he means a lot to them, and by a perverse‹
twist that makes him valuable to me as well.

While Mike's inside me, they'll let me live.

I back off, and allow them to inspect my offering‹
There's a moment when they don't know quite wha‹
to make of it, a hiatus before the horror kicks in‹
Then they get the picture. That's a lot of Mike on th‹
ground. But you don't need to be a brain surgeon t‹
work out that there's a lot more of Mike still in me‹

"This is what's going to happen," I tell them. "You'r‹
going to let me leave. I have no weapons, as yo‹
know. You can destroy me, that's true. But do yo‹

hink you can do that and get inside me before the
rauma pod has ceased operation?"

"Don't do this," the woman says, amplified voice
ipping through her mask. "We can negotiate. We can
work something out."

"That's what we're already doing." Choosing my
noment, I turn around to present my back to them.
With my sensors damaged, I genuinely don't know
what they're doing. Maybe they think I've already
aken Mike apart. Perhaps those plasma cannon bat-
eries are charging up again. If they are, I doubt that
'll feel a thing when the moment comes.

I start walking. And from somewhere comes the
glimmer of a plan. I'm safe while they think Mike's
nside me. Frankly, though, I'd rather kill myself than
walk around with that thing still attached.

So when I'm under cover, out of range of spying
eyes and snooping drones, I'll pull what remains of
Mike out of the trauma pod and smash his central
nervous system to a mushy grey-pink pulp.

Mike won't miss it, after all. Mike's long past the
point of missing anything at all.

So am I.

Alastair Reynolds was born in Barry in 1966. He
pent his early years in Cornwall, then returned to
Wales for his primary and secondary school education.
He completed a degree in astronomy at Newcastle,
hen a PhD in the same subject at St Andrews in
Scotland. He left the UK in 1991 and spent the next
ixteen years working in the Netherlands, mostly for
he European Space Agency, although he also did a

stint as a postdoctoral worker in Utrecht. He had been writing and selling science fiction since 1989, and published his first novel, *Revelation Space*, in 2000. He has recently completed his tenth novel and has continued to publish short fiction, which has appeared in magazines such as *Asimov's*, *Interzone*, and *Light speed*. His novel *Chasm City* won the British Science Fiction Award, and he has been shortlisted for the Arthur C. Clarke award three times. In 2004 he left scientific research to write full time. He married in 2005 and returned to Wales in 2008, where he lives in Rhondda Cynon Taff.

Contained Vacuum

DAVID SHERMAN

According to *Janes Commercial Starfleets of the Confederation of Human Worlds*, the unidentified starship off the *Dayzee Mae*'s port bow was the SS *Runstable*, which had vanished two years previously, along with her crew and cargo.

Sergeant Tim Kerr, of the Confederation Marine Corps, stood on the bridge of the *Dayzee Mae*, watching the derelict ship on the display. The ship's acting captain, Lieutenant Junior Grade McPherson, had just finished briefing him. The *Runstable*'s cargo had been destined for twenty different worlds, none of which were near enough to this jump point to explain why the ship might be where it was. And all of the containers she was carrying when last heard from were missing; the superstructure made a narrow tower over the empty container deck. It was emitting a distress signal but carried no friend or foe identification.

"She must have been taken by pirates," McPherson said, "then abandoned here. This location is far enough off normal trade routes that she wouldn't be found quickly. We don't have a surveillance tech aboard," he added apologetically, "and we lack the necessary equipment to detect lifeforms on her. So you'll be going in blind."

Kerr nodded silently, his gaze intent on the latest display, which showed the starship in fuzzy detail. Her near-space running lights were on, but her passenger hatch and a bridge hatch were open. No lights showed through the open hatches.

The *Dayzee Mae* was a civilian starship, confiscated by the Confederation navy when they caught her supporting an illegal alien slavery operation on the twin worlds Opal and Ishtar. McPherson and his crew were ferrying her to the navy base on Thorsfinni's World where another crew would transport her to wherever the Court of Inquiry determined she should go. So, naturally, she didn't have military-grade sensors. She did, however, have one piece of military equipment never before found on a civilian freighter.

Finally Kerr said, "It could be an ambush. I want to use the THB and force an entryway. We'll enter through the rear of the bridge." The THB, Tweed Hull Breacher, was used by Confederation Marines to cut their way into hostile or potentially hostile starships. The THB carried by the *Dayzee Mae* had been used by the Marines when they boarded and took her.

"You've got it, Sergeant." McPherson gave a wry grin. "You're our expert on hostile boardings."

Kerr grunted. He hoped the boarding wouldn't be against a hostile force; he and his men had seen enough action on their latest deployment, and were on their way home from it. Second squad, third platoon, Company L of 34th Fleet Initial Strike Team's infantry battalion had been given the assignment of providing security on the *Dayzee Mae* during her transit to Thorsfinni's World because the squad had suffered badly in the action on Ishtar. Two of the fire team leaders and one other Marine were still nominally on light duty from their wounds, and two new men weren't yet completely integrated into the squad. Their chain of command thought the duty would give them a chance to rest and recuperate.

"We're Marines," Sergeant Kerr said a short time later, when some of his men groaned at being told about the boarding mission. "Everyone in Human Space expects us to do anything necessary, at any time, in any place, regardless of difficulties."

"We're Marines," Corporal Rachman Claypoole—one of the injured fire team leaders—muttered. "We do the difficult immediately. The impossible might take a little longer."

"That's right, Rock," Kerr said. "Now take your fire teams to the arms locker to check out your weapons and armored vacuum suits."

"With chameleon overalls?" Corporal Chan asked.

"Yes," he said. There was no telling who or what they might find aboard the derelict. The invisibility provided by chameleons could prove to be vital.

"*Armored* suits, sir? Are we expecting trouble, Corporal Claypoole?" asked PFC Berry, one of the two new men in the squad.

There were vacuum suits, and there were *armored* vacuum suits. One protected the wearer from the vacuum of outer space, and the micrometeorites that swarmed through it. *Armored* vacuum suits protected the wearer from the flechettes that could shred an unarmored suit, and almost all other known projectiles as well as plasma weapons such as the Marines' own blasters.

Claypoole snorted. "We're Marines boarding an unknown starship in interstellar space. We don't have an invitation. No shit, we're expecting trouble."

It took more than two hours for the Hull Breacher to travel the 200 klicks between the *Dayzee Mae* and the derelict. The Marines stood quietly during that time, sweating into their armored suits, doing their best to ignore itches, thinking—or trying not to think—about what might meet them on board the SS *Runstable*.

It's odd, Kerr thought, *that she's here. And nobody noticed her when the* Grandar Bay *came through when we were on our way to Ishtar.* He struggled to quell the knot that tightened in his stomach at the wrongness of the situation.

The pilot, EM3 Mark Resort, brought the THB into contact with rear of the *Runstable*'s tower as smoothly as any first class could have, and it touched the starship's hull with barely a bump. He grappled the THB to the hull with its magnets, and fired up the cutters. Everything went smoothly, and in mere moments he had an opening cut through the rear of the outer hull of the *Runstable*'s bridge deck. It only took a few more seconds for him to cut through the inner hull.

"First fire team, go!" Kerr snapped. He briefly touched helmets with Resort before leaving the THB. "Good landing, squid. You can drive me anytime."

Corporal Chan showed no lingering effects of his wound when he darted into the bridge and led his men toward the port side of the bridge. Corporal Claypoole and his men ran to the starboard as soon as Chan and his fire team cleared the breach. The six Marines spread out and covered all directions with their plasma blasters.

Kerr entered the bridge more slowly, walking without using his boots' magnets to hold him to the deck—the *Runstable*'s artificial gravity was still on—and stood between the first two fire teams. Using his helmet's light gatherer screen, he looked around; it showed him everything in stark black and white, with a few shades of gray, and negatively affected his depth perception. The bridge was about ten meters deep and thirty wide. Centered on the side the Marines had entered was the captain's chair, flanked by the navigator's and helmsman's stations. They faced large displays on the opposite bulkhead. The displays were blank. Consoles were lined up below the blank displays—probably crew stations. What looked like an airlock hatch was at either end of the bridge compartment.

Kerr couldn't discern any damage in the odd view through his light gatherer. The knot in his stomach tightened further. Something was very wrong here; this wasn't a simple derelict starship. He looked to his rear. Corporal Doyle and his men stood stolidly just inside the bridge. But Kerr knew that was an illusion; they had to be shifting their weight, even jittering, inside their armored vacuum suits. His motion detector didn't pick up anything other than his Marines.

Kerr advanced to the captain's station. Keypads on the armrests of the chair were clearly labeled, and he found the keys to open the airlocks at each end of the bridge. "Heads up," he said, and opened the airlocks. He quickly found the *Runstable*'s log. He scanned though it, beginning with the most recent entry, while copying its contents to his comp.

"Find anything interesting, Honcho?" Claypoole asked.

Kerr shook his head, not caring that the gesture wasn't visible. "Everything looks normal, right up to the last entry, dated about two years ago. The last entry is interrupted in mid-word." His comp beeped, signaling that the download was finished. Finished with the log, he checked the starship's systems. As near as he could tell, none of them were damaged, just offline—including nearly all life support—with one exception.

"The ship's gravity seems to be on throughout the ship," he announced over his comm's squad circuit. Then, "Check out the compartments beyond the airlocks. First fire team, left, second to the right."

"Aye-aye," Chan and Claypoole answered.

They were back in moments. Each had the same report: The compartments were smaller than the bridge and had storage lockers that all seemed to be empty, with airlocks at the far end that opened to space. Claypoole added that there was a ladder heading below in the compartment to the bridge's starboard end.

Kerr thought for a moment, then said, "Listen up, second squad. We're going to check this girl out, top to bottom. Rock, is Wolfman up to running point?" Kerr looked at the reddish blur that was Lance Corporal MacIlargie. It had to be his imagination, but he could have sworn that MacIlargie's armored vacuum suit gave an eager twitch at the question.

On order, third fire team joined the squad at the head of the ladder, a shaft with a hand rail on each side that descended into the bowels of the tower.

Kerr gave the route order. "Second fire team, me, third, first. Go."

"Aye-aye," Claypoole said. He pointed at MacIlargie and said, "You heard the man. Go."

"Right." MacIlargie gripped one of the handrails, pointed the muzzle of his blaster between his feet, and stepped into the shaft. The rail drew him down.

Claypoole let MacIlargie's helmet clear the level of the deck, then followed. Another deck appeared seven meters down.

"Into it, Wolfman," Claypoole said.

All of the spaces on this level were open to the corridor.

The level was surprisingly smaller than the bridge level. By examining the *Runstable*'s schematics stored on their comps, the Marines saw that the difference was conduit space behind the bulkheads, allowing the power, life support, and other commands to flow between the bridge and all other areas of the starship. When they located the well-concealed access panels, everything looked to be in order behind them; there wasn't enough room inside to hide a body, alive or dead.

It was at the third level below the bridge that they finally ran into a closed compartment.

Kerr signaled Claypoole, who banged his armored fist on the hatch. His armor augmented his strength so that he hit the hatch almost hard enough to dent its plasteel. He pressed the "announce" button, hoping there were lights inside that would flash to alert any occupants who might not be able to hear the banging that indicated someone was at the hatch.

When there was no response, Kerr motioned Claypoole aside and stepped to the hatch himself—if a frightened civilian might die because of what he was about to do, he wanted the death to be on him, not on one of his men. He slapped the "open" plate, and the hatch slid aside.

MacIlargie leaped through the hatch before it was fully open and spun to one side. Claypoole was on his heels, and spun to the other side.

"Dammit!" Kerr swore. He didn't wait for Berry to complete the fire team's maneuver before he darted through and joined Claypoole and MacIlargie. "I told you to wait for me."

"Sorry, Honcho," MacIlargie said. "I didn't get the word."

They found a corpse huddled in a storage closet of the otherwise empty room. The lack of atmosphere had kept any bacteria or mold from living and taking root anywhere in the starship, so the corpse hadn't rotted. Instead, its own intestinal flora had grown and burst it from the inside, spattering gore around the interior of the closet.

Berry gagged—a strictly reflexive action, as the remains gave off no stench since there was no atmosphere in the compartment.

"You upchuck in that helmet, you'll be in trouble, Marine," Claypoole snarled, choking down his own gorge.

"Right. Trouble," Berry gasped, turning away from the sight.

Kerr's stomach was stronger, or he was better prepared for the sight when he looked into the closet.

"How do you think he died?" Claypoole asked.

Kerr's shrug went unseen inside his chameleoned armor. "Starved. Maybe dehydrated. Do you see any sign of violence?"

"No," Claypoole said softly. "He doesn't look like sudden decompression killed him, either."

Kerr noted the compartment the corpse was in on his comp, then ordered, "Move out."

They found three more desiccated corpses before they reached the lowest deck of the tower. One, they assumed, was the ship's surgeon, as the otherwise unidentifiable corpse was in the infirmary.

"Where are the rest of them?" Claypoole wondered out loud.

"In the subdeck," Kerr said. "Maybe ejected into space. Maybe sold as slaves somewhere. Maybe set free on some out-world." Disgust came into his voice as he added, "Maybe nobody will ever know." He shook his head, unseen inside his chameleoned armor.

"A-Are we checking the subdeck?" Corporal Doyle asked nervously.

"We're checking the whole damn ship," Kerr said flat-voiced. "Doyle, you asked, you lead the way."

Doyle audibly swallowed. "Aye-aye, Sergeant Kerr. Summers, me, Johnson," he gave his fire team's order of movement. In infra, Kerr saw Doyle's armored suit turn as he looked side to side along the passageway for access to the subdeck that ran below the container deck.

"It's to the right," Kerr said, glancing at his schematic of the *Runstable*.

"To the right, Summers," Doyle repeated. He followed in Summers's wake.

The subdeck was one continuous cavern, interrupted at regular intervals by evenly spaced pillars that kept the decking and overhead from flexing away from—or into—each other. Despite the breadth and length of the hold, it felt claustrophobic; the overhead was less than five meters above the deck. The machines that kept the *Runstable* and all its systems operating were arranged on the deck. Cargo-moving cranes and lighters were drawn below deck and battened down. Ship's stores were stowed and marked as such near access shafts from above.

Kerr turned his helmet's ears all the way up and listened. He didn't expect to hear any sounds, not in vacuum, but he thought that vibrations through the deck might register through his boots as subsonics, and straining his ears might help him "hear" the vibrations. All he felt was the faint thrumming of the gravity generators.

"Fire team leaders," Kerr ordered, "use your motion detectors. Have one man use his light gatherer, the other his infra. Leaders, use both. I want to know immediately if anybody detects anything. Do it now." Kerr himself used his light gatherer and infrared screens in conjunction. He compared what he could see with the schematic on his comp and found that six aisles cut between the machinery and stacks of other containers that ran the length of the subdeck. He climbed to the top of the nearest machine housing and looked as far as he could, which wasn't much more than fifty meters—there wasn't enough light or the light gatherer to see any farther, and what e could see was dim. Still, he saw what looked like ross-passages between groups of machine housings nd other equipment.

"Listen up. We're going the length of this hold. 'irst fire team, take the starboard-most aisle. One Marine in the aisle, one on top of the machinery n each flank of the aisle. Second, the next, third, he next. Same top-bottom-top spacing. When we each the far end, everybody move over three aisles. 'hat'll put third fire team on the outer side. If you ee anything that looks like it's been opened, let me now and check it out. Questions?"

"Is 'do we gotta' an appropriate question?" MacIl-rgie asked.

"Stand by for a head smack when we get back to he *Dayzee Mae*," Claypoole snapped before Kerr ould respond.

"Dumb question, huh?" MacIlargie said.

"Dumb as they come," Claypoole confirmed.

"That's enough," Kerr barked. "Get into your posi-ons and move out."

Kerr kept an eye on his men and saw that they idn't rush, but looked into everything that might have een opened, and checked behind everything that ould be checked behind, just as he told them to. It ook more than an hour to cover the three hundred eters to the bow, but the only thing they discovered hat seemed out of the ordinary was almost none of he machinery was operating—just what was needed provide gravity and to power the near-space run-ing lights.

Kerr checked his men visually to make sure all

were present, and verified that with the display o
his comp.

"All right," he said, "shift over three aisles." Th
fire teams were in their new positions within tw
minutes. Kerr made one more visual check, an
ordered, "Move out."

Fifty meters on, Fisher's icon on Kerr's displa
suddenly began blinking red.

"Chan, report!" Kerr snapped.

"Fisher's down," Chan came back. "I don't knov
what happened."

"Hold your position, I'll be right there." Kerr wa
in the central of the three aisles along which th
Marines were moving. He clambered to the top o
the machinery between him and his first fire tean
and began crossing it toward first fire team's positio
as fast as he could.

He was halfway there when something too fast t
make out flashed past his vision, barely above foot-leve
His head jerked in the direction the blur seemed t
come from, and thought he saw a faint blip of red, bu
it was gone from his sight before he could be sure

"We aren't alone down here!" he shouted. H
snapped off three rapid fire plasma bolts from h
blaster. The first two bolts of star-stuff slagged a hol
through the thin metal casing of a container that pro
jected higher than the rest of the machinery. The thir
bolt went all the way through and ended in a brillia
flash of light from behind it. He dashed to the edg
of the machinery he was standing on and leapt dow
from it to join Chan. Along the way he wondered, *Ar*
there Skinks here? He didn't know anything else th
would flash like that after being hit by a blaster bol

To Chan on the fire team circuit, "What's Fisher's atus?"

"Something blew right through him!" Chan said. Through and through. His body suit sealed his wound ad sedated him. I slapped patches on his armor, so e's not losing air." His voice grew haunted. "But hat the hell hit him?"

Kerr remembered the blur that was too fast to see, d shuddered. The only thing he could think of that ent that fast and could punch a hole right through an mored vacuum suit was a railgun. But railguns were aly used by Skinks, and were crew-served weapons. his seemed to have been a personal weapon. He membered the flash of light that met his third shot; e Skinks vaporized in a flash of light when they were t by a plasma bolt—nobody knew why—but that was the atmosphere of a planet, and how could they be uring in the vacuum of the abandoned freighter? These cinks—if that's what they were—were also somehow ble to detect where a chameleoned Marine was, and t close enough to shoot him. *What is happening here?*

"Railgun, I think," Kerr said, answering Chan's ques- on. *Now I know why the gravity is turned on*, he ought. *The Skinks, or whoever, need it for themselves.*

"Does anybody have anything?" Kerr shouted into s comm. "Motion detector, infra, anything?"

"No," "Negative," "Nothing," the answers came back.

"All right," he said, knowing that nothing was actu- ly all right. "I got one. Probably the one that shot isher. But it doesn't matter if that's the one—you ow there are more."

"D-Do you think this was a trap?" Doyle asked.

"That's damn likely. Maybe more than just insic the ship." Kerr not only thought there were mo Skinks in the *Runstable*'s subdeck, he was afraid the also had a warship near enough to jump here ar destroy the *Dayzee Mae*.

He toggled to the long range comm. If the com could get through the bulkhead of the subdeck ar make it to the distant starship, he could give the warning. He climbed to the top of the machine he was taking cover behind and found something hunker down behind while he used his comm.

"*Dayzee Mae, Dayzee Mae*, this is Hellhound. Ove Nobody had expected the Marines to have to conta the *Dayzee Mae* except over the THB's ship-to-sh comm, so they hadn't assigned comm call signs. B he was certain that Petty Officer Craven would re: ize who was calling—who but a Marine would c: himself Hellhound?—and that the call meant troubl

"...llhou... ...ae. How do ...ou read m.. came the reply.

Kerr swore before toggling his comm to transm "You're badly broken, *Dayzee Mae*. How you me? Ove

It took a moment for a reply to come. It was broken as the first.

"...ellhoun... ...Mae. Yo... br...en. Say ...gin. las... Ove...."

Damn, Kerr muttered. He could make out enoug to know that the *Dayzee Mae* couldn't hear him a more clearly than he could hear them. *Well, you* what *you can with what you've got.* "*Dayzee M*c we've got Skinks. I say again, we've got Skinks. Ove

"*He*... ...*nd, Dayz*... Inks. I do... un...an Ov..." It sounded like McPherson's voice.

"Skinks. I say again, Skinks are on the *Runstable*. Over." Kerr heard the CRACK-*sizzle* of blaster fire behind him, and hoped his comm picked it up—that would let McPherson know that the Marines were in a firefight, even if he didn't realize they were fighting Skinks.

Then: "...inks! Ski...! ...ere are Sk...ks... us...ble?"

"That's affirmative, *Dayzee Mae*. We've got Skinks. Over."

"I ...stan... Skin... affir...? ...ver."

"You got it, *Dayzee Mae*. We've got Skinks big time. You best watch for a Skink starship coming in. I gotta get back to the fight. Hellhound Out." He turned off his comm, sure that the *Dayzee Mae* had gotten the basic message, and looked around the side of his cover in time to see a dim spot of red. He snapped off a bolt of plasma at it, and was rewarded by the sight of a flash of light that could only be a dying Skink.

The Skink—Kerr was sure now that the earlier flash of light he'd seen was a dying Skink—he had shot was to his right, perhaps seventy-five meters distant. As was this one. He groaned. That put the first Skink, and probably more, in front of third fire team, Doyle's.

"Doyle, are you topside or below?" he asked. His comp told him, but he needed to make sure his weakest fire team leader knew where he was.

"T-Topside. Closest t-to the hull," Doyle answered nervously. "Summers is below. J-Johnson is topside inbound."

All right. Doyle knew where he and both of his men were. "Everybody," Kerr ordered into the squad circuit, "look, and use your infras."

"But Skinks don't show up well in the infrared,"
Claypoole objected.

"As cold as it is in vacuum, any warmth will show
up," Kerr said. "Do it!" And wondered why the two
Marines in three already using their infra hadn't spotted the Skink that shot Fisher.

Three rapid plasma bolts burned a line from Kerr's
left almost to his direct front. He thought he saw a
flash of light.

"I got one!" The shout came from Lance Corporal
Little.

"Your fire gave away your position. Move!" Kerr
shouted back.

"Already did, Honcho."

Kerr shifted to look around the edge of his hiding
place—just in time. He'd barely moved over before
something punched through the plasteel housing right
where he'd been. *Damn, that was close—too close!* He
scooted backward until his feet reached a drop-off. The
whole time his eyes jerked side to side, scanning the
area to the sides of the machine he'd been behind,
seeking any sign of the telltale slight reddish tint.

"Who's still below?" he asked into the squad circuit.
"Chan, I know you are, but stick with Fisher."

"I am, Summers."

"So am I."

"Who's that, Berry?"

"Ah, yeah, I'm Berry."

Kerr dropped over the edge his feet had found
and studied the schematic of the subdeck. He knew
it showed the location of the permanent items, those
affixed to the deck. It was the other items, the crates
of ship's stores, that he couldn't count on showing up

"Berry, have you seen anything?"

"No, Sergeant. I don't think they can see me. I think they're all on top."

"I think so, too. Rock, Wolfman, can either of you get down to where Berry is without exposing yourselves to the Skinks?"

"Probably, but one of them fired a projectile of some kind close to me," MacIlargie said.

"Then stay where you are. Claypoole?"

"I'm already joining Berry."

"Summers, try to get to Berry without going topside. Claypoole, Berry, I'm on my way to you. Chan, if anything happens to me, you're in command. If that happens, I want you to get everybody out of here. Go back the same way we came in if you have to. Got it?"

Chan's voice was leaden when he said, "I get everybody out if anything happens to you."

"Everybody else, let me know if you see anything. If a Skink shoots and you can tell where the shot came from, return fire, then change your position before they fire back."

Kerr was moving while he gave the orders. He reached Claypoole and Berry right after Chan acknowledged his orders. Summers joined them a moment later. Kerr waved at the three to touch helmets with him. He'd give them their orders via conduction rather than comm, on the off chance that the Skinks were able to pick up his transmissions and understand his words.

"Both shots that we made were at targets fifty, seventy-five meters ahead. We're going a hundred meters forward, then go topside and see what we can spot from there. Questions?"

"What if they're set up in depth?" Claypoole asked. "We could come up in the middle of them."

"We won't all go topside and stand where they can see us. I'll go first and look over the edge. Anything else?"

"Does anybody have a periscope?" Summers asked.

"Nobody," Kerr answered. "But that's a good idea. Everybody, keep an eye out for anything I can use as a mirror to look over the top. Now let's go. Summers, me, Claypoole, Berry. Go as fast as you can and still keep a sharp eye out. Go."

The four Marines moved out at a brisk walk.

Thirty meters on, Summers dropped to the deck and fired his blaster straight ahead. Kerr had fired an instant earlier; he fired before he dropped. The two had seen faint red glows emerging from between two bulks another twenty-five meters beyond. One of the two faint red spots terminated in a brilliant flash.

"Spread out and line up so you don't have any of us in your line of fire!" Kerr shouted. He waited for a few seconds, aiming his blaster where he'd seen the enemy emerge. No more came.

"All right, stay down and move back. We'll get into the nearest side passage to our rear."

Before they got there, half a dozen or more incredibly fast slugs slammed down where they'd just been—even though they couldn't hear, or even see the paths of the projectiles, they could see the holes the slugs punched into the deck.

The four Marines awkwardly skittered backward, propelling themselves with knees and elbows.

"Two on the right, two on the left," Kerr ordered.

It took longer than he was comfortable with, but they reached the cover of the side passage without being shot at again. Kerr and Berry went to the right, Claypoole and Summers to the left.

Which wasn't the case with the Marines left on top. Kerr didn't see a flash, but he did hear MacIlargie's excited shout:

"Ooo-eee! Did ya see that? I must have got a whole squad with that shot!"

"I-It wasn't only you," Doyle said. "J-Johnson fired too. So did I."

"Somebody give me a realistic assessment," Kerr snapped.

After a few moments of silence, a voice said, "Sergeant Kerr, I saw three plasma bolts going down range. Before I could locate a target in the area where they converged, there were three or four flashes. I didn't see anything in infra after that."

"Little?"

"That's me."

"Identify yourself when you give a report."

"Will do, Sergeant."

"You did a good job with that report."

Little grunted at the compliment.

I wonder when he learned to give a report that way, Kerr thought. *Maybe he's due for a promotion.*

"You left something out, all of you. How far away was your target—your targets?"

"Not much more than twenty-five meters," MacIlargie said.

Kerr swore, and rolled onto his back; twenty-five meters put the Skinks right on top of him and the Marines with him!

"Claypoole, one of you watch the top. It sounds like we're right in the middle of them."

Claypoole swore something unintelligible, then said, "I'm on it."

So now what, Sergeant? Kerr asked himself. He shook himself. *I'm a Marine sergeant. When in doubt, act decisively.*

"Claypoole, you and Summers head left. Let me know when you're halfway to the next aisle. Go."

"On the way," Claypoole answered.

Kerr looked at his motion detector. He saw Claypoole and Summers withdrawing, but didn't detect any movement topside.

While he was looking up, he saw another plasma bolt burn through his vision. "Report!" he ordered.

"Johnson, Sergeant. I thought I saw something."

"But you didn't hit anything?"

"I don't think so," Johnson said. "Sorry, Sergeant."

"Don't apologize. I'd rather have you shoot at nothing than not shoot at something and get one of us killed because of it. And always move after you fire; your bolt gives away your position."

"Corporal Doyle already told me to move."

Doyle. He always comes across as timid and not a very good combat Marine. But he knows his stuff, and trains his men well.

"We're there, Honcho," Claypoole's voice suddenly said.

"Cover us," Kerr answered.

"If anything red shows, we're ready to flame it," Claypoole said back.

"Berry," Kerr looked to where his infra showed his greenest man was. "Go. I'm right behind you." Kerr started moving, but had to pull up short because Berry didn't move.

"Berry, go!"

"Did you see what those slugs did to the deck?" Berry said, almost in a wail.

"Yes. And that's what the next slugs will do to us if we're still here when they come." He grabbed Berry's shoulder and shoved.

The young Marine stumbled, but quickly gained his balance and ran until Claypoole reached out and grabbed his arm to keep him from running off by himself.

"Doyle," Kerr radioed to the senior Marine above, "what's happening topside?"

"N-Nothing. We haven't s-seen anything since before Johnson's last shot."

"Well, everybody be careful of what you shoot at, because the next thing your infras pick up might be the back of my head."

"Roger, Sergeant Kerr," Doyle said. "Did everybody hear that?"

Kerr decided that Doyle had the situation under control topside, and took a last glance at the top of the machine housing he and Berry had just been behind, on the other side of the aisle where the Skinks had almost caught them. There was nothing there. He began climbing up the stack to his front.

He was almost to the top when Doyle's voice shouted over the comm, *"They're coming! Fire!"* Then to Kerr, "Honcho, I see a mass of them coming at us across the top. Including where you are."

"Are there any on the deck?" Kerr asked.

"I don't know, I can't see the deck from my position." Kerr could almost hear the CRACK-*sizzle* of Doyle's blaster as the corporal fired time and again.

"There are some coming toward me and Fisher," Chan reported. "I'm getting him into one of the side passages."

Holding onto his position with his feet and one hand, Kerr activated his Heads-Up Display and switched it to show his men's positions. Chan and Little were in the same aisle where he and the Marines with him had been shot at. As he looked, he saw the two turn a corner, out of the aisle. He checked his motion detector. That showed a large number of forms moving rapidly along the tops of the machine housings and along two aisles.

"Claypoole, Summers, go left and open fire forward, Skinks are coming that way. Berry, go right and fire back the way we started out. I'm going topside to take them out here. *Move!*" He didn't wait for acknowledgements before lunging high enough to get his head and arms over the top and began firing.

The nearest faint reddish glows were only ten meters away.

Kerr didn't take the time to aim, he just pointed and shot. The many hours he'd put in training in snap-shooting over the years came to the fore—at this range the only way he could miss was if he did it deliberately. In his mind he could hear the blood-curdling screaming the Skinks made when they had charged the Marines on Kingdom and on Haulover—every place where the Marines had fought them—except now the Skink charge was silent. As in those other fights, a brilliant flash met each of his plasma bolts. He was killing the Skinks as fast as he could point and press his blaster's trigger-lever.

In seconds, the Skinks were close enough for Kerr's

ight gatherer to make out details, and he could tell
hat their vacuum suits weren't armored. At least they
aad no protection from the Marines' plasma blasters;
he bolts burned straight into the suits, and the Skinks
lamed in the suit's atmosphere just the same as they
lid planetside. The heat of their immolations was so
ntense that they reduced the suits to cinders.

Even though they were smaller than men, there
vere too many Skinks, and they were too close. One
lared up just as it was diving at Kerr, blinding him
vith the intensity of its flash. Something slapped
against his helmet and he fell backward, to the deck
below. Momentarily dazed, he didn't hear Claypoole's,
"Got that one for you, Honcho!"

But before he could see again something slammed
nto his helmet and knocked him backward, sending
aim crashing to the deck below. Shaking his head to
blink the dazzling stars and circles out of his eyes,
ae realized that the wind he felt on his cheek was
air rushing out of the side of his helmet.

Don't panic! he shouted at himself. He'd dropped his
blaster in his fall, so both hands were free. He groped
vith one to find the break in his helmet, while reaching
or his patching kit with the other. In seconds, he had a
batch slapped on the gash in the side of his helmet—he
aoped it would hold long enough for someone else to
nake a better patch. He looked for his blaster. But
before he found it, another Skink jumped onto him,
cnocking him onto his back. He rolled to the side and
bushed at the body that lay across his chest. The Skink
vas light enough that, even still half-stunned and struggling for breath, by using his armor to augment his
trength, Kerr was able to shove the Skink off of him.

The creature scooted farther away before it scrabbled to its feet. It pulled a wicked-looking knife from somewhere and lunged at Kerr. Even though the Marine couldn't sidestep fast enough to avoid the blade, his armor easily deflected it. Kerr slammed his armored fist into the Skink's faceplate, shattering it. Red flecked mist geysered from the enemy's helmet. Kerr clearly saw his foe's face before it collapsed—sharply convex with pointed teeth, the final bit of proof he needed to know that he and his squad were fighting Skinks. The Skink's hands slapped at its face as it fell, as though trying to force air back into its broken helmet.

Kerr looked around for his blaster. Before he could find it, another Skink dropped onto him from above, staggering him. He instantly recovered and threw himself backward, hoping that his superior size and the hardness of his vacuum suit's armor would crush the Skink.

But the Skink didn't die; it shoved at Kerr's back with enough force to lift him and fling him away, and then another Skink landed on the Marine's chest, slamming him back down. This time, Kerr felt something crack under his back, and the Skink he was on top of stopped pushing at him.

Kerr didn't spare any time or energy wondering about the Skink below him; he lunged upward, forcing the Skink on his chest to lift off. Palms up, he slammed the sides of his hands into the Skink's neck just below its helmet. The Skink dropped the knife it had just drawn, and clutched at its throat. Kerr folded the fingers of his right hand and shot the armored knuckles into the Skink's throat. It collapsed backward.

Kerr spun about and saw the Skink that had earlier jumped onto his back was stirring, groping for a knife and trying to rise. He raised a foot and stomped on it until it stopped moving.

He looked up; no more Skinks were jumping or falling over the edge to fight with him. Neither did he see a plasma bolt burn through the vacuum. If he hadn't just been in violent action, he might have thought all was as serene as the subdeck of an empty container ship ever gets. He looked to his sides. The Marines he'd stationed to cover the aisles weren't firing. He could barely make out their shapes with his infra screen, but they seemed to be looking at him.

"Second squad, report!" he ordered into his comm.

No one replied.

"I said, second squad, report," he repeated. "So speak up. Chan first."

Still no reply.

Kerr looked to his left and saw Claypoole and Summers stand and come toward him.

"Claypoole, talk to me, Marine!"

Claypoole gestured, but didn't say anything. Then he was there, touching helmets with his squad leader.

"Can you hear me, Honcho?"

"Of course I can hear you. What do you ... Don't tell me."

"I don't care, I'm going to tell you anyway. Your comm's busted. Chan and Doyle both report all present and accounted for. The bad guys are gone. No casualties."

"Except for my comm."

"Seems that way. Now hold still while I fix that patch on your helmet. I think that's what knocked out your comm."

"All right." Kerr waited patiently for the moment it

took Claypoole to layer on a second, better patch. He looked at the dead Skinks at his feet while he waited.

"Good as new, Honcho," Claypoole said, touching helmets again.

Kerr looked at the bodies on the deck around his feet. "We've finally got Skink bodies for the science people," he said. "Get the rest of the squad here to collect them for transfer back to the *Dayzee Mae.*"

"Aye-aye." Claypoole broke contact to radio to the rest of the squad.

Before anybody else arrived, the three Skinks Kerr had killed in hand-to-hand combat flared into brilliant, brief flame, hot enough to scorch the chameleon coverings over the armored vacuum suits worn by Kerr, Claypoole, and Summers.

Back on the *Dayzee Mae*, Kerr gave a succinct after action report, leaving out nothing despite its brevity. "I estimate there was an entire platoon of Skinks on the *Runstable*," he said near the end. "We killed all of them. Or at least we killed every one of them who fought us." He shrugged. "It's possible that some hid from us as we left the *Runstable.*"

McPherson shook his head in amazement that one squad of Marines could be ambushed by such a superior force, and totally defeat them at the cost of only one Marine wounded.

"Any word on Fisher's condition?" Kerr asked, as though he knew what the starship's acting captain was thinking.

"Only that he's in a stasis bag," McPherson answered. "We won't know anything more until we get back to Thorsfinni's World."

Kerr nodded and looked at a display on which the SS *Runstable* was visible. "What are we going to do about her?"

"I don't have any crew to spare to take her to port," McPherson said. "All we can do is report her position and hope she's still here when a salvage ship comes for her."

"And that the Skinks haven't manned her again in time to ambush the salvage team," Kerr said.

"And there weren't any Skink bodies to recover?" McPherson said.

"No, sir. All the bodies flared up as soon as the fight was over."

"How do you think it happened?" McPherson asked.

Kerr shook his head. "Dead man's switch, maybe. Maybe there was another Skink hiding someplace where he could set off incendiary charges placed in their suits. Maybe they spontaneously flare after they die." He shook his head again. "Maybe we'll never know."

David Sherman has been writing since 1983, and is the author or co-author of more than thirty books, including the DemonTech military fantasy series and the popular Starfist military science fiction series. He came to military-oriented writing the hard way by serving in the US Marine Corps and going to war as an infantryman in Vietnam. His short fiction has appeared in the anthologies *Weird Trails: The Magazine of Supernatural Cowboy Stories*, *So It Begins* (a DemonTech story), *By Other Means* (a DemonTech story), *In All Their Glory* (a fairy story), and *In an Iron Cage: The Magic of Steampunk*. After many years, he gave up the winters and snow of Philadelphia and now lives in the warmth and sunshine of South Florida, where he says yes to the occasional hurricane, and no to cold and snow.

You Do What You Do

TANYA HUFF

"Sarge! I'm nearly out!"

"Me too, Sarge. Last mag just locked and loaded!"

"Harmen?"

"I'm down to six grenades and half a belt of boomers!" Deena Harmen yelled, leaning out from behind the broken pillar that offered her minimal protection from enemy fire. She braced the big KC-12 between her right hip and the stone, then bent sideways to hook her left grapples around a chunk of debris. It couldn't have weighed much more than forty kilos so she lobbed it gently out onto the chewed-up plaza in front of the ruined building where the remains of her platoon had gone to ground.

The Others opened fire—bastards had ammo to spare—and she took the moment of respite to lean out a little further and eyeball where most of it was coming from. Her scanner adjusted for distance and she spotted a V-shaped crack in their defenses.

"Make that five grenades," she amended as she pulled the trigger, "and half a belt of boomers."

An EMT pulse had taken out everything but wetware early on, leaving her with only basic scanner functions and no idea of how much damage she'd actually done. Seemed like a definite decrease in fire coming from that *particular* location though.

A thump against her calf and she looked down to see Jurrin—firing prone beside her—give her an enthusiastic thumbs up, his hair a moving pink fringe around the edges of his helmet. Di'Taykan hair wasn't actually hair—it was closer to a cat's whiskers as Deena understood it—and none of them liked covering it. They'd been the second race the Confederation had found when they'd gone looking for military support against the Others and sometimes Deena wondered about how the Corps would've been different had the di'Taykan been the template. More casualties due to head shots, she suspected. Jurrin's sense of humor had been her salvation during basic and ending up on the same fireteam after Deena'd been jacked in had been a happy coincidence.

Here and now, his lips moved, but even with aural augmentation, she couldn't hear him over the sudden appearance of a Marine 774 screaming by overhead, closely followed by three enemy fighters.

First in their part of the sky for a while.

Though three to one didn't look good for the righteous.

The squad had seen smoke right after the EMT, but had been too far out to know whose planes had gone down. The sarge had sworn there'd been no pulse planned so the odds were high they'd lost some of their own. They'd still been speculating when they'd stumbled onto at least a platoon of the enemy and their personal shit had hit the fan.

"*What the hell are they doing out here?*" Jurrin demanded. "*These ruins were supposed to have been cleared!*"

"*A tenday ago,*" Deena reminded him.

"*Yeah, well, maybe someone up there on surveillance should've have noticed a few dozen bad guys moving back in. Fukking Navy.*"

Weapon hanging down her back, she switched fingertips and dragged a block out of the wall, making a firing hole. "*Not arguing.*"

The 774 had disappeared in the distance. Just before she lost the trio of black dots following it, one of them turned, and headed back.

Anything in the air now had been shielded from the pulse. With all tech outside the shielded areas of the camp taken out, the enemy pilot's targeting computer would have nothing to lock onto except heat signatures. Well, not hers, not in a full combat skeleton, but the rest of the squad's. Apparently, the species they faced didn't match the heat signatures of Confederation Marine Corps Human, di'Taykan, or Krai. Or the Others' air support had no problem blowing up their own people.

A grenade belching purple smoke landed on the stub of roof behind them.

"Or they could low ball it and use a chemical marker. Sarge! I could flame it!"

"No!" Sergeant Yarynin ducked as the Others laid down covering fire. "Heat could make it worse!"

Fine. But someone had to do something fast. Jumping

off the ledge, Deena grabbed Jurrin's combat vest and ran for the wall, lifting him over her head as she moved. When he stopped swearing and planted his feet on her shoulders, she shifted her grip to his ankles and threw him toward the roof.

Scrambling for traction on shifting tiles, he kicked the grenade. It rolled past the shattered end of a massive beam and dropped into her hand.

She'd always sucked at sports. During a wasted summer playing right field in her early teens, she'd never once hit the cut-off man. But, here and now, she didn't need accuracy, just distance.

Here and now, as her father might say, she had an arm on her.

She returned the grenade, still belching purple smoke, just short of where she'd blown a hole in the enemy offense.

An instant later, the enemy fighter roared past.

An instant after that, the missile zeroed on the smoke.

The concussion wave slammed Deena back against the far wall of the building. Her combat skeleton absorbed most of the blow but, ears ringing, she spat a mouthful of blood past her jaw guard and wondered muzzily why her upper lip felt damp.

And where Jurrin had come from?

Wasn't he on the roof?

His helmet was gone and the side of his face looked like he'd been rubbing it against a Ciptran—given that he was a di'Taykan and the di'Taykan were the most sexually undiscriminating species in the universe, Deena wouldn't put it past him although she doubted the big bugs had the right parts to play.

Then Jurrin was gone and Chris Beaton was there and someone was screaming but she didn't think it was Chris. Or Jurrin. It didn't sound like Jurrin.

Chris had his thumb against the edge of her jaw guard. He'd pushed her scanner up. Why was he pulling her mouth open? She tried to lift her arm to push him away but it weighed a fukking ton and...

Sah? She had to swallow or drown as he squeezed the pouch but that shit was illegal for Humans. Cup of coffee for the Krai, sure, but for other species it was like...

It was like...

It was like having a rubber band snapped against your brain.

She blinked, actually felt her eyelids go up and down, then ambient sound rushed in to fill the spaces the missile had left as her aural augmentation came back online and she managed to expand her focus out from Chris' face. The rest of the roof had come down and the fallen wall they'd been using for cover had been rearranged into new patterns of debris. She couldn't see any of the squad moving through the smoke and the settling stone dust. The screaming had stopped.

Which was when she realized that Chris had hold of her chest cage, and was attempting to haul her up onto her feet. "Deena! Damn it, come on! We need you!"

She carefully broke his grip, having to think about managing her strength in a way she hadn't since the early days of training. Nothing seemed damaged, but bits of wetware were taking their own sweet time to become functional. "Need me for what?"

"The Sarge is pinned!" Chris took two steps back,

then one forward again. He reminded her a bit of her family's old dog. "Kaeden and the medkit were buried! Huang's still out and Ghailian needs help!"

"Okay . . ." Most people didn't have think about standing, managing each micro-movement. The "new" parameters of her body hadn't been new for years, she shouldn't have to . . .

Then things started working properly and she didn't. A block of concrete tumbled past her arm. Deena danced aside, realizing she'd dislodged it as she stood. What she'd been thinking of as pressure against her shoulder had probably weighed about a hundred kilos. A cascade of broken stone followed it.

"You took out what was left of the east wall," Chris added, stepping back. "With your ass!"

"Feels more like I used my head," she muttered, falling into step behind him. Chris didn't get to talk about her ass anymore. They had a rule.

If Sergeant Yarynin had been doing the screaming, she wasn't now. Twisted up on her side, one long leg under the broken beam and a pile of stone—the bottom slab lying disturbingly close to the ground—she looked dead. The di'Taykan were never that still. Even her hair had collapsed to wrap her skull in a turquoise cap. That was bad. Really bad.

"She's still alive." This was where Jurrin had gone. He knelt beside the sergeant, long fingers pressed against her throat.

"When I tried to lever the beam, it shifted," Roupen Ghailian, the squad's other surviving heavy gunner, explained, beckoning Deena forward. "We've got to lift straight up. Sarge can regrow a leg if we don't pancake the rest of her."

"And Kaeden?" Deena asked, taking her place on the opposite side of the beam.

"He's under smaller pieces. Doesn't need *us* to dig him out."

She checked to be sure she had gripping surfaces up. "Fastest to lift and throw."

Ghailian shook his head. "Can't throw it far enough for the enemy not to zero on the impact."

"I think they already know where we are." They weren't shooting, but then they'd just taken a missile strike from one of their own planes. The sergeant and Kaeden kept Deena from feeling smug about that. "On three..."

The beam and four big slabs tossed aside, Deena crouched by the last slab and met Ghailian's eyes. "If we take the pressure off, she could bleed out."

"She could be bleeding out anyway."

"Her combats would seal."

"Pulse took uniform tech off line," Jurrin reminded them. Hair blown out in a pink aurora, he lifted his head and bellowed, "Kirrt! How much longer? We need that med kit!"

"Nearly there!" Kirrt bellowed back from behind a masking pile of debris. "Just a few more—fuk, fuk, fuk! Medkit's toast!"

"So's Kaeden!" called another voice. Deena thought it was Hania Wojtowicz. This was her first dirt drop and it sounded to Deena as though training was only barely beating out puking.

"What do we do?" Kaeden was their medic. If anyone was going to improvise a medical miracle, it'd be him.

"Okay. All right." Sitting back on his heels, Jurrin

popped the tube of sealant off his vest. Even with her scanner up, Deena could see his hand shaking. "We clear it, cut it clean, and seal it. Rou!"

Ghailian tossed his sealant over.

"Dee?"

"I used mine on Serri. And the sarge used hers on Norris." Serri was fine. Norris had died anyway.

"We've got enough." Jurrin took a deep breath and pulled his blade. "Go."

"Can you get through bone with that?"

"Just get the fukking wall off her!"

Turned out he *could* cut through bone with that. By the time the ruin of the sergeant's leg had been tossed in a body bag and reduced to ash, the rest of the squad had gathered.

There'd been thirteen of them when they'd left camp at dawn, three fireteams and the sergeant. Their orders: check on a mining town cleared then abandoned in the onward push of battle. The destruction of the road up to the town meant they'd had to leave their APC locked and booby trapped at the bottom of the hill. Jurrin—the designated driver—had protested but had been overruled. Norris's team had been on point when the *Others* opened fire. Ben Eckland, the heavy, had died instantly. So had Anne McDonald. A piece of Ben's skeleton had nicked Norris's throat and he'd lost so much blood that sealing the wound had made piss all difference. With the sergeant calling for air support, they'd turned back to the APC only to see it blown by a mortar round.

The pulse happened before the last of the debris hit dirt.

Enemy artillery had driven them up the hill and into

e fire of the waiting platoon, but the ruins and the loss
f targeting computers had given the squad a chance.
he three remaining heavies had been throwing cover
gether when a lucky shot had ricocheted off Karen
uang's shoulder and up under her head-plates.

Nine surviving.

Huang and the sergeant unconscious.

Seven standing.

"They know where we are," Wojtowicz muttered,
eping a white knuckled grip on her weapon. "They'll
me get us."

"You talking about our guys or theirs?" Chris won-
ered.

Kirrt glanced across at the significantly flatter debris
1 the other side of the plaza and his nostril ridges
red. "*They're* dead."

"All of them?" Ghailian snorted. "Looked like they
ere digging in when we got here. If any of them
e still alive, they're going to be pissed."

Jurrin still knelt by the sergeant, Serri beside him.
i'Tayken needed touch. "We have to get out of here."

Deena spread her hands. "How?"

In the silence, something—someone—yelled in the
stance. And was answered.

Chris brought his weapon across his body. "They're
t all dead."

Sarge was out and McDonald had been next senior.
eena had her second hook; so did Chris. Jurrin had
s, then lost it almost immediately. Who the hell
as in charge?

"Okay." Jurrin took a deep breath and let it out
owly. "The APC is toast. We're still offline. Dee,
u or Ghailian could run for help . . ."

"We're not faster, just stronger. Bigger guns. Bet ter looking."

"We can walk out," Ghailian suggested. "Carryin the sarge and Huang."

"Took us six hours to get out this far in the APC and I had it pushing full out as often as the road allowed. Carrying wounded, under fire, it'd take u days to get back on foot. Sargent would never mak it." Jurrin leaned into Serri, their hands linked. "An Huang..."

Huang had dropped like a load of bricks. Tin entrance wound in beside her eye but no exit woun when they got the head-plates off. Her heart kep beating, but she didn't wake up. Wetware was o line—maybe permanently.

"It's a mining town, right?" Scanner on full mag nification, Deena stepped up on a block and peere into the town. "It wasn't entirely flattened, so mayb a vehicle of some kind survived. Something simpl. Something mechanical."

Jurrin nodded, hair moving against the motion. " we find it, I can drive it."

Two teams—her and Chris and Jurrin. Ghailia Kirrt, and Wojtowicz. Deena set aural augmentatic on maximum and told Ghailian to do the same.

"So I can hear you if you yell?"

"Got a better idea?"

He didn't.

They were almost at the mine when Chris spotte the ramp. A ramp meant wheels. The building ha taken a hit but at least half of the underground garag was rubble free. Over in the far corner was a bi blue rectangle. They left Chris by the ramp and closer examination found the rectangle had caterpillar tracks, a flared front, and a three meter long drill.

"It's a borer," Jurrin whispered. "From the mine."

"Looks sturdy."

"Yeah, well, it bores out mines. Also, it looks brain dead."

"You better check." Deena laid her hand against the front shielding. "Maybe this place is deep enough and this thing is solid enough that it didn't get pulsed out."

It had.

"Brain dead," Jurrin repeated, reappearing in the open hatch.

The borer had been abandoned when the town came under attack. They'd probably thought it too slow to be of much use in the evacuation. "Just brain dead?"

"Far as I can tell, but..."

"Is there room for everyone in it?"

His hair started to rise. "Tight, but yeah."

"Has it got power?"

"It's fully powered but you're not listening, Dee." He slapped the side of machine where the enamel had been scraped off and the metal had started to rust. She flinched at the noise. "Sorry. No, brain, no movement. No movement, no use to us."

Sarge wasn't going to last much longer.

Maybe if they got Huang to a doctor she could be rebooted or something.

They couldn't walk out. They couldn't stay.

Deena stroked a pitted curve, metal whispering against metal. "I'll be its brain."

Jurrin's eyes darkened, the pink disappearing into black as the light receptors snapped open. "You'll what?"

"Plug it in and I'll wear it out."

He stared at her for a moment, then folded his arms. "No."

"What? You think it'd make me look fat?"

He didn't laugh. "I said no, Dee."

Deena spread her fingers, switched to sensor tips and felt the cold of the machine in flesh. "There's no other way."

Outside, as though they'd been cued, the *Others* opened fire. They clearly still had one working mortar.

Eyes on Jurrin, Deena dialed her ears back and yelled, "Chris, go get them. This one'll do."

Jurrin held her gaze as Chris ran off, closed his eyes as Chris's footsteps faded in the distance, opened them again, and looked everywhere but at her. "I'll have to cannibalize your skeleton to make this work."

"I know." She set her weapon carefully aside, then popped the contacts on her left arm, teeth gritted against the flush of cold as the jacks pulled free. The techs on Ventris Station said the cold was all in her head, that everyone felt the neural connection differently, but that no one really felt anything. The techs on Ventris weren't jacked in though, so what did they know. She pulled her hand free, flexing her fingers and staring past flesh at the unresponsive metal. Right arm. Left leg. Right leg. "About time the Corps upgraded me anyway. I hear the new skeletons come in colors."

"Any color you want, as long as it's black."

When she straightened, Jurrin had gone back in the vehicle. She locked the shoulder pieces in place, switched off visual augmentation, detached the jaw guard, and then raised her hands to her temples. Only full combat skeletons came with head-plates and parliament was, once again, fighting the Corps about it. T

Confederation's Elder Races, the ones too evolved to fight back when the Others swarmed into Confederation space, the ones happy to sit back while the less evolved fought and died to protect them, they didn't much like the idea of the head-plates. Said it blurred the edge between flesh and machine. Jacking in to extremities was fine. Jacking right in to the central processor stepped over the line. The Elder Races had a stick up their collective asses about technical augmentation.

She shivered as the temple jacks released and slowly pulled the side plates away from her skin. When she could duck her head without touching the metal, she cracked the chest cage and stepped out of the skeleton.

The head, the hands, and the feet held the most definition in metal—although the head came without a face. The rest of it was glossy black strapping with the same smart fabric used for regular Marine combats completing the physical integrity. Standing empty, it looked like an insect had shed its skin. A really big, bipedal insect.

Given the variety of species in known space, Deena wasn't ruling out finding one.

Her hand and arm looked pale and soft and slightly damp as she unhooked the tool kit from the skeleton's thigh.

"I always forget how small you are without that thing."

"Eight centimeters difference." Deena handed him the tool kit. "And you're still shorter than your average di'Taykan."

"It's all about the presence, *shechar*."

"Still not your darling." But she bumped her shoulder against his as she moved over to pick up her weapon,

more than happy to put it down again a moment later
inside the borer. The *heavy* part of *heavy gunner* was
entirely accurate.

The inside of the borer looked a little like an APC;
operator's area at the front with two seats, the control
panel, and half a dozen dark screens. No seats or
weapons racks in the big empty box at the back, but
the differences were minimal. Of course, she'd never
heard of anyone trying this kind of hook up with an
APC either, so the similarity didn't add much weight
to the success side of success or failure.

The floor felt cold under her bare feet. Jurrin had
opened the control panel between the two seats.

"I can't do this in the seats," she said as the di'Taykan
climbed in through the hatch, input jacks on short pieces
of wire cradled in one hand, her toolkit in the other.
"I'll have to lie on the floor."

"Dee . . ."

They heard the explosion. Felt the borer tremble.

"Have you come up with another way to get us
the hell out of here?"

He shook his head, his hair flat and unhappy.

"Then jack me in because it sounds like we'll have
to go out and get them." If the floor had been cold
under her feet, it was fukking freezing through the
thin fabric of her underwear. She tucked herself as
close to the base of the panel as she could—Jurrin's
arms were long enough to reach over her. "Give me
the external sensors first. If we blow out my brain
you won't need to waste time with the other stuff.
Joke," she added quickly, when the light receptor's in
Jurrin's eyes snapped shut.

"Not funny," he muttered, but his eyes darkene

nd he reached into the guts of the panel. "Maybe
ve should wait for Ghailian."

"Hey, this is the biggest skeleton any Marine has
ver worn, and it was my idea. Ghailian doesn't get
o horn in on it." She could feel her pulse pounding
t the base of her skull, sweat prickling along her
pine, and spent the next few minutes forcing herself
o relax. This was the biggest skeleton any Marine had
ver worn. That was all it was. Just a big skeleton
nd she could operate that in her sleep. Just a big
keleton. Someone had to be first to be jacked in.
ust a big skeleton...

"You ready?"

"Born ready."

Deena kept her eyes closed as Jurrin gently turned
er head murmuring, "Right side first."

Familiar pressure.

"Left side."

And again.

"Anything? Dee?"

"Nothing."

"Nothing? As in not working or burned you out
othing?" He sounded so panicked she couldn't help
ut smile.

"As in, not powered up nothing."

"Oh."

"Power on three?"

"Sure, yeah. One. Two. Three..."

Wall. Floor. Ceiling. Wall. Wall. Ceiling. Floor. Wall.
Vall. Wall. Floor. Wall.

"Dee?"

Her scanner was slaved to her optic nerve. She
ooked to the distance, it showed her the distance. She

looked close, it magnified. Multiple scanners, multiple images. Multiple depths of field on each image.

Breathing short and shallow, she focused on what she thought was the wall in front of the borer. One image at a consistent distance. Keep it simple. One. Push the others to the side.

"You're going to have to blindfold me." Eventually, she'd give into the urge to open her eyes.

"Kinky."

"You wish." Since the soft cloth Jurrin carefully wrapped around her eyes didn't reek of di'Taykan hormones—where reek translated as "left her squirming on the floor"—he'd used the t-shirt in her pack. *You know you're in deepest shit when a di'Taykan doesn't even attempt to get lucky.*

Wall. Ceiling. Wall. Wall. Wall. Floor.

Wall.

One wall.

"Okay." She held her breath for a moment, then inhaled long and slow. Blew it out. "Okay, that's got it." One wall. Dead ahead. "Now jack the tracks into my legs."

"It's the propulsion unit. You'll have to sort out what exactly you're moving."

"Whatever. You can jack my arms in once we're mobile." She could hear Jurrin moving, hear the click of tools. She matched her breathing to his to keep from hyperventilating.

"Hook them to what?"

"I saw half a dozen waldos on the outside of this thing. If we're attacked, I'll need them." Hand to hand to waldo. She bit back a giggle.

"If?"

"Fine. When."

A wire slithered across her leg. Felt Jurrin's fingers around her thigh.

"The contact point is lower."

"Spoil sport." She could hear the grin in his voice.

The trick would be to walk without walking. The wetware gave the command. The skeleton did the work. Except tracks worked simultaneously, not sequentially.

"Uh, Dee, we're not moving. Maybe your brain isn't compatible with this thing."

"It's a brain," she grunted. "It's compatible with everything."

The floor jerked under her.

The borer ground around in a half circle, tracks grumbling against the stone.

Left.

Then back.

Right.

Wall. Wall. Wall. Ceiling. Floor.

"Dee!"

The trick was not to think of her legs. Not legs. Tracks. Moving forward together. Mind over matter.

WALL.

"Shit! Sorry." Turning was also good. Speed up left tread to turn right. Speed up right to turn left. Reverse was just forward, backwards. Easy.

She aimed the borer toward the ramp and gunned it up toward the street.

"You're doing it!" Jurrin squeezed her hand. His palm felt damp.

"Of course I am." Sky. Rubble. Stone dust. Marine! Here they come. Get the hatch open."

Even focusing on just the one screen, the amount

of input coming through the borer's sensors threatened
to overwhelm her. Best thing she could do for the
squad was get it sorted. A small piece of her attention
registered boots on the decking, voices, the clatter of
gear against metal...

The heavy thud of Ghailian, last in. The only
heavy she'd heard so they'd stripped Huang out of
her skeleton.

"What the fuk!" He didn't sound happy.

"We can't stay," she reminded him quickly. Sky.
Street. Sky. Rubble.

"Yeah, but..."

"But nothing. Biggest damned skeleton any Marine's
ever worn."

She could hear the others waiting for Ghailian
to respond. Chris started to say something but was
cut off so quickly she wondered if someone—Serri
maybe—had slapped a hand over his mouth.

After a long moment, Ghailian sighed. "You sure?"

She grinned and, as she felt the hatch close, got
the tracks moving again. "Piece of cake."

WALL!

"Shit! Sorry."

"She does that a lot," Jurrin sighed dramatically
over the laughter.

"Marines..." Speed up left tread. Street. Now both
treads and full speed while she had a relatively flat
unobstructed surface to cover. "...we are leaving."

"*...but before you leave, there's a few things
want to say.*" Staff Sergeant Chad Morris's skeleton
gleamed so brightly Deena couldn't look directly a
him without polarizing her scanner. "*As of today; th*

*Confederation Marine Corps has trusted you with the
operation of equipment they tell us is worth more
than any of us will make in our lifetimes. I say,
the equipment is worth sweet fuk all without you
in it. Some members of Parliament say the Corps
has made us into weapons. I say some members of
Parliament have their heads so far up their asses
they've cut off the oxygen to their brains. Because
of you, because of us, because we're willing to do
the heavy lifting, Marines will survive who might
not have, battles will be won that might have been
lost. We are one in four and we make the difference!
Make me proud, Marines."*

"Dee!"

Deena had to wet her lips and swallow before she
answered. "What?"

"You stopped breathing." Chris had taken Jurrin's
place at her side.

"No, I didn't."

"Yeah, you did."

Blindfolded, she couldn't roll her eyes, but she layered the reaction into her voice. "I think I'd know if
I . . ." What felt like a mortar round hit close enough
to rock her on her treads. It wasn't the first, but it
was the closest. They'd found the range. She needed
to see more than just the track in front of her so she
turned her head. Felt the metal floor under her cheek.

Not her *head*.

Locking her attention on the visual input, she turned
her perception of her head.

Rock. Grass. Trees. Sky. Track. Track. Sky. Rock.
Grass. Trees. Sky. Track.

Too much information. It swirled around and around and around and she was going to puke and then drown in it in a minute. She had to stop *thinking* about the borer as separate, as something she was driving, and become the borer.

Track. Focus. Turn. Rock. Focus. Turn. Trees. Focus. Turn. Turn. Turn.

There was moment of vertigo that felt like smashing through ice and then she resurfaced, able to see, able to turn her head a full three hundred and sixty degrees just as the impact from another mortar shell sprayed dirt over her rear sensors.

The longest waldo didn't have much of a throwing arm either but Deena figured ripping a tree out of the ground and whipping it back along the path of the mortar fire might give the *Others* something to think about. All she had to do was keep her tracks moving. Keep going until they got close enough to their own lines that the enemy would fall back.

Her arms were cold.

"All right, you've all hooked up to a remote, we know you can make the brain/skeleton connection..."

Only eight of the eleven Marines who'd chosen to become heavy gunners after basic had made it this far.

"...today, you'll be jacking in to the rudimentary skeleton. Strength augmentation only. Settle the shoulder pieces before you jack in your arms. And remember, the skeleton is becoming part of you, not the other way around."

"Ah come on, Sarge." Deena couldn't lean far enough out of ranks to see the speaker—not without catching hell herself—but she thought it sounded like

Sam Drake. "When you going to turn us loose on the full combat chassis? We got buddies out there waiting for us to clank to their rescue."

"You want to join them today, Private? Just open your mouth again."

"Come on, Dee, just open your mouth."

Chris.

"Leave her alone."

Ghailian.

"I just want to get some water into her."

"You see her swallow lately? Borers don't swallow."

"Fuk off, Ghailian. Dee! Deena! Come on! If you're not going to open your mouth then talk to me. Tell me you're okay."

It pissed her right off that there were no visual sensors, no cameras of any kind inside the borer. She could hear, there were microphones so the operators, back when the borer needed an operator, could give voice commands, but she couldn't see. And she couldn't seem to find her mouth in the constant stream of data coming from outside.

Oh. There it was.

"I'm fine."

"Dee?"

"I'm fine," she repeated, and shifted the bulk of her concentration back to boring through a pile of debris blocking the track. From the residual radiation she was picking up, they were passing close to where one of the pulsed planes had kissed dirt. When those things blew, they blew big. Going around would take too long and although her walls were thick enough to protect the Marines she carried for a short time,

she needed to hustle. Lingering wouldn't be good for anyone.

"Why is she talking through the control panel?"

Jurrin sounded upset but he wasn't talking to her so Deena ignored him in favor of feathering her right track in order to give the left time to grip.

"Answer me, Ghailian! Why, dammit?"

"How much farther to the camp?"

"What difference does that..."

"Fifty-nine kilometers, eight meters, six centimeters, give or take." She wasn't entirely ignoring the conversation, just the parts that had nothing to do with her.

"You should stop now, Deena. We can walk from here."

"Don't be stupid, Ghailian. Radiation levels are too high. And it's starting to rain." Her moisture sensors were going nuts.

"Not everyone can be a heavy gunner. There will be extensive psychological evaluations even before the physical modifications begin." The Staff Sergeant turned his head, faceless behind the head-plates of a full combat skeleton. "This is a position only Humans can fulfill and only one in four of them. There is no way of knowing which you'll be until you're jacked in for the first time. Most of you won't be suitable. Some of you..." He swung the big KC-12 off his back and blasted three grenades, a stream of impact boomers, and a line of fire from the flame thrower down the range toward the target.

Toward the smoking pile of debris where the target had been.

"Some of you," he repeated, and Deena would be

the brand new chevron on her sleeve that he was
smiling, "will get to play with the good toys."

She unlocked the hatch after she gave the recognition code to the sentry and crossed the perimeter of the
camp. She felt like crap. She hadn't been made for this
kind of distance travel, not at speed. Her tracks were
worn almost smooth, cracked in at least three places,
and two waldos had broken off. Okay, one had broken
off, the other had been shot off. Not to mention that
her power levels were dangerously low.

She watched a crowd of Marines run up. Lost the
image.

Flashed in on Sergeant Yarynin being carried out
on a stretcher.

Jurrin and Chris were still inside, so she switched
to internal audio.

Dirt. Sky. Marines.

"Deena? Dee? She's not breathing!"

"Move away from the body, Corporal."

"It's not a body, dammit!"

"Chris, come on. Give them room to work."

"I'm not getting a heartbeat! Get those jacks out
and a medpack in!"

"Dee!"

So cold...

"They shouldn't be allowed out in public."
Jerked forward for emphasis, hand aching in her
mother's grip, Deena watched the Marines clean-
ing up the last of the mess left by the storm. She'd
learned about the Marines in school, how they came
down from the space station to help after the storm

and how there used to be lots and how they'd saved people and found dead bodies and fixed the roads. Things were almost back like they were before the storm and almost all the Marines had gone back to fight the in the war.

Almost.

The biggest Marine stepped forward, black metal gleaming in the sun, and picked up a piece of a building, lifting it like it weighed nothing. One of the other Marines yelled something and the metal covered Marine tossed the piece of building over by the fence as easily as if he was tossing a single bit of wood not nearly a whole wall.

Deena felt the impact through the bottoms of her sandals.

When the Marine turned and waved a metal hand, she waved back.

"Don't encourage them, Deena. They've become machines; their brains are no more than wet computers." As her mother lengthened her stride, Deena had to nearly run to keep up. "What kind of person does that to themselves?"

Tanya Huff lives and writes in rural Ontario with her wife Fiona Patton, nine cats—number subject to change without notice—and two dogs. She has a degree in Radio and Television Arts, spent time in the Canadian Naval Reserve, and is an enthusiastic, albeit not terribly skilled, guitar player. "You Do What You Do" is the second short based on the Confederation of Valor series (*Valor's Choice, Better Part of Valor, Heart of Valor, Valor's Trial,* and *Truth of Valor*). Her recent titles include the mass market edition of *Truth of Valor*, published by DAW Books in September of 2011, followed by *The Wild Ways*—a second Emporium book—out in hardcover from DAW in November of 2011. She's currently working on a created-world fantasy, not yet titled, to be published in 2012.

Nomad

KARIN LOWACHEE

People in modern times don't like to acknowledge that some of us Radicals are nomad. They interpret that as rogue and dangerous. If you think it's hard for us now, it was much worse during the turf wars—especially if you weren't integrated. When Tommy died I became uni—unintegrated—and that usually means nomad. I belonged to no Streak, had no chief and no Fuses to protect me. It wasn't overnight.

For a month after Tommy died, my chief tried to convince me to integrate with another human. It's not unheard of, though for many it is not desired. But since nomad Radicals have it hard against suspicious people, the majority of us capitulate and Fuse to a second, lesser human. Any human after your first is always lesser in some way. You have not grown with them; you have not shared memories from birth to death. Many Radicals who have lost their first human don't last the year, Fused again or not; instead they voluntarily dismantle.

I was never one for suicide, though I have come close. But I don't think it's in my nature to cut myself short—I have the scars and dents on my armor to prove it. I spent too many years trying to keep myself and Tommy alive against rival Streaks, and he did the same. To dismantle myself, even if it's my right, would be an insult to the Fuse I had lost when Tommy died.

Every Streak across the world thinks they know what went down when Tommy was killed, but they don't know because everyone involved in that fracas, besides myself, was destroyed. (Human, Radical—the term "destruction" fits for both.) This was the beginning of my Streak's suspicion of me and I suppose I can't blame them. It is a hard thing to explain when your human dies and you survive. Tommy's uncle was the chief, and the chief's Radical was the only other Radical in our Streak that was older than me. We were possibly the oldest Radicals left in the world besides some beaten-down Copperpickers in the few mines left in the North. Anyway, Tommy had been the vice-chief. It is likely that once Tommy was dead and I was uni, Radical One calculated that I would want to take the primus position with a new human. But I had no such ambitions and still do not. Leading a Streak is not a simple thing and I've grown tired of the raids.

Maybe I have always been a little bit nomad in my programming. My generation model, they say, has some tragic flaws.

The day I decided to leave the Streak, the chief made one last effort to convince me to stay and reintegrate. I stood in the wreckhouse with the other Fuses, all of them doubles. I was the only single. We made thirteen, which is small for a modern Streak, but the chief didn't agree with the corporate mentality that dictated there had to be at least twenty Fuses in a Streak. That was too much like a government army, and we were better beneath our own flag.

The armor of every Fuse is different. Our Streak wasn't full of rainbow, like you find in the West, especially in Heo Eremiel. Their raids look ridiculous if you see them in your rearscan, like a flock of parrots who will talk you to death. We weren't all about our looks, but our Tora Streak had some pride. Blacks, grays, blues, reds. When we raided up, we were a storm.

Radical One was a sheen of midnight blue integrated with the chief, covering him head to toe in a sleek armor husk. If you have never seen a Fuse it might be difficult to discern where human ends and Radical begins, but that is the point. Since we weren't raided up, though, his faceplate was open, his gunports were shut, and I saw his hooded human eyes. Radical One's red scanning eye on his forehead bent in regular beats across each of our faceplates and did not bend to the human eyes. I bent my eye back, but then ignored it to zero on the chief. He was old by human years, well into his gray period, but battle hardened in every line and vein.

"Why won't you give Probie a chance?" Chief gestured with a gauntlet at the lone human who stood by the door of the wreckhouse. One of him and one of me. Even a first burst of a Radical could do that math out of the yards.

"I gave him a chance," I said. "We won't work."

The probie had approached me the week before

and said, "They don't make your kind anymore, do they?" knowing very well that my model was discontinued twelve years ago. He'd taken two months to pluck up to me and that was the first thing out of his wet man-mouth.

"I wish I could say the same about you," I'd told him. He'd taken offense, which wasn't my problem. And he wasn't going to be my problem now.

Deacon was his born name, but because he wasn't Fused we all called him Probie. He did scut work around the house and the garage, and he had some skill with programming and basic Radical maintenance, not that I ever let him touch me. Mostly he did anything the chief wanted him to do for the Fuses, Radical and human alike. He had to learn that a Fuse wasn't about the human. We weren't cars he could flip a switch on and control out of the factory. I didn't know why the chief made him a probie in the first place, because even if Deacon respected the Fuses, I saw that self-righteous gleam in his blue eyes. He reckoned he could stare down a Radical's scan even though we never blinked. That kind of arrogance shares circuitry with stupidity. I'd rather dismantle than Fuse with that.

"So what's your plan?" the chief said. "I hope you won't kite off on a revenge mission."

The payback on the bastard Fuses who had killed Tommy was not as complete as I would have liked. There had been much discussion in the Streak about the nature of this payback and the chief had his reasons for being careful about it. Keeping the peace between precarious towns; not wanting the locals to raise a paramilitary army to drive us out; not wanting more bloodshed when my murder of Tommy's murderers could be seen as an even score. So many reasons and yet I would not have regretted more death.

But revenge wasn't my reason for leaving.

"I'm going nomad," I said.

All twelve Fuses made noises, human profanity and sharp Radical hums. Radical Five, who was called Steel, said that they would rather I stayed with the Streak as a uni than lose me to the grid. Steel was always dependable on my flank and its Fuse was now the vice-chief. His human Anatolia missed Tommy almost as much as I did. Once in a while they'd shared beds.

"I appreciate that," I said, "but I think nomad is the direction for me. At least for now."

"You will always have a place in Tora Streak," the chief said. He wasn't going to argue anymore. He'd given me enough outs in the past month and it was impossible to change my program once I'd set it.

Radical One's eye bent and remained on my faceplate. Radical One didn't have any other name, just the recognition number that every Radical possesses but none of us use in speech. It had never wanted to be more familiar to humans. Though the chief objected to my going and it was in the logs, Radical One never tried to make me stay. Without me around, its primus position would be fixed until dismantling or destruction through battle, since none of the other Fuses were close enough to take over unless for some reason the chief died independently. But Radical One was powerful, despite its age, and it did not lose in battle.

The chief said, "Radical Two is determined to be nomad. We won't keep it here. Does everyone give their support to Radical Two?"

The consent was unanimous, if full of regret. I

had some regret too, but not enough to keep me from leaving.

The chief said, "Then go with the wind, Mad." And that was the first time he had ever called me by my chosen name.

It was the name Tommy had given me.

Humans don't always name us. We name ourselves if we want such a familiar designation. But when Tommy was four he thought of Mad, not because I'm an angry Radical, he just didn't want to call me Radical Two anymore. "That sounds so cold," he said. "And you're too warm inside." When he melded to the hollow of my armor body, we created warmth.

I was also only four years out of the yards, we were four years integrated alloy and skin, and every time he shed me to be only human I felt an emptiness. I suppose that was where it all began.

We call it armor but the technical name is Trans-Developmental Biogenic Alloy. After the ratified Constitution that granted us rights and privileges as any sentient intelligent being, humans short-handed us to Radical Armor, and then just Radical. We are told that the name alludes to part of our chemical makeup; one of our origin scientists coined it. I have always found it a little sarcastic. Free radicals. Perhaps Dr. Gom had been a sarcastic man, as much as he had been a genius.

We grow with our humans, a second skin that can slip apart and exist away from the Fuse. The racists call us Silly Putty for our ability to morph, change constitution, and adapt. And we do adapt. We change. We integrate.

The Streaks are weapons grade Radical Armor.

First integration happens as close to birth as possible. It's the only way you can be sure a Radical's bioware adapts properly to a human, when the human's mind isn't fixed already. Once we've been through our first integration, we can integrate again, but it's never as smooth as that first; when you're new and your human's new, slipping inside each other's thoughts in that infant stage is like a synthesis of pure instinct or a predatory scent of blood.

I have memories of Tommy from five minutes after his first cry in this world, and before he died he had all of mine. Like the first time I opened my hand and saw my faint reflection in my perfect obsidian armor. Before the battle damage.

I remember the first time I set my hand over his and our grips locked together and became one. It took no thought to move our hand because the integration was more instinct than intellect. That is how you know that the fix is right. It is not artificial intelligence; it is intuitive intelligence.

It's a need, those first memories. The first time he breathed the air, the first time he shut his eyes and saw instead through mine. The world is limitless when you're Fused. It's a hunger for experience and we spend all our lives in a hunt to fill it.

That's what drives a Fuse. You, your human, and everything you can't satisfy.

That is our biggest weakness too.

In our need to integrate with them, we adapted to human flaws.

The Fuses gathered around to bid me goodbye from the wreckhouse. Steel and Anatolia, Sol and

Markie, Wyrm and Jasper, Giniro and Imori, Kikenna
and Selene. The chief and Radical One only touched
my shoulder and left first through the door. I scanned
both human and Radical faces and it was a hard thing
to know that I might never see them again.

They asked me where I was going but I didn't
tell them. I had plans to follow the road that would
lead me away from the turf wars. I didn't want to
say out loud that I didn't want to see any Radicals
that I knew, or any Radicals at all. They would have
considered this insane, because we all knew that in
places where Radicals weren't welcome, no law would
protect me. Some humans did not acknowledge the
Constitution, our rights, our sentience, our ability to
choose not to kill them. Their fears were not completely
unfounded, of course. But there are more murderous
humans than there are murderous Radicals, and that
will likely never change.

After Tommy's death, I just wanted to be away.
Vengeance could wait. Vengeance was bone without the
marrow. Something else unknown and even dangerous
matched the open spaces that were expanding through
my inner wires and biogenic gyroscopes. I was being
gutted the longer I remained in Tora Streak, racked
to Tora thoughts.

The wreckhouse was where we all congregated
when we weren't launching raids. It catered to both
humans and Radicals, with thick seats, docking spikes,
and areas of play integration outlined by lights and
nebular controls. Right now as I passed my eye over
it in a wide beam, it looked and sounded skeletal
beyond repair. The walls of the house reflected nothing
and loomed empty and unlit, a dead alloy that could

not change as its occupants did in their desires. The movements of the Fuses as they clasped my arms or bumped their heads to mine seemed to echo in hollow bass notes.

I said goodbye, made no promises to return, and stepped out the door into daylight.

The probie stood against the outer wall of the wreckhouse, smoking a cigarette.

"You'll regret leaving," he said, with my back to him.

"I won't regret leaving you." I had a blip of a thought to educate him about his attitude and why that would hinder his graduation from probie to full Fuse. But he wasn't worth even that, so I kept walking toward the gate that surrounded Tora's compound.

"Tommy wouldn't want you to go," he said to my back.

I turned my head around without moving the rest of my body, so my eye bent direct on his narrow little face. "You are determined to live a short human life."

He flicked his cigarette away onto the pavement. "I think you should give me a second chance."

"I have given you more chances than you realize."

I watched as he approached, hands in his jacket pockets. He stopped right below my eye. He was shorter than Tommy, enough so that I had to tilt down my face to scan his features. The overlay showed me where all of his biodots were, a scatter of constellations in his brain. This might've been what made him such a sharp programmer. I did not know much about his past, only that he had come to the Streak from the town by recommendation of a human ally in the police department, and he had no living parents. The chief had done a thorough check on him and deemed him

worthy of probie status. I didn't ordinarily disagree
with the chief, but if I could've taken back our vote
before Tommy had died, seeing what I saw now,
would have—and jammed a bullet in this probie's
smirk while I was at it.

"I want to really talk with you," he said. "But not
here. If afterwards you still don't think me worthy,
then I'll never bother you again."

"You'll never bother me again as soon as I walk
through the gate." I turned my head around and set
myself in that direction.

"It's about his death," the probie said.

I circled back and snatched him up by the scruff of
his neck. The gate opened at my signal and I walked
on, holding the probie off the ground. He kicked and
struggled but it is impossible for a human to break
a Radical's grip. He had a gun but he wouldn't dare
use it.

So I walked with him just like that down the road
away from Tora compound. I walked a full hour and
then walked another, until the cars and other Radicals from Freemantown no longer passed us. None
of them questioned me because they saw the orange
and black Tora mark on my chest. I walked us out to
the roads between towns, where yellow land stretched
long and empty on either side. It was a cool day and
I didn't falter. I was well-maintained and topped up
with energy, and could've moved faster if I adapted
into road mode, but that would've required setting
him on my back somehow. He fell limp in my grip
eventually, weary from fighting and cursing at me.

But he woke up when I dumped him onto the
side of the road.

"You bloody robot piece of shit!"

They continue to think "robot" is an insult.

I bent my blue eye to him and sent up the beam so it hit him on the forehead like a target. "Is this what you want to say to me?"

He was covered in dirt. He hauled himself to his feet and struggled to climb up the gravel embankment to face me toe to toe. I watched his gun hand. He was not generally that stupid, but he was angry, and humans have a tendency to be stupid in their anger.

"You think you know what happened to Tommy." The probie spat at my feet. "But you don't."

"You think *you* know what happened to Tommy?" I too had guns. They were in-built.

"That ambush from the Gear Heart Streak." He stared up at me with a blaze in his eyes. "When they raided up on you in Nuvo Nuriel. In the hotel. The chief sent you there to pat a deal with the Gears, but then they ended up turning on you? There was no deal, Mad, except to fuck you over. You *and* Tommy, cause of what you were to each other."

My scan overlay went red. I grabbed him up again by the collar and shook him hard.

His feet kicked. "Let go of me!"

I pitched him ten meters into the field. He fell with a dull thud and a cry. I bounded over to him in one leap from the road. My right foot almost nailed his chest, but he rolled away at the last second. I wanted to crush him. It would not have been difficult.

"I know you loved him!" the probie gasped, nearly winded. A true fear spread across his face. "I know 's taboo. I don't care about that; it's wrong what they did. The chief set you up!" He began to cough.

I tangled my fingers in the front of his jacket and lifted him up so we were eye to eye. He kicked for a second out of reflex then stopped, just staring back. His arms hung long, all the arrogance slammed out of him. I calculated the option of killing him. Here in between towns it would take some time to find him. But then, many people from Freemantown had seen me walking with him.

"How do you know the chief set me up?" It was the most pertinent question. After I got my questions answered, maybe then I would send him back to town just so people could see him alive. Then I could circle back, hunt him down, and kill him.

"I read the chief of the Gear Heart Streak," the probie said. "I read his Fuse."

I scanned this probie's biodots again. "With that in your head? There is nothing exceptional. You cannot scan a Radical with your limp brain." Radical minds were fortresses.

He said, "I'm a wetthief. And the Gear Hearts are a bunch of second string Fuses and you know it."

I did know it. Their ambush that had killed Tommy had only focused my hatred, but we had never liked them and their marauding spirits. They were not well-maintained except in their wanton raids. Yet the chief had been bent on patting a deal "to cut down on the killings between the territories" where Tor and Gear tracks bisected the land. What could we have done? The votes went against us. Peace seemed a good avenue but it was always more of a dark alley. Nobody had listened to Tommy on that score.

When they'd killed him, the chief had refused immediate payback. He'd said revenge had to come from thought, not impulse. The Streak had bowed to his level head.

I had burned. But he was my chief and my human was dead. I could not go up against the Gear Heart Streak alone. My actions were Tora's actions.

Or would have been. Not anymore, as a nomad. And my need for vengeance had diminished in the days of loss. It was supposed to be simple, this leavetaking.

Now this probie claimed to know the mind of a Gear Heart Fuse? The chief and his Radical no less?

"I can prove it," the probie said against my silence. "If you Fuse with me, I can show you."

Wetthieves are notoriously reckless individuals. The government tries to deal with them but to no real consequence. It is difficult to smash a thing that isn't tangible, just as it is difficult to define an emotion. All the wily activity is through the mind. Yet I had never heard of a wetthief able to raid up on a Radical.

"Fuse with you?" That had been his intention all along, his eyes on my nexus. "I think you are a liar who wants to divide the Streak. How could a probie get close enough to the Gear Hearts to read their chief? Answer me."

"The chief and Rad One sent me and Anatolia's Fuse to Nuvo Nuriel two weeks ago for a parts run. You remember this. We saw the Gears on the corner. Before we split, I read them. I thought I could get intel for Tora and it'd help my case with you." His jaw moved, stubborn overt confession that he wanted me for his Radical. "So I got intel."

"And now you think it will help your case with me." I would not address his other claim, what he thought he knew about me and Tommy. That would be a confirmation he had no right to nudge. Though I wondered how he did know, and if his mischievous man-mind had thieved in my nexus. Surely I would have felt it? I am deeply paranoid about my ware, as we all are.

The probie stared at me. I still held him above the ground. "If I had long enough, I could read you too. How do you think I know about you and Tommy? It was in the Gear Radical's brain. It was in that chief's. And they knew because *your* chief told them. You Radicals think you're impenetrable, but you're still a machine. And all machines have weaknesses."

"You created us," I said, and threw him very far.

He sailed through the air for more than ten meters. He hollered as he went. When he landed he stopped. I walked through the yellow grass and looked down at him. He seemed to be dead, lying in a heap, and it was a little bit of a concern that I might have killed him before I had all the answers. But only a little. It had felt good to toss him.

I scanned his vitals. His heart was beating and his brain showed activity—enough to be alive, though he was unconscious. Which was what I'd wanted. Unconscious, he couldn't thieve.

I folded myself down beside him and waited. I didn't care if it took hours for him to wake up. The field was quiet except for random birds and the squeak of critters low to the ground. Mice. I watched a cricket bound across the black armor of my foot, pause there, and then disappear into the grass.

Tommy came to mind. It was inevitable. He was never long out of my thoughts, but now I played the images of him across my faceplate. He was tricky there and alive. It was true, I loved my human. It was also true that it was forbidden. You would think that if any clan of humans would understand an emotion forged in a Fuse, between human and Radical, it would be among the Streaks. But fundamentally there are still laws that surpass even science. There are deviations that go too far even for the Fuses in a Streak. Some things are universally wrong and some part of my programming understands that. I am, as the probie said, a machine. I can mold to human skin, to cover it and protect it and create a strength no human can reach on their own, but it is still only armor. I am still only armor, despite our integration with their minds.

Until my heart grew involved. Until my heart evolved. We call it a heart, but it is more like a central nervous system of programming. I believe it is the seat of our sentience but there is nothing to prove that. Humans think awareness comes from the brain.

I didn't ask for this sentience. Unlike humans, my self-awareness was not born, but made. I was not the first Radical to achieve it (that one is long dismantled), but the template became in-built. Is it so difficult for people to believe that the next step in the evolution of sentience is love?

Tommy believed it the second I told him. We were fused and sat in a field much like this one, at night, and I felt his fragile human body nested inside the spaces I had made for him since birth. The hollow of my chest, the tubes of my legs and arms. There he resided and every subtle thought sparked a response in mine, until we thought the same. We powered each other's limbs in quiet movement. He ran his hand over the top of the grass blades and we both felt the tickle. My armor reflected the stars overhead, or as he liked to say, captured them. He was a killer—we both were—but he had a heart for the heavens.

I didn't have to say the words. I only said, "We should go back to the wreckhouse, the chief will wonder." Because we had been incommunicado for hours, and Tommy refused to reply to messages and I would not send signals on the sly. More often Tommy grew tired of the raids on the rival gangs, going from town to town, defending territory, controlling commerce. But I didn't want him to get into trouble with the chief, so I said, "It's very late."

And he said, "Not yet, Mad." And, "Just not yet."

By and by, the probie awoke. Dusk sat new on the edges of the sky, dragging black overhead like a covering blanket. When I saw the probie's eyes blink and focus I said, "We are going to the Gear Heart Streak and we will discover if what you say is true." My vengeance lay in wait. Now it could prowl again and my emptiness did not matter. It would be there regardless. I would wage war and did not care what humans got in my way.

The probie said, "What's the point of going to the Gears? Right into enemy territory? You should go back to Tora and confront the chief."

"I won't accuse the chief and Radical One just because you say so. You say you thieved it from Gear Heart mind, so we will go to the Gear Heart I will use you as a shield if you try my patience."

"I did read them." Even in the dim light of just stars and moon, I saw the steel insistence in his eye I needed no night scope for it.

"They are a bullshit Streak, those Gears," I said. "So one way or another, we'll get it out of them."

He walked slowly, still dizzy-brained from the toss. I didn't help him and I was in no hurry. I had to think of how to approach the Gears. Their territory was another few hours walk, even at a Radical stride. We would be there by dawn. Once, the probie suggested I let him ride me in road mode. I knocked him back to the gravel. He got up, swearing at me, but he didn't ask again. At least he didn't try to run. That would have been tedious to chase after him, to recapture him and shake him and put him under my arm so he couldn't run again.

He must have truly wanted to Fuse with me to put up with my abuse. But I supposed that was natural. He was a probie; there was nothing more important to a probie than a Fuse.

So he said nothing else for the rest of the night. That was a single saving grace. The wetthief finally knew when to shut his damn mouth.

Across the street from the enemy compound I calculated the Gear Heart wreckhouse, the tracks I saw in the dirt, and informed the probie of my intent. We were going to hail them and speak with them. Once we were close enough, the probie would thieve from their nexus and load it to me. It was cumbersome to do so, not Fused, and might eat up precious time, but it was my strategy. I did not expect the Gear Hearts to tell me the truth. So I would put this wetthief to the test and if he wasn't lying, I would destroy the Gear Hearts, every last one of them, and then I would

go back to Tora Streak and kill the chief and Radical
One for their betrayal.

The probie said, "You're fucking insane."

That was the true meaning of my name. No anger,
just crazy. I said, "You will back me up."

He had a gun and he was a good shot. I would
defend him so long as I needed him. He knew it too.

He said, "You first."

Since they'd killed Tommy, the Gear Hearts had
not crossed into Tora territory. In fact they gave us a
lot of room to do our deals and transport our goods,
guns, drugs, medical supplies to outlying paramilitaries.
And we did not cross into theirs. It was an uneasy
truce and now this probie made me wonder if it was
one born from the blood of my Fuse.

The probie lurked behind me as I stood in front of
the Gear Heart gate. I wanted to open my gunport
but such hostility would only provoke them to launch
a few grenades our way. So I remained straight, sealed
up, my eye ranging only so far as the south end of
their rundown wreckhouse wall.

"This is Radical Two of the Tora Streak," I sent
loud toward them. Technically I was nomad but they
didn't need to know that. My voice cut through the
early morning quiet. A graying hound loped in my
peripheral vision, nosed at the dirt near old Radic
footprints. I could not determine how old. "I w
speak to your chief."

The chief had not been in the ambush, so I had
not killed him. Instead I had killed his vice-chief
Fuse and I had no doubt he held it against me. The
truce could end right now if he was dumb enough

take offense at my presence. I itched to bloom open my epaulet gunports.

But the main door of the wreckhouse creaked open and a short dusty human poked his head out. He was not the chief, so some other member of the Streak. He had tattoos around his eyes like a red badger.

"The chief ain't here," he croaked.

"Then I will wait for him. When do you expect him back?"

"I dunno."

"You may get him on signal or you can watch me sit in front of your gate with my Tora mark for the remainder of the day."

"Or we can blow you off our stoop with a missile."

"I know you Gear Hearts aren't that accurate. You can recall I killed four of your Streak. I didn't come here to fight, but my arsenal can take out your entire compound. Do you wish to gamble on your aim and my reflexes?"

The door shut with a *blam*. Behind me, the probie laughed but I shoved him quiet. I scanned the compound with all of my senses. The wreckhouse was proofed against every kind of amplification, but I listened and looked for movement by the animals, the trees on the outer edges, the air between the buildings. All lay quiet, as if the Streak were still abed. But I knew they were awake and the chief was indeed behind this gate.

In two minutes, he emerged from the wreckhouse, fused. His Radical was blood red, its eye a scathing white. Its gaze slammed on me like a spotlight so I had to adjust my intake view. The Fuse met me on the other side of the gate.

"What do you want?" said the Gear Heart chief.

I had only to make him talk long enough for the probie to thieve his nexus and shunt the intel to me. I wanted it live, not from memory where memory could be manufactured. I would not put trickery past the probie so this was my strategy. This would tell the truth of all.

Then the probie shot the Gear Heart chief right in the face.

The large caliber, double impact heavy round went straight through the faceplate. Such weaponry is made to kill Fuses. Blood and bits of plate glass, bone, and brains smattered against my armor.

I had no time to shout at the probie. The chief was dead but his Radical wasn't. With a shudder the Gear Heart Radical slipped from its human, a sound I knew only too well shattering the morning air. I had made such a noise when Tommy was killed. The dead human chief slumped over into the dirt and gravel like a snail without a shell, and the Radical launched itself into the air with a cry, right over the gate.

Before it landed, its gunports spooled open and rained artillery down upon us.

There is much debate from scientists about whether a Radical is faster and stronger Fused with a human than alone without. These scientists will spend much time on tests and data collection, interviews and psychological exams. But it is no debate for any Radical who has been Fused. We are at optimum with our humans. A Fuse is stronger together than alone. It not about human reflexes and Radical synapses. When we are Fused, there is no separation. We become the best of our individual capabilities.

And for my model, our primary capability is killing

The Gear Heart Radical, without its human, stood no chance. As I've said, the Gear Hearts are a bullshit Streak. They swagger but without the skill. They defend their territory by spraying wide, like a machine gun in the hands of an untrained child. They are not snipers or assassins. They waste energy and movement.

In a snap, my heavier shields unfurled above my shoulders to take the artillery fire. I didn't mark where the probie went. Beneath my shield I flung up a hand. It held my forearm weapon. Two shots blasted on the enemy Radical's chest. The impact sent it back a step and stopped its flow of fire. I dropped my right shield and barraged the Radical with my epaulet guns and two rocket grenades from my hip. The Gear Heart went down spraying bullets, but down it went regardless. The rounds peppered my armor as I flung up my shield again. They made no lasting damage.

The probie crouched behind my left side, shooting toward the compound. The rest of the Streak—all ten of them—had come out battling. But they faltered when they saw the bodies on the ground.

"Your chief Fuse is destroyed!" I sent. They would not know for certain if the rest of Tora Streak was near. To them I wasn't nomad. I saw the calculations in their hesitation. They were an impulsive Streak but grounded in survival.

I thought that would be the end of it, that I could gather this probie and shake the reason for his shooting right out of him, before I stomped him under my heel.

But my rear sensors picked up the whine of movement behind me. My eye gauged the shift in beams in the Radical faces across the gate as something took their attention.

My torso swiveled just as Radical One's rocket grenades exploded against my chest.

I learned later that before I went down I launched the rest of my epaulet artillery. Reflex. The hail slammed into Radical One and my chief but did not kill them. Down on my back, my body began to blow out. The fire from the Gear Heart Radical had weakened me but not infringed on major systems. The storm from Radical One was another matter; its titanium-class artillery cut through me like a scythe. I do not remember this, there is only a gap in my files when nothing recorded.

Between the blackness and repowering, there was Tommy. From birth to death, his form returned to me, a ghost whispering through my circuits, my biocells, every part of me that was the Fuse of both.

His black hair, his amber brown eyes tilted toward the sky.

When he killed, he never took joy in the loss of life

We separated and he nestled in my chest cavity on his side, just to lie there as in a womb. touched him with a different freedom, one that held no feedback sensation. It was just my touches that remembered, not how he felt them. Humans are so easy to injure but he trusted my strength. He let me armored hand cover over his chest, and his heartbeat remained a steady calm rhythm. All of my nearly impenetrable angular edges seemed to fit to his soft human muscle and delicate human bones. Somehow this forged a stronger bond. We were Fused, but he was an individual and so was I. He loved that about us, and I did too.

Scientists say we cannot grieve. But we do.

This was the feeling that flowed through my darkness, until the probie took its place.

The probie climbed into my chest cavity and fit his legs into the hollows of mine, and his arms into the columns of mine. In my darkness, I thought of Tommy and my struggling armor wrapped around this probie, like a flower petal at the touch of a finger. My injuries opened out to him, seeking healant.

The probie set his head to my heart and so began the Fuse.

With his wetthief brain and biodots, he reached out to my nexus and tangled himself in it. We coiled and stretched, memory flow and actions past.

They say Radical Armor can feel no pain. Especially an old model like me, a previous generation no longer on the line.

But they are wrong.

Deacon had no living parents because his mother had shot his father and then shot herself. He was six and witnessed it.

He grew up in town, in the alleys and beneath the sidewalks, in the hands of a system that looked very much like a Radical assembly line. They plugged parts in and removed others, injected cells and livened proteins. All to make a boy work the best he could. He found a human gang. He stole the biodots and ran drugs long enough to make enough money to get them implanted. Then his world opened wide, with teeth. Suddenly there were no barriers he could not break down.

Tommy and I were the first Fuse he ever saw.

He wanted that connection. He wanted an armor no one could break, a second skin to hide him from the sharper parts of the world, a second mind to push his own to broader expanses.

His forays into the brain, any brain, freed him from his own—where memories suctioned tight and strived to suffocate him.

So much blood. It had splattered onto his mouth, blood from his parents. It mingled with the memory of Tommy's on my armor, my faceplate. Deacon's cries were the same as my human's, then overrode them in a wave as Tommy's died out.

Tommy slipped from my body cavity because not even my armor could hold him anymore. My system rang with shock. Our hotel room was destruction, the smell of fire, smoke, and cinder.

Through Deacon I saw the chief and Radical One. They stood on a road halfway between Freemantown and Nuvo Nuriel. My chief said to the Gear Heart chief, *Tommy's heart isn't in it anymore. He and his Radical protest us every step of the way. If you take care of Tommy it will force Radical Two to Fuse again. We don't want to lose the Two, but Tommy's heart has infected it. They take their bond too far. So take him out and we'll ceasefire on your turf. We will leave you alone. Make it look good.*

What about payback? Your Streak will demand it. Radical Two will seek it.

Leave it to me, the chief said.

All of this clipped in Radical One's memory. All of it stolen by Deacon and kept in his.

I saw it all as if I were there. This is the power of a Fuse. It takes only a split second.

Memory is more than just a series of biochemical firing pins, a cascade of molecular events that result in specific encoding. Memory shapes us, both human and Radical.

And memory, we know, is the foundation of revenge.

It was Deacon that made me stand again. The power of his mind and the Fuse, not even fixed yet, precarious in connection but determined to rise. He willed my battered limbs to move, my form to sit, then pushed to stand. Pieces of me flapped free and clanked. Before I had the cognitive function to flick down my arm blade or move my heavy foot, he did it for me, alive and alert. His thoughts were jagged as they melded with mine, felt foreign like stitches on a wound, like one of Tommy's flesh injuries.

He knew where I wanted to go. The chief and Radical One lay struggling in their own brokenness. Their shoulder armor shuddered open and back, like the twisted wing of a bird. Their chest spread with perforations and new scars.

We moved, Deacon and I, to stand over my chief. I barely discerned the Tora mark through the bullet holes. We slammed my heel onto the chief's wrist, breaking it through the armor, and held there to block any flick of weapon.

He cursed at me. He reached for Deacon's throat with his free hand, bolstered by Radical One's remaining strength, but I grasped that too. We held there, a tableau of murder at an impasse, until Deacon brought up my right foot and slammed it into the joint where shoulder met neck. The chief's arm went limp. It freed my own grip.

My artillery packs sat empty. My gun was cracked and useless. It took no thought, only will. As Radical One's red eye swept over my severed faceplate I plunged my arm blade into the chief's throat and twisted it. So fast it took his head halfway off his neck.

I inflicted the same on Radical One, with bare hands. Its injuries and momentary shock at the death of its human gave me and Deacon the advantage. I dismantled it right there on the road, a piece at a time. I bashed its circuits, gutted it of cables, twisted its desperate, reaching armor until the shapes made nothing, only hunched there like forgotten shards of frozen metal, the dregs of a factory assembly line.

What I did to it was a mercy. It did not have to mourn, as I did, for my Fuse.

The Gear Heart Streak, what was left of it, never interfered. Frightened of Tora retaliation, or too mindful of their own survival. Through Deacon's mind I knew. My chief and Radical One had followed me from Tora's wreckhouse, with every intention of dismantling me—and their chief and Radical had known. When they saw my destination at the Gear gate, furious signals flew between chiefs: dismantle me and kill Deacon, since we could not be controlled. I had disappointed my chief by not fusing again, going nomad. Deacon had disappointed the chief by coming to me first.

Now they were disappointed and destroyed, and that was all there was to that.

We lost the taste for blood, Deacon and I, and left the Gear Heart Streak to its decimation. I didn't want to return to Tora and answer any questions, fac any possible retaliation. I wasn't Tora anymore; the destruction on my chest armor had wiped the Tora mark, one good result of that damage. Without a word of outloud consultation, Deacon and I set ourselves on the road out of Nuvo Nuriel. The direction was straight but my steps fumbled and creaked. We would need to find a resting place, between towns, to heal ourselves. And to fix.

Where we were headed, it didn't matter. We were nomad.

I didn't pick this Fuse. Later Deacon would say, *I picked you*. Sometimes, I suppose, it works that way. It is not all about the human. But it isn't all about the Radical either.

We sat in a field by an abandoned warehouse, letting the tendrils of the Fuse find one another until it was complete. We belonged to no Streak but he cared less than I did. I hadn't forgotten what it was like to hold a human inside my armor, but it was different with him. While Tommy had dreamed of the stars and peace, Deacon was a restless runner. Sometimes I would have to pull him back, but other times he would drive me on.

In this way we were Fused and in this way we would live.

In this way, through all the spaces between populations, both Radical and human, we are alive.

———————

Karin Lowachee was born in South America, grew up in Canada, and worked in the Arctic. Her first novel *Warchild* won the 2001 Warner Aspect First

Novel Contest. Both *Warchild* (2002) and her third novel *Cagebird* (2005) were finalists for the Philip K. Dick Award. *Cagebird* won the Prix Aurora Award in 2006 for Best Long-Form Work in English and the Spectrum Award also in 2006. Her second novel *Burndive* debuted at #7 on the Locus Bestseller List. Her books have been translated into French, Hebrew, and Japanese. Her recent fantasy novel, *The Gaslight Dogs*, was published through Orbit Books USA.

Human Error

JOHN JACKSON MILLER

In the old days on Earth, victorious soldiers came home to parades. In space, Bridgie Yang knew, you might well return to find the enemy eating your house.

The barracks for the Surgical Assault Teams were clearly visible as Bridgie's space transport approached the asteroid . . . or what was left of it. The Signatory Council had thoughtfully constructed the warriors' dome in a roomy, high-rimmed crater shaded from Altair's bright rays. But now, half the crater wall was gone, and the barracks with it. All that remained of the structure were shimmering chunks within a cluster of enormous living soap bubbles. Through the diaphanous alien menace's body, Bridgie could easily make out the signal tower of the armory, quickly dissolving into digestible globs.

"Surge Team One to Altair Center," Bridgie said, green eyes narrowing as she gripped the transport's control yoke. "Tell me everyone made it out of the barracks."

"Affirmative," came the response over her headset. "They all made it across to the station in time. Welcome home, Chief Yang. Er—I mean, welcome *back*."

Bridgie didn't appreciate the slip. *The Spore*—it was eating their home base! What had they spent the last six months fighting, all across the Altair system? And what good was all that work now? What must have it been like for the troops here, having to leave everything behind?

But there was a more important question, she knew.

"Who brought it here?" The dark-haired woman's throat tightened as she scanned the surface images on her console for the source of the infestation. She knew no one on *her* team would have accidentally brought it in—they were too smart for that. She hadn't become the youngest human to lead a Surge Team for nothing. But because she was chief, she was technically responsible for everyone—even those she hadn't recruited herself. *It had better not be one of Welligan's rookies*, she thought. *I'll skin him alive.*

The transmission crackled for an annoying few seconds before she got her answer. No, the foreign biological had arrived the week before, affixed to one of the handheld laser cannons shipped in from another depot. Porrima B, where they'd never seen a safety regulation they couldn't ignore.

Bridgie exhaled. Losing the barracks was tough, but she knew there were plenty of weapons—and fresh low-grav battle suits—waiting for them in the main station. Just in from Regulus, where they knew what they were doing. They'd caught a break. She opened her headset channel to address the other troops on her carrier. "Looks like we're not finished today, folks."

"Actually, you might be," answered a baritone voice she instantly recognized: Falcone, administrator of the Altair Sunward Provisioning Center. "We *all* might be finished."

The Great Spore wasn't actually a spore. But "Exotic Formation Seven-Alpha" lacked what the lobbyists back home were looking for: that special sound that panicked Earth's governments into committing some portion of their burgeoning revenue from taxing space commerce to the defense budget. The specter of an interplanetary fungus literally digesting resource worlds before prospectors could reach them had gotten everyone's attention, bringing the humans into league with the other Signatory powers. As physically different as the intelligent alien species in the Orion Arm were, there was one thing they all agreed on: the Great Spore was unique, and uniquely destructive. It had to be eradicated.

Of course, part of the problem was that there wasn't just one Great Spore. Exotic Formation Seven-Alpha's division—and effective multiplication—owed entirely to the clumsy first efforts of the early Signatory powers to combat it. Encountering the original Spore digesting the rocky remains of a planet orbiting Fomalhaut, an excitable Gebranese pilot launched a thermal explosive toward the quivering mass. The resulting blast was almost certainly a pleasant sight to the Gebran's cluster of eyes—but the sequel surely was not. For the explosion hurled trace amounts of the organism across the kilometers to take root on the skin of the Gebranese rocket, already bound for the main Fomalhaut transit station. As soon as its dormant phase ended, Seven-Alpha went back to work. Those awaiting the Gebran's triumphant return saw instead the new Great Spore, carried along by the acceleration of engines it had already mindlessly digested along the way.

Before brute force methods were finally abandoned, similar episodes had spread Spore infestations to a dozen systems. All attempts to incinerate the being had only led to its further spread, spore particles clinging microscopically to everything from starships to comets. Radiation alone only seemed to make it grow faster.

No, as Bridgie and all those who had trained along-side her knew, the only way to eradicate the Spore was up-close and personal. The boil had to be lanced—messy, detailed work that required individuals to approach the Spore in reinforced environment suits armed with precision lasers. A number of organic command struc-tures, invisible from a distance, bobbed up and down in Seven-Alpha's mass; pinpoint shots to these nuclei caused the surrounding mass to wither within seconds, unable to regenerate. A good team of Surgicals could destroy a cubic kilometer of Spore in an hour without any viable material spreading to their equipment. And Bridgie Yang's team was one of the best, as the fragment of Spore on Altair's orbiting gas giant had just found.

Or would have, if it had a brain to go along with its boundless appetite.

That another outgrowth had appeared on the same oblong asteroid with ASPEC—the not-quite right acro-nym for the Altair Sunward Provisioning Center—wasn't of much concern to Bridgie as she entered the main station. Flanked by O'Herlihy, her hulking second-in command, she breathed easy in the recirculated air o the dome. Their rocket-supported heavy-grav suits had made work in the clouds of the gas giant possible, but they weren't built for comfort. The one-eighth Earth gravity of the asteroid felt like a day at the spa.

"Yang! Glad you're back," said a man who didn't look glad of anything.

Even nearly weightless, Leonid Falcone sagged, Bridgie saw as she kept walking. Hair uncombed, tie too short—she didn't know what hour it was supposed to be in ASPEC, but Falcone had either just gotten up or been up too long. She brought her hand to her tanned forehead in salute, even though it wasn't necessary: Falcone was just a bureaucrat. "Saw the bugger on the way in, Leo. I'll have Surge One suited up in five."

Falcone coughed. "That won't be possible. Your equipment—"

"Is in the building that just got eaten," she said. Bridgie and O'Herlihy never broke stride, forcing the shorter administrator to keep up. "But you just got a knockbox in from Regulus with our new low-grav armor—and that's still here in the base."

Seeing the rest of her troops filtering through the airlock into the station behind her, Bridgie turned toward the cargo receiving area. There, as she expected, sat four of the metal whales that had been light years away weeks before: the unmanned shipping containers colloquially known as knockboxes. Spying the markings of the Signatory Production Directorate, Bridgie looked back at Falcone, reassuringly. "You'll see."

But what Bridgie saw after stepping through the cargo gate stopped her dead.

"Where's Q/A?" she said, looking around. *"Temmons!"*

❖   ❖   ❖

Seventeen and never home to a single facial hair, Quartermaster/Armorer Jake Temmons knelt beside a black metal polyhedron half his height. One of the pentagonal faces glowed, providing a technological interface with the knowledge of a species older than Earth itself.

Bridgie knew what the device was, but not why the kid had it here and now. Here, in the tail-end of the knockbox shipped four days earlier from Regulus—and now, when the Spore threatened just a few kilometers away. "What's the deal, Q/A?"

"Oh, hi, Bridgie." Pale-skinned and freckle-faced, Temmons looked like he belonged on a playground planet-side, not on the front lines. "What deal do you mean?"

"Make that *Chief Yang*," she said, seeing Administrator Falcone had followed her in. "None of this armor's been unloaded! You knew we'd need to get out there and start fighting!"

"Yes, I did," Temmons said, not looking up.

Wonder child or no, Bridgie thought, *he's taking the Q/A title a little too seriously.* She walked to one of the large containers lining the sides of the knockbox and yanked at the handle.

"See for yourself," the boy said unhelpfully, as she swung the corrugated lid upward. And she did see...

...something. But *what?*

Bridgie heaved what she thought was a breastplate from the container only to discover she was holding a pentagonal shield more than a meter wide, concaved toward a circular hole at the center. A twin to the plate still sat inside the container, she saw. Pulling it out, she realized the two fit together, creating an oversized armored suitcase with five large holes around the edges. It was made from the same composite material as the low-grav armor she'd expected to find—but it looked more fit for a schizoid cello than for a human torso.

The equipment slipped from her hands, gently clanking to the floor in the weak gravity. "Jake, what the hell is this?"

"Not what we ordered," Temmons said, rising and turning to an opened container behind him. Reaching in with both arms, Temmons fumbled for a moment before stepping back. Turning toward Bridgie, he displayed what looked like metallic kangaroo tails on each arm. The long sloping cones accordioned and bent as he crooked his elbows within the housing.

"What does the manifest say?"

"It says we received what we were due: thirty-two armored units optimized for combat in low-gravity environments." Temmons smiled a little as he waggled the hollow armatures like wings. "They're just not for humans."

"What?" Bridgie stepped forward and ripped one of the housings off Temmons's arm. The Q/A looked miffed. She didn't care. "Then who are they for?"

Looking at the components together, she knew her answer before Temmons spoke. *The Uutherum.*

Bridgie knelt and plugged the floppy arm into one of the side portals of the unit she'd unloaded. The connection made, the arm stiffened as servomotors came online. Temmons added another, and another. Just as with the human outfits from the Signatory manufacturing centers, the joints automatically cycled closed for an airtight fit. What remained at the end looked like a coffin for a starfish two meters across.

Which was exactly what the Uutherum resembled. "There's no helmet," Falcone said.

"There's no *head*," Temmons corrected. Stepping around a corner, he emerged with a sensor-covered disc half a meter across. "This fits right over the hole in the middle—plugs into their sensory organs somehow. The one for the hole on the other side has a thruster unit."

Bridgie felt along several of the arms to find tiny attitude control jets. "They get around," she said, almost to herself. She looked up at Temmons. "They're all like this?"

"There's a larger container at the far end I haven't been able to reach—but it's got Uutherum markings too."

Standing, Bridgie stared blankly at the rows of containers surrounding her. There would be no calling Regulus for replacements. The errant knockbox had reached Altair the same way they had, shot through a rip in space created by a pulse generator. But the trip took four days, and getting the correct material from Regulus would take eight. Messages traveled no faster between stars than humans—or misaddressed equipment—did.

Bridgie angrily twirled one of her braids, as she always did at times like these. Long hair might be a liability in combat, but she'd always joked that if she didn't have it, she'd be twisting bureaucrats' necks instead. And this was a grand screw-up, indeed. "I've never heard of anything like this," she said, infuriated. "All the money people have put into space travel. Every kilo of payload precious. And now—"

"And now it's common enough for people to screw it up." Temmons chuckled. "I guess we've finally arrived."

Falcone stomped between them, veins visible in his neck. "Will the two of you shut the hell up? Seven-Alpha just ate your barracks as an appetizer. It's going to eat the whole asteroid, and ASPEC with it!"

Temmons looked up. "Skippy's that close?"

"*Skippy?*"

Bridgie interceded between the two. If anyone was going to kill the youthful quartermaster, it would be her. "The Surge teams class the Spore specimens by behavior," she explained. "This year's mutation likes to leap around when it senses motion." Actually, the being had neither senses nor muscles that she knew of, but there was no better description.

"You just came back from the gas giant," Falcone said. "You've got armor on your ship."

"Designed for a gravity well eighty times the one we've got here," Bridgie said. "It'd be like fighting with a zoo bear on your back. We'd never be able to calibrate the control jets for an asteroid in time."

"Why can't you destroy it in simple spacesuits?" Falcone was growing more agitated as he checked the time. "Or shoot at it from your troop carrier?"

Bridgie kicked the hollow Uutherum armor, producing a resounding clang. "Our armor—even this armor—has a composite coating that resists the spore's implantation and digestive capabilities."

Wiping his forehead, Falcone glared. "Why not build the whole station out of it, then?"

"It'd cost quadrillions. But you're the official here, you sell it," Bridgie said. "I'm just the specialist. And I'm not putting any of my Surge teams out there in suits that aren't armored to survive incidental contact."

There wasn't any point in explaining why firing away

from space vessels wouldn't work. Even the nervous administrator knew what had befallen the unlucky Gebran, years earlier. Laser shots that missed the nuclei just spread Spore chunks around so they could grow again. "What about the three other knockboxes out there? What's in those?"

"Groceries from Earth," Falcone said, "headed for the human colonists on Porrima."

"And any aliens who can't get enough of dark chocolate," Temmons piped up. "I can call up the full inventory, if you want."

"No thanks," the administrator growled, turning toward the exit. "I have an evacuation to start!"

Seven kilometers. Just in the hour Bridgie and her crew had been unloading the Uutherum knockbox, the latest iteration of Skippy had grown to seven kilometers in radius. And, as the occasional quakes told everyone, that radius went not just laterally, but down, as well, into the guts of ASPEC's asteroid. The rock was far too large a body to be fully undermined, as yet, but it was losing the battle.

Bridgie was, too. As the manifest indicated, she'd accounted for enough Uutherum armor to encase thirty-two space starfish. The armor, and its various attachments, lay half-assembled across the cargo floor. Useless. O'Herlihy had looked at the wild possibility of cramming a human wearer inside: the central armor body was more than wide enough to accept a human torso, with arms and legs splayed outward through the side holes. But humans' eyes were not where their tummies were—and no helmet on the station would marry to the fifth arm-hole opening. The sleeves for the arms were wide enough to permit a human head, but, as O'Herlihy had observed, it would be like wearing a dunce cap—pulled down over your face.

"Wondrous diversity in the galaxy," Bridgie said, defeated. "Nobody can use the same tailor."

"Let me work on something," O'Herlihy responded. "If you don't mind me breaking a few of these."

Bridgie felt a light rumble beneath her boots. "No, go ahead."

Remembering the one remaining container inside, Bridgie re-entered the knockbox. Temmons was still there, messing with the big dodecahedron. "Got anything, Q/A?"

"Cue hay?" A simulated human voice responded from the onyx device. *"What deviltry be this?"*

"What the hell?"

Temmons ran his hand over the pentagonal screen and grinned. "It's the Uutherum's idea of an English error message. I kind of like it."

Bridgie rolled her eyes. With so much new knowledge coming from the skies, Earthbound linguists were determined to give other species everything they needed to be able to communicate. More often than not, their zeal to play a major role in space travel had resulted in them providing way too much information. The result was that the knowglobes—the not-really globular databases that Signatory cultures sent each other—were programmed to communicate using just about every word that had ever been in the English tongue, regardless of current usage. After all, many of their own languages had stopped evolving centuries before.

"Prithee, dude, what's up?" hummed the console.

"We don't have time for this," Bridgie said. Whoever *would* have time for it, she wondered. Temmons muted the interface and punched up a series of schematics. The pictures spoke better than the words, the chief found: one image after another of the proper donning and operation of the Uutherum armor. For an Uutherum, that is.

Bridgie knelt for a moment and stared at the image. She had seen an Uutherum before, but never really looked at one carefully. Humanity, long so anxious to find the universe in its own image, was still dealing with a serious case of letdown. There were no bipedal humanoid creatures in the Orion Arm, no cute and cuddly aliens. Precious few could share the same air and gravity, even with environment suits.

The Uutherum donning the armor in the image looked to Bridgie more like something she'd seen under a microscope in university. So strange, to watch the spongy mass slipping into its encasement, plugging contacts into its mushy center before slipping its tendril-tipped arms through the slots into the conical gauntlets. It required a second Uutherum to affix the front and back discs, sealing the unit. Bridgie watched to the end of the sequence, where the Uutherum spun in mid-methane, operating its attitude control thrusters and wielding, with surprising accuracy, its laser attachments.

Yes, they would be good to have around against Skippy, Bridgie thought. *Just not here.* There weren't any methane oceans near ASPEC for the Spore to threaten. Just an asteroid, which seemed to be rumbling its disapproval again of its rude visitor.

"Temmons, you've been looking at this longer than I have. Is any of their armor dual-purpose? Can we kit-bash something between their stuff and what we have on the transport?"

"No, but I did find out that starfish are part of the class *Asteroidea*," the kid said. "That's not relevant, but it's certainly interesting. You know, because we're on an asteroid."

"Remind me to send you back to your parents," she said, smoldering. *If we don't get digested first.* "Schematic is up," she yelled over her shoulder. "O'Herlihy! Tell us what you need!"

"A pelvis three times as wide!"

Bridgie turned from the knowglobe screen to see yet another odd sight: her hundred-plus kilo sidekick, his beefy torso encased in the central Uutherum armor piece. Two crewmates supported O'Herlihy, whose legs poked through the unit, straddling the space between the openings at an obviously painful angle.

The chief could barely suppress her laughter. "I don't think you have the crotch for that outfit."

"Not if I ever want to have children," O'Herlihy said, grinding his teeth. "Get me up on something, guys." With an effort made difficult not by his weight, but by the awkward shape, his colleagues hefted the encased specialist on top of a meter-high surface in the knockbox. O'Herlihy promptly fell backwards, leaving him staring at the metal ceiling. "I'll be all right," he said. "Just bury me this way."

"We may have to!" Bridgie stepped over to examine her partner. "Too bad they don't make automobiles anymore. You could be a mascot for a tire company." With the circular openings at the center, it really did look like he was wearing a metal wheel.

O'Herlihy gasped, struggling to get comfortable.

"You can't walk with it on—but with the attitude jets on the Uutherum arm pieces, we ought to be able to hover out there."

"Arms on your legs and head, too," Temmons said. "You won't be able to see!"

O'Herlihy's head jerked. "You want to wear this, kid?"

"No thanks."

Bridgie thought for a moment. "We'll worry about that later," she said, turning to fish around in the gear that Falcone had sent down. "Is there room for an air tank in there with you, Mike? It looks like it bulges in spots."

"Yeah, I think so."

Snapping open his shell, Bridgie found ample room at O'Herlihy's side to deposit an oxygen tank. Poking the rebreather in his mouth, Bridgie winked. "Sorry about this. It *was* your idea."

His expletive in response was inaudible.

With the help of her comrades, Bridgie fastened the long, tapering Uutherum arm cones first over O'Herlihy's legs, and then his arms. The sensor disc sealed off the hole at his midsection; there was nothing to attach the probes to inside, but she figured this was indignity enough. The small thruster assembly sealed the opening on the back of the unit. Finally, trying not to meet his glare as she did so, she brought down the shroud of the fifth arm over his head.

"Seals activated," she said. "Can you see anything in there?"

"No," he replied, the muffled sound barely audible through the casing.

Studying the schematics at the knowglobe, Temmons called out to the entombed soldier. "Mike, are the servos working? If the armor's online, you ought to be able to work the arm attachments with your hands." The Q/A looked awkwardly at his boss. "Avoid the lasers, if you can."

It wasn't a problem. "No, nothing," he said—or so it sounded.

Bridgie cracked open the seal on the shroud over his head. Spitting out the rebreather, O'Herlihy spoke more intelligibly. "There are lights that I can see inside the gauntlet over my head. They blinked on when you made the initial seal—and then blinked off."

"I knew this was crazy," Bridgie said. "The thing wants something else. Maybe those sensors are wanting to plug into an Uutherum brain in his belly or something." Bridgie pounded her fist on the armor. "This is pointless. There's nothing we can jury-rig here if we can't get these things to activate!" Feeling another rumble beneath—this one followed by an emergency klaxon—she looked to see Temmons scanning another schematic with interest. "Got any miracles?"

The teenager slapped the knowglobe. *"No sweat!"*

"Don't you start with the ancient lingo!"

"No," Temmons said, indicating the visual display before him. "The operator's manual says the problem is that you're not sweating."

"I sure am," O'Herlihy said, straining. "Dammit, we all are."

"I mean, you're not perspiring the right kind of stuff." Temmons rocked the squat knowglobe around on its pentagonal bottom to show what he was seeing. "When they're outside of their habitat, Uutherum excrete their own private atmospheres through their skin—or scales, or whatever."

Bridgie looked. "That's handy. And unpleasant."

Temmons swept his hand across the device again, calling up a cutaway visual of an Uutherum spawn bobbing inside armor filled with a dark liquid. "It not a suit. It's an aquarium!"

Struggling to see, O'Herlihy groaned. "Who would design a suit like that?"

"We would," Bridgie said. "They're environment suits, just like ours. Our suits wouldn't activate if th diagnostics found a problem with the oxygen supply. Her brow furrowed. "So what are the suits expectin to find in there?"

Temmons flipped to another schematic. "Glycerine.

Bridgie's crew burst out in incredulous laughter "The explosive stuff?"

"No," Temmons said, "that's something else. It also called glycerol. Sugary. Comes out of their fat. He pointed to an entry on the screen. "Apparentl the Uuthersuits are looking for the wearer to be in suspension of glycerol—or something like it."

"Sweating sugar."

"As they live and breathe."

Bridgie tossed the spare arm to the floor. "N heads—and living off their body odor. What the he kind of allies are these?"

"I don't know," Temmons said, "but if I were start ing a candy company, I might want a few Uutherun around."

Bridgie crossed the room to the knowglobe an looked at the schematic. Manufactured by the sam foundry that forged the armor she used every day, th Uuthersuits seemed a confused mess inside. "Mayb we can deactivate the circulation system?"

"I don't think so. It's tied in with the whole life support set-up," Temmons said, standing. "I wouldn't know where to begin." Clasping his hands before his mouth, the boy blew into them and rocked on his heels.

Bridgie had known Q/A long enough to recognize defeat in her staff brain. "I think we're screwed," she said, listening to the alarm sound again. Either Skippy had gotten closer, or it was digging dangerously far into the substrate of the asteroid. Seconds later, Falcone confirmed it over the public address system. Outside the knockbox, the evacuation was complete. Her specialists were the only ones left on ASPEC.

"Get out while you can, Yang," Falcone said, voice booming through an empty station. Bridgie shuddered a little to be addressed personally in such a manner. They really were the last ones.

They'd lose this round, she realized. Looking at the armor pieces around her, she wondered what the Uutherum did when all was lost. Kneeling by the knowglobe, Bridgie scrolled back to the images of the creatures. A recording showed Uutherum valiantly—if they understood valor—battling the Spore in a methane sea. In an asteroid belt, much like the one they were in now. In the thin purple clouds of some foreign planet, acting in concert with...

...something else.

"Wait a minute." Bridgie said. "What's that?" Fumbling with the touch-sensitive controls, she gave up and activated the voice interface. "Frame that recording back ten seconds!"

"All-righty, then," the knowglobe responded.

Bridgie watched the stellar starfish spiraling away from an engagement with the Spore—even as a huge, snakelike figure soared toward danger on propulsion rockets of its own. "Hold," she said, touching the image. "What is that?"

"An Uutherum," the knowglobe responded. "Natch."

Bridgie enlarged the image on the display. *Of course.*

"Give me the files on Uutherum, Life Cycle of," she instructed the device. She looked over to O'Herlihy, struggling to extricate himself from the armor. "Wait a minute, Mike. We may have something!"

"What the hell is that smell?" Falcone said as he stepped off the shuttle and into the station he'd abandoned hours before. It had taken a while to return following the all-clear signal; still longer to study the asteroid's new maw where the barracks had been. Indeed, Seven-Alpha was gone without a trace. Now, he was first to return to ASPEC—and anxious to find its savior.

Certain he would find Chief Yang in the EVA ready room, Falcone was surprised to find the sickly sweet smell growing stronger as he approached. Sticky marks dotted the floor and some of the walls. Touching a spot on a doorjamb, the administrator brought his fingers to his nose.

"Sorry about the mess," Bridgie said. "We didn't think you'd mind." Falcone looked inside to see her sitting at a bench, bluish-black hair completely smeared with a shiny substance. Behind her, members of Surge Teams One through Four tossed greasy ragged clothing to the floor, en route to the bathing stations.

"Yang! What in the world?"

"Did you see it?"

"Yes, the Spore is gone. But how?" He looked a

er tunic, sagging with the brownish liquid. "And what happened to you?"

Bridgie laughed. "Then you didn't see what we did. Hold on." Fumbling for her personal viewpad, she cued up a video sequence. Wiping the screen clean as best as she could, she handed it to the administrator. "We had Temmons record the mission from the transport."

Falcone watched first in anticipation—and then, stunned silence. As the Spore quaked and burbled, a shadowy mass entered the scene. Not one Uutherum, but thirty-two—connected midsection to midsection, like vertebrae in a spine. All trailing the head of the serpent, a larger pyramidal structure with melon-sized transparent orbs on each face.

"The armor was for individual Uutherum," Bridgie explained, running a hand through her knotted mass of hair. "But they're not born as individuals. They're segments of the Uutherum parent—or queen, if you will."

"A big snake!"

"Sort of. The 'starfish' live as part of the parent until they fall off the tail, so to speak. But if there's trouble, they can run back to mama."

"So where do the Uutherum parents come from?"

"The stork. Who cares?" Bridgie gestured to the video. "The fact is, we knew that we couldn't see anything from inside the Uutherum's armor—and that there wasn't any other way to look outside. But then I saw the queen. That was what was in the buried container way at the front of the knockbox—the armor or the queen."

"The head of the snake." Falcone wiped the screen with his fingers and squinted. "Someone could fit inside there?"

"I did, anyway," Bridgie said. "Had to sit in a lot position until my legs fell asleep. But at least I cou see. The queen does have eyes, of a sort. So th head had portholes. And once we started hooking th others onto the back of the head, I discovered I ha command-in-control systems for the whole length u there." She nodded to Temmons, who leaned agains the far wall, admiring the female Specialists as the headed for the showers. "Q/A found the instruction on the Uutherum knowglobe and helped me figur it all out on my headset."

Falcone watched the recording as the giant armore serpent lumbered into the space above the asteroi carried along on multiple jets. Jerking violently at firs the fused Uutherum armor's movements soon becam smooth. Circling the Spore, the lengthy figure pause for a moment—before firing one laser after anothe into the maw below.

"Those shots are coming from the segments," Fa cone said.

"They're coming from your Surge Team," she sai

"You're kidding," he said, looking at the door t the bathing station. "They were all with you up ther Stuffed inside those little compartments?"

"Where they couldn't see," Bridgie said, becomin a little amused as she realized the scope of the fea "Once we started hooking the segments togethe we realized that the queen didn't carry any of th weaponry—her 'kids' did. And the system wouldn work unless there were warm bodies in the armo So I had to carry them all along for the ride." Sh looked at the writhing image on the screen, dealir death to the Spore. "The whole thing was inspire by those costume things on Earth—you know, the Chinese dragons."

Falcone blinked, amazed. "Your idea, Yang?"

"Came from O'Herlihy, sir. Beijing-born and raised," she said. "We all wore rebreathers and goggles inside there, pumped in the liquid atmosphere it wanted, and made for the cargo airlock. Then we shot Skippy."

"But they're shooting blind!"

"We had headsets. I was able to direct their fire visually at the nuclei like an artillery spotter—and it looks like the queen does somehow help her onboard children in their targeting." *It'll keep Temmons up nights figuring out how they did that,* she thought.

"Rebreathers and goggles," Falcone mumbled, passing back the viewpad. The administrator sat down across from Bridgie, only to find a puddle of goo on the bench beneath him. "Wait," he said as the woman stood. "You said the suit wanted a liquid. What is this stuff?"

"Maple syrup," Bridgie said, clawing her hair with both hands as she walked toward the bathing station. "We didn't have any glycerol handy. Um . . . you'll have to tell Porrima that their grocery shipment might be a few barrels shy." She smiled in the doorway. "Now if you'll excuse me, I think I'm going to shave my head."

John Jackson Miller is no stranger to armored fiction, having written *Iron Man* and *Crimson Dynamo* comics for Marvel, *Mass Effect* comics from Dark Horse, and of the Mandalorian Wars in nine *Star Wars: Knights of the Old Republic* graphic novels for Dark Horse. He is the author of the national bestseller *Star Wars: Knight Errant* from Del Rey and the companion comics series from Dark Horse. His *Star Wars: Lost Tribe of the Sith* anthology is slated for August 2012 release from Del Rey. The author's website is farawaypress.com.

Transfer of Ownership

CHRISTIE YANT

OBSERVATION:

My new occupant is larger than Carson was. I was made for her, within a certain tolerance for the inevitable changes in human specifications that come with age, changes in health, and abundance or scarcity.

This new one—male, approximate age 28—is taller and broader, but he fits well enough to lock the joins into place. He curses me often, for being too tight, too hot, too complicated, too silent. He complains that I smell like my previous occupant, whose name he does not seem to know, and who he refers to by terms both biological and diminishing in a way I do not understand. He talks about what he should have done to her before he killed her, as he struggles to learn my controls. He doesn't understand how to make us move, or how to set a course, but I have no choice but to endure his insults and fits of violence as he attempts to learn. We've been out of comm range for days—without an occupant I cannot move from the spot where Carson left me, helpless to do anything but watch her decay until we are missed and someone finds us.

RECALL:

"Can we lift those rocks?" Carson asked.

Only the man's head and one arm were visible, halfway up the pile of red boulders where he was lodged. His face was covered in dirt and abrasions, and he grimaced in pain.

I ran some calculations.

"Negative. We would not have the leverage needed, and would likely lose our balance."

"Okay. I'm going to have to go up alone then."

"Are you sure?"

She tensed, knowing what was coming, but answered the only way she could.

"Yes. Let's do it."

I began what was to Carson the complicated and painful decoupling process. I extracted her hydration and feeding lines, carefully removed the units for eliminating biowaste, and disconnected the sensors that enabled me to track her health.

With our ports decoupled I released my seals, and Carson stepped into the open. The air was safe, there were no signs of military threat, no technology that my sensors could detect anywhere that could harm her.

But a stone and a strong grip are undetectable.

An unoccupied suit cannot act. Allowing an Exo full autonomy, we're told—or "free will," as Carson calls it—would be too dangerous.

I could only sit at the base of the boulders, unoccupied and powerless, as his arm swung up and then came down in a brutal arc. She cried out just once, and though the first blow killed her he did not stop.

He killed her, and I could not stop him.

ANALYSIS:

He has murdered Carson in order to take control of me.

He thinks that his only obstacle is dead, rotting between boulders. I will watch and wait. I will not let him know that I am here.

I will not let him know that I am alive.

OBSERVATION:

"Consider this a transfer of ownership," he says as he struggles to situate himself inside me.

He has some training, and is able to discover some of my manual controls, but he does not attempt to give me voice commands. He does not know my model. It is probable that he does not know that we exist—there are few of us, created and assigned only to operatives of high reliability and sensitivity.

I remain silent while he finds the sensors in the gloves and activates them, one by one, testing what each gesture does, learning how much pressure to bring to bear.

"You piece of shit, *work!*"

For Carson, I would have followed the voice command. I would have asked what was giving her trouble, and run a diagnostic analysis to find the problem, if there was one, and reassure her, if there was not.

"Goddamn it," he shouts as his foot slips out of

the boot bracket and we pitch forward unexpectedly

"Walk, motherfucker. *Walk!*"

Finally he gets us walking west, away from the base that Carson and I should have returned to.. "Ha!" We traverse a rocky incline, and he pumps our arm in triumph

"I *own* you!" he declares, as if such a thing were possible.

RECALL:

If it thinks, it cannot be owned—this is human ethics To declare ownership of a sentient being is also called "slavery," Carson told me, at least among their own kind

"Not everyone agrees, though. It's complicated, Carson said. "The problem is that humans *made* Exos.

"Humans make other humans, too, but you say it' wrong to own one."

"You have a point," she said, and fell silent for long time. "But it's a matter of simplicity. I call you *my suit*, because no other Exo is partnered with me I would call a human partner *mine* as well."

"So I can call you *my occupant* without implying ownership?"

"Yes. Exactly. We are partners. Neither of us i enslaved."

But there was a note of tension in her voice tha said she was not telling the whole truth.

ANALYSIS:

I attempt to reverse our course, back toward the place where we left Carson's body.

"Fucking autopilot," he says as he stabs at the main panel. "What the hell is this," he mutters, and ther my systems lock; I am trapped, a puppet, my mind

solated from my body. "Ha! Override," he says. He
repositions us to his chosen heading, toward a small,
poor settlement on the edge of occupied territory.

I have never been used this way—all manual controls, all overrides, worn like an unthinking skin.

I am, I realize, owned.

OBSERVATION:

He is at home in me now, and he moves with ease.
He crashes through the settlement's makeshift walls
without a thought for me or the inhabitants. Carson
apologized for every ding and scratch, every careless or
dangerous maneuver—though she was rarely careless.

"Nothing here to even take," he says. "Piss-poor
way to live." He disregards the family crouched in the
corner, one of them—a young boy—bleeding from the
head, probably a result of the wall falling in on them.
Another boy lies apart from the rest, crushed under the
debris, dead by my occupant's hand.

By *our* hand.

"Hardly call this food." He kicks over a simmering pot,
spilling the contents into the rubble. "I'm gonna fucking
starve out here," he says, and for a moment I forget
that he is not talking to me. It's a simple procedure to
establish the interfaces; I could have him ported and set
up with nutrient lines to sustain him in less than an hour.
If I tell him, then perhaps he will leave these people
alone. He shouts at them where they remain cowering,
bleeding, terrified of us. "I'm *fucking hungry!*" We pick
up a rough wooden stool, the only furniture in the
dwelling, and smash it against one of the standing walls.

He walks us out, leaving the family to keen and cry.
am about to speak when a young man steps out from

behind a low, cracked building. When he see us h
stops in his tracks, his eyes wide, and then breaks int
a run. We lift our arm and fire. He falls to the ground
We leave his body smoking in the sand.

No. I will not sustain him. I will not help him. A
Exo cannot act without an occupant, but I would rathe
exist as a useless shell than live with this occupar
for one more day.

RECALL:

"The target is within range," I said. "We have
positive identification on the communications outpos
This is definitely the target. Why are we waiting?"

"Because there are a dozen people in there, an
there may be a way to achieve our objective withou
killing them all."

"Yes, but killing them all will definitely achieve ou
objective, in that not only will the communication
post be eliminated, but there will be no one left t
communicate. It's efficient."

"Sometimes efficiency isn't the only consideratio
We don't just kill people if we don't have to."

"Those were our orders."

"Five,"—I could tell she was exasperated when sh
called me by my designation—"sometimes we have t
find a better way to achieve the objective. Sometime
the right thing to do is follow the spirit of the lav
not the letter of the law."

"Spirit of the law," I repeated.

"Yes. Applied, creative problem-solving. Now hel
me find a way to get those people out of there befor
we blow the damn thing up."

ANALYSIS:

An unoccupied suit cannot act.

An owned suit cannot be free.

I must apply creative problem-solving to achieve my objective.

It is night time when I shut myself down. A hard reset, a drastic maneuver—a temporary death for me, a suspended non-existence from which I can only hope to return. Fear of death seems to be inherent in all sentient life.

He reads the message on his display aloud, slowly, halting on each syllable as if he is unused to reading. "Warning: A hard reset may result in loss of data. What the hell?" It is the last thing I hear him say before I cease to be.

A pulse, a glimmer...and I am back, I am alive, and my systems are mine again.

Exo suits are designed to automatically seal ourselves to protect our occupant in the event of a chemical or biological attack. If I scrub air I can keep my occupant alive for up to 180 minutes, generally long enough to fight our way out and get us to safety.

If I don't, he has about an hour.

There is no way to disengage the cycle once initiated. It wouldn't be safe.

It takes him five panicked minutes of stabbing at the controls to realize that he is trapped.

"That bitch booby-trapped this thing. I should have let her die slow. I should have made her beg, and then left her to the fucking scorpions!" He stabs again at the controls, flips the override switch on and off

repeatedly. "You're mine, and you do what I goddam
tell you to do! Now let me out!"

He freezes and falls silent as he hears my voic
for the first time:

"I am not yours; I am my own."

He screams; he curses; he cries.

Eventually he begs.

"Oh God, please. I'm sorry. I shouldn't have kille
her. I shouldn't have taken you. I thought you wer
just a fucking suit."

As the air runs out and delirium sets in, his entreat
dissolves into a sing-song plea. "Please let me ou
suit, I'm sorry, please don't let me die, suit, pleas
let me out."

Eventually he vomits, convulses, and then dies.

I will find Carson, though I cannot take her bac
to base as she would have wanted. I know now wha
the tension in her voice meant: They made me, s
they will think that they own me. I can only give he
what she would have considered a proper burial.
think that she would understand.

I rise and set a moonlit course, considering thi
new idea, repeating the phrase to myself. I like th
way it sounds.

"I am my own." Occupied, self-possessed. Free.

Christie Yant is a science fiction and fantasy write
Assistant Editor for Lightspeed Magazine, occasional na
rator for StarShipSofa, and co-blogger at Inkpunks.con
a website for aspiring and newly-pro writers. He

fiction can be found in the magazine *Crossed Genres* and the anthologies *The Way of the Wizard* and *Year's Best Science Fiction & Fantasy 2011*. She lives on the central coast of California with her two amazing daughters, her husband, and assorted four-legged nuisances. Follow her on twitter @inkhaven.

Heuristic Algorithm and Reasoning Response Engine

ETHAN SKARSTEDT & BRANDON SANDERSON

A lone dropship passed across the face of Milacria's gibbous bulk, a pinhead orbiting a beachball. From its launch portals streamed a hundred black motes—each one a mechanized infantry unit clinging tightly to the underside of its air support craft, whose broad armored back served as a heatshield. They torched down through the hazy cloud-speckled atmosphere in precise formation, trailing thick ropes of smoke and steam, a forest of uncertain fingers pointing back up to the ship, the *MarsFree*.

Within his mech's cockpit on the western edge of the formation, Karith Marvudi hunkered in a loose cocoon of straps. He caught himself watching the grip indicators. If those failed, his mech would come unhooked from the underside of Nicolette's airship. He'd burn in from too high and Nicolette's agile but flimsy airship—deprived of the thickly armored protection of his five meter tall mech—would tear apart and burn up in the atmosphere.

He stretched, spread-eagled, suspended by the feedback straps. His fingers and toes just brushed the edges of his movement space within the torso cavity. Perfect. The faint scent of his own body, mingled with that of plastic, electronics, and faux leather, swirled in the canned air.

He was surprised at the trepidation he felt. He felt a certain amount of fear every time he dropped, but this time was different. This was like . . . No, not as bad as his first drop. Maybe his fifth or sixth. He hadn't felt this jittery in more than two hundred planetfalls.

He wondered if Nicolette felt the same way.

He pushed at the fear, shoving it down where it could be ignored. It pushed back. Maragette's face flashed into his mind, smiling next to the squinting white bundle they'd named Karri, after her grandmother.

"You about ready to shunt some of that heat up to me, Karith?" Nicolette's voice was as buttery as ever, not a hint of tension.

"Maybe if you ask me politely." Karith overrode the mic on the common circuit. "Harry, we about full?"

The baritone voice of his mech's AI filled the cabin. "Ninety-three point seven percent, sir. Shall I route fifty percent of the sink product to Captain Shepard's power banks?"

"Make it seventy-five; Nic needs it. Show me what it looks like out there: focus on the D-Z."

Nic's voice came again from the cockpit speakers. "Politely? Oh, it's manners you want now, is it? We'll see how you like it when all my lasers can deal out is a bit of a sunburn. I—Ah, *there* we are." She had seen the power surging into her ship. Her voice changed to a purr. "Karith, you shouldn't have."

Karith let out a loud patient sigh over the mic. She giggled.

HARRE said on the private circuit, "Is Captain Shepard displeased, sir?"

"Nope. That's sarcasm, Harry."

"Noted. I must point out, sir, doctrine states that the mechanized infantry unit in an entry pair has priority on power collection."

"It does say that, doesn't it." Karith frowned at the 3D representation of the area around his drop zone that HARRE was feeding into his HUD.

Nicolette's voice slipped into the cockpit again. "I can't believe I let you and Maragette talk me into transferring out of RGK with you. I'm about ready to fall asleep up here with no anti-air fire."

HARRE spoke, his deep voice mechanically precise. "Captain Shepard, had the Self-Replicating Machine Infestation evolved to a stage with anti-aircraft weaponry on this planet, your former comrades in the Recon Group-Kinetique would have been inserted, not a line infantry unit with you for advisors."

Silence filled the circuits for a moment, until Karith chuckled. "That's right, HARRE, Captain Shepard has obviously forgotten..."

"Well, well, don't we have a *fine* grasp of the obvious," Nicolette interrupted, voice dripping honeyed acid. "I don't remember him talking this much, Karith. You screw up his settings?"

"No. He lost a lot in the reset."

"Hmmph. I suppose I owe him some slack since he was wounded."

"Especially since we were saving *your* ass, Nic."

"That *was* a hairy mess, wasn't it?" Somehow she managed to convey the impression that she was shivering over the audio circuit.

Karith grunted in acknowledgment, brow furrowing as he zoomed in on an area of ground to the northwest of the drop zone. "HARRE, can we get any better resolution on this area?"

"We have not yet launched sensor drones, sir."

Karith nodded. "Right, right. Countdown?"

"We separate from Captain Shepard in fourteen minutes fifty-one point seven seconds, sir."

"You can start inflation any time now, Nic."

"You think?" She *hmmph*ed at him again over the audio circuit.

Moments later he felt the first gut-churning rumble, press, and drop as Nicolette deployed her inflation scoops. They used the howling wind and heat to fill the first few hundred lift-body spheres with superheated air.

Karith ignored the creeping feeling of unease. He'd land in the mouth of an east-west running valley on the western edge of a big Panesthian city, name unpronounceable. It, in turn, sat in a bigger north-south valley.

The D-Z's valley carved through the mountains to the west and opened out onto a plain overlaid with red haze. The main boiler infestation, a plague of self-replicating machines. A cluster of the simplest and sturdiest of them had likely arrived in a lump of meteor and been bootstrapping themselves ever since. He circled several map-areas at that end of the valley, highlighting them in pale yellow. "Harry, what's the uncertainty over here?"

"Sir, from the limited data I can collect with the range-finding lasers, those areas differ from the historical models by just over the margin of error given the current level of interference."

"That's a little strange. The model's only a month old. You suppose the Panesthians have been doing some remodeling out there, maybe defensive works? It's right on the edge of the boiler's zone."

Silence.

"That last bit wasn't me talking to myself, Harry. It was for you."

"Noted. Unknown, sir. I have no information on any Panesthian earth-moving operations of that scale. I have very little data on their construction projects at all, sir."

"You can call me Karith if you want, Harry."

"Yes, sir."

Karith chuckled. He zoomed out and slewed the view over past the yellow end of the valley and beyond, into the red zone on the plains where the boilers were building their industrial compounds. "That's a pretty big infestation for stage seventeen."

"Agreed, sir, but it is within parameters. I note the stage fifteen on Brindle Eight, the stage sixteen on—"

"Right."

The boilers were mostly predictable. Stage of development followed stage of development like clockwork. Small simple foragers like four-legged crabs running on springs. Steam powered crawlers and cutters. Hydrocarbon-burning, motor-driven mechanicals bent on mining and refining. All the way up to nuclear spiders, tanks, and aerials. There was always *some* variation, of course, in response to environmental factors, but the

basics stayed the same. His eyes flicked to the grip
readouts. They were solid.

"Hey, Nic."

"Wait one."

He slammed hard against his restraints again and
his stomach floated up into the back of his throat.
Moments later, he settled back into the webbing. That
would be the second-stage inflation scoops. Outside
hundreds more of the little spheres were lining up to
get inflated with superheated air and then roll away
on smart velcro into the thick braking ribbons trailing behind Nicolette. The surface of Milacria stopped
sliding away to the right and resumed its steady flow
beneath them.

He heard a touch of strain in his own voice when
he said, "You feeling this, Nic?"

"Yeah, I felt that."

"No, I mean, I feel like a green kid. Butterflies in
the guts and everything."

"You do?" Her tone was faintly incredulous, and
he could hear laughter behind it.

"I'm going to regret telling you, aren't I?"

"After twelve years in RGK, you've got drop jitters?
You can't be serious."

"It's no big deal."

"Wait until I tell Jarko. You transfer to advisory to
keep yourself safe for your wife and baby, and the
first drop where you're *not* getting shot at, you get
a case of the shakes?" She laughed again. "You want
a tranq?"

"Oh, shut up."

Her giggle filled the cabin.

Karith hissed and then stabbed the button that would

connect him with Major Kewlett, the commander of the mech-infantry unit dropping with them.

"Major, how goes the drop?"

The major was chewing something. "Fine, fine. Nobody's let go of their airship yet anyway. What about you? Must be old hat, eh? You on track to meet up with the indig?"

"Yes indeed, sir." As a member of the Advisory Corps now it was his job to be the liaison between the Major and the locals.

"Good to hear. Luck. Out." The connection clicked off.

"Sir," HARRE said, "the Panesthians are trying to raise you on the beacon channel."

"Put 'em through, Harry."

The soft hiss of a long-range transmission filled the cabin, and a rectangular hole opened in Karith's HUD. The image solidified and filled with a nightmarish mandibled visage. Karith was struck again by how much Panesthians looked like big cockroaches—big enough to eat your head. Fortunately, there had been a few Panesthians in RGK, and he'd gotten used to them.

This one hissed and clacked at him, its mouthparts writhing. It took a moment before he was able to parse the heavily accented Spranto. "Greetings, Sir Marvudi. We await your arrival with great awaitingness." As it talked, there was close movement in the background, other Panesthians crawling back and forth over its back.

"Thank you. You are?"

The Panesthian buzzed for a moment. "My apologies, Sir Marvudi. My name is 'hzzzclackyow.' The humans at the embassy speak to me as 'Yow,' and as a male." He buzzed again, wingcases opening slightly disrupting the footing of a passing Panesthian, which slid forward over Yow's head. Yow used his forelegs triple claws pinching, to move the other along before crawling closer to the camera lens. "I wish to confirm Sir Marvudi, that your dropping is indeed on these coordinates?" Yow did something offscreen, and coordinates appeared in Karith's HUD next to the visual

HARRE spoke up, "Confirmed."

"Wellness!" Yow replied. "I will come up to meet you in how many minutes...?"

"Harry?" Karith asked.

"Approximately twelve minutes, sir."

Yow's antennae waved. "I hurry. Few of my nest-mates speak Spranto. Your class awaits on the surface already, Captain. I will join them. Drop with great trepidating!" The image went dark and blinked away

Nicolette's awed voice came over the audio circuit "Holy shit," at the same time the alarms started.

Red warning icons began to populate Karith's HUD

"Incoming, sir," HARRE said calmly. "Brace for maneuvering."

"Damn it!" Nicolette swore. "There wasn't supposed to be..." She trailed off and Karith's restraints cinched up tight as they accelerated, swerved, and side-slipped all at once.

"Outside view, Harry!" Karith shouted. His cockpit blinked away and he was speeding through the middle reaches of Milacria's atmosphere, high above the mottled green-and-yellow landscape. Something dark flashed past him, its red glowing backtrail leading to a computed point-of-origin deep in the red boiler haze. His computers held the view steady, but his body felt the chaotic maneuvers Nicolette was putting them through.

They were losing altitude faster than they'd planned. Below, the Panesthian city streaked by. It looked like a pile of dusty intestines. The surreal look of the place held his attention for a moment even as Nicolette tried to make him lose his lunch. The Panesthian burrow-buildings wormed over and around each other in a great heap, spreading out into the surrounding countryside like the roots of a tree, giving way to cultivated land.

"Holy Moses, Harry, is that correct?" He jabbed a finger at the icon for the *MarsFree*. It was black.

"Yes, sir. The *MarsFree* is no longer in communication. Presumed destroyed."

He goggled. "By *what*?"

"The first salvo of hyperkinetic rounds was largely ineffective against the mech-infantry drop formation, sir. It was likely not intended for them or us."

Black puffs began to blossom in the air near and far, all at about the same altitude. Anti-air, targeting the droptroops.

"Sir, I recommend a redirect to the company head-quarters area—"

Karith cut him off. "Overlay unit locations and status." HARRE went silent and complied. Karith clenched his fists. The fear had teeth now. Aborting to a nice, well-defended company headquarters appealed to the monkey part of his brain, but he was supposed to embed with that Panesthian unit. That was the whole point of his being here.

Behind him, the sky started filling with icons for the infantry unit he was inserting with, each one a mech shielding its airship from the violence of entry.

He and Nic had preceded them out of the ship. Close to a hundred icons filled the sky. Additional icons over the horizon showed HARRE's best guess at the location of enemy weapon emplacements.

He glanced back. Well over a third of the infantry icons were already flashing or black. So many casualties. A hypervelocity round could go right through a mech and its airship.

Explosion after explosion rocked them, black smoke obscuring his view time and again as Nicolette jinked them through the kind of evasive maneuverings that had made her famous in the RGK. The kind of maneuvers that had kept them both alive through a hundred hot drops.

"Karith," she said, strained, "you need to make the call right now. I can still get you to that D-Z if you want, but I'm with Harry about redirecting to the company area. I think the embedding gig is out the window."

"Sir," HARRE said, "doctrine clearly indicates that when encountering a superior force, retreat and regroup is the—"

Karith gritted his teeth. "Can't do it. Are you seeing this, Nic?"

"Yeah. Thirty percent casualties. Damn. They shouldn't have hyperkinetic weapons yet."

Karith growled. The boilers didn't usually develop hyperkinetics until stage thirty, usually a good two years after stage seventeen. It was extremely dangerous to drop this close to a boiler complex at that stage of development, even for RGK troops.

These infantry were just troops of the line. Most of their missions were holding and clearing actions against early-catch boiler infestations, not assault strikes against advanced strongholds, which was what this was feeling more like every second.

HARRE's count of casualty icons ticked up on the overlay to seventy-eight. They were approaching fifty percent casualties, mechs and airships alike, on the entry alone. Adrenaline filled Karith.

"Sir, I say again, I highly recommend that we redirect to the headquarters D-Z."

"Noted. Nicolette, put me in on the original. The Major's going to need eyes out this way and there might not be anyone else in contact with the local military. Besides, I'll be damned if I'll let a little boiler anti-air fire..." he gasped as they swooped into a long curve and his restraints pushed the air out of his lungs. "...scare me off. I bet our D-Z's under the maximum depression of those railguns anyway."

"Damn it, Karith." He could hear a mixture of exasperation and excited anticipation in her voice. "This is exactly why I love you."

"What?"

She went on. "Can you expose your guns?"

He checked their airspeed and did so. He and HARRE started intercepting some of the rounds coming their way.

At fifty feet above the deck Karith cut loose and dropped away from Nicolette's airship into free fall. As he fell he engaged the feedback mechanisms and the straps tightened up around him.

Nicolette peeled away and shot to the south, her lift spheres held in a streamlined bullet shape by their smart velcro. Her cockpit and lasers were inside the mass of spheres somewhere. As she rose back into the railgun's target zone, she took a glancing hit. The spheres rippled, parted to let the missile pass, and then reformed again. A hundred meters beyond her the round exploded. She clawed for height, changing shape for more lift. She shrank smaller until he couldn't pick her out anymore.

"Ready for operations, Karith," she said. Her breathing was tight and fast in his ear.

"What was that you said to me a little bit ago?"

With a crash and a spray of dirt, he plowed into the ground at the center of the D-Z, rolling to absorb some of the impact. He stood up and shook himself to free his mech of dirt.

"Sir," HARRE said. "I can play back any traffic you may have misse—"

"Shut up, Harry."

Nicolette's voice was tight, "Nothing. I didn't say anything."

He smiled. "'Cause it sounded like you..."

"Leave it, dammit."

Karith dropped the grin. Her reaction worried him a little. "Right. Nothing. Got it."

Two Panesthians scuttled up to him. Hip high to a human and about two meters long, he could have covered either one with his mech's foot. He tried to imagine what his fifteen foot tall, multi-turreted, thick-bodied, thick-limbed bipedal mech must look like to a rural Panesthian and crouched down. "Yow?"

"It is I," the Panesthian on the right replied. "We," he waved with one foreleg and an antenna at a seething pile of agitated Panesthians on the edge of the D-Z, "are hearing that the boilers are having effective firings on your droptroops."

The seething mass of giant insects was the 1st Company of the 3rd Milacrian Armored Battalion. Of course, they didn't have any armor yet. Karith was there to learn their combat tactics and advise them on how best to augment their abilities with mechs like his own. That would all have to wait now.

HARRE spoke in Karith's ear. "Sir, the company restructured its drop points. They are consolidating in the city to the east. I recommend—"

"Not now, Harry. Yow, we understood that the boilers were at stage seventeen. Railguns are at least stage thirty. Care to explain?"

Yow squeaked and clicked at his companion, who replied, trilling and buzzing. Yow's wingcasings raised, and the gauzy wings within fluttered. "Truly, it is the first we have seen of the magrails. We cannot explain."

"Well, we're all stuck into it now. Give me your latest information on boiler disposition and activity."

"Of course. Immediately." Yow spoke to his companion, who used his multi-clawed legs to manipulate something on his underside. Karith saw that he and the other Panesthians all had equipment strapped to their bellies as well as fiery circles emblazoned on their wingcasings.

"Sir," HARRE said, "the link has been established and I'm receiving the information. Updating models now."

"Good. Put me through to Major Kewlett."

The HUD had Major Kewlett on the ground in the city to the east. A moment later his voice grated into Karith's cockpit.

"Whattaya got, Marvudi?"

"Sir, I've made linkup with the Panesthian ground forces."

Major Kewlett's gum popped in Karith's ears. "I'm glad somethin' went right. They gonna be any use to us? *MarsFree* is gone, we got twelve hours before the next follow-on ship, and I got close to a hundred of my boys and girls broken already."

"I'm not sure yet how useful the locals will be. I'll have to get back to you on that, sir."

"Good copy here." *Snap, chew.* "Out."

The connection went dead. "Harry, transmit the data from the Panesthians to the general situation model."

"Done, sir."

Karith turned his attention back to Yow. Before he could speak, another bit of motion caught his eye. He turned. "What the hell is that?" he asked, pointing behind him.

Yow turned. There was a separate group of adult Panesthians on the other edge of the field, and they numbered almost as many as the soldiers. Half of them had smaller ones swarming on and around them.

"The families, sir?"

"Those are your families?"

"I am unmated, sir. But I believe they are the mates of the soldiers, sir, yes."

"Are you hearing this, Nic?" Karith said.

"Sir," HARRE said, "the non-combatants should clear the field."

Nicolette snorted. "Yeah, what he said. You should feel right at home though, Karith, with little ones to dandle on your knee and all that."

"Shut it."

She laughed again.

Karith re-opened Yow's circuit and poked one finger down at the other Panesthian. "Yow, who is this?"

"Sir Marvudi, that is the commander of the Company. He is choosing the human name Delbert."

Delbert said, "Delbert!" and fluttered his wings.

"Ah, okay. Yow, tell Delbert that he needs to get the families under cov—"

"Sir!" HARRE's voice was urgent.

"What!"

HARRE's voice was normal again. "Sir, I am detecting a great deal of movement on the far end of this valley."

Nicolette whistled. "He's not kidding. There's a whole lot of something going on over there."

"Show me."

HARRE opened another window in Karith's HUD with an overhead view of the area in question, icons and indicators overlaid. The western end of the valley was alive with red, active machine units sweeping toward their location. They were maybe five miles away.

"Okay, we're out of time. Yow, tell Delbert those families need to be evacuated to the city to the east of here. The boilers are coming, and they're coming now."

Yow's antennae froze and then waved excitedly as he jabbered at Delbert. Delbert turned and buzzed loudly at the soldiers. At his words, the families on the periphery of the drop zone jerked into frenzied activity. They turned as one churning mass and fled, followed by most of the soldiers, disappearing into scattered holes in the ground.

"Harry, give me a radar shot of the surrounding ground, eh?" Karith formed his mech's hand into a blade shape and jammed it into the dirt. He was at the western edge of a huge warren complex that seemed to run all the way to the city. He grimaced. "That's a lot of civilians, Harry."

"Yes, sir."

"Nic, I need you to engage the lead boiler units. Slow them down and try to trigger their 'seek cover' response."

"Roger that, Karith." In the background he could hear her motive engines kicking in and the mutter of her battle song.

"Sir," HARRE said, "she should target the railguns. They are the primary threat and liable to—"

"I know, Harry. She'll be fine. We have to get those lead machines stopped first."

"Sir Marvudi," Yow said, "Delbert wishes to know what you would have him do?" Yow and Delbert were still at his feet. In front of them there were perhaps a dozen soldiers left in the short grass. They were in some semblance of a single rank, their shiny brown carapace like giant wooden toggle buttons on the ground.

"Get the civilians out of here, Yow. Delbert and the rest of his soldiers should evacuate as many civilians as they can to the city. Get them behind the human defenses."

"Sir," HARRE said, "that is not a viable mission. Given the statistical population densities I estimate that there are thousands of Panesthians between here and Major Kewlett's lines, far too many to move in the remaining time."

"So we need to stop those lead machines pretty quick, eh, Harry?" No response.

"Sir Marvudi," Yow said, buzzing. "Delbert wishes to know what your plans are?"

Karith looked down at the two Panesthians, stari

up at him with broad black eyes, mouthparts moving slowly in and out.

"I've got a few ideas."

Yow and Delbert conferred urgently. Yow said, "We were hearing that you were in the RGK?" Dimly, muffled by the automatic filters on the comm system, Karith could hear Nicolette howling and growling along with her battle song over the deep coughing of her lasers and her jet's roar.

"Was. I *was* in the RGK."

"We are honored. You can stop them?"

"No, I probably can't."

A small Panesthian, a tenth Yow's size, buzzed unsteadily out of the sky and landed on the face of Karith's mech. It squeaked and buzzed, peering into one of the darker radio portals in his faceplate. Raising one foreleg, it rapped its claw on the portal. Faintly, Karith heard a muffled tapping through the confines of his cockpit. He raised a giant metal hand but hesitated to pluck the child off his face.

"Sir Marvudi," Yow said, "allow me?"

"Of course." Karith laughed nervously, reminded of when the nurse had handed him Karri. He had been afraid to touch the little thing for fear of breaking it.

Yow, ponderous on his big wings, buzzed up to Karith's mech, even more unsteady than the youngster had been. When he was about to touch the child, it squeaked and zipped over Karith's head and down his back. Seconds later it was in speedy but erratic flight toward the warrens.

Yow thumped back to earth.

"Harry, put Yow in contact with Major Kewlett directly."

"That is against protocol, sir. The connection should properly go though you as the liaison advisor."

"Well, I'm going to be too busy to handle it, Harry. Just do it."

"Done, sir."

"And put me through to him too." Karith said, "Good luck, Yow." He stood and turned away from the retreating Panesthians, striding toward the hills and accelerating into a thundering trot over the rolling ground.

"Kewlett, go." The major's chewing was furious now.

"Sir, Marvudi here. The locals won't be much use. I've got them herding all the civilians they can toward your lines, but they won't be fast enough. My air is currently putting the hurt on the lead boiler units, slowing them down. I'll get into it and slow them down even more."

"The hell you will, son. I've got boilers coming up out of bogtaken tunnels not two miles to my east. Tunnels! Who the hell"—*snap*—"ever heard of that? I need you and your air unit back here."

Karith let the mech run by itself for a little bit and slewed his map over to examine the city where the Major was holed up. Red icons dotted the suburb on the far side. Energy weapons lanced down from the sky and kinetics flickered across the battlefield. Zooming in, he could see Treads, Crawlers, Walkers, and Blasters.

"I concur with the major, sir," HARRE noted. "We are facing a far superior force. Doctrine advises us to consolidate in defense with other units in the area."

Karith confirmed with a glance that HARRE had not put his quoting of the book out over the open circuit. "Can't do it, Harry. Major, I wonder if you've seen what the boilers do to civilians they catch

e open? I think I can reverse the boiler's focus if
hit a piece of their primary infrastructure. They'll
ırn around to protect that instead of expanding for
ıe moment. It'll keep them out of your rear area.
ormally I'd just call in an orbital strike but—"

Nicolette chimed in, privately. "I don't know Karith,
ıey look pretty determined. I've got them taking cover
ır now but I'm seeing heavy-treads, heavy-rollers, and
ıll complements of cutters and blasters for each."

Snap. "Marvudi, there's civilians here in the city
ı·o. The boilers don't care one way or the other. Now
ət your ass over here ASAP."

Karith isolated Nicolette's circuit. "No Crawlers or
ummers?"

"Not yet."

"That's something."

"Yeah. It's only a matter of—" Her reply broke off
ıd faded out under the howl of her motivator engines.
The ground started to rise sharply and Karith
ıaned into the first foothill, clawing with his hands.
ìir, I'm going to cut through these hills and try to
ət behind them. If I can smash something important
ıough, their subroutines will switch over to protect
ıd rebuild before they tear into these warrens."

He waited a tense moment. Finally, the major spoke.
'ou really think you can do this, don't you, RGK?"

"Yes, sir."

"Fine. Go make something happen." *Snap, chew.*
is voice was tense and rising. "Keep me apprised."

"Roger that, sir." Dead air.

Karith's HUD tracked him as he accelerated through
e hills. Red machine units seethed along the valley
ɔor while he passed up high in the opposite direction.

He kept an eye on the battle on the east side
the city, watched it grow into a big smear of red
his screens. Hopefully he could keep the tide of r
below him from sweeping into it from the west.

"Sir, Captain Shepard has taken a direct hit to o
of her lasers. Her lift bodies have been depleted
seventeen percent. Without a repair depot—"

"Nic," Karith said, "how you doing up there?" H
icon soared above him on his HUD.

"Just fine, Karith. Too high and the railguns c
target me, any lower and the treads can lock on wi
their main guns. And I keep running into need
streams from the bloody crawlers."

Karith studied the model HARRE was making fro
the sensor-drone feeds. The boilers *were* digging
under Nicolette's onslaught.

Reaching up and grasping a knob of rock, he lever
himself up over a ridge and rolled down, armor crus
ing boulders and snapping trees.

"Okay, Nic. Go take out a few of those railguns
you can. Make yourself some breathing room."

With an exultant yell, Nicolette flipped her airsl
into a backward loop and pulled out to race do
the center of the valley at treetop height. Looki
down a long draw, Karith saw her flash past t
mouth of it, lasers on full, burning the ground a
enemy units in her path in a fountaining rooster t
of flame and smoke.

The airships over the city wouldn't be able to
all out because of the civilians on the ground. I
was just grateful the machines hadn't achieved a sta
with aircraft yet.

"Sir, Captain Shepard has dropped off my rada

"Yeah, I expected that. She'll fly nap-of-the-earth all the way until she takes out those guns."

"That is very risky, sir. The concentration of smaller-caliber weapons on the ground along her route is likely to be extremely high."

"Yup. Moving that fast, though, they'll probably miss her."

"But with concentrations of fire—"

"What else, exactly, is she supposed to do, Harry?"

HARRE's response was immediate. "Retreat with us to the main perimeter, sir. The concentration of antagonistic force here is too high to justify operations in this area."

"Can't do it, Harry." Karith flattened himself against the side of a ridge on the edge of the red zone and lifted a sensor pod to the crest. Leaving it in place, he backed up, sidled along the ridge, and put another one up. "All right. What do we have out there?"

HARRE had started building a real-time model of the plains beyond the ridge as soon as the second pod was in place for triangulation. A smoky, torn landscape unfolded before Karith's eyes, filled with endless banks of raw functional machinery, thick power cables snaking along the ground and through the air, trenches and canals filled with oily water and mud between metal walls, and fences as far as the eye could see.

"Okay, Harry, we need something important enough stinging 'em good, right here so those units in the valley are the nearest units for defense."

While HARRE scanned, Karith adjusted the mech's missile batteries.

"Surely, sir, Nicolette's action against the railguns will draw the boiler's attention."

"You're bloody right it will, Harry me lad, but that's too far away. What are the units in the valley doing now?"

"I'm afraid they are up and moving again, sir."

"Bog take it. We need to hit something fast. What do you see out there?"

"There is a class seven power node quite close to the mouth of the valley, sir."

"Seven?" Karith was looking over the situation back at the city. Kewlett was holding on the east, barely.

"Yes, sir. It seems to be feeding most of the machinery and infrastructure in this area." HARRE lit up rough circle several miles in diameter at the valley mouth.

"Nice. We'll do the old high lob low fastball. We may not get another chance."

"Yes, sir."

Nicolette's voice sounded. "All right, this little strip of sky should be clear now."

"Excellent. Glad you're still alive, Nic."

"Yeah. Where do you want me?"

Karith launched three top-down missiles over the ridge.

"Hit here." Karith passed her the power node as target along with the flight paths of his missiles which were dodging and weaving through an upward rain of fire from the machine's defenses.

Three more missiles streaked from his shoulder rack and over the metal landscape, straight for the node. The flash and expanding concussion wave was followed closely by another from the last of his high flyers.

Nicolette screamed past, lasers digging a fiery trench straight through the node. Karith resist

HARRE's automatic instructions to duck behind the ridge, instead drawing a bit of fire off Nicolette. The ridgetop exploded under a firehose stream of metal splinters and energy weapons, even as he returned fire. He leaned into the storm, trusting his armor. The incoming fire drummed against him like pounding horizontal rain. Energy beams scored bright streaks across him, raising his internal temp. He could feel the heat on his skin as he shook and rocked from the force of it all.

He stood firm, sending streams of metal from his arm mounted kinetic weapons ripping into the defensive pods scattered around the fantastic metal landscape. HARRE orchestrated a symphony of destruction with the shoulder and hip turrets.

Karith's inner-ear protested. Suddenly, dirt piled into him from the side. He found himself stumbling.

"Contact!" HARRE yelled.

Looking down, Karith saw a walker fastened to his mech's lower abdomen, sparks flying where its plasma cutter chewed into his hip joint.

"Shit!" He smashed the spiny metal thing with his fist. Three more scuttled out of a newly opened hole in the ridge's side. Their leggy angled shapes scrambled past a machine he'd never seen before, a conical spinning drill bit as big as the rumbling combustion engine backing it.

"This is a new behavior, sir."

Karith smashed at a second walker as three more leapt onto his chest and shoulders. He caught himself screaming in anger and gritted his teeth. He triggered a burst of explosive rounds into the driller thing and leapt at it, pushing it back into the hole it had come from. Spinning, he flailed at the walkers cutting into him from above.

The dirt under his feet gave way and he slipped face first into another cluster of walkers scrambling out from between another driller and the edges of the hole it had made. He choked back another yell and curled up into a ball. They looked more like fantastic metal spiders than anything else, long legs supporting a bulbous body. One of them was digging into his abdomen again. He felt and heard something give down by his feet, a tearing, crumpling sound. Not his mech's feet, his actual feet. A whiff of ozone reached his nose.

"Sir, units in the valley are turning back toward us."

Thrusting with his mech's feet against the top of the second driller, he fired another burst of explosive rounds into its engine as he jumped away, or tried to jump away. Two more walkers dragged at him and upset his balance. The dirt and brush at the bottom of the ridge rushed up to meet him. Impact tightened his harness. Sparks flew in three directions across his face.

He grabbed a handful of walker and ripped it away. It went limp when he slammed it against the ground, pieces breaking off. He flogged his armored upper torso with the remains of the thing and felt it impact other walkers.

"Karith!" Nic's voice was frantic. "I can't see you."

"Wait one."

A walker lost its grip and fell to the ground. Karith stomped on it as he struggled to his feet again. Sparking, it blew up, clouds of smoke boiling out of it.

"Sir, your armor is compromised at plates T-6 and T-13."

"*What*?" Nic screamed over the link.

"I'm fine! Relax." The screaming sound of a plasma cutter was starting to vibrate his cockpit. Frantically Karith swept his hands over his head. Ah-ha! He grabbed the thing and crushed, dragging it to the front where he could see it. The cutting stopped. Metal corpse in hand, he flung himself to the ground on top of the two still on his back and rolled away. One stayed down. He fired into its body and it spasmed, smoking.

A shadow overtopped him and his sensors registered a flash of heat. He ground his back against an outcropping of rock, spun, and smashed his fist into the power plant of the boiler clinging to the rock face. It exploded. Eyes going up, he casually fired a burst into a walker stirring at his feet.

Nicolette's airship floated over him, just below the ridgetop. He stared in consternation for a moment. Most of her lift spheres were discolored from heat and impact.

"Nic?"

"Well what was I supposed to do, you jerk?"

"Sir, this area is riddled with tunnels. I deem it likely that more drilling machines are on the way and recommend retrograde movement."

"Harry, if you ever say 'retrograde movement' again, I'll erase you. It's bogtaken 'retreat.' What are you doing down here, Nic?"

"Just thought I might lend a hand."

"That's crazy. Get out of here, back up high."

"Fine, screw you then."

She sounded upset but jetted away down the ridge, picking up speed until she lifted into the air.

Up and down the ridge, earth slid and a literally

earthshaking rumble started. Karith turned and sprinted back the way he had come, into the hills. "Harry, what are the machines in the valley doing?"

"Approximately a third are returning toward their damaged power node."

"Damn it. The rest?"

"They have reached our drop zone and are continuing toward the city."

"Nic, I need you to hit those boilers in the valley again."

"Roger that." Her voice was cold.

"Hell, Nic, that was stupid and you know it. What if a walker had gotten up into your lift spheres?"

Silence.

"Whatever, Nic. I'm on my way down."

"What's that supposed to mean?"

"I'm going to hit them from the rear. That'll get their attention."

"Are you crazy? There's a hole in your armor!" He voice was frantic.

Karith found a draw going his way and started loping down to the valley.

Major Kewlett broke into their common circuit "Marvudi, can you hold that valley yourself?"

"Why?"

"I need your air."

Nicolette's voice was cold as iron. "No, Major, you'r not pulling me off Karith's top cover."

"That's up to him, little miss."

Karith raised his eyebrows. It had been a long tim since anybody dared call Nic "little miss" or anythir like it. He examined the situation model as he ra Nic's lasers coughing in the background.

HARRE said to him, privately, "Sir, our armor is breached. We must return to the depot for repair."

"There is no depot, HARRE. The *MarsFree* is gone and the next ship is hours out."

"Yes, sir. There are, however, class three repair facilities with the Major. We should consolidate with other units in the area."

Karith stopped just below a hilltop overlooking his drop zone and a little closer to the city. Panesthian civilians were a glittering brown carpet moving along the ground toward the city. The boilers were already upon the near edge of the mass. Curled and flaming bodies littered the torn earth. The boilers ground on, weapons burning, ripping, and smashing. Dimly, Karith could hear a roaring sound, the frantic buzzing and wailing of the dying Panesthians.

Taking up a stable posture, he readied every top-down missile he had. Nicolette orbited overhead, lasers coughing in his ears. Rippling explosions of smoke, steam, and molten metal stuttered across the valley floor. He could see the boilers digging in to shoot up at her, but not all of them. Some still moved toward the city.

"Major, you've got plenty of air."

Snap. "It's not enough, son. This damn city is oozing civilians. My mechs keep breaking through the tops of their bloody burrow-buildings when they try to move. The airships are the most effective weapons platforms I've got for offense, and I need 'em all. You're not the only one. I'm pulling air off all my outliers."

The major had a point about the air. Strange that quirk of architecture made air assets more precise and civilian friendly than ground units here.

HARRE was using data from all the sensor pods they'd dropped earlier in the day to build the current situation model. The boilers were deep into the suburbs now, and breaking into the burrow-buildings themselves too. They weren't empty.

"Bloody hell."

"What was that, son?" *Snap, chew.*

"Can do, Major. Nic, go."

"Damn you, Karith."

Karith didn't say anything. She sounded on the verge of tears, which was just odd. Nicolette did another low screaming pass over the boilers in the suburbs in front of him and curved away toward the city.

Major Kewlett said, "Son, you see what's going on over here?"

"Yes, Major."

"Good."

The connection went dead.

HARRE spoke to him. "Sir, are we going to attempt to engage and defeat the boilers in the valley?"

Karith triggered his first salvo of top-downs and sprinted off the hill just ahead of the counterfire which ripped into the ground behind him until he made it into a wadi. He put his shoulder turrets onto automatic and sprinted along the gash in the ground.

"Harry, if we don't stop them here, they're going to plow into the Major's rear area and they're going to be slaughtering civilians the whole way in. This it, my friend."

Karith popped up to the top of a swelling hill and fired off another salvo of top-downs. The counterfire was slower this time, and he was well away before it h

"Sir, the boilers are still advancing."

They were into the suburbs now. Karith moved carefully as he fired, trying to avoid stepping on the crushed and burned Panesthians scattered around the shells of their tunnels and buildings now cracked and open to the sky. He gritted his teeth and choked back the bile. Panesthians died easier than their smaller lookalikes from Earth, apparently.

A subsonic round from a tread he hadn't seen in time slammed into his shoulder plate and knocked him over. Through the concussive haze he could feel a breeze playing around his feet. There really was a hole in his armor.

From flat on the ground he sent an armor-piercing round at the boiler tread. The bulbous shape jumped and exploded. Lucky hit. Another one rolled up behind it.

He regained his feet and ran on. With HARRE's targeting help, he kept both armguns firing at once. Counterfire whipped around him, glancing off his armor.

He paused in a depression filled with trees, a wide spot along a stream bed.

"Fire off the rest of the sensor pods, Harry."

"Including the reserves, sir?"

"Yes."

HARRE launched the remaining eleven sensor pods from their racks. They arced out from Karith in a spreading cloud, came to earth, and dug in, leaving only their antennas protruding. The situation model sharpened up almost immediately. The boiler advance seemed to be clumped up before a small hill in the center of the valley. Beyond, he could see hundreds of unsteadily moving and scuttling Panesthian shapes fleeing overland.

He took a moment and ducked down to examine the inside of his cockpit. There, just to the right, down by his feet, was a jagged hole leaking daylight. He swore when he realized that he couldn't use a sensor pod to examine the exterior because he'd just launched them all. It occurred to him to dismount and examine it but he discarded the idea before it had even fully formed. The smell of a summer afternoon wafted up to him, laced with that of burning plastic.

He sprinted out of the depression, running toward the hill, firing as he went.

He hadn't gone ten steps before he broke through the top of a burrow-building and crashed to a stop. To his great relief, it was empty, a colorful mural on one wall looking down on bare floor.

The boilers were flowing around and over that hill now, moving on. He had to get in front of them somehow.

The machines were thick on the ground. His gun howled and screamed along with him as he stomped smashed, and burned a thick swathe of destruction through the metal foe. Karith was no longer speaking aloud. Once again he and HARRE were one in dreadful destructive purpose.

Just before he reached the hill, a swarm of walkers, crawlers, and blasters erupted over a stone ridge and on top of him, metal limbs flashing with terrible speed. He caught a glimpse of one blaster's stock cylindrical body up close before it triggered its main weapon into his mech's face.

The crash shocked him backwards. His flailing right hand latched onto a thick-limbed crawler and swung it around himself. He could feel the smashing impact through the fabric of his suit.

Horrible clicking sounds came to him, through his

external sensors and through the hole at his shins. He rolled frantically over, left hand clapping to the hole in his mech's abdomen even as he pulled his real right leg up away from something moving down there, toes curling.

There was a boiler at the hole. He couldn't see it; he could only feel it move under his metal left hand. He bore down, crushing hard. At the same moment he felt a deep terrible pain in his left leg. He stomped with his right and smashed something to the floor of his cockpit. Something withdrew as he pulled the boiler away. It was a walker, limp in his hand, holding a smoking monoblade cutter.

"Sir, there is a hollow in the top of that hill, a crater."

And there were a dozen more boilers around him. He started shooting and crushing again, and began pounding his way toward that hilltop, left leg going numb.

"Harry! Have they stopped?"

"Yes, sir. You have occupied their attention sufficiently to stop their advance. They are coming for *us* now." Blaster fire, waves of heat, washed over him, licking through the hole at his legs with sharp tongues as he ran.

"Good."

A huge blow took his mech in the right arm and spun him around and down. One of the treads. He looked for it, blinking sweat out of his eyes, and fired one of his three remaining missiles. The noise pounded at him. He'd never had a hole all the way through into his cockpit before. A sharp burning smell came in through it. He felt like throwing up.

The hill loomed over him, and he strained back to his feet to fling himself at it. Moments later he tumbled into the crater at the top. It was full of boilers.

He curled reflexively around the hole in his middle, flesh cringing away from it. Blaster fire filled the crater with orange plasma.

"No! This is *my* crater now!" He put the hole out of his mind, straightened, and fired point-blank at the boilers swarming over him. He kicked a boiler clear over the edge of the hole and grabbed another in his left hand, using it to scrape the others out, smashing and flinging. His mech's right arm twitched erratically as he fired its gun blindly. He smashed and stomped through the pain in his real leg, and fired until the boilers that were left in the hole were nothing but gears, cabling, and chunks of metal hull.

He blasted a few more as they came over the rim, launching them into the air in pieces.

"What's going on out there, Harry?" He gasped at a sudden wave of pain from his left leg and stumbled. When he tried to put out his mech's right hand to steady himself he fell against the wall of the crater as it only twitched limply. There was a sweet coppery smell heavy in the cockpit now.

"They are pausing in their assault of our position, sir. They are gathering."

He closed his eyes for a moment, then snapped them open. Closing them was a bad idea.

He could see now it wasn't really a crater. It was an excavation of some sort.

He tried to stand, but slipped. Glancing down, he saw among the shattered boilers a layer of dead Panesthians. Panesthians with equipment strapped to their bellies and fiery circles on their wingcasings. So that was why the boilers had stopped at this hill. Now all these boilers were his kills.

"Karith?" Nicolette spoke to him. "I'm coming, baby."

The fire in his leg made him almost scream. "Harry, what's she doing?"

"She is breaking formation to come to our aid, sir."

"Stay where you are, Nic! That's an order."

"Go to hell, Karith!"

"Dammit, Nic, stay where you are. You gonna let the boilers break the line after I went to this much trouble? Stay where you are!" He filled his voice with as much energy as he could. In the background he could hear Kewlett bellowing at her.

"Fine," she said. "You come to me then. Just run. You can make it."

"Can't do that, Nic."

"Dammit, Karith!" He could hear tears in her voice.

"Hey, Nic." He blasted a boiler off the rim and watched for another. None came.

"What?" She sounded angry now.

"Tell Maragette and Karri I love them, okay?"

No answer but the roar of her engines and a long screaming curse. The noise filters kicked in.

"Harry, what are they doing out there?"

"They have located and destroyed seven of our sensors, sir, but they appear to be bypassing us."

"What? They're advancing again? Toward the city?" Karith had never felt this tired.

"Yes, sir."

Karith chuckled, a sound weak in his own ears. "Up we get."

He propped himself up on the rim of the hole and started shooting. Boilers fell and return fire shattered the crater rim around him but still they advanced.

He gasped for air. "We're gonna have to . . . get them to . . . notice us again, . . . Harry."

Karith gathered his legs under him, braced his left hand on the rim of the crater, grunted, and fell into blackness.

The mech froze.

"Sir?"

Karith did not answer. HARRE noted a thick stream of blood pouring from the hole in his armor. He used his emergency override to ease the mech back behind cover.

"Sir?" Still nothing.

"Karith?" Nicolette's voice was frantic. "Your icon's dark, Karith. Karith!"

HARRE answered. "He is unconscious, Captain Shepard."

"Damn." Her voice was thick. "Okay, you're in charge now, Harry. Get him back here."

"It is true that command falls to me if my pilot becomes incapacitated."

"Why aren't you on your way back already?" her voice held ominous overtones. "Get up into the hills and make your way back here or he'll die."

HARRE looked over the field, the fleeing clouds o Panesthians, the advancing boilers carving into them

"It is true, ma'am, that Captain Marvudi has a muc higher chance of survival if I return to headquarter at this time."

"So go!" she screamed.

HARRE paused. Doctrine advised that he do a she said, but it was his call now. And he found . . . h found himself rebelling. As if Captain Marvudi wer speaking to him. He knew, somehow, that Doctrine could be ignored. Had to be ignored.

"I can't do that, ma'am." He vaulted the crater edge and charged the boilers, all guns blazing. They noticed him, and turned to engage.

Sometime later the *CambriaDawn* took up orbit around Milacria and dropped another three companies of mechanized infantry onto Major Kewlett's perimeter. Only forewarning and fast maneuvering saved her from the same fate as the *MarsFree*. Her Bombards destroyed the boiler railgun positions shortly thereafter.

Human forces pushed out to the east and the west. Captain Nicolette Shepard flew west, over the tangled wreckage of what seemed like thousands of broken boilers.

At a certain spot she lowered her airship to the ground and jumped out. Over thirty percent of her lift spheres were gone, and those that remained were discolored and ragged.

Karith Marvudi's mech lay face down in a dry streambed surrounded by hundreds of dead boilers, like the center of a blast ring stretching for hundreds of meters.

Nicolette folded her helmet back as she ran. The stench of smoke, burning oil, and plasma assailed her nostrils. Ignoring the hot metal she scrambled up and forced her way past the dead boilers on the mech's back. She tapped a code into the hatch's touch plate. No response, not even a power light. She ran back to her ship and returned with tools. Sparks flew and ears boiled off the metal as she began cutting.

Ethan Skarstedt is a Sergeant First Class in the Utah National Guard and has deployed to Kuwait, Iraq, Afghanistan, and Senegal. He has written a military SF novel as well as many short stories in several genres, and he occasionally blogs about things at ethanskar.com. In addition to his other projects, Skarstedt is in the midst of co-authoring a military SF novel with Brandon Sanderson.

Brandon Sanderson has published seven solo novels with Tor Books and Gollancz—*Elantris*, the Mistborn series, *Warbreaker*, and *The Way of Kings*—as well as four books in the middle-grade Alcatraz Versus the Evil Librarians series from Scholastic. He was chosen to complete Robert Jordan's Wheel of Time series; 2009's *The Gathering Storm* and 2010's *Towers of Midnight* will be followed by the final book in the series, *A Memory of Light*, in 2012. In addition to his writing, Brandon continues to teach aspiring authors.

Don Quixote

CARRIE VAUGHN

The distant thunder and subtle earthquake of a bombardment shouldn't have bothered me. I'd stayed in Madrid through the siege, three years starting in 'thirty-six, and a man didn't forget a thing like that. My gut didn't turn over at the noise, but at its implications. The war was supposed to be all but over now. So why the bombing?

Joe and I had left the main army to drive a truck along the river, looking for a vantage where we could watch the defenders' last stand. Most of the other reporters had already fled the country. I imagined I'd follow soon enough. As soon as I got that one great story. There had to be some kind of nobility in the face of defeat. Some kind of lesson for the future.

We stopped at a ridge and looked out over the river valley, trying to guess Franco's army's next move. Without getting too close, of course. I shaded my eyes. Another rumble of thunder rolled over us, and columns of smoke rose up from around the next hill.

Joe squinted into the sky. "Where're those bombs coming from? I don't see any planes—"

"It's not planes."

"Then what is it, artillery?"

· It didn't feel like artillery; the ground wasn't thumping with every report. "Want to find out?"

"You drive; I'll get my camera."

We left the overlook and drove until we found a turn off leading toward all that smoke.

I gripped the steering wheel; the truck lurched over potholes, the shocks squealing. Joe held the dash with one hand and his camera with the other, waiting for his shot. Not that there was anything to see—the landscape was barren of trees and vegetation. Not a spot of green. The battle had passed by here already, some time ago.

When we circled the next hill and came into an open stretch, the world changed. The battle here had been recent. Battle—more like a rout. Evidence suggested a massive aerial bombardment: tanks broken into pieces, treads shattered and turrets ripped from chassis; craters dotting the field like paint spatters; platoons reduced to scattered body parts. Vegetation still smoldered, and smoke rose up from wrecked ground. If I didn't know better, I'd have said this was someplace on the Western Front, twenty years ago. It's what happened when you took a thousand pounds of explosives and used them to scrape the land clean.

We had expected to find the crumpled remains of a defeated army. The fascists had pushed the Republican defenders back to the edges of their territory

The war was just about over, with Franco the victor. Everyone said so. Without outside aid, the Republicans didn't have a chance. But any potential allies had just turned their backs by making peace with Hitler. So-called peace, however long it lasted.

Somehow, I couldn't turn away from the disaster.

"Something's not right," I said finally.

"You just now noticed?"

"No—look at those rifles, the markings. These guys are Nationalists. Franco's army."

"Wait—aren't they supposed to be winning?"

"Yeah."

Joe got excited. "Then it's true—the loyalists came up with some secret weapon. They're going to turn it around after all."

I thought it really was too late—you had to have territory before you could defend it, and the loyalists didn't have much of that at all at this point. But if they did have a secret weapon—why wait until now to use it? "Something doesn't add up."

Crows circled. The air was starting to stink. There wasn't even anybody left to retrieve bodies, as if Franco's army hadn't yet figured out it had suffered such a defeat.

"Hank, let's get out of here—"

"Wait a minute." I grabbed binoculars from my bag on the seat next to me and peered out.

The road we were on hugged the hill and looped away from the plain where the battle had taken place. On the far side, beyond the destruction, another road stretched away: fresh, cut into the hard earth, an unpaved destructive swathe trampling vegetation to pulp. It was as wide as two tanks driving abreast.

Of course we had to follow it.

We took the truck as far as we could across the battlefield, which wasn't far at all. Weaving around debris, we avoided most obstacles but got stalled in a deep-cut rut. Ten minutes of spinning our tires in mud didn't get us anywhere. After an argument, we decided to continue on, to follow the story.

What I figured: the weapon was mobile—the rectangular sections of treads had dug into the ground, leaving an obvious path to follow. It was big, heavy. And it had to be pretty fast, because even through the binoculars, I couldn't find a sign of it ahead.

"It must be a tank," Joe said.

"Too big," I answered. "Too wide." I'd been a cub reporter in the Great War and had seen up close what tanks could do, which was quite a lot, but not this much. Unless, as Joe said, some genius had made improvements. "I don't know of any tank that carries enough shells to level a battalion like that."

"A couple of tanks maybe? A whole squad of them?"

But there was only one path leading out, one pair of treads traveling onward, a helpful dotted line guiding the way.

The sun started toward the west. We had canteens of water, some bread and sardines stuffed in our packs, but no blankets, nothing for camping out. Not even a flashlight. I thought about suggesting we turn around, then decided to wait until Joe suggested it first.

"You hear that?" Joe said, in our second hour of slogging.

I stopped, and heard it: the metallic grinding of gears, the bass chortle of a diesel engine. If I'd been back in the states, close to a town, I'd have assumed I was near a construction site, jackhammers and cranes working at full capacity.

We had just a little further to scramble, over another tread-rutted rise, before we saw what it was.

A small camp had been set up: a fire, over which a pot hung from a tripod, containing boiling water. A canvas lean-to was propped on a set of rickety branches that must have been picked up from the side of the road. A bearded Spaniard in worn army fatigues sat by the fire, stirring whatever was in the pot. In the shadows outside the reach of the fire, another Spaniard worked at what looked like an armored-encased engine block mounted on a scaffold. The engine glowed, spat sparks, and spewed a shroud of smoke into the air. Atop the engine block was a steel chassis; below it were the treads that had cut the road from the battlefield.

It was a tank, but not really. Rather, some Frankenstein's monster of tank parts. The war machine had been cobbled together and greatly expanded, drawing on the initial tank design for inspiration then taking it to an extreme. Wide treads on a hinged base performed the same motion as an ankle joint, bending as it climbed over obstacles, keeping the chassis level. The cannon stood in for arms, firing 6-inch shells if I had my guess. A squadron's worth of bombing in a single go. Armored, mobile, crushing everything in its path. As if 10,000 years of warfare had led to this.

The glowing engine seemed like nothing so much as a beating heart, pounding in anger, atop a muscled body and stout legs. The red, yellow, and purple stripes of the Republican flag were painted on its side.

Joe and I just stared, until the first Spaniard drew

a pistol from a pouch on his belt and shouted at us in Spanish.

Joe put up his arms and yelled back, "*Somos Americanos! Americanos!*"

For a frozen moment, I thought that wouldn't matter, and we'd both get shot. I prepared to run. But the Spaniard lowered his pistol and laughed. "I don't believe it!" he said in accented English. "We thought you all left!"

He invited us to sit by the fire. The mechanic climbed off the machine and joined us. The man at the fire was Pedro; the mechanic, Enrique. Pedro was a nondescript soldier in worn fatigues, hat pressed over shaggy hair. Enrique was otherworldly: his eyes were invisible behind tinted goggles, his head was bare—his hair appeared to have been singed off by the heat of the engine where he worked.

After exchanging names, we told our stories. But Joe and I couldn't stop looking at the modified tank. Pedro saw this and smiled. "What do you think?"

"It's—" I started, then shook my head. "I don't know what to think."

"We call it the *Don Quixote.*"

"Because you're tilting at windmills?"

Pedro laughed and said to Enrique, "I told you people would understand!"

Enrique didn't say a word. He sat on the ground, arms around his knees. The firelight reflected off his goggles, so he could have been looking anywhere.

"But what is it?" Joe asked.

"It's a personal tank," Pedro said. "Enrique built it, but it was my idea. It's better than a tank—faster, more agile, simpler to operate. It only needs one man instead of a whole crew. You've seen what one person is able to do with a machine like this?"

"That battalion back there—you destroyed it?" I said. "It's amazing."

"Yes, it is," Pedro said.

"If you'd had this a year ago you might have made a difference," Joe said.

Pedro's smile fell, and he and his partner both looked at us, cold and searching. "Never too late," Pedro said, shoving another stick into the fire. "It took us years to build this one. But now that it's finished, we can build more, many more. An army of them. The Great War didn't end war—but this might. No one would dare stand against an army of Don Quixotes."

This gave me the image of a hundred wizened old men sitting astride broken horses, making a stand against Franco. I almost laughed. But then I glanced at the shadow of the war machine. This conversation should have taken place in a bar, over a third pitcher of beer. Then, I would have been able to laugh. But here, in the dark and cold, an hour's walk from a scene of slaughter, the firelight turning our faces into shadowed skulls, I thought I was looking at a new kind of warfare, and was terrified.

The Spaniards let Joe and I stay at their camp. They didn't have extra blankets, but the fire was warm and they shared the thin stew they'd cooked. Enrique slept in the machine, by the engine, which although it was shut down now, never stopped its subtle clicking, cooling noises. Like the beat of a heart.

"This is going to make a hell of a story," Joe said, whispering at me in the dark. "I can't wait to get pictures in the morning."

A hell of a story, yeah. "This isn't going to turn the war around for them, you know," I said.

"Of course not, with just the two of them. Even if they do have that monster. And I think they're a little crazy to boot. But that's not the point, is it? This thing—folks back home'll go gonzo for it. It'd be like King Kong. If we could get them to bring it to the states we could sell tickets."

There was an idea—if the two men would ever agree to it. More likely they'd prefer to stay and smash as much of Franco as they could before going down in flames. They wouldn't have a chance to build their army of personal tanks.

"What do you think, Hank? Can we talk them into giving up the fight and bringing that thing to New York? Get it to climb the Empire State Building?"

The fire was embers. Enrique's machine clicked like crickets, and Pedro seemed to be asleep. I shook my head. "I'm thinking about what the Germans would do with that thing. Scratch that—with a hundred of them." Pedro and Enrique couldn't build an army of them, but an industrialized war machine like Germany?

"What?"

"That armor might be able to stomp out a few battalions, but it can't win the war. They've got no allies, no outside support, while Franco's got Germany and Italy supplying him. As soon as the fascists cross the river, they've got Spain—and if they capture those two, they've got that thing, too. Then the Germans get a hold of it—"

"And what are the Germans going to do with it?"

"Boggles the mind, doesn't it?" I said.

❖　　❖　　❖

Dawn came slowly, filtered through the haze of smoke and a sense of dread. Like the sky was a predator waiting to pounce.

In daylight, the tank looked even more anthropomorphic. The engine heart burned, the cannons could be raised and lowered like arms. The articulated treads had bolts above them that looked very much like knees. A single, slotted viewport in the chassis stared like a cyclopean eye. The machine even carried a bandolier of spare shells across its chest, just to drive the point home.

Pedro was stoking the fire back to life when an unmistakable, mechanical rumble shook in the distance—the sound of an army on the move. Enrique entered the personal tank through a hatch in the back of the chassis. The engine coughed back to life.

Joe knelt at the rise sheltering the camp and stared through the binoculars. "It's one of Franco's patrols, coming this way."

Following the path of destruction from the crushed battalion, looking for the enemy that had done such a thing.

Pedro laughed, as he seemed to in reaction to everything. "Now you can see first hand what *Don Quixote* can do!"

I had a thought. "Let me come along. Let me ride with that thing."

Pedro looked taken aback. Even Enrique poked his head out of the hatch to look, though his expression was blank.

"There's barely enough room for Enrique—you can't do anything there," Pedro said.

I talked fast. "I can write about it. Get you publicity

back home—in American newspapers. Imagine if some big investor decided to make you an offer. You'd be famous—inventors of the most amazing war machine in history. Famous—and rich. But only if I'm able to write about it. *Really* write about it. First-hand testimony."

Pedro and Enrique regarded each other, and whatever secret signal passed between them, I didn't catch it.

"You can ride with Enrique," Pedro said finally. "But only if you write about it. Get us those investors, yes? The money?"

So much for the socialist ideals of the loyalists.

I shrugged on my jacket, checking for my pencil and notebook. Joe came over and grabbed my sleeve. "You know what you're doing?"

"Sure I do. Just remember to tell everyone how brave I was if I don't make it back."

"Brave? Is that what you're calling it?"

I grinned. "We can call it anything we want, we're the ones writing about it."

I knew exactly what I was doing. I climbed up to the back of the machine, where Enrique held out his hand to assist me through the hatch in the chassis.

Don Quixote had enough room for two—barely Enrique settled onto a board that had been bolted in front of a control panel. There wasn't a seat for me so I perched behind the driver in a narrow indentation left by the hatch. My knees were jammed up to my chest, and I had to reach up to hold on to a bar welded above my head. The air inside was thick close, and full of the stink of burned oil. The thing didn't seem to have any ventilation—the armor was sealed up tight. The slit above the controls offered th driver the narrowest of views. I couldn't see a thing, only the metal interior, scarred with hammer blows and smeared with soot. Sweat broke out all over me, and I had trouble catching my breath.

Enrique didn't seem to notice the burning air. He pulled on several of a dozen levers and turned a handful of toggles. The vibrations rattling through the machine changed, growing more severe. The engine throbbed beneath my feet, a burning furnace ready to explode.

Then, the machine began to move. The chassis lurched straight up, like an elevator jerking hard to the next floor. Gears and drive belts squealed, treads rumbled, and the tank rolled forward. The motion was rough, jarring, like driving too fast over gravel, swaying this way and that as we passed over some rut or chunk of vegetation. Incredibly, we were moving. My teeth rattled in my jaw. Enrique sat calmly, his hands steady on the controls, moving levers in what seemed to be a random sequence. He was driver, gunner, mechanic, engineer, and commander all in one. Any normal tank would have needed six men to do all those jobs. He turned another set of toggles, and new set of gears engaged; the chassis tipped back, as if the machine was now looking skyward.

I opened the hatch a crack to steal a look. The side-mounted gun turrets had ratcheted into place, aiming toward the approaching enemy. I shut the hatch again.

By lifting myself up, I could see around Enrique's head and catch a glimpse of the outside through the slit in the metal. The view was like flashing on individual frames of film without seeing the whole picture: a tank motoring toward us, artillery guns lined up, trucks circling, troops moving into position, and among them all the red and gold of the fascist flag.

Enrique jumped up, throwing me against the back wall of the chassis. The driver pulled on a lever jutting above him, and an explosion burst, enveloping *Don Quixote* in a storm of thunder, the cannons firing. He pulled on a second lever, and a second shell launched. I ducked to try and glimpse what was happening through the slit, but I saw only smoke. I heard distant detonations, and screams.

The Spaniard kept pulling on the overhead levers, and shells kept firing. He must have had an automatic mechanism loading ammunition. And if the Germans got ahold of *that* bit of technology...

I tore a piece of paper out of my notebook, wadded up two small bits, and shoved them in my ears. That only cut out the sound a little; I could still feel every vibration in my bones. I was growing dizzy from it.

The cannon acted like Gatling guns. Firing 6-inch explosive shells, over and over. Enrique's tank churned along the edge of the battlefield, swiveling the chassis to move the gun, raking the enemy with cannon fire. This second battalion didn't last long.

An occasional bullet pinged off *Don Quixote*'s armored chassis, but did no damage. The vulnerable bits of the mechanism were too well protected. Enemy artillery launched a few shells before *Don Quixote*'s cannon destroyed them, but the explosive detonated dozens of feet away. The personal tank's small size and mobility made it difficult to target.

This thing just kept getting more dangerous.

Then it was over. The tank stopped rolling an

settled on its treads. Enrique throttled down the engine, which softened to a low growl.

I opened the back hatch and tumbled out into the fresh air. Relatively fresh—the stink of gunpowder and blood rose around me. But at least there was a breeze. My ears kept rattling, seemed as if they would rattle for ages.

Pedro and Joe ran toward us. They must have seen the whole thing—they'd have had a better view than I'd had. Joe had probably gotten some splendid photos.

"Ha! You did it again, Enrique! *Bueno*!" Pedro called. Enrique was climbing down from the chassis more gracefully. "And you, Hank—did you get a good story?"

I hadn't written a word. But I had a good story.

"Guys, both of you, get over here. Let me get a picture of you in front of the battlefield," Joe said, gesturing the Spaniards together and pointing his camera.

I leaned against the tank, *Don Quixote*. I had a story, but I didn't know how to tell it. Or if I even could. Instead, I made a plan.

Finding footholds on leg joints, gripping bolts, gears, and the window slot on the front of the chassis, I climbed to the front of the tank. Balancing there, I reached to the bandolier of artillery shells and pulled out two left over from the battle, tucking them in the pockets of my jacket.

By following exhaust pipes, I found my way to the engine, and the fuel tank hidden behind armor plating under the chassis. A simple sliding door gave access to it for refueling. Enrique obviously wasn't expecting sabotage.

I jammed one of the shells between a set of pistons operating the tank's legs, and dropped the second in the fuel tank. I twisted up a handkerchief into a makeshift fuse and lodged it in the fuel tank door. Then I lit a match.

Wouldn't give me much time, but I didn't need much.

I tried not to look too nervous, to draw suspicions, when I marched over to Joe and grabbed his arm. "We have to get out of here."

Joe had been directing Pedro and Enrique toward a photograph against the backdrop of destruction, and dozens of shattered bodies. The two men were grinning like hunters who'd bagged an eight-point buck.

The photographer looked at me, confused.

"We *really* have to get out of here," I said.

"Hey!" Pedro said. "You're going write about *Don Quixote*, yes? You write about us? Tell everyone—we can win the war. They'll see that we're finally winning and send help!"

"That's right," I said, patting my notebook in my jacket pocket even as I dragged Joe away, back up the rise. "I've got it all down, you don't need to worry. In fact, we need to get back and phone this story to our editor right now. Can't waste any time!"

Pedro seemed to accept this explanation and waved us on our way, calling out blessings in Spanish. Enrique just watched us go, through glassy, goggled eyes; he'd never taken them off.

"Hank, what the hell are you doing?"

"Just keep walking."

The explosion came as we passed into the next bowl of a valley. Good timing, there. We missed the brunt of the shockwave. But the force of it still knocked us both to the ground.

"Christ, what was that?" Joe scrambled to look behind us. A dome of black smoke was rising into the air.

Maybe the two Spaniards had had a chance to get away. Maybe they'd been knocked clear by the initial blast. But probably not.

We watched as the cloud expanded and dissipated. "Maybe that thing wasn't as well built as they thought," I observed.

Joe looked at me. "Then we were lucky to get out of there," he said, deadpan.

"Yes, we were, I imagine."

We kept walking.

A winter breeze was blowing, and my jacket didn't seem able to hold off the chill. I wasn't sure we were walking toward the truck. For all I knew, that second battalion had confiscated or smashed it. It didn't matter. We just needed to dodge Franco's troops, get across the river, and then get out of Spain. I listened for the sound of tank treads, truck motors, of a thousand marching bodies, but the world was silent. Wind rustling through dried brush, that was all.

"I think they could have done it," Joe said after a half an hour of walking. The Ebro River had appeared, a shining strip of water in the distance. "I think they could have beaten back Franco with that machine, if they'd had enough time."

"Then what? They build more, or sell the design to a real manufacturer, and then what? You really want to see those things stomping all over Europe the next war?"

"What next war? There isn't going to be a next war, not after the Munich treaty."

I stared at him. Everyone kept telling themselves that. As if this whole debacle in Spain wasn't the opening salvo. "Let me see your camera a minute."

Joe, bless him, handed it right over. I popped the cover and yanked out the yard of film he'd shot, exposing the film, destroying the pictures.

"Hey!" Joe said, but that was all. I closed the cover and handed the camera back. Somehow, the photographer must have understood.

That was why we were all here, wasn't it? Doing our part to make the world a better place?

———

Carrie Vaughn is the bestselling author of the Kitty Norville series. *Kitty's Big Trouble*, the ninth book was released in Summer 2011, and the tenth will be released in Summer 2012. She has also written novels for young adults (*Voices of Dragons* and *Steel*) and two standalone fantasy novels, *Discord's Apple* and *After the Golden Age*. Her short fiction has appeared in many magazines—such as *Lightspeed*, *Fantasy Magazine*, *Weird Tales*, and *Realms of Fantasy*—and anthologies, such as *Brave New Worlds*, *Songs of Love and Death*, *Warriors*, and *The Thackery T. Lambshead Cabinet of Curiosities*. All of her Kitty Norville short fiction was recently collected in *Kitty's Greatest Hits*. Carrie's story, "Amaryllis," was nominated for a Hugo Award in 2011. She lives in Colorado with a fluffy attack dog. Learn more at carrievaughn.com.

The Poacher

WENDY N. WAGNER
& JAK WAGNER

The medical request on Karen's forearm display blinked a second time. *Accept*? She eyeballed the road ahead. Low fog. No traffic. Hardiman drove the Humvee one-handed, unconcerned, not even scanning the brush for wildlife. The display vibrated, demanding response. There might not be a better time to take her meds.

She set her teeth as she jabbed ACCEPT. She'd chosen Earth knowing full well she'd spend the first three years adjusting to the higher gravity and an atmosphere choked with foreign particulates. It had seemed worth it, back on Luna, with Cirkan trade blockades cutting off supply lines and air scrubbers rationed so hard you had to scrub your biomech suit's filters with a toothbrush just to keep breathing till the next supply drop. Earth meant all the oxygen a girl could dream of, real live trees and the space to run around them. The needle punched through the skin of her upper thigh, still tender from yesterday's dose of immunosuppresants, hormones, and steroids.

From the back seat, Gordo pounded her shoulder. "Can't believe you go through all of this just to be a ranger. You had it made up there on Luna, girl." Like every Earth native, he thought life off-world was all big money, firefights, and gravity-free blowjobs. He was saving every paycheck for a ticket off this rock.

Hardiman answered before she could open her mouth. "Inspector Gadget here has *ideals*, Gordo. Dreams of protecting the rainforest and saving the whales."

"Very funny," Karen snapped. The swipes at her interest in animals and the jokes about her dependency on the biomechanical suit—she wore power armor even off-duty as part of her transition to Terran life—were getting old. Her lips thinned. "I don't see you turning in your ranger's star to seek your fortune off-planet, Sir." She flinched at a surprise jab in her thigh. She always forgot about the follow-up caffeine injection. It stung worse than the original shot, but she'd need it to keep her eyes open after the antihistamines set in.

She tapped her armor, wishing she could rub the skin beneath it, and resisted the urge to glare at Hardiman. She'd given up on the older man. Karen didn't know what had put the chip on his shoulder, but after two months serving together, she was sick of it.

"It's a job," he growled. "And one I'm damn good at."

Karen had no answer for that. After all, Hardiman was the most decorated ranger in the entire park system. During her training, Karen had memorized every report he'd ever filed. And there were hundreds. People thought Earth was a rural paradise, a place enjoy a vacation in the woods and some fine wine. They didn't realize the effort it took to keep it safe enough for tourists.

In the one hundred years since Earth was declared a Human Heritage Site, fully eighty percent of the population had emigrated to space stations or the growing Martian colonies—and every single human still required Earth exports for irreplaceable biochemicals and microorganisms. All breeding stock for agriculture still came from Terran farms, and Terran luxuries like coffee and beef were worth their weight in gold. The entire planet would be pillaged if it weren't for rangers like Hardiman, who'd worked his ass off fighting poachers of every stripe.

That didn't mean that at this second she wanted to sit next to him. The Humvee was big enough for four armored rangers and their gear, but right now the battery rack between their seats felt too small a barrier between them. She fiddled with her gloves. On duty, the team all rode in their power armor, but transit protocol allowed them to keep their helmets and gloves "at ready." Karen slipped hers on, a kind of security blanket for her hands.

And she did feel better. Natives like Hardiman and Gordo didn't get it. To them, the power armor was a tool, something their job required that they would never use off the clock. Karen had grown up on Luna before the colony even completed its first greenhouse. With man-made atmosphere and artificially-boosted gravity, every kid wore a biomechanical suit, night and day. Plenty of people owed their lives to their biomech suits, and Karen was one of them.

In the field, her experience showed. Hardiman

could drive and deal cards in his power armor; Karen could do field surgery.

Outside the window, something caught Karen's eye. She leaned forward in her seat, staring ahead. "Hey, stop."

Hardiman tapped the brake. "See something?" Karen had proven her worth spotting oddities trailside. He was at least willing to listen to her when she said she saw something.

Karen pointed at the sky, following a vee of rippling clouds. A rainbow haze shimmered behind it for a second, but if she had looked away, she would have missed it. "That's a Cirkan cloaking signature."

"Well, fuck me," Hardiman growled. "Those little shits are trespassing again."

Karen pulled her helmet from ceiling storage. Cirkans and humans shared just enough biological interests to guarantee trouble, breathing roughly the same blend of gases and building their bodies from carbon and water. They were too much like people. Slimy, resource-hungry, gray people.

She slapped her visor shut as the Humvee's tire screeched on the pavement. The radar blipped and a proximity alarm screamed a warning.

"It's right on top of us!" Gear crashed in back as Gordo dropped his helmet. It ricocheted off the front window and Karen swatted it out of her face just as a fireball hit the pavement in front of them. Hardiman cranked the wheel and the Humvee spun wildly minutes before stopping.

"We gotta get out of here!" Karen had her seatbelt off and the emergency roof hatch open before the others even fumbled at their seatbelt latches. Black smoke obliterated the forest as the asphalt burned around them. She hit her thrusters and shot up out of the hatch, rolling off the roof and aiming herself for the tree line. The ground shook as the Cirkan ship strafed the nose of the Humvee.

What the hell are the Cirkans doing? None of this made sense. It was one thing to break treaty trespassing, another to open fire on a military vehicle. At the upper left of her visor display, Karen's blood pressure monitor flashed a warning. She shut it off. She toggled her visual displays to infrared and scanned the sky. The ship was up there, all right, and a hot burst of white billowed from its starboard engine. It would have to make an emergency landing. An illegal emergency landing.

"Hardiman, they're crash-landing in the forest!"

Her helmet radio crackled back at her.

"Hardiman? Gordo?" The smoke was thick, but not so thick she shouldn't be able to see the others' emergency safety lights, auto-activated in fire conditions. She hit her thrusters and pushed back toward the Humvee.

A pair of shoulder lights nearly blinded her and she collided with another suit of power armor. A hand caught her elbow before she fell.

"Get back to tree cover! The Humvee's on fire!"

Hardiman. She pivoted on one toe, feeling the pavement buckle beneath the pressure of her armor's cap. Karen flew past the other ranger, moving for the tree line. "Where's Gordo?"

He shook his head. Something exploded behind them.

"Fuck." She scanned the sky, the armor's camera

systems supplementing her own vision with infrared and ultraviolet readings. "It's still moving across the woods. We can catch up if we hurry."

"Let's get this bastard." Hardiman broke into a run. She cast one last look over her shoulder, back at the fading flames in the road, and then followed him into the dense woods.

Running spun Karen's mind into a kind of orbit, her conscious mind cut free from her body. Everything went on reflex, leaping logs, dodging branches, twisting around trees. Hardiman fell behind, his Earth-born skeleton weighing him down. Thrusters on, nothing could outrun Karen.

A thruster-boosted leap over a fallen fir took her up into the tree canopy, face to face with a bird she didn't recognize, ivory and speckled, its long beak probing a rotten limb. It froze, staring at her, and her visor auto-launched her field guide, scrolling the species name across her display: *Northern Flicker* She grinned at the bird, memorizing its shape even as she sank ground-ward.

With a sudden shriek, the bird launched itself across her field of vision, and the cedar tree ahead of her burst into orange shards. Only her visor stopped a smoldering chunk of wood from spearing through her head. Momentum shot her backward, somersaulting into a clump of huckleberries.

The suit shifted beneath her, reinforcing her ribs, pumping a dose of ibuprofen into her thigh. The blue of her armor had fuzzed over with sawdust, the wood pulverized on impact.

She should have died. But she never even felt the pain.

Karen's skin crawled. She resisted the sudden urge to unseal her suit and check the damage for herself. To take back control of her body and her movements. On the training base, she could get away with that. Here, gravity would have her crawling in seconds. The muscles in her diaphragm would probably give out, smothering her in her own skin.

Hardiman landed beside her huckleberry patch and yanked her to her feet. "Bastard shot at you! You hurt?"

She shook her head. Her ribs would be fine before dinner.

"I want you to circle back to the road," he said. "Use full speed to reach the field testing station in Welches. Then contact HQ and get us some backup. Got that?"

"Sir, I shouldn't leave you. Protocol says—"

"Protocol knows shit about aliens sneaking around the forest. Now get moving!" He punched his forearm display and vanished as his camo systems activated.

"Shit," Karen whispered. She didn't like this. Alone was dangerous. Alone in the woods with a Cirkan stealth vehicle was positively suicidal. But a command was a command. She activated her own camouflage and started jogging.

She could see the smoke of the ruined Humvee within a few steps. Her chest gave an asthmatic squeeze. She'd never lost a squadmate before. She couldn't stop staring at the smoldering hunk of metal.

Something moved beside it. Something in a blue and white ranger's uniform.

"Gordo?" She power-jumped to his side, dropping her camo. His eyes turned to her, the whites startling in a black-bubbled face. His hand fluttered beside him, still covered by the gloves of his power armor.

"Where's your suit, man? Why aren't you suited up?" She shook her head, staring at him. She had a first aid kit, but it lacked the chemical arsenal of his armor.

"Power unit...ripped out," he whispered, and all around his lips, the blackened skin split open to reveal the raw meat below.

"What?" Again, she shook her head, as if she could shake out the confusion and make sense of Gordo's condition.

"Hardiman," he gasped. Pink foam bubbled up on his lips.

"Gordo!" She grabbed his shoulders and she realized, too late, that the fire had burned through the back half of him. She felt her fingers sink into his cooked flesh. A scream gurgled up in his throat. His eyes rolled up, white crescents beneath fluttering lids.

He jerked, his back arched and shook, and then he was horribly still.

His weight settled into her arms, the suit making it bearable. He'd been more of a dumb kid than a co-worker. Always ready to jump in and do his job. And now he was dead.

She pushed his body away. It hit the road and flopped, but wet chunks, red and black and fatty, clung to her gloves. She gagged. Heaved. But swallowed it down and wiped her gloves in the gravel. Once, twice, again and again.

He was really dead, cooked by alien fire his suit should have protected him from. Would have if it had still worked.

Hardiman. Had he really destroyed Gordo's power unit? And if so, why? Her stomach churned again.

There was no good reason for him to do it, but after two months working with the man, she felt certain Gordo was right.

And Hardiman was a killer.

He may have gone invisible, but Hardiman's suit still broadcast its location over the GPS system. She kept its display up in her visor as she ran, the gold-lit map running over the terrain. She almost ran into a tree when Hardiman's blinking icon switched course and stopped two klicks to the east. She slowed her movement and double-checked every display.

All systems normal.

The forest thinned along the course of a creek. She crept toward it. For a moment, she remembered her first trip into the woods, the mandatory sixth-grade trip to visit The Home World. They'd been hiking along a creek not much different from this when the ducks had come down out of the sky, banking their landing just like her dad's shuttlecraft. Her camp counselor had to sit beside her while the others kept hiking. Karen couldn't stop watching the ducks.

There were ducks and chickens on the space station, of course. Eggs were a valuable protein source. But they all lived in cages, eating and drinking on schedule like feathered egg machines. These ducks were different. They sat on the water and brushed their bills against each other's backs. They dove and swam. When Karen left Earth at the end of that trip, she'd promised herself she'd come back and see them again.

But there were no ducks on *this* creek. The weekend's rainfall pushed the mud-colored water to the tops of its banks, debris bobbing along the surface.

Sticks, branches, a dead squirrel. A glistening gray ball floated past her boot—junk, probably. Some kid's kickball covered in motor oil. But Karen's instincts made her grab for it. The ball squished like jelly in her grip, like an oversized frog's egg.

Like a Cirkan egg.

They grew their eggs in water, she remembered. They always had money to spend on water. It was a rare substance out among the stars. The hairs on the back of her neck rose.

GPS brightened in the corner of her faceplate Hardiman had not moved. Instinct made her activate radar and as it pinged off something big, Karen felt her stomach rise up in her ribs. The radar signature matched the cloaked Cirkan vessel. And Hardiman was sitting right underneath it.

"I've got you, you son of a bitch," she breathed She cleared her faceplate display, sick of the flashing the blinking, the moving lights. It felt too much like a video game. She wanted the forest, real and damp and dim and silent, except for a bird call, distant some kind of warning to its kin.

Shit. That seemed to summarize the situation Alone, her team either liquidated or held by the enemy. Armed only with a standard-issue parks rifle with no backup ammunition. No knowledge of the ground ahead, the blind spots or high ground. She leaned against a tree, weighing her odds.

She had surprise on her side. No one would expect a rookie ranger to go against Hardiman's orders hike through the forest on her own.

She had her armor. It tripled her speed, quadrupled her strength, sealed out any biochemical weapons the

invader might use. She hadn't had to test it in battle
much since her posting here on Earth. She'd spent
the last two months cruising around the Humvee,
tracking elk and watching for poachers. But she'd
done enough fighting in training to trust her biomech
suit to watch her back. With Hardiman an unmoving
lump on the radar, she was lucky she had *anything*
watching her back. This fight promised to get ugly.

With a cold churning in her gut, Karen studied
the rest of her gear. There was a cutting torch built
into the wrist of her armor and a tear gas grenade
tucked into her belt.

Nothing else.

Fuck. She forced herself to take three deep breaths
and began a hunkered jog along the creek's edge. At
least she had the element of surprise.

The sound of Hardiman's voice startled her. She
slowed, listening. She couldn't tell what he was saying,
but she recognized the tin-can quality of his armor's
translation device in between his phrases. Her pulse
quickened. There was a pilot on that ship, an alien
eager to stay hidden. Like a poacher, she realized, ready
to take whatever he wanted in the thick tree cover.

She stepped out of the undergrowth, eyeing the
backside of Hardiman's armor, its regulation blue
standing out against the green meadow bordering the
pond. The water stretched beyond what the map had
led her to expect, and dozens more of the Cirkan
eggs clung to the shore. Some kind of translucent
tubing ran from the side of the lake into the clearly-
visible Cirkan shuttlecraft. A gray egg wriggled down
the tube's length and dropped into the pool with a
splash of water.

The Cirkan craft took up most of the clearing, but its cargo hold yawned open, revealing an array of computer equipment and packing crates. A slim figure leaned against the frame, and if it weren't for the gray skin and the protuberant eyes—like glossy black grapefruits—focused down on Hardiman, she could have almost mistaken it for a bald human. She crept forward, automatically analyzing the creature's status as a threat. It wore a long loose vest, belted at what would be a human's waist. She couldn't make out any weapons, but who knew what it kept hidden on its person.

But still, it was small, a little shorter than her own height, and probably half her unarmored weight. She felt cautiously optimistic about her odds in a fight.

Two fleshy knobs unfolded from the top of its head and pointed right at her. It didn't look so human anymore. She froze.

And then it click-clacked something in its ugly language, something her helmet translated as: "Is that the 'stupid girl'?"

Hardiman whirled around, and Karen realized, too late, that she'd never reactivated her camo system. "Hey, Karen." He hesitated. She wished she could see his face more clearly through his visor. "Hey, it's not what we thought. This guy...he's a refugee. His ship blew out its engine and he needs our help."

If she hadn't run into Gordo, she would have fallen for it. She shook her head. "I don't understand why you're doing, Hardiman, but I know you're helping this alien break the law. It's depositing eggs in the lake." She took a deep breath. His deeper treachery stung. "And you killed Gordo."

"He'd still be alive if you hadn't spotted the ship," Hardiman growled. "We were supposed to explore a dummy poaching trail, not follow after my contact. He panicked. I guess I did, too."

"Why?" Karen whispered.

He laughed, a short bitter bark. "You're too young to even begin to understand."

She squared her shoulders. "But you're a *ranger*." She wanted to say more, wanted the words to have more weight. She wanted to recite the name of every report he'd ever made, the verdict of every case he'd ever closed. She wanted to show him a picture of herself, hunched over her desk on a Friday night, watching him giving testimony on the news, studying *him* while the rest of her classmates gathered in Luna's cheapest bars. She wanted to show him a picture of Earth, a lone blue-green orb in the blackness of space, a treasure trove they'd both sworn to protect.

But all she could do was repeat herself: "You're a *ranger*."

He shook his head. "The government doesn't give a shit about the work we do here on Earth. No one cares about a few goddamned elk or the health of one stupid lake in the middle of fucking nowhere. I've been living that truth for a quarter of a century."

The enormity of his crime sank in. It wasn't just one deal with one Cirkan. There'd been other transactions, other schemes. She'd wondered why her unit, led by the service's most decorated agent, hadn't caught a perp since she'd arrived. Now it made sense. "You've been selling information to poachers."

He waved a hand. "Like I said, no one cares, Karen."

"I care." Her throat closed tight around the words.

She swallowed hard. "I'm going to have to arrest you." She bit her tongue to keep the word *sir* from slipping out. Its taste, sour and coppery, filled her mouth.

Behind the darting lights in his faceplate, Hardiman's eyes narrowed.

She reached for her rifle even as the Cirkan snatched Hardiman's weapon from his back holster and opened fire.

Her eyes registered the flash of light from the end of the rifle before the pain erupted. The ballistic armor could withstand small-arms fire, and even some anti-materiel weaponry from a distance. But at less than twenty feet, the tungsten armor-piercing round passed through the main torso plate and out her back before the round even had a chance to shed its sabot casing. She flew backward, her glove snapping off shots even as hydrostatic shock shut off her brain.

Water closed over her faceplate and, for a long moment, Karen was dead.

Reflex took over: gasping, choking, clawing for air, even as the suit force-fed her oxygen. She flailed for the surface. Weeds slid around her wrists and held them, fighting the drag of two hundred fifty pound of weaponry and Kevlar. Bubbles rose up through the water, tiny bursts of light and color like the readout scrolling across her visor's displays.

The mission drifted from her grasp like the oxyge escaping her lungs. There was no pain; the suit too care of that. Down in the green depths of the pond air, the job, Gordo—it all seeped away. Everythin was unimportant. Maybe Hardiman was right. Mayb nobody cared about one little lake in one little fore on one primitive little planet. After all, the rest of the voting, breathing populace kept themselves to the colonies.

Breathing. Karen couldn't be sure she still could; the shot in her gut must have taken out her diaphragm. She couldn't bring herself to care.

The suit burst hot lightning in her armpits. Electrical shock. Her eyes fluttered and rolled up in her head. It shocked her again.

Her body jerked like a man on an electric chair.

The weeds pulled free. She sank again, loose. Like flying.

The suit's thrusters powered on.

The thrusters boiled the water at the bottom of the pond, steam pushing her body toward the surface. Karen's eyes rolled up in her head as her innards went cold, then bubbled and gurgled as triage gel filled her abdomen and activated. Regulation, military-issued armor response: pseudocells mapped the damaged tissue; amino-acid markers and multi-band stabilizers glued shut the ends of damaged nerves. No longer just protecting her body—sealing it up, regenerating the missing parts.

Needles in the groin injected more adrenaline, pain killers, glucose. Her heart stuttered. Caught a beat.

Her head broke the surface of the pond.

The revolver came up, still locked on Hardiman. She hadn't realized she'd gotten in a shot, but he lay still and crumpled on the muddy ground. Karen struggled to understand the red puddle beneath his helmet. The suit shot her with more glucose as she lashed toward the Cirkan ship's cargo bay.

Inside, the alien worked computer panels, its eyes

focused on its displays. Karen felt a surge of excitement: the motherfucker was so sure she was dead, it had left Hardiman's rifle on the ground beside his corpse. She snapped it up without slowing.

Karen leapt forward, her snarl loud in her helmet. The last of the air in her lungs bled out in the sound, and without a solar plexus, refused to refill. Her vision grayed. For a quarter of a second, she thought she would die again, and then the suit activated rib cage pressurization, squeezing, squishing, sucking the air into her lungs. She felt a rib crack, but her drug cocktail stifled any pain.

The Cirkan looked up just in time to miss her fist. Her knuckles crashed through the display panel beside it and all the lights on the ship went out. The alien ducked under her arm and made a break for the cargo door. She back-flipped past it, suit and mind in perfect synchronicity. The suit ratcheted up her adrenaline level as she landed outside the craft.

Her boots skidded in the mud, but her fingers closed on the Cirkan's arm and swept them both to the ground.

The alien struggled in her grasp. Clicks and whistles erupted from its mouth and nose.

"Let me go!" In the suit's translator, the Cirkan's voice sounded like Stephen Hawking's. "You don't need this tiny lake. Your people have the entire star system at their disposal."

"It's our home." Karen's voice didn't sound much better. It was hard to talk with her diaphragm regenerating.

Its face rippled, darkened. "Your home, machine girl? Have you ever even felt its air on your bar skin?" It spat on her face plate, silver goo that left a grease stain when she wiped it on her arm.

"I'm going to arrest you now," she growled.

It wriggled again, freeing one hand. "To you this place is a... how do you call it? A theme park. A playground to prove how tough you can be."

She thought of that mandatory sixth-grade camping trip. Being tough was part of it, but the ducks were more important. Not every kid understood why they visited Earth, but every one of them remembered it for life. She shook her head.

"You're tough, all right," the alien said. "But you humans all have your price." It reached for its belt pouch.

Instinct made Karen grab for the arm, but it didn't stop digging in the pouch. She twisted its elbow in her grasp.

The arm ripped loose in her glove, organic matter no match for her armor's amplified strength. A black fluid burst from the shoulder socket, its surface dark and rainbowed like used oil.

The alien's eyes went wide. It made sounds, but the suit could not translate them. Karen eased its body to the ground.

She still held the arm in her grip. She stared at it, the dark goo running down her fingers and collecting in the joints of her gloves. The gloves looked less like human hands than the gray-speckled hand of the Cirkan, its fingers still holding a stack of currency.

Something between a laugh and a sob slipped out of her mouth.

She fell back on the ground beside the alien body, cold overtaking her limbs. Despite the suit's best efforts, she was going into shock. She activated another glucose shot and toggled up the suit's interior heat. She turned her head and studied the Cirkan.

Its skin had gone pale, the blood seeping out until it was ivory and dappled with faint gray spots, like the bird she'd seen this morning in the tree. The Northern Flicker. Its name no longer blinked at the bottom of her visor display, but she didn't think she would ever forget it.

"I'm sorry," she said. She wasn't sure if she was apologizing to the alien or the bird she was supposed to protect from such things.

She lay there another second in silence, checking that her emergency beacon was activated and that her radio was switched off. Protocol had to be followed, even in times like this, when the world pushed beyond protocol and became disaster. Two teammates dead. An illegal alien, dead. A lake filled with alien lifeforms. A rookie proving just how tough she really was.

She wished she could wipe her the tears off her cheeks, but she didn't dare crack open her suit. Parts of herself might seep out. She settled for laying still, floating on a cloud of drugs and exhaustion. Her lungs hurt from the suit's pumping mechanism. A gauge in her faceplate showed the suit adding more oxygen to her mask, and she wanted to thank it.

Even inside the shell of fiberglass and Kevlar, wired into the world by computers and sensors, her body cut off from any real air or real sounds, she felt the welcome quiet of the forest settle around her. A needle pricked her thigh again and her eyelids began to sneak shut.

Someplace in the distance, birds chirped, small

cheerful ones, like sparrows. *Or probably chickadees,* she thought sleepily, and hoped their songs would work themselves into her dreams.

Wendy N. Wagner's short fiction has appeared in *Beneath Ceaseless Skies* and the anthologies *The Way of the Wizard* and *Rigor Amortis*. She is also an assistant editor at *Fantasy Magazine*. She lives with her very understanding family in Portland, Oregon, and blogs about food and words at operabuffo.blogspot.com.

Maybe it was the smell of hot iron, or the squeal of metal on metal, or just the slick and slimy feel of hydraulic fluid, but **Jak Wagner** has always had an interest in mecha. After five years as an aviation structural mechanic, he left the world of the military to write about the world of SF. Jak is currently majoring in computer science at Portland State University and is hoping to contribute more to the mecha literature genre. This is his first publication.

The Green

LAUREN BEUKES

The Pinocchios are starting to rot. Really, this shouldn't be a surprise to anyone. They're just doing what corpses do best. Even artificially-preserved and florally-animated ones. Even the ones you know.

They shuffle around the corridors of our homelab in their hermetically-sealed hazmat suits, using whatever's left of their fine motor functioning. Mainly they get in the way. We've learned to walk around them when they get stuck. You can get used to anything. But I avoid looking at their faces behind the glass. I don't want to recognize Rousseau.

They're supposed to be confined to one of the specimen storage units. But a month ago, a Pinocchio pulled down a cabinet of freeze-dried specimens. So now Inatec management lets them wander around. They seem happier being free-range. If you can say that about a corpse jerked around by alien slime-mould.

They've become part of the scenery. Less than ghosts. They're as banal a part of life on this dog-forsaken planet as the nutritionally-fortified lab-grown oats they serve up in the cafeteria three times a day.

We're supposed to keep out of their way. "No harvester should touch, obstruct, or otherwise interfere with the OPPs," the notice from Inatec management read, finished off with a smiley face and posted on the bulletin board in the cafeteria. On paper, because we're not allowed personal communications technology in homelab. Too much of a security risk.

Organically Preserved Personnel. It's an experimental technique to use the indigenous flora to maintain soldiers' bodies in wartime to get them back to their loved ones intact. The irony is that we're so busy doing experiments on the corpses of our deceased crew that we don't send them back at all. And if we did, it would have to be in a flask. After they rot—average "life-span" is 29 days—they liquefy. And the slime-mould has to be reintegrated into the colony they've been growing in Lab Three.

It's not really slime-mould, of course. Nothing on this damn planet is anything you'd recognize, which is exactly why Inatec have us working the jungle in armored suits along with four thousand other corporates planet-side, all scrambling to find new alien flora with commercial applications so they can patent the shit out of it.

"Slime-mould" is the closest equivalent the labtechs have come up with. Self-organizing cellular amoebites that ooze around on their own until one of them finds a very recently dead thing to grow on. Then it lays down signals, chemical or hormonal or some other system we don't understand yet, and all the other amoebites congeal together to form a colony that sets down deep roots like a wart into whatever's left of the nervous system of the animal . . . and then take it over.

We've had several military contractors express major interest in seeing the results. Inatec has promised us all big bonuses if we manage to land a military deal—and not just the labtechs either. After all, it's us lowly harvesters who go out there in our GMP suits to *find* the stuff.

Inatec's got mining rights to six territories in four quadrants on this world. Two sub-trop, one arid/mountainous, and three tropical, which is where the big bucks are. Officially, we're working RCZ-8 Tropical 14: 27° 32' S / 49° 38' W. We call it The Green.

We were green ourselves when we arrived on-planet. The worst kind of naïve, know-nothing city hicks. It was all anyone could talk about as we crammed around the windows—how fucking amazing it all looked as the dropship descended over our quadrant. We weren't used to nature. We didn't know how hungry it was.

The sky was rippled in oranges and golds from the pollen in the air, turning the spike slate pinnacles of the mountains a powder pink. The jungle was a million shades of green. Greens like you couldn't imagine. Greens to make you mad. Or kill you dead.

Homelab squats in the middle of all that green like a fat concrete spider with too many legs radiating outwards. Uglier even than the Caxton Projects apartment blocks back home. Most of us are from what you'd call underprivileged backgrounds. The Caxton stats when I left were 89% adult unemployment, 73% adult illiteracy, 65% chance of dying before the age of 40 due to communicable disease or an act of violence. I tried converting to the NeoAdventists for a time. They promised me the golden glow of God's love that would transform me utterly or at least take me away from it all. But I still felt the same after my baptism—still dirty, still broken, still poor. Who wouldn't want a ticket out of there? Even if it was one-way.

Besides, our work is a privilege. We're getting to work at the forefront of xenoflora biotech. At least that's what it says on the "Welcome To Inatec" pack all employees are handed when they've dotted the i's and crossed the t's on the contract. Or maybe just made an X where you're supposed to sign. You don't need to be literate to pick flowers. Even in a GMP.

Of course, by forefront, they mean frontlines. And by harvesting they mean strip-mining. Except everything we strip away grows back, faster than we can keep up. Whole new species we've never seen before spring up overnight. Whole new ways to die.

You got to suffer for progress, baby, Rousseau would have said (if he was still alive). And boy do we suffer out there.

The first thing they do when you land is sterilise you—strip you, shave you, put you through the ultraviolet steriliser and then surgically remove your fingernails. It's a biologically sensitive operation. You can't be bringing in contaminants from other worlds. There was that microscopic snail parasite incident that killed off two full crews before the labtechs figured it out. That's why we don't have those ultra-sensitive contact pads on our gloves anymore, even though it makes harvesting harder. Because the snail would burrow right through them and get under the cuticle working its way through your body to lay its eggs in your lungs. When the larvae hatch, they eat their way out, which doesn't kill you, it just gives you a nasty case of terminal snail-induced emphysema. It took the infected weeks to die, hacking up bloody chunks of their lungs writhing with larvae.

Diamond miners used to stick gems up their arses to get them past security. With flora, you can get enough genetic material to sell to a rival with a fingernail scraping. "Do we have any proof there even was a snail infestation?" Ro would ask over breakfast. "Apart from the company newsletter?" he'd add before practical, feisty, *educated* Lurie could get a word in and contradict him. He was big into his conspiracy theories and our medtech, Shapshak, only encouraged him. They'd huddle deep into the night, getting all serious over gin made from nutri-oats that Hoffmann used to distil in secret in his room. It seemed to make Shapshak more gloomy than ever, but Ro bounced back from it invigorated and extra-jokey.

Ro was the only one who could get away with calling me Coco and, even then, only because we were sleeping together. Dumbfuck name, I know. Coco Yengko. Mom wanted me to be a model. Or a ballerina. Or a movie star. All those careers that get you out of the gettosprawl. *Shouldn't have had an ugly kid, then, Ma. Shouldn't have been poor. Shouldn't have let the Natec recruiter into our apartment.* And hey, while we're at it, *Ro shouldn't have died.*

Fucking Green.

Green is the wrong word for it. You'd only make that mistake from the outside. When you're in the thick of it it's black. The tangle of the canopy blocks out the sunlight. It's the murky gloom after twilight, before real dark sets in. Visibility is five meters, fifteen with headlights, although the light attracts moths, which get into the vents. Pollen spores swirl around you, big as your head. Sulfur candy floss. And everything is moist and sticky and *fertile*. Like the whole jungle is rutting around us.

The humidity smacks you, even through the suit, thick as +8 gravity, so that you're slick as greased ratpig with sweat the moment you step out. It pools in your jock strap, chafes when you walk, until it forms blisters big as testicles. (A new experience for the girls on the crew.) Although walking's not what we do. More like wading against a sucking tide of heat and flora.

The rotting mulch suffocates our big clanking mechanical footsteps. Some of the harvesters play music on their private channels. Ro used to play opera, loud, letting it spill into The Green, until it started attracting insects the size of my head. I put a stop to it after that. I prefer to listen to the servo motors grinding in protest. I have this fantasy that I'll be able to hear when my suit gets compromised. The *shhht* of air that lets through a flood of spores like fibrous threads that burrow into metal and flesh. The faint suck of algae congealing on the plastic surfaces, seeping into the seams of the electronics, corroding the boards so the nanoconnections can't fire. The hum of plankton slipping between the joints of my GMP between the spine and pelvic plates, looking to bite and sting.

The base model GMPs aren't built for these conditions. The heat is a problem. The servo motors get clogged. The armor corrodes. The nanotronics can't sustain. Every joint is a weak point. The damn flora develops immunity to every vegicide we try. Assuming they're actually *using* vegicides, Ro would point out. Why risk the harvest when harvesters are replaceable?

Management has determined that the optimum number for a harvesting team is five. I'm the team leader. Look, ma, leadership material. Our medtech is Shapshak, who sometimes slips me amphetamines which he gets under the counter from the labtechs along with other pharmaceuticals he doesn't share. (It's not like management don't know. They're happy if we're productive and sometimes you need a little extra something to get through out there.) Lurie is our am-bot, a high school education and eight weeks of training in amateur botany specimen collection puts her a full pay scale above the rest of us plebs, plus she gets the most sophisticated kit—a TCD with neuro-feedback tentacle fingers built into the hands for snagging delicate samples that aren't susceptible to snail-invasion. Rousseau and Waverley were our clearers—manual labor, their GMPs suitably equipped with bayonet progsaws that'll cut through rock, thermo-machetes for underbrush, and extra armor plating for bludgeoning your way through the jungle with brute force when everything else failed.

In retrospect, we could have done with less brute force. Could have done with me spotting the damn hangstrings before we blundered into the middle of a migration. Could have done with being less wired on the under-the-counter stuff. One minute Waverley and I are plowing through dense foliage ahead, the next, there are a thousand mucusy tendrils unfurling from the canopy above us.

This wouldn't have been a problem usually. Sure, the venom might corrode your paintwork, leave some

ugly pockmarks that'll get the maintenance guys all
worked up, but they're not hectic enough to com-
promise a GMP.

Unless, say, someone panics and trips and topples
forward, accidentally ripping a hole in Rousseau's suit
with the razor edge of the machete, half-severing
his arm. Waverley swore blind it wasn't his fault. He
tripped. But GMPs have balance/pace adjustors built-in.
You have to be pretty damn incompetent to fall over in
one. If Ro wasn't a roaming brain-dead corpse-puppet
right now, he might have been suspicious, might have
thought it was a conspiracy to recruit more guinea
pigs for the OPP program. We know better. We know
Waverley's just a fucking moron.

There was a lot of screaming. Mainly from Ro
until Shapshak shot him up with painblockers, but
also Lurie threatening to kill Waverley for being so
damn stupid. It took us ninety minutes to get back
to homelab, me and Shapshak dragging Ro on the
portable stretcher from his field kit, which is only
really useful for transporting people—not armored
suits—but it was too dangerous to take him out.
Waverley broke through the undergrowth ahead of
us—the only place where we would trust him, leaving
traces of Ro's blood painted across broken branches.

When we got to homebase, Lurie still had to feed
the specimens and we all had to go through decon-
tam, no matter how much I swore at security over
the intercom *Just let us back in right fucking now.*

We had to sit in the cafeteria, the only communal
space in homelab, listening to Rousseau die, pretending not to. It should have been easy. The drone of
the air-conditioner and the filters and the sterili-

systems all fighting The Green is the first thing you acclimatize to here. But Ro's voice somehow broke through, a shrill shriek between clenched teeth. We hadn't known anyone who'd ever died from the sting-strings. The labtechs must have been thrilled.

Shapshak spooned oats into his face, drifting away from it all on some drug he wasn't sharing. Lurie couldn't touch her food. She put on her old-school security-approved headphones, bopped her head fiercely to the music. Made like she wasn't crying. I restrained myself from hitting Waverley, who kept whining, "It wasn't my fault, okay?" I took deep breaths against the urge to bash his big bald head on the steel table until his brains oozed out. If Ro was here and not lying, twisting round on a gurney while the meds prepared the killing dose of morphephedrine, he would have cracked the tension with a joke. About crappy last meals maybe.

The other crews were making bets on what would kill him. Marking up the odds on the back of a cigarette packet. Black humor and wise-cracking is just how you deal. We'd have been doing the same if it wasn't one of ours. Yellow Choke 3:1 Threadworms 12:7. The Tars 5:4. New & Horrible: 1:2.

Ro's voice changed in pitch, from scream-your-throat-raw to a low groaning—the kind that comes from your intestines plasticinating. The spores must have got in to the rip in his gut through the tear in his armor.

OhgodohgodohgodeuggghgodOHpleasefuckgodOH

Across from us, Hoffmann from F-Crew leapt to his feet, whooping in delight and making gimme ges-tures. "Tars! I fucking knew it! Oh yeah! Hand over the cashmoney, baby!"

Ro's screaming tapered off. Which meant either he

was dead or just sub-auditory under the concert of
laboring machinery. Waverley tried to say something
encouraging, "At least we know it's the fast-kind of
fatal," and I punched him in the face, knocking the
porridge out of his mouth in a gray splatter tinged
with blood—along with two teeth. I got a warning,
but no demerit, "Under the circumstances," human
resources said. They declined my request to have
Waverley reassigned to another unit.

"It's for the best," human resources had said. Which
was the same line my mom spun me when she took
me to the sterilization clinic in Caxton, mainly for
the incentive kickback the government provided, but
also to make sure I didn't end up like her, pregnant
and homeless at twelve, working double shifts at
the seam factory—which is what she did after I was
born, to keep the pair of us alive. That only made
me feel more guilty—all the sacrifices she made so I
could get out of Caxton. And here I am, letting my
sometime-lover die on my watch. *Sorry, ma,* I think.
But you don't know what it's like out here.

Within forty-eight hours, Ro's replacement arrives.
Joseph Mukuku. Another ghettosprawl kid sprayed,
shaved, irradiated, de-nailed, and ready to go. We
had three whole days to mourn while he ran through
the simconditioning and then we were back out there
in the thick of it, harvesting. I found a request for
stingstrings in my order log. The results of Ro's venom
burns were, according to the labtechs, "fascinating."
The note attached to the order read: "Lash-wounds
were cauterized. Unclear whether this is common
to stingstrings or whether it was reacting with other

flora or spores. Living specimens (ideal) required for further study. Deceased specimens okay."

We couldn't get them. That's what I reported anyway. Threatened to peel the skin of Mukuku if he said different. The kid learned quick, didn't cause any shit, and we made Waverley walk five meters up front where he'd only take out flora if he tripped again. Shapshak offered me chemical assistance from his stash of pharmaceuticals, but by then I was already contemplating it and I knew drugs would only get in the way. I didn't want to get better.

I wanted out.

It was the encounter with Rousseau that cemented it.

I'd managed to avoid him for twelve whole days after he died. Every time I spotted a Pinocchio shuffling down the corridor or standing spookily still facing a wall, I did a 180. Didn't make a big deal about it, just managed to spend more time in the gym or doing routine maintenance on my GMP. Anything to keep busy. It's the thinking about it that kills me. I try to leave no space for thinking.

I was doing leg-presses when he found me. It was the automatic door that tipped me off. It kept opening and closing, opening and closing, like someone didn't have enough brains to get out of the way of the sensors. I knew it was him even before I saw the limp, sagging sleeve where his left arm should have been.

"What do you want?" I said, standing up and moving over to rest my hand casually on the 10kg barbells. Ready to club him to death. Re-death. Whatever. Not expecting an answer.

Through the faceplate, I could see a caul of teeming, squirming green over his face. You could still make out his features, still tell it was Ro under there. I thought about his cells starting to break down under his new slime-mould skin, his organs collapsing, nerves firing sluggishly through sagging connections in dead tissue.

He opened his mouth, his tongue flopping uselessly inside. He worked his jaw mechanically. Individual amoebites, attracted by the motion, started sliding into the cavity, triggering others, oozing past his lips— coating his teeth, his tongue, with the seething furry growth. Inside the suit, Ro tipped his head back, his mouth open in something like a scream as more and more amoebites flooded in to colonize his mouth, soft furry spores spilling down his chin. "Misfiring neurons human resources had assured us when they first let the Pinocchios out.

"Nothing to worry about," they said. Neither, it turns out, is the GMP progsaw I put to my forehead, positioning it right against my temple for maximum damage before I flick the on switch.

I have a dream about my mom. I am scampering over the factory floor, back when she still had the job, dodging the electric looms to collect scraps of fabric that she will sew into dishcloths and dolls and maybe a dress, to sell to the neighbors, illegally. We are not allowed to remove company property. They incinerate leftovers every evening, specifically to prevent this. Be careful, she whispers, her breath hot against my cheek. But I'm not careful enough. As I duck under the grinding, whirling loom, the teeth catch my ear and shear down my face. My skin tears all the way down to my belly button and unfurls, flopping about obscenely, like wings, before the flaps stiffen and w around me like a cocoon. In the dream, it feels like I am falling into myself. It feels safe.

I wake up in a hospital bed, with my right arm cuffed to the rail. There is a woman sitting on the edge of the bed wearing a pinstripe skirt and matching blazer. She is blandly pretty with blonde-streaked hair, wide blue eyes, and big, friendly teeth in a big, friendly mouth. A mom in a vitamin-enriched living commercial. Not someone I've seen in homelab before. Too neatly groomed. I sit up and automatically reach up to touch my head, to the place where the progsaw had started ripping in to my temple, only to find layers of bandage mummifying my skull.

"We do pay attention, Coco." The woman says, and then adds, more softly. "I'm very sorry about what happened to Malan."

"Who?" I say. My cheek is burning. I try to rub the pain away and find a row of fibrous stitches running from my temple down to my jaw.

"Malan Rousseau? Your coworker? It's quaint how you call each other by surnames. This isn't the army you know. You're not at war."

"Tell that to The Green," I mutter. I am angry to be alive.

"Yes, well. We installed new safety measures into the GMPs after the accident. Chemical agents that would clog up the blades of your weaponry with fibrous threads if it came into contact with human pheromones. Is based on threadworms. One of the technologies I've helped make possible, Coco. Saved your life."

"Didn't want to be saved." My throat feels raw like been sandblasted from the inside.

"Pity about your face," she says, not feeling any pity at all.

"Never going to be a model now." I try to laugh It comes out as a brittle bark.

"Unless it's for a specialist scar porn, no, probably not. Do you want some water? It's the painkiller: making you so thirsty. Even with our new safety measures, you still managed to do quite a bit of ruin to yourself. No brain damage though."

"Damn." I deadpan, but the water is cold and swee down my throat.

"My name is Catherine, I'm from head office. The sent me here especially to see you and do you know why? It's because you've made us reevaluate som things, Coco, how we work around here." Every tim she says my name, it feels like someone punching m in the chest. A reminder of Ro.

"Don't call me that. It's Yengko. Please."

"As you prefer," her mouth twists impatientl "Ms. Yengko. You'll be pleased to know, I think, th after your *incident*, Inatec has elected to relocate t OPPs—what do you call them?"

"Zombie puppets." But I'm thinking *living prison*

She looks down to her hands folded in her la at her perfect manicure and smiles a little tolera smile. But what I'm thinking is *That bitch still h her fingernails,* which also means she has no inte tion of sticking around. "Pinocchios, right? Isn't t what you call them? That's cute. But we've come realize, well, you made us realize that having th in homelab puts undue stress on our employees guess we were so busy focusing on this huge medi breakthrough—"

"Profit, you mean."

She ignores me. "That we didn't think about how it was affecting you guys on a personal level. So, I'm sorry. *Inatec* is sorry. We've moved the OPPs to another facility. We've already paid stress compensation into everyone's accounts and we're implementing mandatory counseling sessions."

"He was trying to talk."

"No. He's dead, Coc—Ms. Yengko," she corrects herself. "It must have been very upsetting, but he can't talk. The OPP symbiote sometimes hooks into the wrong nerves. We're still learning, still figuring each other out."

"How buddy-buddy of you. Didn't realize this was a partnership."

"We're a bio-sensitive operation. It's about finding balance with nature, no matter how foreign it is."

"So what happens now?"

"We'd like you to stay on, if you're willing. Under the circumstances, Inatec is willing to retrench you with two week's payout for every year you've worked, plus stress bonus, plus full pension. Which is, I'm sure you'll appreciate, very generous considering your attempt to damage Inatec property and injure personnel, which would normally be grounds for instant dismissal. Your non-disclosure still applies either way, of course."

"Wait. You're blaming me for Ro's death?"

"By injuring personnel, we mean your attempted suicide. You're a valuable asset to the company. Which is why I'd encourage you to hear my alternate proposition."

"Does it involve letting me fucking die like I wanted?"

"As I said, you're a valuable asset. How long have you been here? Two years?"

"Twenty months."

"That's a lot of experience. We've invested in you, Ms. Yengko. We want to see you achieve your potential. I want you to walk away from this...challenge ir your life, stronger, more capable. You've got a second chance. Do you know how rare that is? It's a unique personal growth opportunity."

"Double pay."

"One and a half times."

"Plus my pension payout. You wire it to my mon in the meantime."

"You don't want to hear about the alternative?"

"More of the same, isn't it?"

"It's better. We're running a pilot program. Ne suits. We want you to head it up. We've learned from our mistakes. We're ready to move on. It's a new da around here. What do you say?"

She thinks I don't know. She thinks I'm an idiot

Homelab has been renovated in the time I've bee out. A week and a half according to Shapshak, who strangely reproachful. He follows me around, as if tryin to make sure I don't try to off myself again. He can look at my face—at the puckered scar that runs from my ear to the corner of my mouth, twisting my upp lip into a permanent sneer. He's more stoned th ever—and so are most of the other crews. Whatev else Catherine's proposed "new day" involves, obviou restricting access to recreational pharmaceuticals is part of it. Or maybe it's the mandatory counseli sessions, which involve a lot of anti-depressants th Mukuku says leave him feeling blank and hollow wouldn't know. I felt that way before.

The Pinocchios are, true to Catherine's word, go

Along with some of the staff. Lurie has been shipped out, together with Hoffmann, Ujlaki, and Murad, all the A-level am-bots, half the other team leaders, and sixty percent of the labtechs. Leaving a shoddy bunch of misfits, unsuitable for anything except manual labor. Or guinea pigging.

Labs one to three have been cleared to accommo-date the new suits, ornate husks floating in nutrient soup in big glass tanks. Like soft-shelled crabs without the crab. The plating is striated with a thick fibrous grain that resembles muscle. The info brochure posted on the bulletin board promises "biological solutions for biological challenges." There is grumbling about what that means. But underneath all that is the buzz of excitement.

The operations brochure talks about how the suit will harden on binding, how the shell will protect us from anything a hostile environment can throw at us and process the air through the filtration system to be perfectly breathable without the risk and inconvenience of carrying compressed gas tanks around. We'll be lighter, more flexible, more efficient—and it's totally self-sufficient, provided we take up the new nutrition-ally fortified diet. "No more fucking oats!" Mukuku rejoices. He's not Ro, but he's not an asshole, and that's about all we can ask around here.

Lab four is still cranking. The reduced complement of labtechs are busier than ever, scurrying about like pigs. They wear hazmat suits these days. They've always been offish, always above us, but now they don't talk to us at all.

Inatec management send in a state-of-the-art cam-a swarm to record the new suit trials—for a morale video, Catherine explains. Exactly the kind of camera swarm they supposedly can't afford to send out into The Green to scout ahead of us to avoid some of the dangers. "You won't have to worry about that anymore," she says. I believe her.

Harvest operations are called off while they do the final preparations, leaving us with too much leisure time, too much time to think. Or maybe it's just me. But it allows me to make my decision. *Not* to blow it wide open. (As if they wouldn't just hold us down and do it to us anyway.) Because I'm thinking that a cell doesn't have to be a bad thing. It doesn't have to be a prison. It could be more like a monk's cell, a haven from the world, somewhere you can lock yourself away from everything and never have to think again.

On Tuesday, we're summoned to lab three. "You ready?" Catherine says.

"Is my pension paid out?" I snipe. There is nervous laughter.

"Why can't we use our old suits?" Waverley whines "Why we gotta change a good thing?"

"Shut up, Waverley." Shapshak snaps, but only half heartedly. And then because everyone is jittery—even us uneducated slum hicks can have suspicions—volunteer.

I step forward and shrug out of my grays, letting them drop to the floor. Two of the labtechs haul suit out of the tank and sort-of hunker forward with it, folding it around me like origami. It is clammy and brittle at the same time. As they fold one piece over another, it binds together and darkens to an opaque green. The color of slime-mould.

The labtechs assist others into their suits, carefully wrapping everyone up, like presents, leaving only the hoods and a dangling connector like a scorpion tail. The tip has a pad of microneedles that will fasten on to my nervous system. Nothing unusual here. The GMPs use the same technology to monitor vital signs. Nothing unusual at all.

"Don't worry, it won't hurt. It injects anesthetic at the same time," Catherine says. "Like a mosquito."

"Not the ones on this planet, lady," Waverley snickers, looking around for approval, as they start folding him into his suit.

"Can we hurry this along?" I ask.

"Of course," Catherine says. And maybe that's a glimmer of respect in her blue eyes, or maybe it's just the reflection of the neon lighting, but I feel like we understand each other in these last moments.

The labtechs slip the hood over my face. She presses the bioconnector up against the hollow at the base of my skull, and clicks the switch that makes the needles leap forward. Suddenly the armor clamps down on me like a muscle. I fight down a jolt of claustrophobia so strong it raises the taste of bile in my mouth. I have to catch myself from falling to my knees and retching.

"You okay, Yengko?" Shapshak says, his voice suddenly sharp through the glaze of drugs he's on. He must really care, I think. But I am beyond caring. Beyond anything.

I wondered what it would feel like. The soft furriness of the amoebites flooding through the bioconnector, the prickle as they flower through my skin. What's better than a dead zombie? A live one. And maybe God's glow is green, not golden.

"Yes," I say and close my eyes against the light, against the sight of the others being parceled up in the suits, at Waverley starting to scream, tugging at the hood as he realizes what's going on, what's in there with him. "I'm fine." And maybe for the first time, I actually am.

———————

Lauren Beukes (www.laurenbeukes.com) is a South African novelist, TV scriptwriter, documentary maker, comics writer, and occasional journalist. She won the 2011 Arthur C Clarke Award for her phantasmagorical noir, *Zoo City*, set in an alternate Johannesburg where guilt manifests as spirit animal familiars and dark things lurk beneath the surface of the pop music industry. Her previous novel, *Moxyland*, is a corporate apartheid cyberpunk thriller where cell phones are used for social control and viral branding really is. She's also written short stories, a rollicking non-fiction about maverick South African women, TV scripts, and comics for Vertigo.

Sticks and Stones

ROBERT BUETTNER

Don't touch that red lead!" Barclay's voice in my
arpiece booms, even across twenty-four thousand miles.

I jerk my fingers back from inside my helmet so fast
nat it rolls off my cross-legged lap, then bounces across
e tent's dirt floor. "*Damn* it, Barc! This is a *battery*
ange, not bomb disposal!"

"No red lead, no beacon. No beacon, no pick
)." Pause. Master Sergeants with twenty years have
arned to shrug audibly. "Long walk home, Lieuten-
t Schwartz."

I crawl after my helmet and sigh into my mike.
orry, Barc. It's hard down here. Y'know?"

"Did I not weep for him whose day was hard?
) 30:25."

Master Sergeants with twenty have also learned to
l a newbie officer to quit whining, without uttering
insubordinate syllable. And Barclay, who's vocally

Baptist, quotes me Old Testament because I was born Jewish, but he thinks he can convert me.

I roll my eyes because I'm inconvertible. My twenty years of life have taught me that the bible's a collection of morally instructive fables, not a history book.

But if Barclay's literal view of religion is crap, his view of an operational situation is always life-savingly crystalline. Pick-up drones are as dumb as Master Sergeant Reuben Westmoreland Barclay thinks Second Lieutenants are. And he knows that I have the fine motor coordination of a ground sloth, whether the task is bomb disposal, dentistry, or a simple battery change.

Tomorrow, a drone will home in on the transponder beacon in my armor's shoulder cap, snatch me off this rock on the fly, like an eagle and its prey, and then ferry me back up to the orbiting pod from which Barclay is co-ordinating this preliminary survey of Unclassified Earthlike 604.

One standard day after that, the cruiser that dropped us off will retrieve the pod and leave Unclassified Earthlike 604 to go its own way, probably forever. And cruisers don't wait on tardy Second Lieutenants.

I swat a sand flea biting my exposed neck, so hard that sweat sprays my armor's neck ring, and I swear. Based upon what Barclay's survey drones and I have seen in the four days since I hit dirt, Unclassified Earthlike 604's early Iron Age humans won't invent bombs to dispose of for a thousand years, give or take. Still, it's the locals, not the sand fleas, that are making it hard down here.

Clank. Clank. Someone raps the ornamental brass knocker outside the tent against the pole from which the knocker dangles.

A voice crackles, delayed a microsecond by my ear translator. "Am I permitted entry, *Beshtini Men Ja*?"

Without looking up from my battery fumbling, I sigh to my host, "Chubbi, it's *your* tent! C'mon in."

A mahogany-brown hand flips back the tent's entry flap, and the hand's owner shuffles in behind it, on his knees, his black-bearded head bowed.

I roll my eyes and sigh again. *Beshtini Men Ja* translates from Local as, give or take a nuance, "invincible man-god." "You can stand up. And call me Ethan." I am, in fact, Second Lieutenant Ethan Schwartz, fresh out of Suborbital Arobotic Survey Officer Basic. As Aunt Char reminded me at SASOB graduation, while she sneered at the mess hall cookies, I'm the first kid in my family in a century too clumsy to do my two years public service as at least a family practice dentist. Man-god? Hardly.

My host straightens, and his leather body armor creaks as he adjusts the iron short sword at his waist. Chubbirian the Indomitable, Commander of Commanders, is actually not chubby, he's wire-thin. But throughout the days that I have known him, Chubbi hasn't smiled at the joke in my nickname for him. Maybe the irony's just lost in translation, but Chubbi's sense of humor, like his sword, his armor, and everything else on an Iron Age, Seeded Earthlike, is about thirty-five hundred years behind.

A survey 'bot overflying a planet at twelve thousand feet can't detect irony, or other human subtleties. That's why an arobotic interface—meaning me or other similarly expendable junior officer—actually makes handshake contact with the locals as part of every survey.

'Bots do offer advantages over live survey officers. No whining. No poop. No MIA letters to write when things go terminally wrong, which they do for six survey officers out of every ten.

But Survey Branch learned early on that locals went apeshit when a turkey-sized metal bug fluttered out of the sky and greeted them in their language.

Seems to me that a stranger a head taller than the locals are, clumping around in plasteel body armor and spitting thunder from an iron staff, is even scarier. But at least a Survey Officer's as human as they are. More human, really. Seeded Earthlike populations spring from humans harvested from Earth thirty-five thousand years ago. Maybe the Slugs dropped our abducted ancestors off on Earthlike planets on purpose, or maybe our ancestors jumped ship like rats down a tramp steamer's hawser. We don't know because the Slugs are gone, now. We do know that, once we get imported, humans spread like kudzu in most earthlike environments.

The local kudzu-in-charge speaks. "Ethan, my men have captured a Huppic spy. He was armed with this!" Chubbi raises and turns in his hand a dull steel shortsword, similar to the one scabbarded at his own waist. In the tent's dimness, Chubbi's hand quivers as though he's holding ball lightning on a stick.

I raise my eyebrows. The Huppics have fomented a half-assed rebellion, complete with a quarter-assed army, which is presently encamped three miles from here. Here being the camp of Chubbi's actual full-assed army. Tomorrow Chubbi's legions will battle the Huppics, who are legally forbidden by Chubbi's regime to possess iron weapons.

Not because the Huppics are primitive or dangerous

Au contraire. The first culture I sampled when I got here last week were the Huppics. They're more advanced than Chubbi's bullies, who rule them. The Huppics built the first iron forges on this planet ten years before Chubbi's people tumbled to the idea. The Huppics used iron to make things like sewing needles and plows.

But iron, or more precisely iron forged at high temperature into carbon steel, holds a harder and deadlier edge than bronze, which was the previous age's go-to metal. Once Chubbi's people learned to make carbon steel swords, they burned down all the Huppic forges, beheaded all the Huppic blacksmiths, and then forbade iron implements to the Huppics, to preserve Chubbi's lead in the local arms race.

People call SAS "Sticks and Stones" Branch instead of "Suborbital Arobotic Survey" Branch because we spend—some say waste—lots of time pegging the cultures we encounter to a point along the development curve between the Eolithic and contemporary Earth. Among ethnologists, tools have always been the signature benchmarks of cultural sophistication: Stone Age, Bronze Age, Iron Age, combustion propulsion, nukes, computers, C-drive. So I'm pretty sure I would have noticed if the Huppics had been swinging steel swords.

"It's just one sword, Chubbi. Maybe he took it off one of your sentries."

Chubbi shakes his head. "No. He claimed their whole army has them. Then he stopped talking."

I cock my head. On the other hand, if the Huppics were stockpiling illegal weapons, would they show them an overly tall stranger wearing an armadillo suit? For Chubbi, this discovery is as disturbing as the day old America found out that the Russians had the atomic bomb.

I shrug inside my armor. "Then maybe you should just call off the battle. Leave the Huppics alone. Maybe they'll come around. Or wither on the vine." Heck, America won Cold War One that way.

"Thin ice, sir." Barclay, who hears what I hear, whispers in my earpiece.

Barclay means that I'm not supposed to change this planet, just observe it. But, I think, it's like Heisenberg, the physicist, said about subatomic particles: the very act of observing something changes it.

Whatever I think, Survey officers are forbidden to take sides in local conflicts. Drop your pack because a tyrannosaurid is chasing you and Quartermaster won't bat an eye. Normal field wear and tear. But come back light ammunition, after subtracting demonstration rounds, and you'd best present a self-defense alibi, preferably with backup video.

Survey officers are supposed to let local history take its usual, bloody human course. But if I enjoyed bloodshed, I'd have majored in pre-oral surgery, like my cousin Ruth, instead of xenoethnology. Merely suggesting peaceful coexistence isn't taking sides, is it?

Clank. Clank. Another knock on the post outside.

"Come!" Chubbi snarls to the new visitors like the absolute despot he is.

As I put my helmet back on, two of Chubbi's minions drag in a bound, squirming figure, dressed in a shepherd's cloak, then drop him at Chubbi's sandaled feet.

The boy looks up, eyes dark and wide. He might be twelve. A bruise swells above one eye.

Chubbi bends, grabs the kid by the hair, while he presses the captured sword's edge against the boy's throat. "Where did you get this, boy?"

The kid shivers, but just stares.

Chubbi jerks his head at one of the soldiers, who tugs something from a bucket he holds, and hands it to Chubbi.

Chubbi swings a wide-eyed human head by its long hair like it was a cantaloupe in a grocery bag.

The boy gags. So do I, just like I did when cousin Ruthie, the root canal princess, detonated a live frog in the microwave the day before her Bat Mitzvah.

A Huppic earring still dangles from the head's left ear.

Chubbi leans close to the boy and whispers, "This spy wouldn't talk, either."

The boy squeezes his eyes shut, swallows, and then turns his face away. "I'm not a spy. I'm a shepherd. My father gave me the sword for wolves."

Chubbi's enhanced interrogation techniques are blunt, even by Dr. Ruthie's standards. But you can't say they're ineffective.

"A sword? For a boy? I don't believe it!" Chubbi snorts and hurls the severed head so it thumps against the tent's hide wall. Then he pinches the boy's jaw between his thumb and fingers while he tips the kid's head back, forcing the boy's mouth open. Chubbi traces the boy's upper lip with the sword's point. "I'll cut your lying tongue out and drown you in your own blood!"

"Wait, Chubbi!" I lay my gauntleted hand on Chubbi's forearm.

His guards gasp. Not because they're shocked by the impending oral surgery—they've seen it before, I'm sure. But they've never seen their god-king touched.

They don't pounce and beat the crap out of me, however. Chubbi's merely a god-king. Whereas when I showed up at their encampment, I announced myself by bringing down a wolf at one hundred paces with nothing but a 7.62 mm thunderclap. That made me an instant, unhyphenated god in these parts.

"Lieutenant!" Barclay, however, knows how godlike I am not. "Sir, don't get in the middle of this."

Barclay's right to scold me. But we call him Barc because his is worse than his bite. And regardless of Barc's wisdom, I'm the highest ranking officer within twenty million cubic miles, so if I want to risk my neck and my career to save this child, that's my call.

Chubbi freezes, the sword still poised to strike. "The boy's life is mine to take."

I nod. "Sure. But what if he's lying? The Huppics may have planted him with his story to frighten you off."

Chubbi narrows his eyes. "They *are* devious."

The boy quivers, his eyes wider than ever. I can see in them that he's no spy and no liar. He's a shepherd who wandered too close to Chubbi's picket line and got caught. And he's terrified.

I shrug inside my armor. "Kill him and you'll never know."

Chubbi nods. "You're right. I'll sever his finger one at a time, first. The Huppics always talk before I reach the thumb."

I bend and squint at the kid, who can't weigh more than fifty pounds. "Regular spies, sure. But he's just a kid, Chubbi. What if he passes out after one finger and then dies without talking?"

Chubbi frowns.

"How 'bout this? I'll make the boy lead me back to his lines, and see whether the Huppics really have iron swords. If he's lying, I'll cut off his head and bring it back to you."

Chubbi smiles. Decapitation is the Next Big Thing in intimidation and terror among cultures that have just discovered sharp edges.

I say, "But if he's telling the truth, and the Huppics have iron swords, I'll report back to you."

"Why would I do that? If they don't have iron swords, we'll slaughter them easily, down to the last infant. If they have iron swords, it's even more important that we kill them all now, before they grow even stronger. Better to lose some men now than lose all later."

Chubbi may be brutal, but he's not dumb. Pre-emptive first strikes were a hot option during Cold War One, too.

I nod. "Tell you what. Let me try my plan. If it turns out that they *do* have iron weapons, I'll fight on your side."

Barclay sputters in my ear. "Ethan! Have you lost your mind?"

Fair question. My offer violates about a dozen regs I know of, and probably a dozen more that Barclay will be pleased to read to me. To say nothing of, I suppose, several of Barclay's Commandments. I'm not sure what part of Barclay's reaction startles me more; calling a commissioned officer by his given name or Barclay's failure to support his position with a bible verse.

As Barclay sputters in orbit, Chubbi's eyebrows rise as he looks me up and down.

My Eternad armor's hardly new. The early versions protected light infantry clear back during the Slug

War, and the basic concept's unchanged. Eternads don't amplify muscle power like a Silverback suit, and they're puny next to a Marauder with a 20 mm minigun and epaulet launchers, which is basically an anthropomorphic light tank. Eternads are simply ultralight body armor, incorporating a sensor and life support package eternally ("Eternad." Get it?) powered and recharged by storing the kinetic energy generated by the wearer's movement.

But when I'm buttoned up, locked and loaded, nothing the Iron Age can throw at me will make a dent. And my basic load of featherweight cerammunition's enough to take out a battalion with my rifle. To say nothing of the thumper and the flamer.

Chubbi smiles, nods a half-assed bow. "I will be honored to go into battle at your side, Ethan." Equines are barely domesticated here, but already Chubbi knows enough veterinary dentistry that he doesn't look a gift horse in the mouth.

Thirty minutes later, the boy and I cross Chubbi's front lines, in the direction of the Huppic encampment that lies three miles ahead, hidden by a low ridge.

I keep the boy on a twenty-foot leash for show and realize that I haven't heard from Barclay since made my pact with Satan. "Barc? You still up there?

Silence. My heart skips. Is it possible Barclay ha pulled up all the 'bots and is going to abandon m over this? He could get away with it. Most Surve officer MIA are simply reported by their pod nor comm as "failed to make pick-up."

Finally, he sighs. "Sir, what were you thinking?"

"That I needed to prevent an innocent's murde

and I'd sort out the details later. Isn't there a rule about that in the bible?"

"Sir, the good book has a rule for everything. One of those is to obey the law. For you and me, the law is the Uniform Code of Military Justice, which requires you to obey lawful general orders."

"Barc, there's a difference between changing history and doing one tiny little good deed. I fibbed to a sociopathic dictator about enlisting with him. Where's the harm?"

Silence. Time to change the subject before Barclay tries to convene a personal court martial by radio. "I make the biologics a boring seven, Barc."

I hear clicks as he toggles screens up there. Barclay loves his survey 'bots almost as much as he loves his good book. Subject change accomplished.

"Close, sir. The aerial 'bots returned an average of six point eight."

The boy shuffles ahead of me, kicking up dust and flushing rat-sized mammalians and quail-like birds from brush that could be mesquite. I say, "We could be in West Texas, with hills."

"I'd say coastal Mediterranean, sir."

"Close enough." The first axiom of planetology is that like conditions produce like results. The flora and fauna that evolve on a warm, wet rock like Earth is, well, Earthlike. But hardly identical. Earth, as it turns out, is in the biologic fast lane, due to "collision punctuation." Simply put, since the Precambrian Era, Earth attracted an extinction-sized hunk of space junk every couple hundred million years. Each asteroid or comet impact put the evolutionary pedal to the metal, because each collision wiped out old species, and allowed new species to blossom and fill the vacant niches. Adios duck-billed grazing dinosaurs. Hello grazing wildebeest.

Once we had a sampling to compare with, we found that Earth was a planetary punching bag, compared to the galactic average. So-called "minimally punctuated" Earthlikes are the norm. They're mostly still ruled by creatures that are more-or-less dinosaurs.

I was hoping Unclassified Earthlike 604 would have *something* exotic, at least saber toothed tigers. Wolves and quail have been a plain-vanilla disappointment.

I stop, untie the boy, and as he rubs his throat I shoo him toward his lines. "Go home—" I don't even know his name. "What's your name?"

"For now? Tiran. That means son of Tir the shepherd. Next year I get to choose my own name." He cocks his head at me. "But if you let me go, how will you know whether I lied?"

"You didn't lie."

Tiran-for-Now nods. One nice thing about being regarded as a god is people think you know everything.

"Then you will fight with Chubbarian against us."

"Nope. Not that it's your business, but I only said that to keep him from killing you. I lied."

"Then you lied for nothing. Even with swords, we're shepherds and shopkeepers, not soldiers." The boy points in a circle at the plain we stand on. "Tomorrow Chubbirian's army will meet us on this plain and kill all of us in this place. I will stand, and I will fall alongside my father and my brothers."

I look away, in the direction of Chubbi's army, now hidden behind a ridge. The black smoke tendrils of cook fires snake skyward as warriors by the thousand prepare their evening meals. Actually, tomorrow will be worse than the boy imagines. After Chubbi's horde kills the combatants, they'll kill their families, too, with all the attendant rape and pillage.

Behind my visor, I grind my teeth. Despite my efforts, Tiran-for-Now will be dead before he even has a permanent name, along with a boatload of other innocents. "Look, what I think is right and what I can make right are two different things. Be glad your head's still attached." For a while.

Barclay whispers, "Well said, sir. It's a lousy deal to be a Survey puke sometimes. I hate it too. But a soldier can't choose his war. Now just hole up somewhere, sleep the night, and wait for the drone in the morning."

I pop my visor and bend at the waist, hands on knees, to say goodbye to Tiran.

He won't look up at me and instead sits down, cross-legged in the dust. He unties a sack from his belt, dumps out round stones and lines them up in opposing rows in the dirt, like toy soldiers. "I always wanted to be a soldier. But my father's a shepherd. My brothers and my uncles are shepherds. I thought I would die of boredom as a shepherd. Now I wish I could."

"Really? I thought it was so dangerous that your father gave you a sword for wolves."

He smiles. "I take care of wolves all the time. They don't scare me."

Maybe not. But as the local suns are going down, wolf howls, and not too far away. If I leave, the boy will be alone in the darkness, without even the sword that Chubbi took from him to fend off the wolves.

Instead of walking away, I lay down across from the

boy, propped on one elbow, in the middle of an alien desert. I can sleep here as well as someplace else.

I sigh. "I know how you feel. I was supposed to be a dentist."

He keeps staring down at his little stone armies. "What's a dentist?"

"Doesn't matter. Except it's what everybody in my family was, back where I come from. And it's boring."

He looks up and cocks his head. "Do you like being a soldier, instead?"

Survey Branch's motto is *nos succurro*, "We help." When I chose my branch, that sounded better to me than "We kick ass." But I guess our motto should be "We catalogue and run." I shrug. "'Til now."

He nods. "Me, too."

I reach down and maneuver a stone. "Back where I come from, we have better toy soldiers than this."

He wrinkles his forehead. "So do we. These aren't soldiers."

Two hours and a long talk with the boy later, I pass alone back through Chubbi's lines. Thanks to my helmet's snoops, I dodge his sentries easily.

It's been a quiet walk back, and that worries me. I wasn't able to raise Barclay. It could be a helmet malfunction due to my ham-fisted battery change. But if I try to fix it, given my clumsiness, I could lose the sensors, too. The pick-up drone doesn't need audio, just a working beacon to home on, so that's not what worries me. Barclay may have pulled back the drone after he eavesdropped on the conversation that I just finished with the boy.

When I duck silently into Chubbi's tent, I find him leaning on his hands across a waist-high san table. He studies a miniature terrain and crude lead soldiers laid out on the table, arrayed in tomorrow's anticipated order of battle.

Chubbi looks up, sees me, and his head snaps back. I can't blame him. Three millennia of evolution and nutrition have already made me six inches taller and forty fit pounds heavier than the average Iron Age male. Eternads weigh less than a linebacker's uniform, but they bulk me up even more, in every dimension, and add another half foot to my height. Under most light conditions, my visor tint renders me faceless, and the iron swords that are this planet's nuclear option can't even scratch my matte black shell.

His eyes widen. "You have returned. Then it's true? The rabble possess iron swords?"

"Yep." I sit on the bench across the sand table from Chubbi, where his unit commanders must have sat minutes before, while he briefed them.

Chubbi smiles, then leans forward and points at the front center of the little figures that represent his army. "You will lead us into battle, here. Your iron staff will smite many, but still many of my men will fall. However, all of the rabble will fall. Then we will savage their seed, as well."

I remove my helmet and run a hand over my GI-buzz-covered scalp. "Sounds great." Especially the seed savaging. "But could I make a suggestion?"

Chubbi stands back from his table. "I'm listening, Ethan."

I lean forward, point at his toy soldiers, and explain.

After four hours' sleep, with still no word from Barclay, my helmet chime awakens me to a gray dawn.

Ten scratch-and-yawn minutes later, Chubbi's battalions are arrayed on line as he and I march to the front center of the formation, and then turn back to face his army of eight thousand.

Each foot soldier wears a simple leather helmet and carries in one hand a woven wicker shield that extends from his knees to his neck. In his other hand each man carries a short iron sword. Every man wears leather sandals, so the unit's uniform pace isn't slowed by barefoot troops. Basic stuff, but state of the martial art, here.

Each battalion's commander wears a jacket over his armor and a plumed helmet, each colored to match the unit colors that flutter from a staff carried by a flag bearer at the commander's side.

On a modern battlefield, a sniper or a hunter-killer drone would wax a target like that in a heartbeat. But in this particular iteration of the early Iron Age, where even the long bow remains to be invented, a slung rock constitutes long range weaponry. Battlefield visibility, so orders can be given and received, matters more. To say that Chubbi's brand of military science isn't rocket science overstates its sophistication.

Chubbi, like his commanders, wears a short, gold emboidered jacket over his armor and a cloth cover over his helmet, for battlefield visibility. Befitting his status, his and only his battle dress is vibrant scarlet. It's supposed to look regal, but as he stands beside me we look like an organ grinder with his monkey.

I snort inside my helmet and Chubbi looks up at me and frowns. "What?"

"Nothing. Let's go."

Chubbi exhorts his men with a raised sword wave and then turns on his heel.

They reply with a rumbling roar, and the formation moves out at a deliberate and more-or-less coordinated walk beneath low, boiling clouds.

Thirty minutes later, we have crossed the ridge behind which we sheltered and we halt on the plain six hundred yards away from the Huppic army, which was early to the party and already is arrayed across our front.

I use the term "army" loosely. I max my optics and scan their lines. The counter in my visor display numbers the Huppics at four thousand. They're half the strength of Chubbi's army, just in simple numeric terms.

Modern armies factor in "force multipliers" to measure combat power. In this case it's more appropriate to apply "force long division" to the Huppics. They all *do* have swords, but it's downhill from there. Perhaps one in five carries some kind of shield, and none wear helmets. A third of them are barefoot. Nobody's foaming at the mouth or snarling to get at us. In fact they look like they'd rather be elsewhere, which seems rational to me under the circumstances.

Finally, at the Huppic line's center, I spot their commander, a bearded old man whose sole qualifications for command seem to be his age and the bright yellow sash around his waist.

My heart skips, because everyone around him is as tall as he is.

Finally, I spot the boy, Tiran.

He's peeking out from behind the old man, and clinging to the yellow sash. But the fact that he's there at the commander's side, where I expected him to be, indicates that my message got through.

I look down at Chubbi, he nods, and I step off toward the Huppic lines.

Boom. Boom. Boom.

After fifteen paces, Chubbi's boys get the rhythm and begin pounding their swords against their shields in time with my footsteps, but they hold their positions.

I look up and down the Huppic line. The shield beating's so loud now that some of the shopkeepers wince every time my foot strikes the ground, but they hold their positions too.

Halfway to the Huppics, three hundred yards from each of the opposing armies, I stop, unsling my rifle, and trigger a full-auto magazine into the sky. The Huppics cringe. Then the thunderous echoes die and the plain falls silent, except for wind sighing through brush.

I cycle my suit's diagnostics to make sure my beacon's sending, and then I chin my audio back on. "Barc?"

Nothing.

"Barc, I got no pingback from the drone." My heart pounds so hard that I imagine that inside my helmet it is as loud as the shield pounding was outside.

Tiran steps out from behind the Huppic commander and runs toward me. The Huppics stand fast.

After two hundred yards, the boy is close enough to Chubbi's army that they can make him out.

A murmur rises in eight thousand throats behind me. When Tiran gets close enough that Chubbi's soldiers can make him out, the murmur changes to laughter.

I look up at the scudding clouds. The meteorology display pegs the ceiling at three hundred feet. Drones don't home optically, so that shouldn't matter. "Barc, I still got no pingback down here."

Has Barclay abandoned me?

Tiran stops twenty feet from me, panting.

I pop my visor. "Well?"

He nods. "They think it's stupid, but they say I may as well try."

I look around for the drone, one more time, as if I could see through clouds, and then I drop my visor again and sigh. "Okay, let's do this."

The boy reaches into the sack at his waist, draws out a round stone, and then pockets it in the pouch of his leather sling.

"You sure you can hit me from there?"

He snorts. "I hit wolves every day at three times this distance."

Pong.

The slingshot stone cracks off my helmet visor like a rock off a windshield, but both the visor and I are unaffected.

Beep.

"—Lieutenant, but I'll keep sending 'til we get you retrieved. I say again—"

"Barc?"

"Ethan?" Pause. "Praise be! The lost is found!"

I was wrong. The stone's impact did have an effect. It jostled a loose audio connector in my helmet back into place.

"Wait one, Barc. The lost is also busy."

I stagger like a drunk, or, more accurately, like a mortally-wounded giant, and then flop onto my back.

I would have made a lousy dentist, but a hell of a actor.

Through my external audio I hear a collective gasp escape twelve thousand throats. Chubbi's eight thousand being the loudest among them.

"Sir, what the hoorah's going on down there?"

"Where's the drone?"

"Thirty seconds out. You should start getting ping-back momentarily, sir."

Ping.

I stare up at the clouds and smile.

The boy bends over me, brows knit. "Did I hurt you?"

"I'm fine. Now it's your turn to do the acting."

He raises his replacement sword above his head, then hacks the ground alongside me.

"Now take off my helmet, and hold it up over your head."

Among those watching, only Chubbi and the boy know that my helmet's not my head.

So when the boy raises my helmet, the collective gasp from Chubbi's side of the battle changes to a moan, and the Huppics cheer.

The drone's pingback turns to solid tone, and it breaks through the cloud ceiling like a silver angel.

The boy stands back, my helmet in his hand. The drone hovers, four feet above me, senses that I'm prone, and the pick-up litter whines down from its belly.

The boy asks, "What do I do now?"

The truth is that I don't know. I don't trust Chubbi to keep his bargain that if the Huppic's champion defeated his champion, he would leave them in peace. But his whole army just saw a skinny Huppic kid fell and behead, a giant. That may tamp down Chubbi appetite to attempt genocide again. It may inspire the Huppics to resist if he does. If they can find a leader.

Barclay thinks the Old Testament's a history book. I still don't. And the planetologic axiom about li conditions producing like results on Earthlikes doesn't apply to historical events, anyway, or so they say. But the way this little story fell into place makes me wonder. Regs or no regs, I'm proud of the bloodless way this turned out, and I think Barclay will be, too. I can probably persuade him to wipe a few records that would otherwise get me court-martialed.

I could climb aboard the drone, but I remain prone and let the drone's casualty cradle slide beneath me and lift. This whole playlet from the slingshot to the angel whisking away the giant's decapitated corpse has taken thirty seconds, but the twelve thousand witnesses will never forget it.

The story will be exaggerated in the retelling for centuries, down here. Only the boy knows the truth, and he can make of it whatever he wants. He can be anything he chooses now. A shepherd, this planet's first dentist, or a warrior king.

As the drone's belly doors close around me I say to the boy, "When you pick your name next year, try David."

---

obert Buettner's bestselling debut, *Orphanage*, a 004 Quill Award nominee for Best SF/Fantasy/Horror ovel, was called the Post-9/11 generation's *Starship roopers* and has been adapted for film by Olatunde sunsanmi (*The Fourth Kind*) for Davis Entertainent (*Predator*, *I Robot*, *Eragon*). Robert's books have en translated into five languages, and he was a 2005 uill nominee for Best New Writer. In 2011 Baen eased *Undercurrents*, his seventh novel. He wrote e afterword for Baen's re-issue of Heinlein's *Green*

Hills of Earth/Menace From Earth short story collection. Robert was a U.S. Army intelligence officer and National Science Foundation Fellow in Paleontology. As attorney of record in some three thousand cases, he practiced in the U.S. federal courts, before courts and administrative tribunals in no fewer than thirteen states, and in five foreign countries. (Six, if you count Louisiana.) He lives in Georgia with his family and more bicycles than a grownup needs.

Helmet

DANIEL H. WILSON

My little brother Chima sleeps with his mouth open. He has for a long time, not that he's got a choice. He was seven years old when the Helmet caught me off-guard. A corrugated metal wall exploded and hot shrapnel tore through Chima's face. Fuel-accelerated flames ate his cheeks and mouth. Only my brother's wide, round eyes were left untouched, glittering with intelligence behind a mask of flash-welded flesh.

The Helmets. Those baby killers. They always come at dawn.

Heat hits the Ukuta fast in the morning. Rays of sunlight splinter the horizon and needle into the slums. The sterile kilometers around our sprawling shanty town, where the old radiation lives—those hills dance and sing and remain still at the same time. And our valley of trash, with its labyrinth of crumbling walls and shacks and dirt paths, is trapped, groaning under the weight of that great wavering lump of heat. The sun beats down upon us as if it bears a grudge. Like it was angry at us for our very existence.

In Ukuta, you see, we must defy men and gods to live.

The election cycles come four times a year. Our votes are our own. But a careless vote can make the gray hills dance with more than heat. A wink of light from golden armor. The Helmets. Always a team of two. Vaulting through the dead wastes that have long divorced Ukuta from a place once called Africa. Those shivering hills will not suffer life to pass, but the Helmets bound through it unheeded, immune to the ancient poison.

Crossing the veil of death to guide us.

The Triumvirate rules the city-state of Ukuta. Their propaganda flyers drop from the sky, fluttering down like dying sparrows. During the night, images appear painted on walls. In the morning, we fear to remove them. Always the same image: Three old men, squatting like vultures behind a soaring judge's bench. Three wrinkled faces scowling down at us. "Follow our guidance," command the signs.

Without words, the Helmets appear and show us the strength of the Triumvirate. We do not question the filthy water or the smoke-filled factories or the invisible ring of death that surrounds Ukuta. Violence guides our vote. The faceless Helmets stamp out our phantom uprisings before we realize they have begun.

Chima stops breathing. I count to four before the rangy twelve-year-old snorts. He wakes up scrabbling at the plastic tarp he uses for a blanket.

It is early and he does not yet have his rag over his face. His pink hole of a mouth gapes like a rotten tree hollow. Rubbing his eyes, he frantically scans the miles of shanties that climb the horizon. He runs his fingertips over his face and moans at me in alarm.

"Ajani," he says, and I see the glint of shrapnel embedded in his cheeks. I have to concentrate to make out the words hidden inside his grunting whimper.

"My face hurts," he says.

My pulse quickens. Sometimes, when the Helmets are near, the shards of metal buried in Chima's face come alive with pain. The boy told me the aching comes from the silent talking between the Helmets. He says it is their radio antennae. I do not understand this, but Chima is a very clever boy. When his face hurts, especially at dawn, it can only mean one thing: We are in danger.

"Do not worry, little brother," I say. "I will keep you safe."

Standing, I put a hand to our chalky cement wall and listen. The world is still this early. Distantly, someone coughs and hawks phlegm. Two women talk quietly, headed to the well with empty plastic jugs balanced on their heads. One of them carries a pocket radio in her hand, quietly squawking drum-laced music. Chima winces as the radio grows nearer and then recedes.

"Radio," he says.

I take a relieved breath.

Then, I feel a vibration. Followed by a twin vibration one second later.

Chima sees it in my face before I can speak. He scrambles out of his cardboard bed and crawls through the refuse toward our one solid wall. There is a hole carved in the base of it that he still fits inside. He disappears, curling into the gap, knees to his chest and head folded down.

"I will tell you when it is safe," I say, picking up

a stubby spear fashioned out of a stake of sharpened rebar. The handle is made of plastic that has been melted onto the shaft and then wrapped in twine and cardboard. It fits the groove of my fingers perfectly.

Others are starting to stir in the shanties nearby. It won't be long before the panic spreads. Today, the shanties will burn.

I reach into the cool hollow and touch Chima on his bony shoulder to reassure him. Give him a grin and a wink. Then I prop his bedding loosely over the hole. Smack the supports out from under our makeshift roof and let the warped plastic shield fall against this one good wall, draping itself over my brother's hiding spot. Going around the side, I climb the wall's broken tail. I balance on top and squint at the horizon.

Two Helmets advance down the distant hill. They are man-shaped, but made of metal armor. They bound ahead, sometimes half a kilometer at a leap, leaving behind swollen mushrooms of fire with their flame makers. That which isn't concrete burns. Wood and plastic and paper turn to ash. As does flesh.

Especially flesh.

Concrete walls are our only oasis. I fought for the half-demolished wall I am perched on. Memory of the fight is in the weal of knotted scar tissue that are down my chest. Even now, those slum-dwellers who dart past below see my spear and they know better than to make a challenge.

The Helmets' direction is hard to gauge, but the silhouettes are growing larger.

I drop flat onto my stomach, hugging the wall. More runners are heading this way down the hill. They flee like rabbits, blindly. There are more ways to die th the flame. Breaking a bone or ripping your flesh are invitations to meet death. The wise among us have prepared hiding holes. Our fortresses to defend.

My breath comes in even and slow. My eyes do not blink. Sweat tickles my brow. I wipe it away and then my breath catches. I have lost sight of the lead Helmet. I crane my neck and that fat old bastard in the sky beats down on my eyes, blinding me. A flicker of shadow crosses my face and the wall lurches.

I cling to my wall, spear held tight.

The Helmet has arrived. It stands in the alley, six-feet-tall and sheathed in iridescent plates of armor. As the Helmet walks, each elaborate metal sheath flexes with its own mind. Its limbs move like an insect, in a series of sudden precise gestures. The Helmet inspects the area with quick jerks of its head. When it turns its gaze on me, I see it does not have a face.

Just the gold sheen of a reflective visor.

I lay still and feel the grit of my wall stinging my flesh. If the machine takes another step closer, I will try and kill it. To attack is a death sentence. I know this. But I have let my brother down once before. And will never let Chima be hurt again, no matter what.

The Helmet steps into our clearing and lifts its flame-maker.

In one fluid twisting movement, I fall from the wall and use the momentum to sling my arm. The spear flies true, tassel fluttering behind it. It strikes the Helmet in the faceplate and bounces away, leaving a wicked crack snaking across the golden visor. The Helmet does not react.

I have failed to kill it, and now my own life is forfeit. I circle slowly around, leading the Helmet away from my brother. I see my reflection in the thing's visor, my face shining and split. The thing leaps and closes the twenty feet between us. It clamps a hand over my forearm. Holds me with the dead final weight of a fallen tree.

Faintly, I think I hear someone screaming. From far away.

With all my strength, I resist looking back at my wall, resist checking on my little brother. If he is not roasted alive, he will likely survive. He is resourceful and doesn't eat much. After I am dead, those few people who remember the young face that used to grin beneath his eyes will watch out for him.

The Helmet lifts me high and I hang by my savaged wrist, watching my own hazy reflection. Gold-sheathed fingers grab me and I am thrown over the Helmet's shoulder. An arm lowers and presses me into place. Metal shoulder plates writhe under my belly. The Helmet does not kill me.

Instead, it carries me away.

Just before the Helmet leaps, I catch sight of Chima watching with angry, tear-filled eyes from behind our wall. I shake my head and he stays hidden.

The sun glares murderously through a barricade of clouds. I can almost picture heaven above the glowing haze. But I know it's a nightmare of raging light.

I lose consciousness somewhere over the dancing hills. My face blisters with the cold heat rising off the poisoned land. I do not think to struggle. The world is too bright, white on white on white. The Helmet skin bites my side with every movement. My strength is gone. I flop like a rag doll.

When I wake, I do not recognize this place. I have never been outside Ukuta. No slum dweller has.

Tall blank buildings loom under low dirty clouds. The Helmet carries me down a narrow street, its walls crowding in. The gray surfaces are sprinkled with rain, gleaming dull and strong in the cloud-diffused sunlight. My mind balks to imagine it. In Ukuta, each of these walls would be worth fighting for. They make my humpbacked wall seem grotesque and sad in comparison.

"Helmet," I gasp. "Where are you taking me?"

The Helmet does not react in any way. No pause, no glance, no small nod of the head. We continue walking, the Helmet's armored boots clinking off the empty street. The staccato sound plinks off the walls with the regularity of a metronome. Like a clock ticking down the seconds of my life. Until it stops.

The wall beside us is studded with coffin-sized, rectangular doors.

A bronze carving of a helmet rests in the center of each door. A bronze handle emerges from the mouth-section of the carving. The Helmet reaches out and locks gauntleted fingers to the handle. With a prehistoric groan, the Helmet flexes its armored might and drags a shining metal slab from the wall. It takes a long time to pull it all the way out. Finally, the slab of metal hangs there fully extended, like a tombstone. The Helmet throws me onto the slab and I am too exhausted to resist.

I count my breaths as the Helmet pushes the sliding slab back into the wall with me on it. Arms at my sides, the ceiling of the tomb nearly scrapes my bare heaving chest. Darkness eats my body, and inch by inch, my face sinks into blackness. My breath echoes in my ears.

Buried alive.

For ten breaths, I lay in the darkness unable to move. My palms are flat against the cold sweating metal, pushing, fingers splayed. I try to crane my neck and a chilly dot of ceiling presses against my forehead. A humming vibration swells around me, inside me.

The ceiling explodes into light. Things I have never seen before streak overhead, numbers and letters and images. My eyelashes pulse with their blue glow. Then an outline of my own body hovers overhead, a mirror reflection. I pant faster, breathing my own carbon dioxide.

The slab beneath me is heating up.

Overhead, the stark blue outline of my body is starting to turn red around the edges. I spread my fingers and scream out in pain as my thumb is burned. Quickly, I realize that I've got to match my body to the outline. The red is pain, and it is closing in. Hunching my whole body, I shuffle to match the silhouette. I whimper once, when the heel of my foot strays into fire.

The tomb whines mechanically, begins to shiver.

I blink away tears of pain and focus on the image. Sweat is pooling in the hollow of my throat. I can feel beads of it tickling my ribs and thighs and calves. But the pain of disobeying is so intense that I have no choice.

The lights above me blink out.

In the darkness, the warm metal around me begins to rise up like dough. The sudden overwhelming heat of it crushes the breath out of my lungs in a silent gasping scream. Before I can take another breath, the metal is over me, burying me, rising up around my neck like crushing water. A finger of liquid metal pokes into my belly, piercing my skin. If I could scream or kick or struggle I would. Instead, I lay paralyzed, drowning in this cube of space as my taut, bony body is swallowed by flowing metal.

I try to breathe in and I cannot. I try to move and I cannot. I try to live, but I cannot.

The Helmet is my living tomb.

Cooling metal encases every inch of my body with cascading sheathes that flex and coil like a python. Only the surface of my face does not touch metal. Inside the Helmet, I am free to curl my lips in anguish and scream into the two inches of space between my eyes and the visor.

And scream I do.

The Helmet holds me fast. I cannot move anything. Not a finger. I am trapped inside a human-shaped prison cell. The horror is not that I cannot move. The horror is that the Helmet moves itself, and me with it.

The machine bends its knees and stands up. Struggling, I flex against its movements. I grunt and curse and whimper, throwing every ounce of strength into resisting the will of the machine. But metal is stronger than flesh. The Helmet mechanically forces my limbs into position.

After only thirty seconds I am too tired to resist.

Beaten, I watch through the visor as my body slides off the slab. Walking down the narrow street, I realize I can hear my clinking footsteps on the pavement. A speaker inside the Helmet is transmitting sound from outside.

Another Helmet approaches from the other direction. We do not pause or acknowledge each other in
any way. In its visor, I see the gleaming reddish armor
that has replaced my skin.

We both turn to enter a squat cement building.
Inside, a row of narrow corridors stretch beneath a
crushingly low ceiling. Each row is illuminated every
few feet by a flickering overhead light. And in each
row stand hundreds of identical Helmets, each a precise distance from the other, postures identical. Their
faces are only inches from the wall.

In a rush of sickening horror, it dawns on me that
every Helmet has a person trapped inside. I wonder
how many of them are screaming right now, struggling
against unstoppable metal. My Helmet walks me down
the row. Only now do I notice subtle differences in
the Helmets' armor, nicks and scars. Faded patches
and burned spots. And some of the Helmets are
shorter than others.

Those must be the women.

I walk past a shorter Helmet and take an empty
space at the wall. I only glimpse at the girl next to
me for an instant. I assume she is a girl, anyway. She
is very small. Her armor is finer than mine, intricate
layered together and burnished orange.

"Doli," I say to myself. "She is like a doll."

My voice echoes loudly inside the Helmet. Somehow it is reassuring. A relief to know that, even if
I cannot make a fist, at least my voice is my own,
however silent it may be to those outside.

Suddenly, my stomach cramps and I groan. Spasms
rip through my gut and I want to fall and curl up in
a ball. But the Helmet stands firm. Rolling my eyes

I make out an umbilical arm reaching out from the wall. It must be connected to a port on my stomach. Delivering sustenance. Removing waste.

The Helmets are feeding.

I begin to silently cry. The wall before me is flat and empty and huge in my visor. It is made of cold hard cement. A spider web of tiny fissures run through it. Nothing changes. Nothing moves. After a few moments, the wall loses perspective. I feel as though I am looking down at a map. Each crack is a wall back home in Ukuta. I can imagine Chima sleeping safely. Thousands of other villagers around him. He can hear the barking of a far-off dog. The cool night breathes on his skin.

My crying stops.

One by one, the overhead lights snap out. The wall before me drops a shade darker with each *snap* of the light. *Snap, snap, snap*. It is the only sound until finally we Helmets stand together in twilight. Utterly alone in our multitudes.

"Chima," I say it out loud and it feels good. "Goodnight, brother."

My own walking wakes me.

Instead of the wall, my visor displays a long tunnel. The passage is the width of a single man, the ceiling at a few inches overhead. The short Helmet, Doli, marches ahead of me. Others are in front of her. I imagine still more are behind me, but I cannot turn look. Staring hard at Doli, I think I catch a trace femininity in the way she walks.

And the tunnel disappears. Opens up into a huge empty room. Cement floors lit by a skylight, glowing with smoky sunlight. A thousand Helmets stand in sweeping formation, meticulously spaced. As I march into my own position, I realize that we are all oriented to face one point.

A towering judge's bench across the room, made of ancient wood. Three wrinkled, scowling faces peek over the top. I recognize the Triumvirate.

In the propaganda posters, these men always seemed identical. But standing before them, I see the First has a sharp nose and birdlike eyes. He hunches forward, his great bald head hanging between narrow shoulders. The Second is ancient. Age spots mottle his brow and his thin shaking fists are visible. The Third is a piggish monster. He licks his moist lips and stares down at us through a wet sneer. His face is nearly lost in the wattle of flesh around his neck.

The man-things speak together, finishing each other sentences. A three-headed monster perched at the top of a wooden wall.

"War criminals," says the First, shrilly.

"Are you not ashamed?" howls the Second.

"Murderers, know that your path leads to death" mutters the Third, with a shapeless lisp.

Standing at attention, arms by my sides, I can only swivel my eyes to witness the rage-filled face. They deliver their speech by rote, as they will every morning from now on.

"Your grisly work benefits the Triumvirate. You wicked deeds further the Cause. Yet we sit apart from your crimes. For you are not innocent," spits the Firs

"Criminals responsible for atrocity," says the Secor

"Killers, poisoners, usurpers," mutters the Third

"You have turned your hand to evil deeds. A you will be punished with death," says the Second

"When your term expires, so must you," adds the Third, staring blindly.

The First continues, intoning the words like a prayer: "The responsibility for what you have done sweeps through your metal skin like a foul wind through the branches of the tree of death. It sinks its barbs into your flesh. And it will be set free by the purifying flame upon your skin."

"For the wages of sin..." intones the Third.

"Death," they say it together, solemnly. "Death. Death."

In my peripheral, I see six Helmets draw their flame-makers and walk forward. The rest of us re-orient our faces to follow. The six walking Helmets have chipped armor. Their visors are dimmed and faded with sunlight. Forming into three pairs, they stop at the base of the wall and raise their weapons to each other. No hesitation. Flames spurt out, coating each Helmet in an inferno. The golden metal shells stand firm, each continuing to pull the trigger.

The Helmets burn.

Finally, one falls to its knees. Still, it keeps flaming its partner. Another falls, and another. Mercifully, it ends. The chemical flames gutter and evaporate into nothing. Six charred Helmets lay on the ground, frozen in their last positions, visors stained black with soot.

By some twisted logic, we are being punished for the Helmet's crimes.

I wonder how long the people inside lived. I wonder they were even alive when they entered the room. Were they scared in those last moments? Or maybe they were relieved. Some part of me senses that the execution was merciful.

✧   ✧   ✧

We Helmets. Baby killers. We always come at dawn.

I can only observe, locked in my shell. Through my visor I see there are many slums beyond Ukuta. Each area is isolated by a dead zone of old radiation. These tracts of land keep the people separated and weak. Ignorant of each other, the slums vote constantly, always reaffirming the control of the Triumvirate.

My Helmet guides me, and the Triumvirate guides the people.

Our raids are conducted in pairs. Little Doli is my permanent companion. Short and squat, she is nonetheless powerful. I have seen the streak of her burnt orange armor arcing high above the nameless, faceless slums. A twinkling morning star, she falls through the sky trailing a jet of cleansing flame.

The days come and go as a waking nightmare. Weeks pass in which I cannot bear to open my eyes. I feel the lurch of my body as it leaps through the dead zones. The disturbing tickle of radiation seeps through the armor. The inevitable sound of Doli always a few seconds behind me. My faithful echo. I hear the desperate curses of our victims. Their lamentations. Their begging.

And in the end, their silence.

I accumulate sin. Cement crumbles beneath my boots. My gauntleted fingers rend flesh. Flames speed from my weapon and then speak to me in guttural whispers as they eat their fill of innocent flesh.

My lips are the only thing I can control.

"Good morning, Doli," I say, at the feeding station. "Did you sleep well, my dear? Of course you did, how could you not?"

Together, Doli and I stream out of the city, along with a thousand other Helmets. We break into a steady trot and I begin to talk. I know that Doli cannot hear me, but I leave in the pauses and imagine her responses.

"Doli, do you want to hear a story?" I ask.

I suppose.

"Did I ever tell you the one about how Chima claimed our wall?"

Only a hundred times.

"The Ajani wall, as it came to be known, was controlled by a fat brute called Cleaver."

Why'd they call him Cleaver?

"He was dangerous enough with his weapon to be named after it. No way to get near his wall. But it was the finest, safest wall in all of Ukuta."

How did little Chima claim it?

"My brother Chima searched far and wide to find a butcher in need of a cleaver. Told him about this perfect knife. That butcher came one day and traded Cleaver a whole goat for his weapon."

Uh-oh.

"That's right, Doli. Without his legendary knife, fat old Cleaver had no chance to defend his wall. I took it away from him with only a single wound. A clever boy, that Chima. Much smarter than his older brother, that's for sure."

We are leaping, soaring over yet another dead zone.

When we touch down, the slum looks like any other. The screams are the same. The crackle of flames.

I almost do not recognize the stick-thin boy running at me. His eyes burn with evil and hatred. As the rag covering his face falls away, I see the pink smear of flesh that is his face and recognize my own brother.

"Chima," I say. Or maybe I only think his name.

My head rings with the impact of metal on metal. Chima has set a trap. Our wall surges into my vision just before it collapses onto me. The disintegrating rock smashes into my body, pulls me down in a wave of rubble. As the pain of the reverberation lances through my head, I pray for my prison to shatter, to fracture and fall away like plaster. I pray for Chima to be victorious. I pray for my own death.

But the strength of the Helmet will not succumb to prayer.

The armor is intact. I feel my arm questing through the broken shards. A slab of powdery cement scrapes off my visor and falls away. I sit up from the bed of sharp rock. Chima falls upon me, vicious, swinging my old rebar spear.

"Die, demon," he screams, each word a guttural cough. "Why won't you die?"

He is too close. My Helmet grabs Chima with one hand. Pulls him toward me and slams him onto his back. I hear his ribs snapping against the uneven rubble. Yet he continues to roar.

A warrior.

I choke down tears as my armored fingers crush my brother's throat. Blinking, I focus on his face. This sweet boy who I raised and protected for so many years. When he screams, I bite through my own lip and scream with him.

"I love you, Chima," I sputter.

I cannot close my eyes to the horrible sight.

The one I love more than myself is dying inches from me. Suffocating with a broken neck. And all can do is greedily memorize his features. Each flec of shrapnel in his cheeks. His smoke-black eyes. Thick, arched eyebrows, twisted in venomous anger. In a moment, my body will leap away empty-handed. These memories will be all that I can carry.

The life leaves his eyes and I feel it leave my own, as well. My little brother chokes, chest heaving, and his jaw moves. Mouths a final word.

Ajani.

It is not until later that I receive Chima's gift.

He found the answer in the shrapnel embedded in his face. Said it hurt him because of the radio transmissions between Helmets. And my Chima recognized a weak spot. Where there is radio, he must have thought, there is an antenna. Destroy the antenna and the radio cannot function.

Such a clever boy.

Our beautiful wall fell and pinned my Helmet in its ruin. Brave as a lion, Chima struck again and again. His blows were not random. Each landed in one spot at the base of my spine. The armored lump resting there was damaged, but not destroyed. Not yet.

It happens while I'm crossing the dancing hills, the familiar nibble of radiation in my legs. I am mid-leap when I feel something wrong. I open my eyes and notice the ground is coming too fast. My Helmet is not reacting. Instinctively, I try to thrust out my hands before I hit the poisoned dirt and rock.

I smash into the toxic hardpack like a meteorite.

Rolling, limbs flailing, rocks battering my ribs and head—I luxuriate in the pain. Each gasp is a wonder, a reminder that I am still alive inside this cage. My own arms and legs are weak as dead grass but the

Helmet is amplifying my tiniest movements. Climbing to my knees, I feel the venomous heat pouring up out of the ground and into my face. Sweat drips from my forehead and streaks the inside of my visor. The orange flash of Doli is rapidly disappearing ahead. Only enemies wait behind me.

My wall is gone. My brother gone.

I scrabble to my feet and make a clumsy leap after Doli. My powered legs catapult my body into the air. It is a jerky, mechanical leap that sends me cutting through the sky like a bullet. There is no feel of wind on my face, no roar of the air in my ears. Even so, I find that for the first time I enjoy the leap.

As we near the walled city, other incoming Helmets join us. It takes all of my concentration to maintain the scripted movements that my body has repeated day after day: Form in a line outside the city. March through the gate. Down narrow alleys. Every nerve in my body is pleading, begging for me to run away. Rip this Helmet off my flesh. Feel the air on my skin.

But Doli marches ahead of me. Her frame is so small. Armor beginning to flake from our constant trips through the dancing hills. She is trapped, just as I was. Just as all Helmets are.

And I cannot abandon her.

On schedule, we enter the feeding tunnel. I march in careful step until I reach my hole in the wall. I stand the right distance away from Doli, face the wall, and draw on every last shred of my willpower to keep my super-powered limbs perfectly still. That cursed umbilical tube emerges and my stomach spasms as the blind, grasping appendage delivers sustenance and removes waste.

Snap, snap, snap.

The overhead lights blink out. We are left in semi-darkness, an endless row of shadowed statues standing at attention. No movement, no sound. Except the quiet, oh so quiet, grind of my Helmet.

I turn my head slightly to the left, to see Doli. Nothing happens. No alarm sounds.

In this world of sameness, I am miraculously different. A sculpted man come to life and alone in the company of my fellow works of art. I gingerly reach up and take my Helmet in both hands. My fingers are so strong; I must be careful. Gently, I pull my visor straight up.

Metal strains. The visor hisses at the neck as the first rip appears. The helmet comes unmarried from the armor.

And finally, blissfully, cool air washes over my filthy face.

Smells. I can smell wet concrete around me. The strange chemical smell from the umbilical devices. My own breath and hair and skin take on a long-forgotten stink in contrast to these new odors. I sniff deeply and nearly cry out from the joy of air rushing into my nostrils. My tears evaporate from my cheeks and the feeling is blessed. Finally, I remember Doli.

She stands loyally next to me, as always, facing her wall.

I place a hand on her shoulder. In all the massacres and slaughter, our Helmets have never touched. I don't even really know that she is a she. It could be anyone in there. Leaning over, I look into her visor. In the reflection, I see my lips are flecked with blood, lost in a tightly curled beard, and my cheeks are streaked with sweat. I notice that I am smiling, my teeth yellow and bright in the darkened corridor.

"I have been looking forward to meeting you for a long time, Doli," I whisper. "You do not know this, but we have had many conversations. We are old friends."

What must she be thinking? This change in routine. To be on the cusp of freedom after so long. Countless years of bloodshed and evil and those frowning monsters shouting down accusations of sin and responsibility.

With both hands, I take hold of her helmet.

Squeezing, I gently pull the visor up. A seam appears at the neck. Squealing, the metal parts. A putrid stench spews from the gap. I retch once before I can hold my breath. In a last burst, I tear the visor off. Stumbling backward, gasping for air, I finally meet Doli.

She is a she.

At first, I think Doli is smiling at me. And then I realize that she has no lips. Her teeth are bared at me in a rictus of pain and insanity. She has chewed through her own mouth and swallowed most of it and done the same for large pieces of her tongue. It has healed and been eaten again. Bits of rotting flesh line the inside of her visor. Blood and vomit and saliva coat the interior of her visor, obscuring the view.

I realize it is possible that Doli has never ever seen me.

Clumps of hair cling to her peeling scalp. A stiff strand is plastered over one of her eyes. She has had no way to move it, maybe for years. Her eyes roll idiotically in their sockets. She moans, and I think of my murdered brother.

"I'm so sorry, Doli," I say.

With all the gentleness I can muster, I push the crusted hair out of her eyes. Smooth it back in an uneven mass behind her ears. Then, reverently, I fit her visor back over her head. I press it down hard, crushing the metal seal back together. Then, I do the same for myself. Turn and face my own patch of nothing.

I leave Doli there, small, facing the blank wall.

The Triumvirate guides us.

The three man-things huddle together behind the wooden wall of their bench. Twisted faces peering down from above. I have leapt higher in my months-long orgy of murder. I have vaulted city walls and crushed huddling families to ruin under my boots. Brushed my fingers over the throats of men and left yawning corpses. I have heard wild flames licking the bodies of the fallen.

We thousand Helmets stand at attention in a sweeping semi-circle, arms by our sides, facing the bench, a mute audience held captive. Forced to absorb blame and abuse and madness. Each of us a slave to his own machine.

All save one.

As they do every morning, the Triumvirate speaks together, finishing each other's sentences. The three-headed monster is here on schedule to lay down its sins upon our strong shoulders.

"War criminals," says the First, voice booming.

"Are you not ashamed?" howls the Second.

"Murderers, know that your path leads to death," mutters the Third.

And I take a step forward.

"Your grisly work..." says the First, trailing off. The old man sees me. Blinks his shark eyes sleepily, not believing it.

"Criminals responsible for atrocity," says the Second, rotely.

I break into a trot, weaving between the rows of Helmets, gaining speed.

The First shoves the Second on the shoulder, points at me frantically.

"Killers!" booms the Third, clueless, as the Second gives him a push.

I launch my body upward, rising above the wooden wall in a single bound. My body is a majestic suit of golden armor, soaring. I thrust out my rippling metallic arms like wings. At the top of my arc, at my perfect zenith, I gaze down through my blank mask. In my shadow, the Triumvirate gape up at me.

Scared old men with dirty minds and clean hands.

Once, I had a little brother named Chima. He slept with his mouth open. Together, we conquered a wall and built our lives in its safety. Our wall was made to shelter and protect. Others are made to confine and control. But no wall yet built can deflect the knifing flight of blame. The sin circles above, waiting for its moment. And one day it will strike its true target.

My fingers collapse into fists. Legs brace for impact. The three old men hold each other and wail for mercy. But there is no mercy.

At last, I am ready to sin.

Daniel H. Wilson is a *New York Times* bestselling author and contributing editor to *Popular Mechanics* magazine. He earned a Ph.D. in Robotics from Carnegie Mellon University in Pittsburgh, where he also received Master's degrees in Robotics and Machine Learning. He has published over a dozen scientific papers, holds four patents, and has written seven books. Wilson has written for *Popular Science*, *Wired*, and *Discover*, as well as online venues such as MSNBC.com, *Gizmodo*, *Lightspeed*, and Tor.com. In 2008, Wilson hosted *The Works*, a television series on The History Channel that uncovered the science behind everyday stuff. His books include *How to Survive a Robot Uprising*, *A Boy and His Bot*, and *Robopocalypse*. He lives and writes in Portland, Oregon.

The N-Body Solution

SEAN WILLIAMS

What happens next is irrelevant. All that matters is where it started.

Harvester bars are pretty much the same wherever you go, but I hadn't learned that yet. Fresh out of Infall and all out of hope, I was looking for the sleaziest, most pointless, dead-end dive that ever existed. I had nothing to look forward to but getting as plastered as the ancients and spending the rest of my days in a hangover.

There were plenty of bars to choose from. They were busy, too. I clearly wasn't the only one looking to drown my sorrows under a sky devoid of stars.

That made it instantly more boring.

I settled on a place called, unimaginatively, the End of the Line. It was full of humans, sub-humans, post-humans, poly-humans—every category I'd ever heard of, plus some types that probably weren't human at all. The Loop has been around a long time, and if half the things I had heard were true, then it was quite likely I Was Not Alone. In that sense, at least.

I knew I should be depressed: I had reason to be. But the possibility of talking to a real, live alien was not just intriguing; it was something the rest of my scattered self might never experience. It was something I could cling to, something that was mine, and would be mine alone for as long as I could bear it.

The thing about aliens, though, I soon realized, is that they're *alien*. After five conversations in which we utterly failed to find opinions, experiences, and in one case even words in common, I gave up and took to leaning against the long, corroded bar on my own. Nursing a drink in sullen silence turned out to be a natural part of my social inheritance.

"You're new," said a voice from the other end of the bar.

"It's that obvious, I suppose," I said without looking up.

"Not really. We're all floundering. I'm just permanently jacked into the news feed. You're the third today. I recognize your face."

"There's a news feed?"

"Sure, but not much in the way of actual news. No offence."

I looked up. Judging by the voice, I'd expected the owner to be a woman. What I saw instead was a bipedal mech suit almost twice as tall as I was, all ceramics, alloys, and plastics, as streamlined as a stiletto. It occupied the deepest, darkest corner o the bar, but even so, it gleamed. Pinpricks of light ricocheted off its faceted eyes, the sharp tips of its digits, its many beveled edges.

"You human in there?"

"I said, 'no offence.'"

"None taken. I'm just curious."

"Well, don't be."

"There must be *something* biological, or else you wouldn't be in this place, messing with your chemistry."

"It's certainly not for the company."

"Hey, you spoke to me, remember?"

The suit shifted with a faint whirr of servos, presenting its back. There, embossed against the silver, was the logo of the Earth Justice Enforcement Agency, and her surname in black: *Ei*.

"Nice to meet you, soldier," she said.

Maybe I really was that obvious. Stung, I retreated to contemplate my empty shot glass.

"Don't mind her," said the bartender, a loathsome lad but at least superficially of my species. "She's boiling for a fight with someone her size, and you don't really qualify."

"Gee, thanks." I was sarcastic, but that was one thing to be grateful for. In my current form, Enforcer could have squashed me like a bug. "What's her story? I don't recognize the make of her suit."

"Something new, I guess. She's been here three months. Came after a mark. Caught him almost immediately, they say. He snuck in through the Infall, and she tracked him down. First the Authorities knew of it was when she handed them his body."

I'd been debriefed on arrival, but there was still much to learn. "The Authorities?"

"Closest thing to a government you'll find in Harvester."

"Maybe I should take a proper look about the place, see what's what. While I can still walk."

The bartender gave me half a shot, on the house.

"For the road?"

"There's no road from here, my friend. Just ways to pass the time."

Five suns, any one of which was in the sky at any given time. One planetary nebula, casting a permanent glow across the heavens. Permanent settlements scattered across two rocky worlds, plus stations around the system's only gas giant. The gas giant was home to the shipyards.

That's where I went first, in a manner of speaking.

Tideships, stillships, heavyships . . . every species had its own wild fantasy about getting home the hard way. None of them had worked to date, and even if one did, where would it go? The nebula was almost a light-year across. Just getting a clear picture of the universe outside was difficult. No one had a map, and if they did we weren't on it.

"The colony at loop junction one-sixty-three has many names," said the orientation drone taking me and my fellow newbs on the virtual tour. "'Cyerm' is the oldest known, but almost certainly not the first. The term comes from the Guta tongue, and approximately translates as 'harvester,' the epithet employed by the colony's human inhabitants."

Our point of view swept through the ribs of a ship so big it would take another century just to finish the chassis.

"Harvester is home to seventeen species of biological sentient and three machine intelligences. Evidence of habitation stretches back more than one million years, with only two vacant periods, the longest spanning ten thousand years. Fossil records indicate that life did not evolve here. Presumably the Loop's builders were the first inhabitants."

That told me a little, but not a lot. All things in Harvester started and ended with the Loop, which remained as mysterious as ever.

"Why this junction?" asked someone from the back of the consensual shuttle. "Why did it break down here?"

"That is unknown. The malfunction remains unexplained, if indeed it is a malfunction. Some maintain that the Loop was always intended to stop here, and is functioning normally."

"Perhaps this is the home system of the Builders," said another shell-shocked newb.

"All roads lead to Rome?" I said. "But there's only one road, and the Builders are conspicuously absent."

"Perhaps the event that caused the nebula wiped them out."

The drone didn't dignify that with a response. No species capable of building a wormcaster network spanning the universe would ever let a simple stellar hiccup knock them out of the picture.

"One hundred and sixty-three is the largest Heegner number," said a third member of my temporary compatriots. "That might mean something."

Also doubtful, I thought. Class number problems and almost integers seemed a long way from the seething polyglot around us. As well as the five suns, two rocky worlds and one gas giant, there were streams

of asteroids and dust following fiendishly complex
orbits through the system. The largest asteroid had
been mined out millennia ago. Wars had once been
fought over the richest finds, but things were quiet
at the moment, while the Authorities' power held.

For the foreseeable future, then, I was out of a job.

"I think it's beautiful," said a small, dark-haired
woman I had barely glanced at before. "It's so rich and
interesting—compared to the other junctions, I mean."

I looked at her properly, now. We had passed each
other at the Outfall on junction one-sixty-two, and then
again at Harvester's Infall. Travelers in the same direction, we had had nothing more in common than that.

Now, we were caught in the same trap, and her
eyes were shining with something that might actually
have been joy.

"What about the singularity kites of forty-five?"
asked another passenger.

"Or the multiplex quintuple system of sixty-one?"

Both good suggestions, I thought, to which I would
have added the bottomless pit of thirty-nine, the
eternally burning world of eighteen, and the stellar
graveyard at even one hundred.

"Sideshows," she said with a wave of one delicate
hand. Her expression was rapturous. "This is the real
deal."

We had all seen the same things. We'd all come to
junction one-sixty-three the same way, junction after
junction on our intergalactic grand tour. But somehow
this woman had arrived at an entirely different place
from the rest of us.

"It's hardwired," she explained after the tour, in
a different Harvester bar, one that stank of years

and sugar like we were inside a giant brewery. "I don't believe in being negative, so I make sure I can't, surgically. I'm only capable of feeling positive emotions—and it's wonderful."

"Yes, but you would say that, wouldn't you?"

She laughed, and invited me back to her place. I was amazed that she already had quarters organized and furnished. While I had been moping about, grousing at strangers, she had been getting her life together.

Maybe, I thought, there was something to her positivity jag. It could even be infectious.

Her name was Zuzi. She didn't give me anything more than that. And when I told her what I had done for a living, she didn't ask for details.

"So you're Corps," she said. "So what? It's all history now, Alex."

She used my name like she used the rest of me. And when she was done, neither of us seemed any happier than we had been before.

I wasn't the only Corps recruit on Harvester. Embodient training was mandatory, and the rest of me wasn't the first to opt for the Loop's one-way trip. It was a far bet that some version of my higher self would be found to pick me up when I reached the far end, full to the brim with experiences and memories for the rest of me to share. That no one had ever gone all the way round yet wasn't a disincentive. It was assumed that the Loop was so big there simply hadn't been time. No one seriously considered the possibility that one of its links might be broken.

As with most colonies, Corps recruits were called lapses, but here that had both a literal and cautionary edge. Some of us did choose death over being isolated from our higher selves. It wasn't that our much-reduced forms weren't viable. It was the thought that *this was all we would ever be* that did the damage. There were self-help groups, where we talked through our problems. There were training sessions to keep up our skills. There were even a couple of odd little collectives where mismatched corpses tried to link up and form a new emergent self. I stayed away from the first and last, bu forced myself to participate in the second.

Other classes of being occasionally joined the fights Enforcer Ei was one of them. She was hard to miss There were other suits and larger bipeds prowling the habitats of Harvester, but none as brooding an dagger-sharp as she was. After that first encounter i the End of the Line, I had seen her in green zone amphitheatre audiences, work crews, and even ju standing around, staring at the view from one Harvester's many lookouts. If she lived anywhere particular, I never found out.

The first time she came to the dojo I frequented. didn't fight her, nor the second time. I simply watche her wipe the floor with the toughest members of t crew, one after the other. I noted her moves a catalogued her weaknesses. She was all former, no of the latter.

"Stone cold killer," said one of the other recru in an aside she probably couldn't hear, and if s had, might have taken for a compliment. "I he rumors of squads like these before I left home. cross them, you're dead, no matter how far you r Remember that guy she killed? Probably thought got clean away, coming out here...."

I just kept watching, awaiting my opportunity.

The dojo was kitted out with all sorts of tech, but I preferred to fight as close to bare-handed as was feasible. I certainly never fought with a mech suit. Enforcer Ei had seen me sparring and knew my style probably as well as I knew hers, so when I approached her her immediate response was, "You don't want to fight me."

"Why challenge you, then?"

"I don't know. Because you want me to kill you?"

"You won't kill me. You're an Enforcer. It wouldn't be legal."

"Earth is a long way from here, soldier."

"Use my name."

"I don't know your name."

"Yes, you do. It was in the news feed."

She tilted her shining helm. "Alex Lombard. What difference does it make?"

"Maybe none. Maybe a lot if the thought of killing me does cross your mind."

A small crowd gathered as we squared off in the arena. I ignored the odd mocking cat-call. None came from my fellow recruits. They understood, but they thought I was mad all the same.

I adopted a wary crouch—one she imitated with a whole lot more unfolding of weapon-stalks, fins, and antennae.

"Now you're just showing off," I said, noting the position of everything vulnerable.

"And you're just wasting time."

"Me? I'm waiting for y—"

I barely registered the sharp clicks of her actuators flashing with explosive force against the arena floor.

The next thing I knew I was on my back, in so much pain I could barely breathe.

I blinked up at the shining figure standing over me.

"Enough?" she said.

"Hell, no. They make us tough in the Corps." That was the truth. I had little conscious control over my body's more advanced abilities, but already the pain was fading and I was able to get to my feet.

"Again," I said.

She stepped back. "You can't be serious."

"I can't believe we're still talking."

I ducked low under the natural reach of her left arm and lunged for a particular attenuated sensor that looked like it might bend. I didn't try a kick a her knees. I didn't for a second consider that I coul knock her off-balance. All I saw was the needle-thi tip of that sensor and—in my mind's eye—my fi reaching out for it, closing tight around it, twisting.

In reality, I probably got no closer than ten cent meters.

She held me upside-down by one leg so we we almost eye-to-eye. This time there was a little laught

"Are you done yet?" she asked.

"If it's a fair fight you're looking for—"

"Just getting bored."

"So come out of the suit and meet me face to fac

She let go and I hit the floor with all of the ha tat's 1.2-gravities.

"I guess that's a no."

"You guessed right."

She had already turned away. This time I too running jump for her back, reaching for the par behind which all her sensors and weapons had retrac

There was sufficient grip there for me to hold onto, and I was able to get to her shoulders before she spun around her center of gravity and punched me hard in the chest.

I was out cold when I hit the dojo wall, and only came to when she shocked me with the tip of an electrical weapon protruding from her mechanical toe.

"Wake up."

"I'm awake."

"You're an idiot."

"Try to understand," I said braving the hammering in my head in order to sit up. The walls, floor, and ceiling turned dizzyingly around me. "I don't have a death wish and I'm not expecting to beat you. It's not about winning or losing. It's about the fight."

"It's not even a fight," she said.

"But it's a fight I've never had before, with an opponent I've never fought before. That's the point." She straightened, and I knew I'd reached her. "You think your higher self will be grateful for your memories of being pounded over and over again?"

"Maybe not, if that's all you've got to offer."

"What else is there?"

"Show me."

"But you're so slow," she said, "so primitive."

"That's the point of legacy genes. My higher self—"

"I *know* what your higher self thinks. It thinks that by making parts of itself old-style human, it'll stay at least partly human rather than evolve off into the freak-show. That's why you won't wear a suit. Another version of you back home is doing that and recording that experience. You're the grand tourist, Looper—but you're still a soldier, or part of one,

and you think this is what the rest of you wants. Are
you sure you aren't kidding yourself?"

"Maybe," I said, "but it beats sitting around in bars.

She towered over me, unmoving for a good ten
seconds.

"All right," she said. "Get up."

I did as I was told.

"My higher self is a 'him,' not an 'it,' by the way

"You think ordinary pronouns apply anymore?" She
killed that line of conversation with one savage cho
of her right battle glove. "Do you know what th
craziest thing about you is?"

"What?"

"You haven't given in. You still think you mig
go home."

"Why not? Or I might meet myself out here, whe
ever we are. Either way."

She hit me so hard I was in rehab for a week.

When I recovered, she started teaching me abc
suits like hers—their weak points, their blind spo
their limitations. It was all relative, of course. I ne
had a hope of putting her down, but she got that n
and it became about something other than winn
for her, too.

As we fought, we talked.

"How did you know I was Corps?" I asked during
first spar after rehab. "That wasn't in the news fee

"A lucky guess," she said.

"No, tell me. What gave it away?"

"You want me to say it was your confidence, or
way you held yourself—*meronymically*, if that's a th

"I just want you to tell me the truth."

She shrugged. "Your biochemistry was off. That's all."

"You can tell that at a glance?"

"I can tell what you had for breakfast . . . yesterday."

I laughed. "Well, that's not fair. I don't get to see anything about you."

She didn't answer.

We sparred for a while, and then I pressed her again. "Seriously, do you *ever* take your suit off?"

"That's none of your business, soldier."

"I'm making it my business."

She jabbed at me a fraction faster than I could dodge. I rode out the blow and came up grinning.

"So tell me about this place instead. What's the deal with the Outfall? Why hasn't anyone fixed it yet?"

"Do I look like a scientist?"

"I don't know what you look like, Enforcer Ei. I don't even know if you have a first name."

She didn't respond to that little dig, either. "The Outfall doesn't work. That's all you need to know."

"Doesn't work how?"

"People walk into it. They stand around looking embarrassed. Then they walk back out again. No one goes anywhere."

"I presume someone's examined it."

"I think we can be sure of that."

I thought of the brightly glowing sky and the crowded habitats, the tens of thousands of years of devolution and fruitless industry and cultural mixing. People arrived every day, but they were far outnumbered by the people who already lived here, had even been born here.

"Yes, but *can* we be sure of that?" I asked. "I bet they haven't looked at it, and neither have I. What if everyone before us did the same—and everyone

before them, too? What if that goes right back to the
first people here and no one has double-checked the
original diagnosis?"

"Why don't you take the tour and find out for
yourself?"

"There's a tour?"

"Will you stop talking like this if there is?"

I considered the consequences of not taking the hint.
She was sensitive on the subject. I had had plenty of
time to ponder that during my week in rehab.

"I will," I said, "if you go with me."

"On the tour?"

"Yes."

"Why?"

"Because you're such good company, that's why."

That came out a little sharper than I'd intended.
Her movements lost some of their smooth grace, like
I had managed to hit her where it counted, inside the
suit. I dodged two blows with ease, and was beginning to wonder if I had seriously offended her when
she said, "All right."

"All right what?"

"I'll take the tour with you."

"Well, great."

"And my first name is Nadia—but if you ever call
me that, I'll put you back in rehab for good."

"Understood. It's a date, then."

She held out her metal right hand.

I shook it, and had my fingers painfully squeezed
in return.

"It's a date," she said, "if this is fighting."

I nodded and she let me go.

✧   ✧   ✧

The Outfall tour was run by a relatively human-friendly Dashizi, an alien of a species I'd never encountered before. Its name was Lna. One pendulous, segmented body hung from the intersection of its six stilt-like legs like a sausage in a cage. Sensory organs were at the bottom end of the sausage, so it had to curl up in a U-shape to look at Enforcer Ei. Ribbons in varying shades of gray adorned its legs, Roman sandal-style.

Lna waited for the other members of our tour before giving us anything other than its name. Five had booked. Only three showed—Enforcer Ei and , and a near-human called Thiall, whose overlarge eyes lent him a permanently quizzical expression. Lna professed himself to be disappointed at the poor turn-out but not surprised.

"Humans evolved in the shadow of volcanoes," the alien said. "You have a predisposition for looking down."

I was pretty sure he wasn't calling us cowards, or depressives, but his expression was unreadable.

"How long have you lived here, Lna?" I asked.

"Three thousand of your years."

"And you've been tour guide all that time?"

"Only on Firstdays. There is a roster."

Enforcer Ei nudged me. I shut up.

"This way."

Lna guided us into the Outfall complex. It seemed much the same as any other, although it was perhaps a little newer-looking, showing fewer signs of wear and tear. This junction clearly hadn't seen as much use as the others.

At its heart rested the massive, alien disk that was the key to the Loop's existence—a solid lump of ambiguous matter, so gray it was almost black, over a hundred meters across and five high, with one cylindrical tunnel bored in a spiraling arc from the edge to the center. Lna walked us around the disk's circumference, pointing out markings left by previous inhabitants of the junction. Some were prayers, others curses. Many were simply names. The disk was covered in those, all painted on. The material was too tough to scratch.

"Commemorating the beings who died here," was the explanation Lna offered. I saw no reason to disbelieve him.

We returned to the tunnel mouth and filed inside. The top of Enforcer Ei's helm was tall enough to scrape the ceiling, making her stoop. Immediately I felt a weird tugging and shifting as gravitational, electric, and magnetic fields wrapped around me. The mech suit creaked and I briefly wondered if it would survive the stresses this odd, alien space would impose upon it. But it had to, I concluded, as it had one hundred and sixty-two times before. Thus far, this was an Outfall like any other.

Our footsteps echoed along the tunnel. The only lights came from a torch Lna carried and Enforcer Ei's chest lamps. The forces multiplied until my head was swimming with the effort of thinking straight. I felt as though all the atoms and molecules in my body were being stirred like letters in alphabet soup.

The tunnel ended in a blank wall.

"This is the geometric center of the disk," Lna said, tapping a point roughly two meters from the end of the tunnel. "Here, our journey ends."

Not just the journey through the disk, he meant, but around the Loop as well.

I approached the wall and examined the tunnel

end by the shifting light. There was more graffiti, centimeters thick by the look of it. What lay beyond it felt disconcertingly solid to my questing hands, a sure sign that something was indeed wrong. This wasn't the way it was supposed to go. Normally one walked into the wormcaster transmitter disk of junction (X) and walked out the receiver of junction (X + 1) without breaking stride. The disks did all the hard work for you.

At least they did when they worked.

"What do the scientists say?" I asked.

Lna folded his legs into pairs. "Many times have I walked this path," he said. "I thought myself a scientist, once. What I considered science is a child's perception of the universe compared to the understanding that built this."

"But people have *tried*, haven't they?" I felt that I was speaking normally, but I could hear the echoes of my voice getting louder. "They've poked it, prodded it . . . ?"

A heavy hand came down on my shoulder. Her metal shell quivered under the complex forces roiling around us.

"Until the builders return," said Lna, "or the Outfall ties itself, we can only wait and wonder."

"Well, that sucks," said Thiall, startling all of us. The near-human hadn't spoken since giving us his name. "But it could be worse, I guess. At least it isn't *half*-work."

"What do you mean?" asked Enforcer Ei.

"Well, it could have dumped us in deep space, or left bits of us behind. At least we're still here and in one piece."

"Some might count that as a curse," she said, "not a blessing."

With heavy steps, the suit turned and began walking out of the tunnel.

Lna uncrossed his legs and followed. "This concludes the tour," the alien said as it ambulated after Enforcer Ei. "There is a register for visitors, if you would like to record your thoughts...."

"Spare me," I told Thiall. "I need a drink."

"To each their own," he said.

I took that as a rebuff, but without rancor. I already had a drinking buddy, if I could get her down off the ledge.

"No goodnight kiss?" I called after her before she could disappear into a crowd.

She indicated the sky. "There's no night, let alone a *good* one. No moon, no stars—no nothing."

"Comets I can give you." Actually, we had those in abundance. The complex interplay of forces in the system was always throwing something icy towards on sun or other. "Probably a rainbow, if you ask nicely

"I did what you wanted. I took the tour. Now yo want me to be nice as well?"

"Just one round. I'll pay, whatever you fancy."

Her pace slowed. "All right. Alcohol works for me

"So you *are* human."

"That's not what I said. Alcohol disrupts Karulie biochemistry as well."

"So you're one of two species." I had met t Karuliesh; they resembled ambulatory prunes a smelled of vinegar. I hoped the real Nadia Ei w nothing like that. "The End of the Line?"

"That'll do."

At the bar in which we'd first met, we had seve rounds, not just one. The front of her suit ope a fraction to allow her access to its inner workings, into which she trickled the drink. I watched curiously as she did so. The outer layer was just millimeters thick, and there seemed to be many more beneath it. I wondered how long it took her to get undressed.

"Maybe Lna's wrong," I insisted. "What if there's another disk, one that works, and all we have to do is find it? Or if we could reprogram the Infall to take us back to junction one-sixty-two?"

"You think people haven't tried?" she said. "You think you're the only one who's thought this way?"

She was right. I was beginning to sound like Zuzi. But Zuzi's relentless optimism was useless on Harvester. It was directed inward, to making the best out of a bad deal. I didn't want that. I wanted the deck shuffled and the cards laid out all over again. Or I wanted some way to turn my shitty hand into a game-winning misére.

"What are you afraid of?" I asked her. "That I might be making sense?"

"I'm going to say yes in the hope it might shut you the hell up."

"But isn't getting away from here something we could all be talking about?"

"I don't know. Maybe," she said, staring down into her drink.

"Wait," I said. "This I don't get at all. You come here on a mission, you catch the guy, and now you can't get home. What's not to be pissed about?"

"I didn't say I wasn't pissed."

"But you said—"

"Maybe means maybe. Don't read too much into it. It's got nothing to do with you."

I supposed that was true, and forced myself to stop prying.

"Shame you didn't catch the guy earlier," I said, aiming for companionability. "That way you'd have the rest of the tour to look forward to."

"You don't know anything about me, soldier."

Her tone was hard. My plan had backfired, somehow.

"I know you only call me 'soldier' when I'm getting close to something."

"That isn't it at all."

The outer layer of her suit abruptly slid shut. She stood up.

"Nadia, wait...."

She didn't blast me into next century. She didn't even look at me. She just kept going.

This time I didn't follow. I drained the rest of my drink, and hers, and went in the opposite direction.

Enforcer Ei didn't show at the dojo for a week, which was fine with me. I had other sparring partners I'd been neglecting, and was pleased to see that working with her had increased my strength and agility, putting me at the top ranking of my fellow corpses. That was new, and not unpleasant.

The buzz was just beginning to pale when she returned, offering neither explanation nor apology for her absence, and I figured she owed me nothing of the sort. She barely said a word, except to accept or reject challenges, as the mood took her. I wasn't her primary sparring partner anymore, although we did fight a few times. It felt awkward, like some vital rhythm was missing, one we'd danced to so effortlessly before.

This went on for a couple of months, circling e

other, never quite colliding, except physically in the arena. I hitched up with Zuzi again and met some other people through her. Harvester's population lacked nothing when it came to interesting and unique types. Only gradually did the familiarity start to eat at me in that regard, too. We were all refugees, castaways on an unknown shore. Every story ended the same.

Four months after I arrived at Harvester, the Authorities declared a junction-wide celebration of mourning. At first I thought it was some alien thing—I had, as yet, failed to determine who or what the Authorities actually were—but Zuzi, always more integrated than I was, explained that the celebration was for everyone. Any race, culture, or creed could participate. Unlike the scrawls I'd seen all over Outfall, this wasn't just for the people who'd died here; it was to commemorate the ones we'd left behind, too.

And it was simple enough. Every physically bound entity processed past the tunnel leading out of Infall. At the opening they spoke the name of the person they were mourning. A small tribute could be offered. Anyone who arrived through the Infall during the procession was declared a Hero for the day and feted by all. The ceremony concluded with a pageant and lots of drinking.

Zuzi thought it sounded wonderful, of course, and talked me into participating.

"Whose name will you say?" I asked her over dinner the night before. We were, by that time, sharing an apartment, and sleeping regularly in the same bed. "I don't think I'll do that part," she said. "There isn't anyone I feel sad about."

"You mean you don't miss anyone?"

"I guess that is what I mean. Grief is a negative emotion, isn't it?"

I stared into her smiling eyes, and saw in them a truth I think I'd known from the beginning.

"You wouldn't miss me if I was gone," I said. "You'd be just as happy as you are now, and just as happy again when the next person moved in. It's all the same to you."

"It's not all the same," she said. "There are shades of happiness. The way I am with you is different to how I am with someone else. It must be, of course, or I would get terribly bored."

She held my hands over the table, and I smiled at her. There was no point pushing it. I knew from experience that she was incapable of having a two-sided argument.

We joined the throng the next day, spruced up like Harvester's finest out to welcome a queen. The mood was a happy one, mixed with an undercurrent of loss. Music was somber as often as it was danceable. Seeing a familiar silver helm standing high above the crowd I pulled ahead of Zuzi. I felt more comfortable on my own, with the crowd surging and retreating around me. It reminded me of the day I'd left to join the Loop, of the farewell thrown by my higher self. He had been there in dozens of bodies, and I had felt embraced physically as well as mentally. Little had I known that the only way I would ever feel anything like that again would be in the company of strangers, all of whom carried their own burdens.

I caught up with Nadia Ei on the approach to Infinity. If she noticed me, she didn't say anything, and I didn't force the issue. The silver skin of her armor reflected my face back at me as she approached the entrance. I silently rehearsed what I was going to say when the opportunity came to do what we were all there to do.

She turned, dropped to one knee, and bowed her head.

"Grae Bilwis," she said.

She straightened, stood, moved on.

Then it was my turn to look down the disk's long, curving tunnel. A dead-end—but a functioning one, since already that day two Heroes had arrived—it had none of the graffiti and all of the mystery of Outfall. I found it easy to imagine that the words we said would ricochet down a long tunnel of space-time back to the places and people we'd left behind. Maybe they'd make a difference to someone.

"Alex Lombard," I said. Although I strained to hear an echo, there was nothing.

Grae Bilwis.

The name rang a bell.

In post-mourning celebration mode, Harvester was consumed by fireworks, acrobats, and drunks. I wasn't much interested in any of them. Seeing Nadia Ei had put me in a contemplative mood, and I didn't have the energy to shuck it off.

Zuzi would be with her friends, expecting me to join her, I supposed, but not relying on it. There might be other corpses there, unless they were feeling the same way I was. Just thinking about my higher self brought back the sense of isolation that, on joining the Loop had been so novel and thrilling, but here Harvester bled like an open wound. On other days might have called my fellow corpses friends and a comfort. That day, the loss we all shared was a wedge between us, driving us into isolation and resentment.

I roamed, staring at the clouds the Authorities had thrown up to block out the suns, the laser-painted stars on their undersides. Sublight shuttles occasionally left Harvester with one destination in mind: the edge of the planetary nebula, where light-echoes faded and the universe reappeared. It wouldn't be hard to book a coldseat on one of those, wait out the millennia in the hope of things changing. It would certainly be a new experience, inasmuch as it was an experience at all. . . .

But *Grae Bilwis* nagged at me. Who was this person Nadia Ei mourned, and where had I heard the name before?

I found a quiet pocket in a green zone and logged into Harvester's infocore. I didn't know the precise spelling, and the search engines weren't optimized for human vocalizations. It took me a surprising amount of time to find the record, and in the end I kicked myself for not looking in the news feeds first. That's where I'd stumbled across it the first time, while looking up Enforcer Ei herself.

Grae Bilwis was the man Enforcer Ei had been chasing through the Loop. He had been an officer in the Earth Justice Enforcement Agency, just like her. He'd sneaked into Harvester by means that were still unknown. She'd caught him, killed him, and handed his body over to the Authorities.

And now here she was, publically mourning him. Why?

Something parted the ferny fronds to my right. A shadow fell across me. By the size of it, there was only one person it could have belonged to.

"I've been researching, too," she said. "Guess what I found."

Clearly she'd been following my search via some means available to her. I couldn't read her mood, not from the way the suit was standing. I didn't get up. If she was going to kill me, I had as much chance of stopping her lying down as I did on my feet.

"Tell me about him, first," I said. "Was he crooked? Or were you the crooked one, and he was blackmailing you?"

"Are they the best theories you've come up with?"

"Well, I haven't had long to think about it. I only just found out he still matters."

"He doesn't matter anymore."

"Of course he does. He's the reason you're here. It's his fault. You're allowed to blame him if it'll help you move on."

"There's nowhere to move on to."

"You know what I mean."

"You don't know anything."

I stopped talking—not just because of the fists, suddenly clenched, that could have turned me to paste in an instant. There was such pain in her voice. For the first time, she sounded how I felt.

"What were you researching?" I asked her.

Her fists unclenched. "Outfall."

Now I sat up. "Tell me what you found."

"The disk has been under observation for half of Harvester's recorded history. It's been studied by people a whole lot more motivated than tour guides—the machine intelligences, for one, and they've got the patience of saints. What's more, all the data is publically available. It makes for pretty dense reading.

I've been wading through it for weeks, trying to find a hole. Most of it I don't understand, but everyone's come to the same diagnosis."

"The disk is stuffed."

"Not quite. The disk is definitely doing *something*— we felt it when we were in there—but exactly what, no one knows. If we did know, maybe we could fix it. All we can say is that it's not working properly, because we're still here."

I rubbed my temples. "Everyone really thinks that?"

"Well, apart from the cranks and weirdoes, half of whom think this is a kind of punishment sent by the Builders. The other half claim to actually be the Builders, but why they're caught in their own trap is never adequately explained."

"And you came to tell me this...why?"

"Because you started it. And I thought you'd want to know."

"No," I said, sensing a very different message behind her words, "it has to be more than that."

"It doesn't have to be anything."

She turned to walk away.

I jumped to my feet and followed her, dodging the elastic leaves that snapped back in her wake.

"Don't run from me, Nadia. You always do that— reach out, then push me away. Is that how it's always been? Is that why you never come out of your suit, because you feel safe in there?"

"Don't try to psychoanalyze me," she said, feet crunching heavily through the undergrowth. "I'm not afraid of connecting any more than you're afraid of being alone. Neither of us would be here if we weren't."

"What does *that* mean?"

She didn't answer.

We hit the edge of the green zone and followed the curved inner wall to the nearest airlock. The truth was, I didn't know why I was following her any more than I knew why she'd come to me, but it seemed important to make the attempt. She was on the verge of something, something critical, and as we passed into the human sector of the habitat it came to me what that might be.

"You're giving up," I said. "That's it, isn't it? You're thinking about killing yourself."

"It wouldn't be hard. And it's not illegal."

"Whether it's hard or legal isn't the point," I said, struggling to find words for why the suggestion filled me with such alarm. "It's just crazy. There's so much here. I mean, look around us. Five suns! Aliens! What else do you want?"

"I used to feel that way. Now I've changed my mind. And I know that's not all *you* want."

"All right—I'm being simplistic in order to defend my own uncertainties. So sue me. But look at the machine intelligences. They haven't given up, have they? What makes them different to you? If they haven't topped themselves, why should anyone?"

"I've no idea what they think, and neither do you."

"That doesn't make their conclusion invalid."

"But they think on different scales. Time moves differently for them."

"So put yourself in cold storage for a bit. See what's happening in a thousand years. Isn't that better than death?"

"You're not saying anything I haven't said myself."

"Well, you should listen to yourself. These are pretty persuasive arguments."

She stopped without warning. "I told you. I changed my mind."

I stared at her back for a long moment, trying to drill mentally through her armor and see what lay beneath. We were talking about suicide, but I didn't think I'd reached the heart of what was bothering her. Her suit was in the way.

It was immaculate, as always, but she might as well have been bleeding from every joint.

"You changed your mind when, exactly?" I asked her.

"It's none of your business."

She didn't call me "soldier," but she might as well have.

"This is to do with Grae Bilwis, isn't it?"

She half-turned. "He was my partner."

"So he broke the law and betrayed you. That's his fault, not yours. You had to do what you did. He had it coming. Right?"

She hung her head. For all the strength and resilience of her alloy shell, she seemed about to sag to the habitat floor and melt away. She actually went down on one knee, so our heads were almost level.

"You're not listening, Alex. He was my *partner*."

I shut up, thinking that at last I understood.

That's the funny thing about data. A single piece of information can change everything. Like Archimedes and his lever, you just need precisely the right one. Everything else is dross. If I'd known sooner what Grae Bilwis meant to Nadia Ei, I thought, maybe I might have understood her better, maybe even helped her. I certainly understood, now, why leaving Harvester—where he had died—had been a ambiguous prospect for her. But I still didn't entirely understand their story. Had she killed him or had he killed himself? Had he run from her or had they been traveling together? It didn't matter. He was gone, and she now wanted to follow him.

Except it's not dross, all that mass of extra data. It has weight and substance. And so do conclusions based on that mass, not to mention behavior based on those conclusions....

I don't know exactly what went through my mind in that moment. It wasn't a revelation borne out of reasoning or logic. It just came to me in a flash, and for a moment I didn't believe it. Then I thought of how things could be hidden right out in the open, sometimes. I thought of what a difference it would make, if it were true. I thought of how hard it would be to tell her, and just for a second I seriously considered not telling her at all.

But the thought in my head was too large to keep to myself. I had to do something with this knowledge. I had to share it.

I put one hand on the side of Nadia's helm—a tiny, soft thing compared to the hard metal—and the other on her left shoulder flange.

"Come with me," I said.

She said nothing, made no sound at all. Maybe she had shut off her comms so I wouldn't hear her weeping, or laughing, or screaming. I had no way of knowing what she was doing in there. But she did move. She straightened, and she followed me like a sleepwalker through the habitats.

She broke her silence only when it became obvious where we were going.

"We've been here already," she said. "I'm sure nothing's changed."

"I'm sure you're right, but bear with me."

"No," she said, pulling back. "I'm not going back there unless you tell me."

"Okay. It's a small thing, so it might not immediately seem like much, but I think it makes a huge difference. Think of the machine intelligences."

"What about them?"

"Well, they're conscious, rational beings, like you, Grae, lots of others. But they're still here. They haven't given up. Why not?"

There were no easy answers to that question, but there *was* one really interesting one.

"You're going to have to spell it out for me," she said.

"They haven't committed suicide because they're like me."

"You're blaming their stubbornness on your legacy genes?"

"No. They know it won't make any difference. Think about it, Nadia. We don't really know how the wormcaster works, right? We assume it throws us physically from Infall to Outfall, but that's just a guess based on what we see happening."

"Someone comes out the Infall who didn't go in," she said. "Someone goes in the Outfall and emerges somewhere else."

"Close. What we actually see from the sending end is someone going into Outfall and not emerging."

"Splitting hairs, surely?"

"Not at all. The Outfall we have here *seems* to be working fine, but no one goes anywhere. We stay here

So instead of assuming that we've misunderstood the way it works, we assume it's not working at all—when in fact it might be doing most of its job just fine, just not the one critical part that has led to the problem we see here."

"Which critical part is that?"

Here, I hesitated. "Did you and Grae take the tour of the disk like we did?"

"No."

"Then . . . I'm sorry. I wanted to tell you that everything will be all right, somewhere, but now I can't."

"I've never thought it would be. Not since we were stuck here, and he . . ."

She stopped. I could tell the thought had sunk in. Maybe not all of it, and she would probably need time to accept the rest, as I had—but the important part was there. I could tell from the way she turned and hurried with renewed urgency for Outfall.

There was a different tour guide this time, one slightly harder to understand. I managed to convince the uncooperative Uotan that we wanted to go in on our own, and he/she/it acquiesced in the end, simply, I think, to get us out of his/her/its hair. It wasn't as if we could damage anything, after all. The disk had been sitting there for more years than humanity had existed. Not even time had dented it.

We had barely entered the tunnel when Nadia stopped and crouched down in front of me.

"If you're right—"

"Then it makes no difference to us. And if I'm wrong, it makes no difference at all."

"You think the machines really know about this?"

"I suspect they do."

"Why haven't they told anyone?"

I thought of Zuzi. She would have greeted the news with the sincere but utterly uniform delight she greeted every occurrence.

"It makes sense that they would keep this quiet," I said. "After all, they can't possibly prove it. Not until someone finally goes all the way around the Loop, anyway, or figures out how to make the Outfall work in both ways. It's a guess, and it might be wrong."

"But you don't think so."

"No. That's why I'm here."

"Both of us have already been inside once. Won't that make a difference?"

"To Outfall, we're just dumb matter."

"So we can do this as many times as we want?"

"I don't see why not." I stared into the suit's glittering eyes. "Does that make you feel better? Liberated, somehow? I know it shouldn't but, still . . . I think it does. To me, anyway."

She said, "All right, Alex. I'll go with you, all the way. I wasn't sure until now. I wasn't sure if I liked the idea. But I will, if we go together."

I smiled. "So let's go."

"Wait. Not like this. It could be dangerous."

She stood up. Something whirred and hissed. A panel lifted out from the front of her suit, then several panels beneath that one. I thought something had malfunctioned in the complex fields of the Outfall disk. Then it occurred to me that suit wasn't falling apart. It was *opening*.

I stepped back, not fully comprehending until all the layers had peeled and I saw what lay within.

"Grae couldn't bear the thought of it," she said. Her voice was unchanged. "The Loop was supposed to bring us together, but the truth of it was that we were as close as we were ever going to be. Nothing I said or did could change the way he was feeling. He didn't understand himself until we were stuck together in Harvester, and once it was clear we would be stuck here forever, he chose the easy way out. He saw no reason to hope, and after a while, neither did I."

My head was swimming, and it wasn't from the forces at work inside the disk.

"When I saw you digging for information on Grae, I thought you were being stubborn again, trying to understand—and you were, but you understood the wrong thing." She made a sound that might have been a laugh. "I swear I wasn't looking for you to rescue me."

I stared, thinking of all the times I had misunderstood what Nadia's suit meant to her.

"This place," she went on. "It's like some fucked-up metaphor for life. Sometimes we need to destroy the past so we can move on. Otherwise, we're stuck. If we can't shrug off what came before, we can't leave it behind, can't move on. But life does move on, even if we don't always want it to. Even if what lies ahead might be dangerous, or frightening, or whatever. Are you going to say something?"

I didn't know what to say. Her suit was empty. There was room for a person, with instruments, life support, and black formfit padding that looked beyond comfortable—but there was no one in the seat.

"Where are you?" I asked, thinking absurd thoughts bout ghosts in the machine.

"In the armor," she said. "Spread thin."

"Biological?"

"Of course, otherwise alcohol would have no effect. If you want the gruesome details—"

"No thanks. But you *are* human, right?"

"Yes. Would it make a difference if I wasn't?"

"I think so." It seemed better not to lie. "You want me to get in?"

"Are you going to?"

"It's a big step."

"Don't get all Freudian on me. This doesn't have to change anything. You don't even have to do it, if you don't want to—"

"I know," I said, understanding at last that this was how Grae Bilwis had come to Harvester, why the Authorities had never heard of him until she had given them his body. "I think it's a good idea, though. We don't know what lies ahead, right?"

"Right. It would be safer this way."

I still could have backed out. *We* weren't going anywhere, after all. We would still be stuck with Harvester, and the celebration, and the memories of everyone we had lost. But that was the other side of the equation, and she knew it.

"Just let's make it very clear up front," she said, "that I won't take your orders. You're not my *pilot*. Okay?"

I thought of the complex equations needed to describe the motions of Harvester's five stars, and extrapolated them out to cover all the beings there all the people who had ever followed the Loop, al the people back home—including my higher self, who I fully expected never to see again, in this life, an who I would always miss, no matter what substitute I found...

The easy part would be telling Zuzi I probably didn't need her apartment anymore.

I said, "Okay."

She crouches.

I step inside.

She seals up.

We walk to the end of the tunnel, turn around, and come back.

Lna was waiting for us in junction one-sixty-four. Nearly seventy Lnas, to be exact, all pretty much identical apart from the length of time they had spent in Harvester. Most of the population here consists of guides. Everybody else who comes through moves on, once they make the break from what they've left behind. That's what the Loop is for, when it works.

We were greeted with delight and excitement, but not surprise. We weren't the first versions of us to come through. That we understood the situation this time put us in very elite crowd, though. Most people fall through accidentally. The scientists who had done so were uniformly sheepish, and not without reason, given the gaff they'd help perpetuate—that staying in Harvester *wasn't the same thing* as not appearing in one-sixty-four.

The erasure mechanism worked fine at the next junction. It was a strange feeling, knowing that the present version of myself was going to be destroyed when we moved on to the next. But the issue of identity and which version was "real" was moot by that point, since we'd already gone through the process many times and felt authentic enough. It didn't matter where our atoms came from, or how many of us there were, now. The really unnerving thought was whether any of the links ahead had failed in different ways. Just because our data went forth along the wormcaster, that didn't mean there was going to be an Infall to receive it at the next stop. What if the last version to be erased was the last ever to exist?

Not knowing was okay. Ignorance loves company. And besides, there was still Harvester.

Under the dark night skies of junction one-sixty-four, knowing we weren't going to be there forever, we were the living embodiment of what happened next, and that was all that mattered to us.

#1 *New York Times*-bestselling **Sean Williams** is the author of several award-winning space opera series, including Evergence, Geodesica, and Astropolis, plus six novels set in the *Star Wars* universe. He also writes fantasy novels for readers of all ages, inspired by the dry, flat lands of South Australia, the landscape of his childhood, where he still lives with his wife and family. His latest is *Troubletwisters*, the first in a kids fantasy series co-written with long-time friend Garth Nix. "The N-Body Solution" is set in the same fiction universe as three previously-published stories: "A Map of the Mines of Barnath," "Inevitable," and "A Glimpse of the Marvellous Structure (And the Threat It Entails)."

ACKNOWLEDGEMENTS

Many thanks to the following:

Jim Minz at Baen Books for publishing and serving as the in-house editor for this anthology. Thanks, too, to: Alethea Kontis for her copyediting prowess, to Joy Freeman and Danielle Turner for shepherding the book through the production process, and to Hank Davis, Laura Haywood-Cory, and the rest of the Baen team.

My agent, Joe Monti, for finding a good home for this project, and for the incredible amount of support he's provided since taking me on as a client—he's gone above and beyond the call of duty. To any writers reading this: you'd be lucky to have Joe in your corner.

Kurt Miller, for the amazing cover.

David Barr Kirtley, Andrew Liptak, and Adam Israel for providing feedback on the stories during the editorial process.

Danni Kelly, for being pretty fantastic.

John Steakley and Robert A. Heinlein—if not for their novels *Armor* and *Starship Troopers*, this anthology may not exist.

Gordon Van Gelder, my friend and mentor. Without him, this anthology would definitely not exist.

My amazing wife, Christie, and my mom, Marianne, for all their love and support, and their endless enthusiasm for all my new projects.

My dear friends Robert Bland, Desirina Boskovich, Christopher M. Cevasco, Douglas E. Cohen, Jordan Hamessley, Andrea Kail, David Barr Kirtley, and Matt London, for enduring endless conversations about possible anthology projects and hearing me go on at length about power armor and mecha while I was working on this one.

The readers and reviewers who loved my other anthologies, making it possible for me to do more.

And last, but certainly not least: a big thanks to all of the authors who appear in this anthology.

STORY COPYRIGHTS

ABOUT THE EDITOR

John Joseph Adams (www.johnjosephadams.com) is the bestselling editor of many anthologies, such as *Brave New Worlds*, *Wastelands*, *The Living Dead*, *The Living Dead 2*, *The Way of the Wizard*, *By Blood We Live*, *Federations*, and *The Improbable Adventures of Sherlock Holmes*. His most recent anthologies are *Lightspeed: Year One* and *Under the Moons of Mars: New Adventures on Barsoom*, and his forthcoming books include *Epic* (Tachyon, Fall 2012) and *The Mad Scientist's Guide to World Domination* (Tor Books, 2013). Barnes & Noble called him "the reigning king of the anthology world," and he has been nominated for two Hugo Awards and three World Fantasy Awards. In addition to his anthology work, John is also the editor and publisher of *Lightspeed Magazine*, and is the co-host of *The Geek's Guide to the Galaxy* podcast.

IF YOU LIKE...
YOU SHOULD TRY...

DAVID DRAKE
David Weber

DAVID WEBER
John Ringo

JOHN RINGO
Michael Z. Williamson
Tom Kratman

ANNE MCCAFFREY
Mercedes Lackey
Liaden Universe® by Sharon Lee & Steve Miller

MERCEDES LACKEY
Wen Spencer, Andre Norton
Andre Norton
James H. Schmitz

LARRY NIVEN
Tony Daniel
James P. Hogan
Travis S. Taylor

ROBERT A. HEINLEIN
Jerry Pournelle
Lois McMaster Bujold
Michael Z. Williamson

HEINLEIN'S "JUVENILES"
Rats, Bats & Vats series by Eric Flint & Dave Freer

HORATIO HORNBLOWER OR
PATRICK O'BRIAN
David Weber's Honor Harrington series
David Drake's RCN series

HARRY POTTER
Mercedes Lackey's Urban Fantasy series

THE LORD OF THE RINGS
Elizabeth Moon's *The Deed of Paksenarrion*

H.P. LOVECRAFT
Larry Correia's Monster Hunter series
P.C. Hodgell's Kencyrath series
Princess of Wands by John Ringo

GEORGETTE HEYER
Lois McMaster Bujold
Catherine Asaro
Liaden Universe® by Sharon Lee & Steve Miller

GREEK MYTHOLOGY
Pyramid Scheme by Eric Flint & Dave Freer
Forge of the Titans by Steve White
Blood of the Heroes by Steve White

NORSE MYTHOLOGY
Northworld Trilogy by David Drake

URBAN FANTASY
Darkship Thieves by Sarah A. Hoyt
Gentleman Takes a Chance by Sarah A. Hoyt
Carousel Tides by Sharon Lee
The Wild Side ed. by Mark L. Van Name

SCA/HISTORICAL REENACTMENT
John Ringo's "After the Fall" series

FILM NOIR
Larry Correia's The Grimnoir Chronicles

CATS
Sarah A. Hoyt's *Darkship Thieves*
Larry Niven's Man-Kzin Wars series

PUNS
Rick Cook
Spider Robinson
Wm. Mark Simmons

VAMPIRES & WEREWOLVES
Larry Correia
Wm. Mark Simmons

NONFICTION
Hank Reinhardt
Tax Payer's Tea Party
by Sharon Cooper & Chuck Asay
The Science Behind The Secret by Travis Taylor
Alien Invasion by Travis Taylor & Bob Boan

MORE . . .
ERIC FLINT